D0991106

GEORGLO PUBLIC LIBRARY

RECEIVED NOV - 4 2004

FIC Jonke

Jonker, J.
The girl from Number 22.

PRICE: $22.37 (3797/   )

The Girl From
Number 22

Also by Joan Jonker

When One Door Closes
Man Of The House
Home Is Where The Heart Is
The Pride Of Polly Perkins
Sadie Was A Lady
Walking My Baby Back Home
Try A Little Tenderness
Stay As Sweet As You Are
Dream A Little Dream
Many A Tear Has To Fall
Taking A Chance On Love
Strolling With The One I Love
When Wishes Come True

Featuring the McDonoughs and Bennetts

Stay In Your Own Back Yard
Last Tram To Lime Street
Sweet Rosie O'Grady
Down Our Street
After The Dance Is Over
The Sunshine Of Your Smile
Three Little Words

Non-fiction

Victims of Violence

The Girl From Number 22

JOAN JONKER

headline

Copyright © 2004 Joan Jonker

The right of Joan Jonker to be identified as the Author of
the Work has been asserted by her in accordance with
the Copyright, Designs and Patents Act 1988.

First published in 2004
by HEADLINE BOOK PUBLISHING

10 9 8 7 6 5 4 3 2 1

Apart from any use permitted under UK copyright law,
this publication may only be reproduced, stored, or transmitted,
in any form, or by any means, with prior permission in writing
of the publishers or, in the case of reprographic production,
in accordance with the terms of licences issued by the
Copyright Licensing Agency.

All characters in this publication are fictitious and any
resemblance to real persons, living or dead, is purely coincidental.

Cataloguing in Publication Data is available from the British Library

ISBN 0 7553 2122 7

Typeset in Times by Avon DataSet Ltd,
Bidford-on-Avon, Warwickshire

Printed and bound in Great Britain by
Mackays of Chatham plc, Chatham, Kent

Headline's policy is to use papers that are natural, renewable and
recyclable products and made from wood grown in sustainable forests.
The logging and manufacturing processes are expected to conform to the
environmental regulations of the country of origin.

HEADLINE BOOK PUBLISHING
A division of Hodder Headline
338 Euston Road
London NW1 3BH

www.headline.co.uk
www.hodderheadline.com

I am dedicating this book to all my readers, who have enriched my life so much with their letters and their friendliness.

As one of my characters would say, 'I love the bones of yer.'

Hello to all my friends.

This is another of my one-off stories. The characters will be strangers to you until you get to know and enjoy them. You will love the goodies, and from the depths of your easy chair you can hiss at the baddies.

Take care.

Love,

Joan

Chapter One

'I'm going to the shops, Ada. Is there anything yer'd like me to get for yer?' Harriet Watson looked up to where her next-door neighbour was standing on the top step. 'Save yer going out yerself.'

'No, I'm going to the shops meself, girl, but thanks all the same. I haven't made up me mind what to get for the dinner yet.' Ada Fenwick opened the door wider. 'If yer want to come in and wait a few minutes, Hetty, I'll come with yer. I've only got to wash me hands and comb me hair.'

'Yeah, okay, I'm not in a hurry.' Hetty smiled at what she was about to say. 'I've even got time for a cuppa.'

'Ye're a cheeky sod, Hetty Watson. Ye're certainly not backward in coming forward. And I suppose yer'd like a biscuit to dunk in the tea?'

Hetty squeezed past her neighbour of twenty years. 'It pays to be cheeky sometimes, queen. But I'll repay yer kindness by giving you afternoon tea, eh?' Her mousy-coloured hair was neatly combed, and with her slim figure and the smile that was never far from her pretty face, she looked much younger than her thirty-eight years. 'We could always buy ourselves a cake to bring back, and make a proper job of it.'

'Don't be going all posh on me, Hetty Watson. Next yer'll be asking me to go to Reece's tea dance with yer.' Ada's ample body shook with laughter. 'Someone told me once, bragging like, that Reece's dance hall had a sprung floor, and it would need it if I started doing me stuff on it. I used to be quite a raver in me time. Jimmy will tell yer, the boys used to queue up to dance with me.'

'To hear you talk, anyone would think yer were like Two Ton Tessie O'Shea. Ye're not fat, Ada, ye're pleasantly plump. Yer can certainly move when ye're in a hurry. While I'm puffing and panting, you sail along as though ye're floating on air.'

Ada's bonny, rosy face broke into a smile. 'No, girl, I only float on air after two bottles of milk stout. Anyway, I'll go and make that pot of tea, girl, before I forget I promised yer a drink. Once I get started on the old days, I don't know when to stop.'

1

Hetty looked around the room and nodded. It was like a little palace as usual. You could see your face in the sideboard, it was so highly polished. The net curtains on the front and back windows were pure white, and the panes of glass gleaming. 'Have yer got any bright ideas for what to get in for the dinner?' she called. 'It's a worry every day, trying to come up with something for a change.'

Ada came in drying her hands. 'It's a toss-up between a sheet of ribs, which would please Jimmy and Danny, or sausage and mash. We had stew last night so we can't have that again, or I'll be getting complaints. The kids aren't fussy. They're like me, they'll eat anything that's put in front of them.'

'Me too. I'm not a fussy eater,' Hetty said. 'It was easy before Sally and Kitty left school and started work, they weren't fussy then either. But now they expect me to do miracles with the few bob they hand over.' Her elder daughter, Sally, was eighteen, and her younger, Kitty, was seventeen. 'So shall we stick with ribs tonight, sausage tomorrow, and to hell with whether they like it or not? I'm not going to start cooking different meals for everyone, they'll have to eat what's put in front of them. As me mam used to say, hunger's a good sauce.'

The kettle began to whistle, and Ada made for the kitchen to turn off the gas and pour the boiling water into the brown teapot. 'Yeah, we'll do that, girl,' she shouted back. 'Not that mine would moan no matter what I served up, but I like to please Jimmy and Danny. I think they deserve to come home to something they fancy after putting in a hard day's work. And when the two youngest start work and are bringing a few bob in, then I'll listen to their likes and dislikes.'

Hetty pushed her chair back and walked into the kitchen. 'You bring the cups in, queen, I'll carry the pot.' She turned her head to add, 'And don't forget the promised biscuit.'

When they were sitting facing each other across the table, Ada said, 'I haven't seen much of Eliza the last few days. D'yer know if she's all right?'

Eliza Porter was an elderly woman who lived across the street from them, and most of the near neighbours kept an eye on her. 'She waved to me this morning when she was taking her milk in, so she's all right.' Then Hetty frowned. 'Mind you, come to think of it, I haven't see her going to the shops for a few days. Shall we give a knock on our way out, and ask if she needs any shopping?'

Ada nodded. 'Yeah, we'll do that, just to make sure.' Again she nodded her head, but this time it was towards the plate. 'Yer may as well dunk that last ginger snap, then I can take the empty plate out. I'm not going to ask if yer want any more, 'cos our Danny would blow his top if there were no ginger snaps.' Danny was her eighteen-year-old son, and her pride and joy. 'Honest, he's like a big soft kid sometimes.'

'Oh, don't be trying to kid me, Ada, for I know yer love the bones of him, and yer spoil him rotten. But I have to admit if he was my son I'd spoil him too. He's a lovely lad, and it'll be a lucky girl who gets him.'

'She'll have to be more than lucky to get past me,' Ada said jokingly. 'I'll want to know everything about her and her family, right down to how many blankets they have on their beds.'

'For heaven's sake leave the lad alone and let him enjoy himself.' Hetty tutted. 'He's only young once.'

'And he's making the most of it, girl, believe me! He's out every night at one dance hall or another, having the time of his life. And I don't begrudge him one minute of it. He may as well enjoy himself before he settles down. His mates tell me he's a smashing dancer, and he's got all the girls after him. But Danny never mentions girls to me, so I can't see there being anyone in particular . . . not yet, anyway.'

'He wouldn't tell you if there was, queen, not the way you dote on him. He knows he'd get the third degree if he even mentioned a girl's name.'

'Ay, I'm not that bad! I'm only thirty-seven years old, young enough to remember what it was like to have a mother who wanted to know every time I took a breath. She was so strict with me, I used to have to tell her fibs, just so I could go out.' Ada chuckled. 'I have to confess, though, that I asked for it. I was a cheeky little beggar when I was at school, and a damn sight worse when I left. I thought the world was there for me to enjoy meself, and I led me poor mam and dad a merry dance.' She became serious, and said, 'I made it up to them, though, when I learned a bit of sense. I met Jimmy, we fell in love, and suddenly I realised what I'd put me parents through.'

'Yer were the only child, weren't yer, queen?'

Ada nodded. 'I didn't know, 'cos in those days nobody mentioned having babies, not in front of children, anyway. I must have been about thirteen when I heard one of me aunties talking to me mam, and I heard her saying something about when I was born the doctor had told me mam, and me dad, that she mustn't have any more babies, for her life would be at risk. It all went over me head, really; I didn't understand. And I was too young to ask anyone about it. All I knew was, me mam never had any more babies after me.'

Hetty was leaning forward, interest in her eyes. In all the years they'd been neighbours and friends, Ada had never mentioned this. 'When did yer eventually find out?'

'When I met Jimmy. He asked me about having any brothers or sisters, and I told him what I'd heard me auntie saying. When I'd been out with him a few times, I asked me mam if I could bring him home to meet her and me dad. I remember she seemed really pleased that I'd asked her, and both her and me dad really liked him. And a few weeks later, Jimmy made it seem like a joke when he asked if I'd been such a bad baby that they'd decided not to have any more. It was me dad who told us, with me mam sitting blushing like mad. But when I heard the real story, it made me pull me socks up, I can tell yer. I made up for all those years when I'd never told them how much I loved them. And I thank God that I did, for me mam was only forty-seven when she died. I took time off work to help me dad nurse her. I was courting Jimmy at the time, and he would call every night to see if he could do anything.' Ada swallowed hard to rid herself of the lump forming in her throat. 'She was only bedridden for four weeks, and she wasn't in a lot of pain, thank God. But me dad was out of his mind when she died. He idolised her. He never went back to work, he just seemed to fade away. And six months after me mam died, he passed away. The doctor said he'd died of a broken heart.' She sniffed up. 'I should never have told yer all that, I've upset meself now. Ye're the first one I've ever told the full story to, and I'm sorry, girl, if I've upset yer. But yer can blame yerself, for you were the one what started it.'

'I know, I was being nosy. I'm sorry I've brought it all back, queen. I should have minded me own business and kept me mouth shut.'

'No, it does me good to talk about me parents, even though it does make me weepy. Never a day goes by I don't think of them, and thank God I made it up to them for the worries I caused when the only person I thought about was meself. And I was also able to give them the love they deserved.' Ada smiled at her neighbour. 'Anybody watching us two over the last fifteen minutes would have thought they were in the Gaumont watching a sad movie and clutching their hankies wringing wet with tears. So let's liven ourselves up and press ahead with our daily chores.'

Hetty looked round. 'From the looks of things, yer've done all yer chores, except seeing to the dinner for the family. My living room doesn't look like this, it's a shambles. I cleaned the grate out, washed the breakfast dishes, and was about to start polishing when me mind went on strike. It told me to stop work and go out and get some fresh air in me lungs. So I threw the duster on the couch, combed me hair, and here I am.'

'That mind of yours will get yer in trouble one of these days. It sounds bolshie to me. If yer were working in a factory, it would make yer into a

4

real troublemaker, and yer'd have the whole factory out on strike. I can see yer now, standing outside the factory gates, with all the workers behind yer carrying big banners and chanting slogans about low wages.'

Hetty looked at her neighbour with eyes wide. 'My God, Ada, yer don't half let yer imagination run away with yer. I wouldn't say boo to a goose, and you've got me bringing a whole factory out on strike. Plus ruddy banners!'

Ada chuckled. 'There's worse things yer mind can make yer do than bring workers out on strike, girl, but yer'll have to put yer foot down hard if it does.'

Hetty's eyes narrowed. 'I don't know whether to ask what it is, or leave well alone. Me mind says don't bother asking, 'cos there's nothing can be worse than starting a revolution in a factory. But me nose is telling me not to be so miserable, 'cos it would like to know. So go ahead and I'll keep tight hold of the table.'

'Before I say a word, Hetty,' Ada said, laughter building up inside her, 'yer do believe that all is pure to the pure, don't yer? And don't be looking at me with that blank look on yer face, it was an easy question. You are pure at heart, aren't yer?'

'Yeah, I suppose so. As pure as you are, anyway.'

Ada pursed her lips and wagged her head from side to side. 'Ooh, that was the wrong answer, girl. Yer should have thought of something else.'

'Why? You're pure at heart, queen, aren't yer?'

'That's debatable, girl. Sometimes I have very un-pure thoughts in me head. Perhaps we'd better leave things as they are, and get down to the shops.'

'Not on your ruddy life, Ada Fenwick. I'm not moving from here until yer tell me when I should put me foot down when me mind tells me to do something.'

'Okay, yer asked for it.' Ada was really enjoying herself. 'Can yer imagine yerself in bed one night, and your Arthur is getting very amorous? And just at the height of his passion, your mind tells yer to go on strike! Where would that leave your Arthur if yer didn't put yer foot down and tell yer mind to sod off?'

A grin spread slowly across Hetty's pretty face, then it gathered momentum until she was roaring with laughter. 'Oh, you are a case, Ada,' she said, wiping her eyes. 'Yer don't know my Arthur very well, do yer? If yer did, yer'd know he wouldn't let a little thing like my mind, or my foot, put him off. When my husband's feeling passionate, queen, not even a storm would put him off. In fact, we'd both be making more noise than the storm.'

'Oh, he's that good, is he? Mmm, I'll have to have a word in his shell-like ear, and ask him if he'll pass on any tips to my Jimmy.'

'Yer've pulled me leg over a few things, queen, but I'm not falling for that one. What yer seem to forget is, I live next door, and the walls are not very thick.'

Ada held her hands up in mock horror. 'Oh, girl, ye're not saying yer stand with yer ear glued to the wall, are yer?'

There was a look of triumph on Hetty's face as she tried to even the score. 'I don't need to, queen, not with you having such a loud voice.'

Ada leaned forward and patted her hand. 'Good for you, girl. I think that just about makes us quits now. So I'll swill me hands and comb me hair, while you carry the dishes out for me. Then we'll knock and see if Mrs Porter is all right.' A grin crossed her face. 'I know we won't be going in her house, but just in case, I don't think we should tell her what we've been talking about. Not at her age.'

Hetty stacked the cups and saucers on top of the plate, and pushed her chair back before picking them up. 'I won't even tell Arthur what we've been talking about, never mind a woman of eighty-two. She'd think we're a couple of brazen hussies.'

Ada opened a drawer in the sideboard and took out a comb. 'You speak for yerself, girl. I'm proud of being a brazen hussy. Even if the only man in my life is me own husband. We have a very healthy sex life, and it doesn't half make life worth living.'

'I've left the dishes on the draining board, queen,' Hetty said, coming in from the kitchen. 'I'll help yer wash them when we get back from the shops.'

When Ada had closed the front door behind them, and they were about to cross the cobbles to a house opposite, she put a hand on Hetty's arm. 'Ay, girl, yer can't really hear me through the wall, can yer?'

'Of course not, soft girl. I was only acting the goat, same as yerself.'

'Thank God for that,' Ada said. 'Yer had me worried. I mean, if you could hear me and Jimmy, what about Danny and me two kids? If I thought for one minute that they could hear, I'd die of humiliation.'

'Well, if ye're that worried, queen, there is an answer to yer problem.'

'What's that, girl?'

Hetty was lifting the knocker on Eliza Porter's door when she answered. 'Yer could behave yerselves.'

'There's another solution, girl. I could always join a ruddy nunnery!'

The door was opened by eighty-two-year-old Eliza, and she was smiling. 'Somehow I can't see you in a nunnery, Ada. The life wouldn't suit yer.' The old lady's hair was pure white, and she had it combed back and pleated into a bun at the back of her head. She was a slim woman, with faded blue eyes, who held herself straight and was always neat and tidy. She was the oldest resident in the street, both in years and in the time she'd lived in the same small two-up-two-down house in the narrow street. Gentle and kind, she was very much loved by all the neighbours, old and young alike. She was smiling when she asked, 'You're not on your way there now, are you, Ada? You haven't called to say farewell?'

Ada was really fond of the old lady, and she felt like putting her arms round her and holding her tight. But Eliza was so frail, Ada had to be content with a kiss on the cheek. 'I did try the nunnery last week, Eliza, but they wouldn't have me. I didn't have the right qualifications, yer see. And me and me mate haven't come to wish yer a fond farewell, but to ask if yer want anything from the shops.' She gave the old lady a sly wink. 'I'd have been there and back only for Tilly Mint here. I was soft enough to invite her in, just while I combed me hair, like, so I'd look respectable, and she's done nothing but gab for an hour. Honest, I couldn't get a word in with her.'

'Why, you cheeky article!' Hetty said with fire in her voice. 'Yer've talked the ear off me without stopping to take a breath, and ye're standing there like little Miss Innocent, putting all the blame on me. It's the last time I call to see if I could do yer a favour.'

'Which brings us to why we came and knocked on Eliza's door.' Ada was pleased to see the old lady smiling. 'If yer want anything from the shops, sunshine, me and Hetty could go on a message for yer. We've got to go to the butcher's, the greengrocer's and the bread shop. Anything yer want, all yer have to do is say, and we'll be only too happy to get it for yer.'

'That's very thoughtful of yer to think of me, ladies, and I appreciate it. But I've got all the food in that I need to last me a few days. My son and his wife came yesterday, and they brought tea, sugar, bread, margarine and some biscuits. And Edith, next door, she was kind enough to get me some stewing beef this morning, which will do me today and tomorrow. There's really nothing I need, but I'm beholden to yer for asking.'

'That's fine, girl. As long as yer larder is full, yer can't come to any harm.' Ada smiled. 'How are John and Vera keeping, and yer grand-daughter?'

'They're very well, Ada, thanks.' Eliza's son and his wife had lived with her when they first got married, and their first baby was born there, a girl they named Patricia. But they found the living conditions cramped in the small two-up-two-down, and they moved to a six-roomed house in Knotty Ash. They never failed to visit Eliza, though, even though they had to get a tram and then a bus from their home. Their daughter was a mother herself now, and Eliza had two great-grandchildren, Brian and Pauline, whom she doted on.

'Next time they come, sunshine, tell them me and Hetty were asking after them. And Pat and the children. Ay, they must be quite grown up now?'

It was Hetty who told her, 'They're the same age as your two younger ones. Don't yer remember, each time you had a baby, Pat gave birth two months later. We all remarked on the coincidence at the time. Aren't I right, Eliza?'

Eliza nodded. 'Yer've got a much better memory than me, Hetty, for I would never have remembered that far back.'

There was a chuckle in Ada's voice when she said, 'My mate has got a good memory, but I wouldn't want her mind. Yer see, her mind is stronger-willed than she is, and it orders her around. I wouldn't stand for it meself, but then I haven't got a good memory. So between the two of us, we've got one good mind and one good memory. As long as we stick together we won't come to any harm.'

Hetty decided it was time to move before her mate had the old lady blushing. 'We're keeping Eliza standing, queen. I suggest we go about our business and let her get back to that lovely comfortable rocking chair she's got.'

'Yeah, I often think of that chair,' Ada said, well aware she was rubbing her mate up. 'In fact, I've promised to buy meself one when I've got the money. I've seen the one I'd like, in the window of that furniture shop on Stanley Road.'

Enough was enough, Hetty thought as she pulled on Ada's arm. 'Come on, there's a good girl. And if yer behave yerself, I'll take yer along to that shop one day, and I'll ask the kind man if yer can have a little rock in it.'

Ada entered into the spirit of things. Clapping her hands in glee, and speaking in a childish voice, she said, 'Oh, thank you, Mummy. Can we go there now, Mummy? I'll cry if yer won't take me there today.' Stamping one of her feet in temper, she went on, 'I'll tell Daddy on yer when he comes in from work.'

Eliza watched the smaller woman pulling the larger one away, promising she'd buy her a lollipop if she stopped crying. And the old lady had a smile on her face as she closed the door. She lived alone, but her life wasn't lonely, thanks to the wonderful neighbours she had.

'I'm not having that sheet of ribs, Ronnie Atwill, yer can give it to some other poor sucker.' Ada jerked her head back in disgust. 'That poor bloody sheep died of starvation, there's no ruddy meat on his bones. I feel so sorry for him, if I'd known when his funeral was, I'd have gone to it and taken a bunch of flowers.'

Hetty opened her mouth to say ribs didn't come from sheep, but she noticed the spark in her neighbour's eyes and kept quiet. The butcher was used to Ada, and he'd give back as good as he got. And the customers in the shop would get a laugh out of the confrontation.

'Do yer really feel sorry for the sheep, Ada?' Ronnie asked. 'If ye're that partial to lamb, why don't yer have some nice lamb chops?'

'I don't want no bleeding lamb chops, I want a sheet of healthy-looking ribs, with bags of meat on them.'

'What have yer got against pigs, Ada?'

'Dirty buggers, pigs are. Have yer never seen the way they wallow in dirt? Ugh, I could be sick at the thought of it.'

Ronnie's young assistant, sixteen-year-old Barry, had two customers in front of him, and when he'd asked them what they wanted, they'd told him to leave them for a while to give them time to make their minds up. They lived in the next street to Ada and Hetty, and many's the laugh Ada had given them. So there was no way they were going to leave that shop until the matter of the ribs was sorted out. And the young lad thought of the saying that if yer couldn't beat them, join them, and he folded his arms and leaned back against the chopping block.

'Yer wouldn't be inconsiderate enough to be sick in me shop, would yer, Ada?' Ronnie asked, laughter in his blue eyes and a rosy glow to his cheeks. 'If yer did that, I'd have to close the shop while I cleaned the floor, then yer'd get no chops, no ribs, just sweet Fanny Adams.'

'I'm fussy where I'm sick, Ronnie Atwill, thank you very much. And why did yer go all round the world, bringing Fanny Adams into it, instead of just saying I'd get bugger all?'

'Because I don't swear in front of ladies, that's why. And to get back to what your feller's having for his dinner tonight, would yer consider having a sheet of bacon ribs, even though yer think pigs are horrible?'

Ada shook her head. 'Not on yer life, I want a sheet of lamb's ribs and I'll stand here until I get one.' She winked at one of the women whose back entry door faced hers. 'It's coming to something when yer can't have what yer want, isn't it, Dora?'

'Ye're right there, queen, no doubt about it,' said Dora. 'I was only saying to Helen as we walked here that the world isn't what it was years ago. Didn't I, Helen?'

Helen wasn't going to argue when her neighbour was twice the size of her, and known to have a quick temper. 'Yes, yer did, Dora, they were yer very words.'

Ronnie could see two more customers coming in, and he decided they'd had enough fun for one day. After all, business is business. 'I'll tell yer what I'll do, Ada, seeing as it's you, and you and Hetty are two of me favourite customers.' He felt Dora's eyes on him, and quickly added, 'Along with Dora and Helen, of course. So I'll take this sheet of ribs out and find one that will take yer fancy.' He knew he had customers waiting, but a joke was a joke, and if he didn't say it now, he'd forget it. 'By the way, Ada, do yer prefer a sheep what came from Wales, or Scotland?'

Ada pretended to ponder. It was a serious business this. In the end she turned to Hetty. 'What do you think, girl? Wales or Scotland?'

'I'm quite happy with the sheet of ribs Ronnie's got in his hand,' Hetty said. 'I don't care where it came from.'

'Okay, that settles it,' Ada said. 'Find another sheet of lamb's ribs, exactly the same as the one yer've got in yer hand, and they'll do for me and me mate.'

While young Barry was serving the other customers, Ronnie came out of the stockroom with two sheets of bacon ribs that were thick with lean meat. 'How do they look to yer, ladies?'

'Oh, brilliant, Ronnie,' Hetty said. 'My feller will be in his element.'

Ada nodded in agreement. 'See what yer can do if yer try, Ronnie? Now those ribs come from a sheep what got well fed and had lovely green fields to play in.'

Ronnie wrapped them up separately, then handed them over. 'That will be three bob each, ladies, and they'll taste a treat.'

As Ada handed her money over, Ronnie said, 'Seeing as yer like lamb so much, Ada, I'm surprised yer've never asked me for a sheep's head. They make lovely soup.'

'Go 'way, yer dirty bugger.' Ada pretended to retch as she leaned on the counter. 'I've gone off sheep now. I've a good mind to ask yer to take these ribs back, and I'll have a sheet of bacon ones.' She shuddered. 'Just imagine lifting the lid off the pan and seeing two eyes staring up at yer.'

Dora nodded. 'It doesn't bear thinking about.'

Helen forgot her neighbour's temper for a minute, and, with real feeling, said, 'My mother used to say sheep's head soup was delicious, and good for yer.'

'She would,' Dora snorted. 'She was soft in the head and you take after her.'

Timid as she was, Helen wasn't going to stand for that. 'My mother was a very clever woman, and a real lady. That's more than can be said for yours.'

Hetty sensed trouble brewing and tugged hard on Ada's arm. 'Come on, queen, we've still got a lot of shopping to do before the shops close for dinner.'

Ronnie chortled when he saw Ada being pushed through the door. 'See yer tomorrow, ladies. Ta-ra!'

'Yeah, see yer tomorrow, Ronnie,' Ada called from the pavement. 'Ta-ra for now, lad.'

Hetty kept her eyes straight ahead, but she could feel the daggers coming her way. And to nip any criticism in the bud, she said, 'When we get to the greengrocer's, yer won't ask Stan if he's sure the cabbage comes from Ormskirk, will yer? After all, I'd like to get home in time to put the ribs in steep.'

Ada managed to look surprised, even though she was chuckling inside. 'I didn't know they grew cabbages in Ormskirk! Well, I never! It just goes to show yer learn something new every day.'

Round the table that night, when the Fenwick family were tucking into their dinner, Ada told them about pulling the butcher's leg about the sheep's ribs. And she went on to say how she'd pretended to feel sick when he asked why she didn't buy a sheep's head to make soup. When she came to the part about lifting the pan lid to see two eyes staring at her, her husband and son, Danny, thought it was funny. But the two youngest, Monica and Paul, looked absolutely horrified.

'Oh, you, Mam!' twelve-year-old Monica said, pulling a face. 'That's terrible, that is. It's enough to make yer feel sick.'

'They don't really make soup with a sheep's head, do they, Mam?' Ten-year-old Paul had gone right off his dinner. 'Yer wouldn't ever do it, would yer?'

'Yer mam is pulling yer leg,' his father told them. 'Yer know how she likes her little jokes. She'd faint if she saw a sheep's head, never mind making soup with it.'

'The only sheep's eyes yer'll see round here,' Danny said, laughing, 'is when me mam wants to cadge some money off our dad to go a matinee to see her heart-throb, Cary Grant. And if the sheep's eyes don't work, she gives him cow's eyes.'

That cheered the children up, and the atmosphere round the table became light and cheerful again. 'I know it's a daft question to ask, Danny, but are yer going out tonight?'

Dimples appeared in the handsome face. 'As yer said yerself, Mam, it was a daft question to ask. Of course I'm going out.'

'Jazzing again, I suppose?'

'Right again, Mam! Ye're doing well tonight.'

'When are we going to meet this girlfriend of yours?' Jimmy asked. 'Yer not ashamed of us, are yer? Or has the girl got two heads?'

Danny stared at him blankly. 'Girlfriend? That's the first I've heard of it, Dad. Who's been spreading that story?'

'Nobody has been spreading any story, son,' Ada told him. 'It's just that me and yer dad don't think yer go to dances every night to dance on yer own. Which means yer dance with a member of the opposite sex.'

'Mam, ye're breaking the record tonight, yer've been right every time.' Danny was like his father in looks, with fair hair, hazel eyes, and a very happy disposition. And he only had two more inches to grow before he reached his father's six foot. But his humour came from his mother. 'I'll come clean and tell yer the truth. There is a girl, and she's a smashing dancer. But unfortunately she's pigeon-toed, bow-legged, and wears big thick glasses 'cos she's very short-sighted.'

Monica and Paul sat open-mouthed. Their Danny going out with a girl who was bow-legged and pigeon-toed? Why would he do that when half a dozen nice-looking girls in the street were after him?

'Ah, God help the girl,' Ada said, wanting to laugh at the expression on the kids' faces. 'My mam always said yer should never mock anyone 'cos yer never knew what the future held for yerself. Apart from being bow-legged, pigeon-toed and short-sighted, has the girl got anything good going for her? There must be something, or why would yer bother dancing with her? I mean, if her toes are turned in, and her legs bent out, it must be hard going trying to dance in a straight line.'

'When yer love someone, Mam, yer don't mind putting up with little inconveniences. You did, didn't yer? Yer told me yer didn't pretend not to know me dad when his glass eye fell out on the dance floor. Now, that's what I call true love.'

Paul's eyes were like saucers. 'Me dad hasn't got a glass eye!'

'Not now he hasn't, sunshine,' Ada said. 'We saved up and bought him a real one.'

'They're pulling yer leg, son,' Jimmy told him. 'What happened was, I had a fight with this bloke who was as big as a mountain, and he gave me a belting black eye. Me face was so swollen, yer couldn't see me right eye at all, and everyone thought I'd lost it.'

'Can we leave your eye where it is for the moment, and get back to the business of our son and his girlfriend? I'd like to know her name, where she lives, what does she look like, and what did she have for her dinner last night?'

12

Danny threw his head back and roared with laughter. 'Mam, there is a girl in me life, and last night she had stew for her dinner. You should know, you made it. There's only one girl in my life at present, and that's you. And I'm quite happy with things as they are.'

Ada was delighted, for she doted on her first born. But her last born wasn't a bit happy. 'No wonder yer get yer own way all the time, crawling to me mam. I think I'll have to try it and see where it gets me.'

Ada stood up and began to collect the plates. 'Yer don't have to butter me up, Paul, 'cos I have the same amount of love for all me kids. Danny gets a bit more, I admit, but then he's a working man, and bringing a wage in. And he gives you and Monica tuppence a week pocket money, so he's not a bad brother, is he?'

'No.' Monica and Paul shook their heads. Their brother was the nicest-looking lad in the street, and they were proud of him. But they weren't going to tell him that.

THOROLD PUBLIC LIBRARY

Chapter Two

Ada was peeling potatoes by the sink when she heard the sound of the front door being pushed open so hard it banged against the wall. She always left the door ajar when the children were due home from school, but they never usually made that noise. She wiped her hands down her pinny and walked into the living room as her son came in through the other door.

'What in the name of God d'yer think ye're playing at, son? Yer nearly took the ruddy door off its hinges. And if yer've knocked any plaster off the wall, yer dad will have yer life.'

Paul was puffed after running, and moving from one foot to the other. 'Can I have a jam butty, Mam? I'm starving.'

'Why can't yer walk home instead of running and making yerself out of breath? It would only take yer five minutes longer, and yer wouldn't die of starvation in five minutes.'

'I wanted to go down the yard, Mam, that's why I ran. I was dying to go to the lavvy.'

'Everything is a drama with you, son.' Ada tutted. 'Ye're starving with hunger, and ye're dying to go to the lavvy.'

'I can't help being hungry, Mam!'

'Okay, you win! Go on, down the yard, and I'll make yer a jam butty. But I warn yer, the jam will be scraped on and then scraped off again. We're not made of money, and jam is a luxury we can do without.'

Paul grinned, then made a dash for the kitchen door. He was halfway down the yard when he heard his mother shout, 'In case yer can't taste it, I may as well tell yer now that if yer could taste it, yer'd know it was raspberry.'

'Who are yer talking to, Mam?' Monica slipped her coat off and threw it on the couch. 'If it's our Paul after a jam butty, then I'll have one as well.'

Ada lifted her hands in the air. 'I give up! The pair of yer are going to eat me out of house and home.'

14

'Yer won't be saying that in eighteen months' time, Mam, when I leave school. I'll be bringing in a wage packet then like our Danny.'

'Don't try throwing yer weight around now, on expectations that in eighteen months' time yer'll be bringing a wage in and we'll all be rolling in money. At fourteen, sunshine, yer'll only be earning peanuts. And while I admit that even peanuts are better than nothing, they won't bring you the change in lifestyle yer seem to be looking for. Mind you, yer won't be as badly off as I was at your age. I started work at fourteen earning seven and six a week. My mam took five, and out of the half-crown I was left with, I had to buy me own clothes. I didn't know what it was like to have a pair of stockings that didn't have a ladder in. And me dresses came from a second-hand stall at the market.' Ada grinned as the memory of those dresses came back. 'They weren't the height of fashion, and they'd been well worn before I got them, but it didn't stop the boys from giving me the eye. And me mam helped me as much as she could, even though money was scarce for there were a lot of men out of work.'

Monica was looking very glum. 'I hope I get a job what pays more than seven and six a week. If I was left with half a crown, I'd have to stay in every night. A pair of stockings cost about one and eleven.'

'Wages have gone up since I was fourteen, sunshine, so don't look so miserable. I don't know what the going rate is, but I would think yer'd be on at least thirty bob a week.'

The girl was bucked up by that. 'Ay, Mam, if I did get thirty bob a week, how much would I have to give to you?'

'That's something I would have to discuss with yer dad when the time comes. But if I were you, I'd forget about work for another eighteen months. It's no use talking about what might happen, 'cos things can change a lot in that time.'

Paul popped his head round the door. 'Ah, ay, Mam, where's me jam butty? Yer said yer'd make me one, and I'm starving.'

'You wash yer hands, young man, before I do anything. No clean hands, no sandwich.'

'I'll wash me hands, Mam,' Monica said, sticking her tongue out at her brother. 'And I'll have one of the raspberry jam sandwiches, even though I won't be able to taste the jam.'

Paul got to the sink first, and he wouldn't budge as his sister tried to push him aside. 'Ye're sneaky, you are. All girls are sneaky. Just 'cos I asked for a sandwich, you've got to ask for the same. And stop pushing me or I'll kick yer.'

Ada stood at the kitchen door with her hands on her generous hips. 'Stop messing and behave yerselves, ye're not babies any more. And there's room for both of yer at the sink if yer'd give each other a chance. Talk about sister and brotherly love, it's a pity yer don't show some for each other.'

Paul was first to leave the sink, and he reached for the towel hanging on a hook on the back of the door. 'We do love each other, Mam,' he said with mischief in his eyes. 'We just don't say it 'cos it would sound daft. I'd feel a real cissie.'

'I'm not saying it,' Monica declared with passion, ' 'cos ye're a little twerp.'

'That settles it,' Ada told them. 'Yer've just talked yerselves out of a butty.'

With his tummy asking him if his throat was cut, Paul opted for desperate measures. Falling down on to one knee in front of his sister, and clasping his hands together, he said, 'I do love you, Monica. I think you are the best sister any boy could have.'

His sister giggled. 'And I love you, Paul, very much. I think we both deserve a butty now, even if we can't taste the jam that our mam scraped on and off.'

'I'm in two minds,' Ada told them. 'The pair of yer think it's a joke, which it isn't. Yer should love each other without me having to tell yer. It should come natural. Yer dad and his sister, yer Auntie Ethel, they love each other.'

Paul, still on one knee in front of his sister, asked, 'Is that why our Auntie Ethel went to live in Wales, Mam, because she loved me dad so much?'

Ada couldn't keep the laughter back. 'Ye're a holy terror, Paul, and if yer don't get up off that knee I'll be tempted to push yer over. And I wouldn't let yer dad hear what yer've just said, he wouldn't think it was funny. His sister met a man from Wales, fell in love with him and went to live there. But because they're miles apart doesn't mean they don't love each other. They're family, and the ties will always be there.'

'We never see me Auntie Ethel, though, Mam. Why is that?' Monica asked. 'She could come here to see me dad, or he could go there.'

'It's about eighty miles to where they live, right in the middle of the country. They'd have to get a bus, a train, then another train. Same as us if we went there. And it would cost a lot of money in fares, which neither of us can afford.'

'When me and Monica are working we could go,' Paul said. 'If it's in the middle of the country, there'd be cows and sheep and forests. We could go there on holiday. That would be great, wouldn't it, Mam?'

'It would that, son.' Ada pulled on the lobe of her ear, a habit she had if she wanted to stop herself from laughing. 'There's a lot of talk right now of when you two start work and are earning. I'll be a lady of leisure then, and able to go into town to buy meself a new dress, or whatever takes me fancy. The trouble is, it'll be eighteen months before Monica leaves school, and nearly four years before you do. In the meantime all I can do is try and manage from week to week, with dreams of life getting better in the future.'

Paul got to his feet and rubbed his knee. 'Yeah, yer have got a long time to wait, Mam. Nearly as long as me and Monica have waited for those butties yer promised.'

'Ye're a cheeky monkey, Paul Fenwick, and if it wasn't for wanting yer out from under me feet, I'd change me mind and not make those butties. But I will make them on one condition. And that is that you and yer sister set the table for me. I'm sure that's worth a butty what nearly has raspberry jam on. With a good imagination, yer could pretend yer were actually tasting it.'

'With a really good imagination, our Paul, yer could close yer eyes and pretend yer were sitting in the middle of a field in Wales, with horses and sheep nudging yer shoulder, wanting some of yer butty.'

Ada looked at her daughter with pride. She was good at English, was Monica, always top of the class. And she was a marvellous storyteller, with lots of imagination. It would be a pity if she ended up working in a factory, which was all most working-class people could look forward to.

'I'll make yer sandwiches,' she said, heading for the kitchen. 'If I don't put a move on, I'll not have the dinner ready for the men coming in from work.'

'I'll put the tablecloth on, Mam,' Paul said, opening the sideboard cupboard to get the white cloth out. 'And our Monica can put the knives and forks out.'

'What are we having for dinner, Mam?' Monica called through. 'I hope it's something I like. As long as it's not tripe. I hate that.'

'Bacon, egg and mashed potatoes,' Ada shouted. 'And ye're going to eat it whether yer like it or not. It's not a ruddy hotel, yer know.'

A few minutes later the children stepped into the street with their sandwiches. Paul turned left to call for his mate, Eric, whom he was going to play footie with, while Monica turned in the opposite direction to knock for her friend Freda. Before being called in for dinner, they'd spend the time making plans for what they'd do when they left school. It was the same every night, and they always ended up by both saying the first thing they were going to buy was a pair of long stockings.

Ada was mashing the potatoes when there came a loud hammering on the front door. She threw the masher down and ran through the living room, afraid something dreadful had happened to one of the children, Her heart beating like mad, she opened the door only to gasp in surprise at the sight that met her eyes. For in front of her stood a neighbour from a few doors away, Doris Smedley. And Doris's hand was gripping Paul's ear, practically lifting a very frightened boy off his feet. 'This son of yours, this holy terror, has just broke me kitchen window, Ada Fenwick, playing bleeding football in the entry. What have yer got to say to that?'

'The first thing I'll say, Doris Smedley, is that if yer don't remove yer hand from my son's ear, I'll clock yer one.'

'My hand stays attached to his ear until yer tell me what yer intend doing about me broken window. I haven't got the money to have a new pane fitted, and even if I had I don't see why I should fork out when this terror was the one what done it.'

Paul kept screwing his face up with the pain. 'She's hurting me, Mam. Make her leave go of me.'

'Take yer hand away, Doris,' Ada said softly, 'or I'll do as I said, and clock yer one. Now that wouldn't do yer window much good, would it? So let Paul go, and act yer age.'

It was with great reluctance that Doris let go of Paul's ear, but she had a healthy respect for Ada Fenwick's left fist, having seen it in action. 'Well, are yer going to get me window fixed, or do I have to send my feller round to yer?'

'No, yer don't need to do that, Doris, I've got a feller of me own. And I will discuss your broken window, after I've asked yer how old your Fred is now?'

Doris's eyes narrowed. 'What the hell has my son's age got to do with me blasted broken kitchen window?'

Unnoticed by the two women who were staring each other out, Danny Fenwick had been walking up the street when he heard, and saw, what was going on. He didn't want to interfere, for he thought it wasn't right for him to do so. It would mean taking his mother's side against another woman and he didn't think that fair. So he stood and watched, ready to get involved if necessary.

'Your son's age doesn't have anything to do with your broken window, Doris, but when he was Paul's age, he had a lot to do with my broken bedroom window. Or has your memory failed yer? I didn't drag him by his ear to complain to you, did I? I came up to you, on me own, and explained what had happened. I asked yer in a civil manner if yer would

18

pay for having a new pane put in, and what did yer have to say to that? Yer told me to bugger off 'cos yer had no money.'

A few of the neighbours had come out to see what the commotion was about, and they formed a little group. Arms folded, they waited with interest to see what the outcome would be. Doris could see them out of the corner of her eye, and was sorry she'd come down on the bounce. For she'd forgotten the incident with Ada's bedroom window. 'I didn't have no money then, and I haven't got no money now. My feller doesn't earn very much.'

There were mutterings from the group of women, that her husband wasn't so short of money he couldn't go down to the corner pub every night. He was a dreadful man, a lousy husband who wouldn't think twice about giving his wife a clout if she spoke out of turn.

Danny knew her husband well, and disliked him. In fact nobody in the street had a kind word for Dick Smedley. And it was rumoured his workmates couldn't stand him, either. They'd nicknamed him Smelly Smedley. And although Danny remembered the incident all those years ago, he didn't see how it would help anyone to rake it up now. He'd been brought up in a home where there was plenty of love, with never any violence, and he had sympathy for the woman. So he smiled at the group of neighbours as he passed, and walked up to his house. 'So, our Paul's been a bit heavy-footed, eh, Mrs Smedley?'

Doris nodded. 'Yes, he has, lad, and I want to know who's going to pay to have a new pane of glass put in?'

Danny looked up at Ada. 'How much will it cost, Mam?'

'Bob Gibbons from the next street, he'll do it for half a crown. He's very obliging, and he'd do it tonight, after he's had his dinner. No mess, quick and tidy. But I don't know whether I've got half a crown in me purse right now. It might have to wait until yer dad gets in.'

Danny put his hand in his trouser pocket. 'I've got one handy, so yer may as well take it, Mrs Smedley.' And believing her husband would use the broken window as an excuse to cause a rumpus, he added, 'If yer went straight round to Mr Gibbons right now, he might do it straight away, save having any mess when yer husband comes home from work.'

Doris grabbed the money, and after a hurried, 'Thanks, lad,' she scarpered. There'd be ructions if her husband came home and found the broken window. She'd get the blame for it because she was handy for him to bawl at. But with a bit of luck he might be working late, and that would give her time to have it fixed. Bob Gibbons was a nice bloke, and noted for being understanding. A glazier by trade, he always had a sheet of glass handy, ready to cut if one of the neighbours needed help.

Later, across the dinner table, Ada told the family she'd never been so glad to see anyone, as she was to see Danny. She would have given Doris Smedley the money to have the window fixed for she knew the poor woman would get merry hell off her husband when he came in. But Ada admitted she was in a bit of a temper because of the way her Paul had been hurt and frightened. 'She had no right to take it upon herself to punish the lad. It was that what got my goat. If there was any punishment to dish out, she should have left it to the parents.'

Paul had hardly spoken since the incident; it had really scared the life out of him. There'd be no more playing footie for him, unless it was in the park. 'I won't do it again, Mam, honest. And our Danny needn't give me any pocket money until I've paid him back.'

Ah, God love him, Ada thought. It wasn't often he got into trouble, and he wasn't cheeky like some of the kids. 'Consider yerself lucky, sunshine, that me and yer dad are going to give a shilling each towards the window, and Danny said he'll pay the other tanner. But because ye're getting off light, that doesn't mean what yer did wasn't naughty, 'cos it was.'

Jimmy kept his face set when he looked at his son. 'There'll be no more playing football in the entry, or in the street. Play in the park if yer must kick a ruddy ball, but don't let me see yer or yer'll really be in trouble. We can't afford to be forking out for windows, so just bear that in mind next time yer mate Eric brings his football out.'

'He was stupid playing football in the entry,' Monica said, thinking her brother was getting off scot-free. 'He should have had more sense. But then boys don't have much sense. If they're not playing football, it's cowboys and Indians.'

Paul gave her a look to kill. 'Listen who's talking! It's not as stupid as playing with silly dolls. When you had a doll, yer used to talk to it as though it was a real baby. And if that isn't stupid, I don't know what is.'

'All right, that's enough now,' Ada told them. 'An hour ago yer were swearing undying love for each other, just to get yerselves a jam butty. If that's your idea of love, then I'm ruddy glad yer don't hate each other, or life wouldn't be worth living. A little understanding and tolerance would go a long way. Boys have boys' games, and girls have their own. I had a rag doll when I was a kid, and I used to talk to it, and take it to bed with me. I used to love that doll because it was something of my very own.'

Her husband chuckled. 'Seeing as it's confession time, I may as well tell yer that when I was Paul's age I broke a neighbour's window, when me and me mates were having a game of rounders. In fact I broke more than her window, 'cos the ball was a hard one. It went right through the window

20

and knocked an ornament off the mantelpiece. And I ended up getting a hiding off me dad. He put me across his knee and belted me with me mam's shoe. I couldn't sit down for a few days, but it taught me a lesson.'

Paul's eyes nearly popped out of his head. 'Did yer mam have to pay for the ornament, and the window?'

'She paid for the window, son, which she could ill afford 'cos money was a lot tighter then than it is now. Because of the fright I got, I have never forgotten the woman's name. Mrs Fothergill it was. And to make up for the ornament, I had to do all her messages for a month, bring a bucket of coal in for her every night after school, and swill the yard and lavatory every Saturday. When the month was up, she gave me a penny for sweets, and with that penny in me pocket I felt like a millionaire.'

'What kind of sweets did yer buy, Dad?' Paul asked. 'Did they have liquorice sticks in those days, and black jacks?'

Jimmy smiled. The way his son spoke, anyone would think it was a hundred years since he was Paul's age. 'Yes, they had those sweets, son, and I was sorely tempted. But I didn't spend the penny, I gave it to me mam.'

'I'm beginning to feel like the odd man out,' Danny said, his dimples showing. 'I'm the only one here who hasn't broken a window or had a doll. I never noticed, like, but I must have led a really dull life.'

'There's plenty of time yet, son,' Ada told him. 'It might not be windows yer break, but a few girls' hearts.'

'Oh, I've done that already, Mam! At the last count it was twenty-two. One girl took it so bad, she threatened to jump off New Brighton Pier.' He chuckled at the look on his mother's face. 'It's all right, Mam, she chickened out. She was at the dance the next night, and she had the cheek to tap me on the shoulder in the excuse me waltz.'

'She didn't jump off the pier, then?'

Danny shook his head. 'No, I pulled her up about that. I told her she had no right to say things and then not do them. And d'yer know what her answer was? She said she got the ferry over to New Brighton, determined to jump, only to realise when she got there, she'd forgotten to take her bathing costume with her.'

Paul thought he had the answer. 'She didn't intend to jump, she was only saying that to frighten yer.'

Danny put on a surprised expression. 'Is that what you think? No, I can't see her doing anything like that.'

'Of course she did,' his brother said, with all his ten years of experience behind him. 'She wanted to get her own back on yer 'cos yer wouldn't let her be your girl.'

'There speaks a man of the world, Danny,' Ada said. 'Yer want to take what he's saying on board, for he could be hitting the nail on the head.'

Danny nodded his head slowly for his young brother's benefit. 'Yeah, he could have a point. If she excuses me in a dance tonight, I'll have a word with her.'

However, Paul wasn't going to leave it there. 'Is she ugly, or something? Is that why yer don't want to go out with her?'

'Sadly, although I really shouldn't talk about anyone behind their back, ye're right. She's even worse than the pigeon-toed, bandy-legged, short-sighted girl I told yer about. This girl has got huge buck teeth, and can't close her mouth. She looks as though she's laughing all the time. If yer told her someone had died, she'd look really pleased.'

Jimmy was highly amused. 'If yer told her a joke, how would yer know whether she thought it was funny or not?'

'I couldn't tell yer the answer to that, Dad, 'cos I didn't see the point in telling her a joke.'

'These dances yer go to, son,' Ada had this question for him, 'aren't there ever any pretty girls there?'

'Oh, yeah, plenty of them! That's why I'm going to leave the table now, and nab the sink before yer start doing the washing up. I want to get there early so I'll have the pick of the bunch.' Danny pushed his chair back, then, ruffling his mother's hair, said, 'Give me fifteen minutes, Mam, 'cos I need to shave.'

He was in the kitchen when Paul shouted, 'Why d'yer have to go looking for pretty girls when there's Sally next door? She's really nice, is Sally.'

Danny's head appeared round the door. 'Because I've known Sally since the day I was born, and she's like a sister to me. And no bloke would want to go out with his sister.'

Ada lifted her hand to silence Paul when she saw he was about to speak. 'Leave it now, son, and let him get ready. And leave yer plate where it is. I'll take it out later, with the others.'

She gave a little sigh, but kept her thoughts to herself. She'd never mentioned it to her family, but over the years, when Danny and Hetty's daughter Sally were growing up, they had been really good mates. And both mothers had been hoping the pair would one day find romance together. They would have been over the moon to have the two families united. But while Sally did at one time seem keen on the boy next door, nothing had ever come of it. The two were, as Danny said, like brother and sister. They would always be there to help each other, but that vital spark of love was missing.

Danny was whistling when he reached the entrance to the building, and he took the flight of steps leading up to the dance hall two at a time. He could hear the strains of a waltz, and he softly hummed the melody as he handed sixpence over to the attendant for his ticket. Dancing was in his blood, and he was never happier than when he was gliding across the dance floor, keeping in perfect time with the music.

When he pushed the door of the hall open, he could see there were several couples on the floor, all very experienced dancers who enjoyed having the space to twist and twirl without bumping into another couple. Their style and grace was putting off the learners, who preferred to wait until the hall was crowded, when any mistakes they made wouldn't be noticed. There were groups of girls standing at the edge of the floor, waiting and hoping to be asked to dance by one of the group of lads standing near the doorway.

There were three girls whom Danny danced with regularly. He never saw them away from the dance hall; they were only partners when they were dancing. All three were good dancers and one of them was there now, with the other girls lining the side of the floor. She saw him come through the door and waved. He walked towards her, his dimples showing when he grinned, and causing a few of the young girls to sigh with hope. If only he was walking towards them, they would be overjoyed. But it was a slim, blonde-haired girl who reached for his outstretched hand when he asked, 'Are yer dancing, Janet?'

The girl's pretty face lit up. 'Are yer asking, Danny?'

'I'm asking.'

'Then I'm dancing.'

The music had changed to a slow foxtrot, and Danny clasped the girl's hand and pulled her gently on to the floor. The slow foxtrot was his favourite dance, and holding his partner close he led her into each step. They were perfect partners, moving with grace and ease across the floor. And he was sorry when the dance came to an end. 'Ye're no sooner getting into it than they stop,' Danny grumbled as he walked Janet back to where her friends were. Releasing her hand, he told her, 'I'll be back for the quickstep. So if anyone else asks yer, tell them ye're spoken for.'

'It depends who it is,' Janet said, smiling. 'If it was Cary Grant, then I'm afraid he'd win hands down.'

Danny pretended to be horrified. 'Cary Grant! He's old enough to be yer dad, and he can't dance for toffee.'

'Oh, I wouldn't have me mind on toffee if Cary Grant came and stood in front of me and asked me for a dance.' Janet giggled. 'I wouldn't be worrying about anything because I'd be flat out on the floor in a dead faint.'

'Yeah, I suppose ye're right,' Danny said, deadpan. 'I think Cary would call it swoon, and not faint. Yer see, a long time ago, when he was a lot younger, all the ladies used to swoon when they saw him.' He was chuckling when he turned away. 'I can't see Cary Grant making it here tonight, he'd never manage to get on and off the tram at his age. And even if he did, the steps outside would defeat him. So, to save yer being a wallflower, I'll step in for him when the quickstep comes up.' Danny winked at her, before walking off to join the group of lads standing by the door. The girls were for dancing with, his mates were for having a laugh with, and talking about work.

He was listening to one of his mates, Greg, sounding off about the lousy wages he was getting, and the miserable sod he was working with, when the double doors opened and two girls came through. They both waved to Danny, for they were the other two girls he regularly danced with. Betsy, who had auburn hair and a slim figure, was fantastic at the tango; no other girl could match her. Dorothy, on the other hand, with her black hair and deep brown eyes, excelled at the quickstep and the rumba. They always came to the dance together for they lived in the same street and were good friends. But their arrival coincided with the sound of a quickstep starting up, and this put Danny in a bit of a dilemma. For Dorothy was looking at him, expectation in the smile on her face. But he'd promised Janet now, and he didn't want to let her down. He chuckled inside, thinking Janet wasn't the type to let him get away with it. If he chose Dorothy now, then next time he asked Janet she'd tell him to get lost in no uncertain terms.

'Are yer dancing, Janet?' Danny asked, feeling Dorothy's eyes boring into his back. 'Seeing as Cary Grant hasn't been able to make it.'

'I suppose yer know Dorothy's here, don't yer?'

'Yeah, I saw her come in with Betsy. Why?'

'Well, perhaps yer don't know she's giving yer cow's eyes. I don't mind if yer dance with her, Danny. I'll get asked up, if that's what's worrying yer.'

'I asked you before Dorothy even got here, so I don't see why I should back out on yer, even if she is giving me cow's eyes. The worst thing she can do is trip me up in the middle of the floor, just when I'm doing me intricate steps, what I'm famous for in every dance hall in the city of Liverpool.' He took Janet's hand and pulled her on to the dance floor. 'Anyway, surely to goodness I can dance with who I like. Why should I be frightened of Dorothy? It's a free country.' He waited for the right beat, then swept forward, carrying Janet along with him. After a few seconds, he whispered, 'Ay, have yer ever seen Dorothy's dad? D'yer know if he's a big feller or not? I don't mind facing a little twerp, but I don't fancy taking on a bloke what looks like King Kong.'

Janet wanted to laugh, but she could see Dorothy staring at her so she kept her face straight. 'I have seen him, yeah. I don't live far from them. I'd say he was in between a twerp and a King Kong.'

'In that case, I'd better be diplomatic. The next dance with Dorothy, then the tango with Betsy. After that I should be free to ask you again.' They had reached the corner of the dance floor, and Danny was silent as he executed his famous twirl. Then he said, 'They might put a rumba on, though, so then I'll be back to Dorothy.'

Janet liked Danny, and wished he would ask her out one night. But she knew he was too fond of dancing to waste a night sitting in a picture house. One day, perhaps he'd surprise her, you never know. 'While ye're dancing with Dot, ask her about her dad. Not outright, like, but in the course of a conversation. If she says he's about the same height as herself, then yer'll be safe to ask me up again.' Her pretty face creased with laughter. 'If I don't see yer again tonight, I'll know her dad is a six footer.'

'Ay, I'm no midget meself, yer know. Five feet ten in me socks, and five eleven when I've got me shoes on. And I'm only just eighteen, so I'm still a growing lad.'

'Ah, well, in that case, Dot's father should be a pushover for yer.'

'I wouldn't go as far as to say that,' Danny said. 'And in the interval, when all the girls disappear to the ladies' room to renew their lipstick, don't you be getting too friendly with Dorothy, either. I know what girls are like for a bit of gossip.'

The music came to an end, and Danny was leading Janet back to her mates when she said, 'I don't stand gossiping while I'm putting me lipstick on, Danny, I don't have time. I'm far too busy listening to the other girls pulling each other to pieces.'

Danny left her with a smile, and rejoined his mates. She had a good sense of humour, did Janet. That was one of the things he liked about her. More than could be said for his mate, Greg, who was still moaning about his wages and the miserable sod he worked with. 'It's a waste of a tanner, you coming here,' Danny told him. 'Why don't yer stay at home? Yer could moan to yer heart's content there, and it wouldn't cost yer anything.'

'It doesn't cost me anything to come.' Greg had a smirk on his face. 'Me ma pays for me.'

Another mate, Paddy, said, 'I don't blame her. She probably does it so she doesn't have to listen to yer moaning all night.'

Danny cocked an ear. The four piece band were playing a rumba. And there wasn't a girl in the hall who could do a rumba as well as Dorothy. So he made haste towards her. 'Are yer fit, Dorothy?'

Dorothy's deep brown eyes widened, and when she spoke there was a hint of sarcasm in her voice. 'Oh, I thought yer'd be asking Janet for this one. Yer seemed to be getting quite matey with her.'

'Did I? Oh, well, if yer don't want to dance, I may as well ask her.'

Dorothy was quick to tell him, 'I didn't say I didn't want to dance, I was only remarking that yer seemed friendly with Janet. Yer know I enjoy doing the rumba with yer.'

'Shall we get on the floor before the dance is over, then?'

There was no doubt that Dorothy was outstanding when doing the rumba. Many couples left the floor to stand at the side and watch. And Danny, his head and chest swollen with pride, matched her step for step. They made a perfect couple, and both knew it. But Danny wasn't quite as serious as Dorothy, he could always see the funny side. And when they came to the part of the rumba where he bent her backwards over his left arm, he looked down at her, his dimples deepening, and asked, 'By the way, Dorothy, is your father a big bloke?'

Chapter Three

It was Monday morning and Ada was struggling to turn the heavy handle on the mangle. She stopped to wipe the perspiration from her forehead, saying aloud, 'I hate ruddy Mondays. I don't know why we can't spread the wash over a few days and make life easier for ourselves.' With a deep sigh, she turned the handle again with her right hand, while with her left she held the sheet as it came through the rubber rollers at the back. 'It's a flaming custom that's been passed down from generation to generation. In fact it's probably a habit from the year dot. Washday every Monday, and fish day every Friday. Not that I dislike fish, I'm rather partial to it, but I hate Monday!'

The sheet came out from the rollers, and Ada folded it several times so it wouldn't touch the stone floor. She stood for a while to catch her breath, then opened the kitchen door and stepped down into the yard. The large pocket in her pinny was bulging with wooden pegs, and she took three out and put them in her mouth before throwing the sheet over the clothes line. Then she opened it up and spread it along the line, pegging it at intervals. There was a breeze out, and soon the sheet was blowing in the wind. She leaned back against the wall and watched it as her head filled with notions. 'I'd swap places with my feller any day. I'd do his job, and he could take over the housework. He wouldn't know what had hit him. I'd give him one week, and he'd throw the towel in. In fact he wouldn't last the week.'

'Ada Fenwick, are you talking to yerself?' Hetty's voice floated over the wall. 'Yer want to be careful, 'cos it's a bad sign, that is.'

'Well, it's Monday, isn't it? I'm entitled to have a moan. It's the worst ruddy day of the week, and from this week I'm going on strike. Instead of one big wash, I'm going to do a bit each day and make life easier for meself.'

'No matter how yer do it, queen, it's still the same amount of washing. And it's not all bad today, the weather is just the job for drying the clothes quickly. We'll have them all dry by teatime, ready to iron in the morning.'

'Thanks for telling me that, sunshine, it gives me something to look forward to. A stack of ruddy ironing!'

'My goodness, you are down in the dumps, aren't yer? When yer've put the washing out, why don't yer come here and I'll make us a nice pot of tea. I might even stretch to giving yer a few biscuits to dunk.'

Ada, still leaning against the yard wall with her arms folded, called, 'Considering you've got nearly as many to wash for as I have, can I ask why ye're feeling so pleased with yerself?'

'I've had the wireless on while I've been doing me washing, and Victor Silvester and his dance band have been on. It's a wonder yer didn't hear me singing along with all the old tunes he played. I haven't half enjoyed meself.'

Ada pulled herself away from the wall. 'Why the hell didn't yer tell me he was on? Yer know he's a favourite of mine. If yer'd used yer brains and given me a knock, I could have been as happy as you are.'

'If you hadn't been so busy moaning and talking to yerself, queen, then yer would have heard the radio through the wall. And I was singing so loud me throat's gone all dry.'

'Then the sooner we get our washing out, and the tea made, the better. So let's shake a leg and get it over with. I'll be at yours in about twenty minutes. I've been washed, I only need to comb me hair to make meself presentable.'

'Who d'yer want to make yerself presentable for?' Hetty asked. 'Is it Ronnie in the butcher's yer've got yer eye on, or Stan in the grocer's?'

'Ah, ay, sunshine, credit me with a bit of taste. My Jimmy would knock spots off those two! If I was looking for a feller, it would have to be someone with loads of money. And d'yer know why I'd like someone with loads of money?'

Hetty knew her mate inside out, and she grinned. 'Yeah, I bet I can quess why yer'd like a sugar daddy.'

'I bet yer can't! Not unless ye're a blinking mind reader.'

'A penny if I guess right? Scout's honour?'

'Oh, go on then, I'm as daft as you. A penny it is, if yer get it right.'

'Yer'd like to have enough money to take all the washing to the laundry, so there'd be no more Monday morning blues.'

Ada shook her head slowly. 'D'yer know what, Hetty Watson, you should be sitting in one of those booths they have at fairgrounds. Yer know what I'm talking about: they have a gypsy sitting there with a glass ball on a table in front of her, and she entices people in by saying she'll tell them their fortune if they cross her palm with silver.'

'Yeah, I'd like that,' Hetty said. 'I've never told yer this before, but I am a bit of a fortune-teller. For instance, I'll tell yer what your fortune is now. I haven't got no glass ball, but I'm getting a sensation running through me whole body. And it's saying that if yer don't get back in the house and do what yer've got to do, then we'll be late getting to the shops. So get yer skates on, girl.'

It was eleven o'clock and the friends were leaving Hetty's house, having finished off a pot of tea and a plate of biscuits. She was closing the door behind them when one of the neighbours opposite waved to them. Her name was Jean Bowers, and she lived next to Eliza Porter. 'Have yer got a minute to spare, ladies?'

'Yeah, of course we have,' Ada said. 'As long as yer don't want us to help yer hang yer washing out. A bit of a sore subject, that is.' She linked her arm through Hetty's and together they crossed the cobbles. 'D'yer want something from the shops, sunshine?'

Jean shook her head. She was a pretty woman, with fair hair, blue eyes, and a round happy face with rosy cheeks and dimples. 'No, I'll be going to the shops meself soon, Ada. And I'm probably worrying for nothing, but I haven't heard a sound from Eliza's house all morning. Usually I hear her raking out the grate, or the water running in the kitchen, but I haven't heard a thing this morning. I thought she might be having a lie-in, as she sometimes does, but never until this time.'

'Have yer had a word with Edith?' Hetty asked. 'She usually gives Eliza a knock before she goes to the shops.'

'That's just it,' Jean said, clasping her hands. 'Edith went out early this morning, to visit her mam, and she asked me if I'd see to any shopping Eliza wanted. And I've knocked a few times but got no answer, and I'm starting to get worried. I don't know what to do for the best.'

'Have yer looked through the window?' Ada asked, walking towards the house next door. 'She may be asleep on the couch.' With a hand shading her eyes, she tried to see through the net curtains, but they were heavily patterned and it was impossible to see anything. She was frowning when she joined her two neighbours. 'I can't see anything. But if my memory serves me right, doesn't she leave a key on a piece of string in the lavatory, in case of an emergency? I'm sure she told me once, oh, years ago, that she was afraid of locking herself out, so she kept a spare key in the lavvy.'

Jean was very flustered. 'Trust this to happen when it was my day to keep an eye on her. Even if there is a key, I couldn't just walk in on her, she'd get a fright.'

'If ye're so concerned about her, that's the only solution if she's not answering the door to yer. For all we know she might not be feeling well, and it's better to be safe than sorry. If yer nip through yours and get the

29

key from her lavvy, I'll go in, sunshine,' Ada said. 'And I'll shout out when I open the door, so she won't get a fright.'

Hetty nodded her head in agreement. 'Ada's right, queen, we can't just do nothing. And if Eliza's not feeling well, she'll be glad to see us.'

'Okay, you stay here while I slip through my yard to hers. If the key is where yer say it is, Ada, I'll bring it back to yer.' Jean pulled a face. 'I'm hopeless in an emergency, I go to pieces. So, coward that I am, I'll let you go in first.'

While Jean was running through her house to get into next door's yard, Ada said, 'If I ever have an accident, sunshine, don't send for Jean, will yer? Get someone who'll tell me a few jokes so I can laugh. Then I'll know I'm not on me death bed.'

'Jean's got a good sense of humour,' Hetty said. 'She's always got a smile on her face.'

'Not today she hasn't, sunshine, or haven't yer noticed?'

'That's because she feels responsible for the old lady. I'd be the same if I was in her shoes.' Hetty wagged a finger in her friend's face. 'Besides, you're a fine one to talk. Yer had a face on yer like a wet week until I put a cup of tea in front of yer. A real ray of sunshine yer would have been to someone on their deathbed, I don't think!'

Ada chuckled. 'Yer don't have to tell me that, 'cos when I looked in the mirror to comb me hair, I didn't want to think the miserable face staring back at me was me own.' Again she chuckled. 'I pretended it was you, on one of yer bad days.'

'You cheeky article!' But Hetty couldn't help smiling. 'Even on one of me bad days, I'm a damn sight better-looking than you, queen.'

'That's a matter of opinion, sunshine,' Ada said. 'And there's one way to settle the matter once and for all. When we get back from the shops, we'll stand in front of the mirror in my house and ask, "Mirror, mirror, on the wall, who is the fairest of them all?"'

'How soft you are, Ada Fenwick. That mirror over the mantelpiece in your house is cracked to blazes! I went home from your house one day thinking I looked seventy years old, with me face full of wrinkles. It was only when I happened to glance in me own mirror that I realised I didn't have any wrinkles, it was that ruddy mirror of yours.'

Ada put a hand across her mouth, and her eyes bulged. 'D'yer mean I've gone through life thinking me face was lined and wrinkled, when really I've got a complexion as smooth as a baby's bottom? Well, fancy that now! As soon as I get home, that mirror is going in the ruddy midden, and me wrinkles with it.'

Jean Bowers came rushing out of her house dangling a key on a piece

30

of string. 'Yer were right, Ada, it was hanging on a nail in the wall.' She handed it over. 'I've changed me mind, and I'm coming in with yer. I can't go through life being a coward.'

'That's not being a coward, girl,' Hetty told her. 'Ye're worried about the old lady, that's all. Same as me. I'm concerned about her, too, and that doesn't make us cowards.'

'There's only one way to find out why Eliza hasn't opened the door to yer, Jean, and that's to go in and see if she's all right.' Ada slipped the key in the lock, and said softly, 'I'll go in first and call her name, so she won't get a fright.' She jerked her head. 'You two follow me in.'

There wasn't a sound as the three women huddled together in the tiny hall. Then Ada called, 'Eliza, it's Ada. You know, the nosy parker from over the road. Where are yer?'

A faint voice came back to them. 'I'm in me bedroom, Ada. Will yer come up, please? I've had a bit of an accident.'

Ada pushed her two neighbours aside and made for the stairs, fearful something serious had happened to the old lady. 'I'm on me way, Eliza. Hetty and Jean are with me.'

When the three women crowded into the room, it was to see the old lady sitting on the side of the bed, still in her nightdress. 'Oh, I am so glad to see you.' Her lips quivered as she tried to smile. 'I thought I was going to be here all day.'

Jean rushed to sit beside her on the bed, and she took a frail hand in hers. 'Eliza, yer've had me worried to death. I've knocked at least six times in the last hour, and when I didn't get an answer, I didn't know what to do. I mentioned it to Ada and Hetty, and fortunately Ada remembered about yer leaving a spare key in the lavatory.'

'I heard yer knocking, sweetheart, and I shouted as loud as I could. But me voice isn't very strong now, and yer couldn't have heard me.'

'Well we're all here now, Eliza,' Ada said, 'so tell us what's happened, and why ye're sitting up here?'

'I've been very silly,' Eliza said. 'I know that when yer get to my age yer shouldn't be in a hurry to do things 'cos yer can go dizzy and lose yer balance. So as a rule, whether it's getting out of a chair, or out of bed, I give meself a minute for me brain to get organised. However, I forgot the golden rule this morning, got out of bed too quickly, went dizzy, stumbled, and twisted me ankle. I was afraid I'd broken it at first, but now I think I've just sprained it. Thank God it happened by the side of the bed, and I was able to sit down.'

'What time did it happen, sunshine?' Ada asked. 'Have yer been sitting there long?'

31

Eliza nodded. 'I woke at the usual time of seven o'clock. When yer get to my age, yer don't need much sleep. I have tried a few times to stand up, but it's too painful.'

'Yer must be hungry, queen,' Hetty said. 'I'll go and make yer a cup of tea and a piece of toast.'

'While Hetty's doing that, sunshine, we've got to try and get yer down the stairs.' Ada put a hand on her chin as she weighed up the situation. 'I might be able to carry yer, 'cos I'm strong, and there's not much of you. Or me and Jean could carry yer between us. I could lift you under yer arms, while Jean took yer feet. One way or another, we'll get yer down those stairs in time for the promised tea and toast. Which way would yer like to be carried down, Eliza? Which would be the least painful for yer?'

Jean thought she had a brainwave. 'Why don't you and me join hands, Ada, and make a chair to carry her down?'

'I don't think so, sunshine, the stairs are not wide enough. But what I could do is give yer a piggyback, Eliza, what d'yer think to that? I'd be very careful not to let your foot touch the wall or the stairs.'

'I couldn't let yer do that, Ada, yer might end up straining yerself.'

'Yer haven't got much choice, sunshine, 'cos the banister isn't wide enough for yer to slide down, and there's no men to help out. So it's either a piggyback off yours truly, or you spending the rest of the day up here. My Jimmy would carry yer down in no time, but the trouble is, he ain't here. So it's Hobson's choice, I'm afraid.'

'You'll be all right, Eliza,' Jean said. 'Ada's very strong, and I'll walk down in front, just to make sure ye're safe.'

'I'll be walking down backwards, Jean,' Ada told her. 'I'd feel safer doing it that way. Eliza can put her arms round me neck and I'll hang on to the banister rail to let meself down each stair.' She bent and grinned into the old lady's face. 'If all else fails, sunshine, we'll slide down, with you sitting on me knees. My backside is well padded, I wouldn't feel a thing. But I do think a piggyback is the best way.'

Eliza managed a smile. 'It must be seventy years since I had a piggyback. Me father used to give me one every Saturday when I went to meet him coming home from work. It won't be as easy for you as it was for him, though.'

'Oh dear, oh dear, oh dear! Have some faith in me, sunshine, I'll not let yer down. Now I'm going to turn me back on yer, so yer can put yer arms round me neck. And when yer've got tight hold, Jean will help yer off the bed as I stand up straight.' Ada glanced over her shoulder and winked. 'And this is no time for shimmy-shaking, either, so behave yerself.'

32

'I'm more worried about you than I am about meself,' Eliza said as she put her arms round Ada's neck. 'All this trouble I'm putting yer to, just because I'm a stupid old woman who can't remember how to get out of bed.'

'Ay, doing stupid things isn't reserved for the elderly, sunshine,' Ada said, standing upright and taking Eliza's weight. 'Not a day goes by when I don't call meself for all the stupid nits going.'

'Me too!' Jean said, her hands round the old lady's thin waist, trying to lighten the load for Ada. 'Ask my Gordon, he'll tell yer how forgetful I am. I can have something in me hand one minute, then the next I can't remember what I've done with it.'

'Right, I'm ready for the off,' Ada told them. 'You walk down the stairs in front of me, Jean, and yer can guide me feet. In five minutes we'll have yer lying on the couch, Eliza, and we can have a look at this ankle of yours.'

When she'd been sitting on her bed, all alone and worried in case nobody missed her until the next day, Eliza thought she'd never laugh again. But the performance of getting down the stairs was so hilarious, all three woman ended up giggling and laughing. Jean was supposed to be walking in front of Ada and telling her when to step down to the next stair. But to do that, Jean had to walk down backwards herself, and with Eliza's backside practically in her face, it was no easy task. 'Don't take this as personal, Jean,' Ada croaked, 'but I wouldn't like to climb a mountain with you as a guide. Yer might get us up there, but God help us when it came to finding our way down.'

'If we were climbing a mountain, I wouldn't have a backside in me face, and a pair of dangling legs.' Jean patted Eliza's bottom. 'Not that yer haven't got a nice little bottom, girl, or a pair of legs many a person half your age would be proud of. It's just that I have to keep me eye on the step below me, or I'd end up falling down the lot. And while I don't mind ending up at the bottom of the stairs with you on top of me, I draw the line at Ada falling on me as well.'

Having made a pot of tea, and a plate of toast, Hetty came from the kitchen to find out what the commotion was about. Standing at the bottom of the stairs, she said, 'What in the name of goodness is taking yer so long? And for the life of me I can't see what yer all find so amusing. Eliza is in agony, and it's nothing to laugh about.'

'I'm all right, sweetheart,' Eliza told her. 'In fact I'm enjoying meself. I have to say, though, that it's a different kettle of fish for Ada. I'm nearly choking the poor woman to death.'

'Yes, I have noticed me mate is croaking a bit. But it's nothing for you to worry about, queen.' Hetty winked before realising they all had their backs to her. 'There's a few people will be pleased if she loses her voice for a while.'

'If yer haven't come to help, then bugger off, Hetty.' Ada's voice was rough. 'To make yerself useful, yer could take over from Jean, give her a break.'

'Okay, Jean, yer heard what me boss said. You go and pour four cups of tea out, and we'll have Eliza on the couch in no time.'

When Jean had made her escape to the safety of the kitchen, Hetty climbed the few stairs to reach the old lady. 'Now let's get down to business, and we'll have no more laughing out of the pair of yer. Not until we've got the patient in the living room in one piece. There's only four stairs now, Ada, so if yer come down another two, then I'll relieve yer of Eliza. I could lift her down the other two, she's not heavy. Are yer fit, Ada?'

'Fit as a fiddle, sunshine.' Ada wouldn't complain for the world, but her neck was sore. Eliza was small and thin, but it was still a heavy weight for Ada's neck to support. It would have been easier if she could have carried the old lady, but she needed the use of the banister for safety. 'Let's get it over as quickly as possible.'

Hetty's presence gave Ada more confidence, and she managed to get down the two steps without fear of tripping with her frail neighbour. And from the next to bottom stair, Hetty put her arms round Eliza's waist and carried her through to the living room, and the couch. 'There yer are, that wasn't too bad, was it?'

The old lady was shaking a bit, but that was from shock, not cold. Heaven knows what would have happened if Ada hadn't remembered the spare key. But she was soon tucked up with a cover over her knees, a cup of tea in her hand, and a plate of toast on her lap. 'I don't know how to thank you. You've all been marvellous.'

'No thanks needed, sunshine, we're getting a nice cup of tea in return.' Ada felt she hadn't really been fair on Jean, so she gave her a big smile. 'It's all down to Jean, anyway. She was the one who was worried enough to find out why yer weren't opening the door.'

The laughter was back in Jean's eyes now Eliza was safe and well. 'I'll put the key back in the lavatory, sweetheart, but I hope yer never have the need for it again.'

'Drink your tea, sunshine, and eat some of the toast,' Ada said. 'Then we'll have a look at yer ankle. If it's broken, I'm afraid we'll have to send for the doctor, 'cos none of us would know what to do. If it's only a sprain, though, a couple of days resting on the couch should do the trick. We'll all be keeping an eye on yer to make sure yer do as ye're told, and we'll take turns making yer cups of tea and bringing meals in to yer.'

Hetty nodded in agreement. 'We'll make sure yer don't starve, queen, yer can depend on that.'

Tears came to the faded blue eyes. 'I am so lucky to have such kind neighbours. What would I do without you?'

'Oh, I know what yer'd do if we didn't keep our eyes on yer,' Ada said, chuckling. 'Yer'd have a different fancy man in here every night and get the street a bad name.'

Hetty agreed. 'None of our husbands would be safe. We'd have to lock them in every night, or tie them to a chair.'

Eliza finished her tea and passed the cup and saucer over. 'You are all lucky with the men you married. They're good husbands and fathers.'

Ada put her cup on the table with Eliza's. 'Now let's have a look at this ankle of yours. That's unless yer've been having us on, and were playing the wounded soldier 'cos yer wanted some company.'

The old lady smiled. 'Yes, I'm fond of doing tricks like that, Ada. I put yer through all this just so I could see yer happy faces.'

'We'll be a lot happier when we've seen that ankle, sunshine, so I'm taking this cover off yer.' Ada dropped down on to her knees. She didn't need to touch the thin leg, for she only had to look at the ankle to see it was swollen to twice its normal size. 'Hetty, come and have a look at this, will yer? I'd say it was a sprain, meself. If it was broken, Eliza would be in agony and the foot would be out of shape. What do you think?'

'I think ye're probably right, queen.' Hetty knelt at the side of her mate, and smiled into the old lady's face. 'I'm going to touch yer ankle, queen, and if it really hurts, then shout out.' She gently touched the area around the ankle, then when there was no cry of pain, she ran her hand over it. 'Did that hurt very much, queen?'

'Me ankle is very sore, sweetheart, but your touching it didn't make it any worse.'

'Then it definitely isn't broken, or yer'd have been screaming the house down. What we'll do is put a cold compress on it, and see if that eases it for yer. Have yer got anything I can use, like an old pillowcase or something?'

Eliza pointed to the cupboard in the alcove at the side of the fireplace. 'Yer'll find what yer want in there, sweetheart. Don't worry about looking for an old one if all ye're going to do is wet it. I'm quite well off for sheets and pillowcases.'

'Ay, don't be sitting there like Lady Muck, telling us how well off yer are.' Ada opened the cupboard door and smiled when she saw the sheets, pillowcases, tablecloths and tea towels in neat piles. She took out a pillowcase and passed it to Hetty, before saying, 'Yer put me to shame,

Eliza. My cupboard looks a shambles compared to yours. If Jimmy or one of the kids want anything, they just pull it out and leave the rest crumpled up.'

Jean came through from the kitchen carrying a bowl of water. 'While ye're near the cupboard, Ada, would yer get one of the big towels out, please?' She put the bowl down on the table. 'Eliza will need a thick towel under her foot so the couch won't get wet.'

Hetty stayed on her knees and passed the pillowcase to Jean. 'Soak it in the water, girl, and then wring most of the water out.'

Ten minutes later, the old lady had a cushion under her foot to keep it raised, and a cold compress wrapped around the swollen ankle. 'The compress will need changing quite often, so if you want to go to the shops, Jean, me and Hetty will stay here until yer come back.'

Jean shook her head. 'No, you were on yer way to the shops when I nabbed yer, so you do yer shopping first and I'll sit with Eliza.'

Struggling to her feet, Ada nodded. 'We'll be back as quick as we can, to relieve yer. Then yer can get yer own shopping done, and whatever Eliza wants.' She bent to kiss the old lady's cheek. 'A couple of days, sunshine, and yer'll be running around like a two-year-old. Until then, sit back and let us spoil yer.'

Linking arms with Hetty as they walked down the street, Ada said, 'Poor old soul. It must be rotten to get to that age and live on yer own.'

'Yeah,' Hetty agreed. 'From all accounts she is someone who was always on the go, kept her house spotless, and helped anyone in the street who was down on their luck.'

'Growing old is something that comes to all of us, sunshine, it's the one thing we can do nothing about. But don't let's make ourselves miserable by thinking of it. We've got a good way to go to reach Eliza's age.'

They were outside the butcher's by this time, and Hetty asked, 'What are yer getting for tonight's dinner?'

Ada chuckled. 'I put it to the vote last night, and all hands went up for Cumberland sausage fried with onions, on top of mashed potatoes.'

'That sounds good, queen,' Hetty said. 'Yer won't mind if I copy yer, will yer?'

'Of course I don't mind. Yer know what they say, sunshine, about copying being the most sincere form of flattery.'

When they walked into the shop the butcher raised his brows. 'Ye're late today, ladies. I'd almost given yer up. In fact, and Barry here will tell yer it's true, I was beginning to think I'd got me days mixed up, and today was Friday.'

'We got waylaid, Ronnie,' Hetty told him. 'One of our neighbours needed help.'

'Yeah, we haven't half had some excitement, Ronnie. It's been like something yer see in the pictures.'

Hetty looked up at her friend, puzzlement on her face. She hadn't found the events of the morning exciting. Worrying, yes, but never exciting. She was about to query Ada's remark when a sharp kick in the shin told her it would be to her advantage to keep her mouth shut.

'I could do with a bit of excitement,' Ronnie said, 'so what's been happening?'

Ada leaned her two elbows on the counter, a sure sign she had a tale to tell. 'One of our neighbours is elderly, in her eighties. She's a lovely old soul; everyone in the street thinks the world of her.'

Now Ronnie wanted a bit of excitement to liven things up a bit, but he didn't want any sad news. 'Ay, ye're not going to tell me she's died, are yer, Ada? It's nourishment I want, not ruddy punishment.'

'Of course she hasn't died, yer soft nit! She fell over in her bedroom and twisted her ankle. She couldn't move 'cos she was in agony. She couldn't get down the stairs, so she was sat on the edge of the bed from seven o'clock until one of the neighbours knocked. And although she shouted down the stairs, Jean, the neighbour, couldn't hear her. And Jean was worried about her, what with not hearing any noise from the house and getting no answer. So she told me and Hetty. We looked through the window and couldn't see any sign of life.' She put her hand on Hetty's shoulder. 'Me mate here will tell yer I'm not lying, Ronnie.'

'No one said yer were lying, Ada, so just get on with it! Is the old lady still sitting on the side of the bed? And if she couldn't open the door to yer, how did yer know she'd hurt her ankle?'

Ada stood up straight and put her hands on her hips. 'Who's telling this story, Ronnie Atwill, you or me?'

The butcher held his hands up in surrender. 'You are, Ada, but ye're not half spinning it out. Why not let Hetty tell us? She'll be quicker.'

'Because it wasn't Hetty what went for the ladder, that's why!'

It was hard to know which face showed the most surprise, Ronnie, his young assistant Barry, or Hetty. But Hetty was quick to avert her face, and she left it to the butcher to ask, 'What ladder, Ada? Where does a ladder come into it?'

'Because we couldn't get in the house any other way, soft lad, and we had to find out whether the old lady was all right or not. So yer know Bob Gibbons, the glazier who lives a few streets away? Well, I had to run round to his house to borrow a ladder. He was at work, and of course he had all his big ladders with him in his van. But his wife was very helpful, and let me take the one he keeps in the yard for emergencies. It's what yer call an extending ladder, like two ladders in one. It wasn't half heavy to carry. I bet me shoulder's black and blue with the weight.'

When Ada stopped for breath, and for inspiration, Ronnie asked, 'Yer didn't carry that heavy ladder on yer own, did yer?'

Hetty said a little prayer asking God to forgive her for telling lies, but she had to help her mate out. 'She did, Ronnie, all on her own. I would have helped, but she didn't ask, she just ran off without saying where she was going.'

'Well, when I left yer, I didn't know Bob was going to be out at work and I'd have to carry the bloody ladder meself, did I? Anyway, I managed to carry it, even though it did take it out of me. And carrying the ladder was the easy part. The worst part was climbing up it, and then having to hold on with one hand while shoving the window up with the other.'

'And don't forget to tell Ronnie yer were also worried about people looking up yer clothes and seeing yer knickers.' Hetty was getting into the spirit of things now. In her mind's eye, she could see Ada on top of the ladder, hanging on like grim death. 'Ronnie won't get embarrassed, he's a married man.'

'Yer didn't climb through the window, did yer, Ada?' Ronnie thought she was having him on at first, but she looked so serious he started to believe her.

'There was no other way of getting into the house, Ronnie, unless we'd broken the door down. And there was no point in me lugging a big ladder the length of three streets if I wasn't going to make use of it.' Ada gave a good imitation of a heartfelt sigh. 'I was terrified climbing through that window, though. I had to hang on tight when I cocked me leg through. Me heart was in me mouth the whole time. I've always been afraid of heights, so how I did it, I'll never know. I just kept telling meself there was an old lady in the house, and she could be very ill for all we knew.'

'It was your good deed for the day,' Hetty said, her head nodding slowly. 'Wasn't it, queen? You saved the day.'

'I don't know about being a good deed,' Ronnie said. 'I think it was a very stupid thing to do. Yer could have been killed.'

'It wasn't as stupid as you falling for it, sunshine.' Ada bent double with laughter. 'If only yer could have seen yer face, Ronnie. It was a picture.'

Ronnie pursed his lips for a few seconds, his mind working overtime. 'The look on my face won't be a patch on yours when I tell yer we've got no Cumberland sausage in.'

The two women looked stunned. 'How did yer know we wanted Cumberland sausage?'

'We heard yer talking on the way in, and I said to Barry, they're going to be disappointed.'

But Ada had detected a smirk on the young assistant's face. 'Oh, well, in that case we'll have to walk along to the Co-op. It's not far; the walk will do us good.'

The butcher grinned. 'Tit for tat, Ada. You pulled my leg, I pull yours. So, was it a pound of Cumberland for both of yer?'

'Ye're a cheeky bugger, Ronnie Atwill,' Ada said. 'But because Hetty's got corns what are giving her gyp, we'll take the sausage off yer to save her the walk.'

Now Hetty had never had a corn in her life, but she didn't relish another kick on the shin, so she smiled. 'Suits me, Ada, and it's very thoughtful of yer to remember me corns.'

Chapter Four

Ada was wiping her wet hands down her pinny when she came through from the kitchen after washing the breakfast dishes. She'd put a light under the kettle, promising herself a quiet half-hour with a cup of tea. Then she let out a sigh when her eyes caught sight of a few finger marks on the front window. That would be young Paul's fault, knocking to tell his mate to wait for him and they'd walk to school together. She was forever telling him off about it, but it was like talking to the wall. When he got home today, though, she'd give him a right telling off, for now the windows wanted cleaning. And although she wasn't in the mood, she knew she'd only worry herself silly for the rest of the day if she didn't give the panes a good going over with the shammy leather. She'd always prided herself on having the cleanest windows in the street, and the whitest front step, and she wasn't going to lower her standards, even if it did mean her cup of tea would have to wait.

The water was hot in the kettle, so Ada poured it into the washing-up bowl with some cold water from the tap. Then she added a large tablespoonful of vinegar before throwing in the shammy leather. The vinegar had been a tip from her mother when she was only about ten years old. She could see her mother's face now, as she told her that the secret of sparkling windows was adding a drop of vinegar to the water, and having a good shammy leather. It was a tip Ada had never forgotten.

In front of the window was a small round wooden table, upon which stood a very healthy aspidistra plant that was Ada's pride and joy. And as she lifted it from its spot, she said, 'I'm sorry to disturb yer, sunshine, but if I don't clean the windows I'll be the talk of every wash-house from here to the Pier Head.' The plant was placed on the table, while a chair was taken out and carried to the window. The draw curtains were pulled back and the nets taken down, before Ada wrung the water out of the shammy leather and climbed on to the wooden seat of the dining chair. She didn't feel very safe on the chair which was old and rickety, so while her right hand went to work on the top two panes of glass, her left hand clung to the wall. And she let out a sigh of relief when the top panes were clean enough to pass her inspection, and she was able to climb down from the chair. 'One of these days I'll have enough money to buy a pair of steps like Hetty's got,' she told the aspidistra as she put the chair back under the table. 'They're not half handy. And a damn sight safer than a ruddy chair.' Then she patted the rail at the top of the chair. 'I shouldn't moan about yer, God knows. I've had yer since I got married, and yer were second hand then!'

After rinsing the shammy leather and wringing it out, Ada walked back with the intention of cleaning the bottom windows. But her attention was caught by the sight of two neighbours opposite, Jean Bowers and Edith Benson, who lived on the other side of Eliza Porter. They were deep in conversation, their faces serious as their heads kept nodding. There was no reason why the two women shouldn't be talking to each other, for they were good friends. But the smiles that were usually on their faces weren't there, and that was what made Ada wonder if anything was wrong with the old lady. And, she told herself, the only way to find out was to ask. So the shammy went back in the water and Ada took her pinny off, threw it over the back of a chair and made for the front door.

'If I'm pushing me nose in where it's not wanted, ladies, then just tell me to take a running jump. But from yer faces, I got the impression yer weren't telling each other jokes. So I'm here to ask if there's anything wrong?'

'We were discussing Eliza,' Jean said. 'We both think she's gone down the nick since that incident with her ankle. Oh, she's not complaining, Ada, but we feel she's changed, don't we, Edith?'

'She's not steady on her feet, although if yer ask her, she says she's fine.' Edith had been Eliza's neighbour for twenty years, and she was really fond of the old lady. 'Another thing, she's not eating very well. I take her dinner in to her, and when I go back she says it was lovely, and her plate is empty. I haven't told her I know, but I happened to look out of the back window when I was upstairs yesterday, and I saw her emptying her plate in the bin.'

Jean moved a few feet away and beckoned them to follow. 'One thing she does have is good hearing. I'd hate her to know we were talking about her.'

'I've asked yer before to let me and Hetty share the responsibility of looking after her, but yer've always insisted yer can manage. It's too much for both of yer, though, with yer own families to look after. So let me and Hetty take a turn to give yer a break. Eliza won't think anything, 'cos we often call in. We'll give her a knock on our way to the shops and see what

41

we think of her. She won't know you've been talking to me, and we'll just pretend it's a friendly call. Perhaps she's just feeling under the weather, or hasn't got over the shock of spraining her ankle. It takes a long time for anyone as old as Eliza to get over a shock. If it's not that, and she really is failing, then perhaps yer should tell her son.'

Edith nodded. 'We were talking about that before yer came over. But we'll see what you and Hetty think before doing anything. It's no good worrying him unless it's really necessary.'

'That's true, just leave it for now,' Ada agreed. 'I'll have to finish cleaning me windows, then I'll give Hetty a shout over the yard wall. It'll be about half an hour before we get to Eliza's. If we are concerned about her, I'll call and let yer know. If yer don't hear from us, yer'll know we both agree that there's nothing to be concerned about. Is that all right with you two?'

Jean smiled. 'I feel a bit better already. Yer see, both me and Edith are inclined to imagine trouble. My Gordon says I go looking for it. So I'm glad you and Hetty are going to see the old lady. I think yer've both got more sense than us.'

Ada chuckled. 'If my feller heard yer saying that, he'd laugh his head off. He thinks I was at the back of the queue when they were giving brains out.'

It was Edith's turn to chuckle. 'At least yer were in the queue, even if yer were at the back. Me, now, I didn't even know there was a queue.'

Ada stepped from the pavement on to the cobbles. 'We can't all have brains and beauty, sunshine, so thank God for small mercies.' She began to cross the street. 'Me and me mate will give yer a knock on our way back from the shops. But if we don't, that means we don't see any need for it. Ta-ra for now.'

'I knew it was too good to be true,' Hetty said with feeling. 'I did tell yer that it would take a while for the old dear to get over the shock, didn't I?'

'All right, sunshine, keep yer ruddy hair on!' Ada couldn't help laughing at the expression on her friend's face. 'Yer looking at me as if I had disagreed with yer diagnosis.'

Hetty's face went blank. 'What are yer talking about? Where did yer get the word diagnosis from, and what does it mean?'

'I don't know what it means. I heard a doctor saying it while I was in the hospital for an examination when I was pregnant with our Paul. The doctor wasn't talking to me, like, he was talking to another doctor. I took it to mean it was his opinion.'

'When yer were expecting your Paul!' Hetty's voice came out in a squeak. 'That's over ten years ago! How could yer remember a word like that for ten years, and still not know what it means?'

'What good would it have done me, in those ten years, to know what it means? Just how often would I be able to throw it into a conversation without people thinking I was bonkers?'

'It would have satisfied yer curiosity.'

'But I've never been curious! I had other things on me mind at the time, being eight months pregnant and as big as a ruddy house. The last thing on me mind was a lesson in English.' Ada was having a good laugh inside, but she managed to keep her face deadpan. 'And d'yer know what, Hetty, I'm sorry I brought the word up now, 'cos it's been a waste of time. Neither of us are any the wiser, and I'm fast losing the will to live.'

'Don't be so ruddy dramatic, girl, 'cos yer'd never make an Ethel Barrymore.' Hetty decided to get her own back. 'Ye're too big in the bust for it, and yer voice is too common.'

'Oh, well, we can't all have everything we want in life, sunshine. At least I'm not as unlucky as you.'

'What d'yer mean? Why d'yer think I'm more unlucky than you?'

'Well, for starters, I haven't got a mate what is fat, and as common as muck.'

Hetty leaned her elbows on the sideboard while she eyed her friend from head to toe. 'I see yer point, girl, but I could have done worse. Ivy Thompson is twice the size of you, and she's so common I can't understand a word she says.'

'If yer shut up and listen to what I was going to tell yer fifteen minutes ago, then I promise I won't tell Ivy what yer said about her. And that'll be doing yer a big favour 'cos yer know how handy Ivy is with her fists.'

Hetty pulled a face. 'That, Ada Fenwick, sounds very much like blackmail to me.'

'Never mind it sounds like blackmail, it is ruddy blackmail!' Ada clicked her tongue. 'I'll get this out if it kills me! I promised Jean and Edith that we'd call in to see Eliza before we go to the shops, to see what we think of her state of health. And seeing as we'll have to spend some time with her, not just run in and out, like, then we'd better get our skates on if we want to catch the shops before they close at one o'clock for their dinner.'

'In case yer haven't noticed, girl, I came all ready to go out,' Hetty said. 'It's you that's keeping us back, not me.'

Ada lifted her coat from one of the hooks behind the door. And keeping her back to Hetty, she slipped her arms into the sleeves while saying, 'Oh, and I offered to help Jean and Edith with taking turns with the old lady. Yer didn't mind me offering your services, did yer?' Without waiting for a reply, Ada went on, 'No, I didn't think yer'd object.'

'It would have been polite to have asked me first, girl. Yer know I wouldn't object to helping Eliza, I'll be happy to. But it would have been nice to be asked.'

'So, sunshine, yer'll be happy to help, will yer?'

'More than happy, girl.'

'Then can we stop wasting words and get on with it.' Ada waved her neighbour towards the front door. 'And not a word to Eliza about what I've told yer. Let her think it's just a friendly call to see how she is.'

Hetty was on the pavement when she looked up and said, 'I'm not thick, Ada.'

Ada banged the door behind her, made sure it was properly closed, then faced her mate. 'Let's see now. Er, how can I put it? Sometimes ye're not very quick off the mark, sunshine, but, er, no, I wouldn't say yer were thick.'

Hetty narrowed her eyes and pursed her lips. 'If Mrs Grogan wasn't on her knees scrubbing her front step, I'd clock you one, Ada Fenwick.'

'If she's still doing her step when we come out of Eliza's, sunshine, yer could ask her for her opinion.'

The pair began to cross the cobbles. 'What would I want to ask Mrs Grogan for her opinion on?'

'Yer could ask her what, in her opinion, the word diagnosis means. Or whether she thinks ye're thick or not. There's loads yer could ask her to pass the time away.'

Hetty lifted the knocker on Eliza's door. 'I don't know about me being thick, you're as soft as a ruddy brush. In fact, come to think about it, whatever I am, you made me.'

The old lady's eyes lit up when she saw her visitors. 'What are you two laughing at now?' She stood aside to let them pass. 'Don't yer ever have bad days, when yer don't feel like laughing?'

Ada waited until they were sitting down before answering. 'I'm going to be very truthful with yer, Eliza, even though what I'm going to say may shock yer. In fact, yer might throw us out and tell us never to darken yer door again.' She paused, straight-faced, to add a little drama. 'Me and Hetty aren't always laughing and joking, like people think. There are times when we're just the opposite. Yer wouldn't think so, but before we came out, we were throwing punches at each other, and our language was foul.' Another pause for effect. 'Hetty, who everyone thinks is a quiet, respectable woman who wouldn't hurt a fly, well, she threw a cushion at me. But instead of hitting me, it hit the clock on the mantelpiece. The clock what had been left to me by me parents fell to the floor and was smashed to smithereens. I bet me poor mam and dad are turning in their graves right now, for that clock was their pride and joy.'

The old lady bit on her bottom lip to keep back the laughter that was bubbling up inside her. Laughter that wasn't only brought about by Ada's very unlikely tale, but also by Hetty's face, which was a picture no artist could paint.

'May God forgive you, Ada Fenwick,' Hetty said when she found her voice. 'I enjoy a joke with the best of them, but to bring yer dead parents into it, well, I don't know how yer'll sleep in bed tonight.'

Eliza leaned sideways and patted Hetty's arm. 'What Ada said was all in fun, sweetheart, and I'm sure God has a sense of humour.'

'I'll tell yer who else had a sense of humour, Hetty, and that was me mam and dad. Our house was always full of laughter. What we lacked in material things, me parents made up for with love and laughter. I bet any money they're looking down on me now, and they'll be laughing so much their haloes will have slipped sideways.' Ada chuckled. 'I remember we didn't have a clock, 'cos me mam had pawned it just after they were married, and she never had enough money to redeem it. They used to rely on the neighbours to wake me dad up for work.'

'So the one in your house wasn't left to yer by yer parents?' Hetty seemed surprised. 'It looks so old, I took it for granted.'

'No one will ever know how old that clock is.' Ada laughed. 'When me and Jimmy got married we got some wedding presents, and I had a few things in me bottom drawer. But no one thought about a clock. So I scouted around and bought that one from a second-hand shop for threepence. It looked on its last legs then, and I've been expecting it to conk out any time since. But it's still going strong after twenty years, so I'd say I got a good bargain.'

'It's not a bargain, girl,' Hetty told her, 'it's a miracle.'

Ada nodded her head slowly as she asked, 'Is that your diagnosis?'

'Oh, don't let's go back to that, girl, or Eliza will think we've only come to confuse her.'

'Ye're right there, sunshine, 'cos I'm confused meself. So let's pretend we've just come in, and we'll ask our dear friend and neighbour how she is.'

The old woman smiled. 'I feel a lot better since you two came in. It would be hard to feel lonely or miserable with you around.'

'Oh, were yer not feeling very good before we came?'

45

'I was feeling a little bit down,' Eliza told them. 'When yer get to my age, and yer live alone, it gets very boring talking to the wallpaper.'

'I know how yer feel, sunshine, 'cos my wallpaper never has anything interesting to say when I talk to it. I often wonder whether it would cheer up a bit if I watered the flowers on it.'

Hetty decided it was time for her to contribute something to the conversation. 'Your wallpaper hasn't got flowers on! If it has, then I must be going blind.'

'Oh, it has got flowers on, sunshine, red roses they are. But I have to admit yer need very good eyesight to see them. The paper's been on the wall so long they've almost faded away. It was nice when it was first put up, I was really proud of me room then. It was so bright and airy it was a pleasure coming down in the mornings.' A wide smile spread across Ada's chubby face. 'But good news is on the way. I've moaned so much about how miserable the room looks that Danny offered to pay for the paper if Jimmy shows him how to put it up. And I intend to keep on moaning until they keep their promise. I don't think either of them were serious, they only said it to shut me up. But they're going to get their eye wiped, 'cos one day I intend to get busy with the scraper, and they'll be laughing the other side of their faces when they come in from work one night and find the walls stripped bare.'

Hetty's brows shot up. 'Yer wouldn't do that, girl, would yer?'

'Of course we would!'

It only took Hetty's brain a second to absorb the implication of that remark. 'Where d'yer get the "we" from? Surely yer wouldn't get the children to help yer?'

'Would I heck! I'd be frightened of them falling off the ladder! No, I'm going to ask me very best mate to give me a hand.'

'Who would that be?' Hetty feigned ignorance. 'Someone in the street?'

'Yeah, she only lives four doors away from you. I was thinking of Ivy Thompson.'

Eliza was really enjoying this, and her eyes moved from one to the other. Ivy Thompson was the street bully, and Ada was about the only woman in the street who wasn't afraid of her tongue or her fists. But that didn't mean they were bosom pals, and the old lady couldn't imagine Ada asking favours of a woman whose language turned the air blue. So how was the tale going to end?

'You do surprise me,' Hetty said, knowing full well what the out-come would be, but stringing it along because Eliza was showing great interest. 'I thought she'd be the last person in the world yer'd ask a favour of.'

'Oh, she is, sunshine, she definitely is! I was only pulling yer leg, yer should have known that. There's only one person I'd ask for help in any situation, and that's the woman who's really me best mate. And as I can see ye're getting jealous, I'll put yer out of yer misery. You're the one I'm going to ask to be me labourer.'

'Well, I do declare! You are one cheeky article, Ada Fenwick, and if yer think I'm coming to do your dirty work while you stand by and watch, then yer've got another think coming.' Hetty nodded her head to show she meant business. 'Yer'll not get me scraping paper off yer walls unless I'm the gaffer, and you're the apprentice what will keep the cups of tea coming every half-hour.'

The old lady leaned forward and put her thin hand over Hetty's. 'Don't forget the biscuits, sweetheart. Cups of tea are no good unless they come with a biscuit in the saucer.'

Ada was happy to see how the old lady had bucked up. It was surprising what a funny tale and a laugh could do. And they didn't cost anything. 'Oh, we've got a rabble-rouser in our midst, have we? I always had a sneaking suspicion that when yer were younger, yer were a real trouble-maker. And I've proved meself right. Ye're the type that would bring men out on strike for the sake of an arrowroot biscuit.'

The two friends sat back with smiles on their faces as they watched tears of laughter rolling down Eliza's cheeks. And both were thinking they'd call and tell Jean and Edith there was no need to alert the old lady's son. Not yet anyway.

Hetty linked her arm through Ada's after they'd waved to Eliza, who had insisted on coming to the door to see them off. It meant they couldn't knock on Jean's or Edith's, for the old lady would have seen and heard them.

'We'll let them know after we've been to the shops,' Ada said. 'I don't think there's any reason for concern, do you, sunshine?'

'She seemed a bit quiet when we first walked in, but she soon brightened up. I think that's part of her problem, in as much as she's on her own too much. She enjoys having someone to talk to, and make her laugh. I'm glad yer told her about decorating yer living room, and how yer'd keep her informed of the progress.' Hetty looked sideways to see her friend's face. 'Are yer really going to strip the wallpaper off, or did yer make that bit up to give her a laugh?'

'Oh, I didn't make it up, sunshine, I'm in dead earnest. That wallpaper is giving me the willies, and I'm going to make a start on stripping it one day this week.' Ada chuckled. 'It depends what day you have free. I need

47

someone to gab to while I'm working, 'cos I move quicker when me mouth is on the go.'

Hetty was more level-headed than her friend. 'Hadn't yer better make sure when Danny will have the money to buy the paper? Yer don't want to have to sit for weeks with nothing on the walls, that would really give yer the willies.'

'I intend to drop a hint when we're having our dinner tonight. Danny is buying the paper, but it's no good papering without painting the woodwork 'cos one thing would be laughing at another. So it means Jimmy will have to fork out for the paint. That leaves me trying to get round the two of them at the same time.' The pair turned the corner into the main road. 'I'll cut down a bit on me shopping for the next few days, then I can put a few coppers towards the cost. Every little helps.'

'Well, when yer do start, girl, I'll get stuck in with yer, yer know that. Between us, we could have that room stripped in a few hours.'

'I'll see what I can do while we're having our dinner. That's about the best time, 'cos they're usually in a good mood when they're eating.'

Hetty squeezed her arm. 'Ay, I've just thought of a good nickname for you, girl. How about Crafty Clara?'

Ada stopped in her tracks. 'But me name's nothing like Clara!'

'I know, but I couldn't think of anything that went with crafty and Ada. But I'll think about it during the day, and I bet I come up with something what goes with Ada.'

'Ye're not half slow, sunshine, 'cos I can come up with a lot of words that would go with Ada. At least three came into me mind right away.'

'Go 'way! What are they, girl?'

'When I tell yer, yer'll kick yerself for not thinking of them. What about Adorable Ada? Or Adaptable Ada? Even Admirable Ada? Any one of those would suit me.'

'Oh, I've just thought of one that would really fit the bill,' Hetty said with delight. 'How about Abominable Ada? It came into me head just like that.' She clicked her middle finger and thumb. 'Just like that.'

'Well, if we're going to play silly buggers, how about Horrible Hetty? Hideous Hetty? Or even Helpless Hetty?'

'If I'm helpless, horrible and hideous, girl, yer won't want me in yer living room scraping paper off yer wall, will yer?'

Ada was straight-faced, but laughing inside. 'Don't be so ruddy quick off the mark, sunshine, I haven't finished yet. I kept the best one till the last. How about Heavenly Hetty?'

'Yer just saved yerself by the bell, girl, but it was quick thinking, I'll give yer that much. So is that all settled now? Can we get on with our shopping?'

'We certainly can. And when we're in the butcher's, and I ask for three-quarters of stew instead of the usual pound, don't ask me why. It's because I want to save sixpence to go towards the wallpaper.'

'That's a good idea, girl. Yer can make up for the lack of meat by putting some barley in.' Then Hetty had a brainwave. 'Ay, d'yer know what would be a good idea, girl? When ye're having yer dinner tonight, yer could say yer'd seen some wallpaper yer liked, and yer've put sixpence deposit down towards it. If yer said it in a casual way, it would sound more like a gentle reminder than you pushing them into doing it soon.'

They were walking through the butcher's door when Ada said, 'Ay, that's a good idea. So Heavenly Hetty is not just a pretty face after all.'

Ronnie greeted them with a grin. 'Late again this morning, ladies. It's getting to be a habit with yer. Or are yer trying to give me a heart attack, thinking two of me best customers have left me for another butcher who is better-looking than me.'

'Yer've got no worries on that score, Ronnie,' Ada told him. 'We could never find another butcher nicer-looking than you. Me and Hetty have tried, though. We walked the length of Scotland Road, but every butcher's shop we went in, there was an ugly mug behind the counter. And we decided that being greeted by an ugly mug every day would put us off whatever we were buying.'

Ronnie's chest expanded by about six inches 'That's a nice compliment, ladies. Yer've made me day a lot brighter.'

'I wouldn't get too cocky, Ronnie, not until yer've seen the other butchers. One of them looked like Frankenstein's monster, another favoured Charles Laughton as the Hunchback of Notre Dame, and the last one was the image of Count Dracula.' Ada began to shake with suppressed laughter at the sight of Ronnie's face. 'Me and Hetty didn't have a good night's sleep for weeks. We kept having nightmares.'

Hetty nodded vigorously. 'My husband got real worried about me. In fact he wanted me to see a doctor 'cos I was keeping him awake at night screaming with fright. I kept on seeing Dracula pushing his coffin lid aside and sitting up with this horrible look on his face and long fangs hanging out of his mouth.'

Ada put a hand on her friend's arm. 'All right, sunshine, ye're quite safe in here. I won't let anyone get to yer. And yer can see that although Ronnie's got big teeth, they're not nearly as big as Dracula's fangs. And he hasn't got no hump on his back.'

49

'Ay, I've got a smashing set of teeth, and they're all me own.' Ronnie grinned, revealing a set of strong white teeth. And after showing them off to Ada and Hetty, he turned his smile on the other two customers who were in the process of being served by young Barry when the two friends had entered the shop. Now they were being entertained, they were in no hurry to hand their money over for the meat which was wrapped and sitting on the counter. They didn't want to laugh out loud, for it would show they were listening, and that was bad manners. So they bit on their lips when the butcher turned full circle, saying, 'Even if I say it meself, I'm tall and slim, with no sign of round shoulders. I don't want to sound big-headed, but I think I'm in very good shape.'

'That's nice to hear, lad,' Ada said. 'I admire people who look after themselves. Me and Hetty keep in good shape, too! Don't we, sunshine?' Without waiting for an answer from her mate, Ada went on, 'I'm shaped like a Mersey ferry boat, and Hetty's shaped like the twenty-two tram.'

Hetty's laughter was joined by the other two customers'. And by that of young Barry, who had lifted his white apron to cover his mouth and smother his chuckles. Ronnie was a good boss, but his sense of humour didn't stretch to being made fun of. 'Not the twenty-two tram, girl, more like the bus what goes into the city centre.'

There was a sharp intake of breath from Ronnie, and the smile dropped from his face when he saw a large figure coming through the door of his shop. And when the ladies' eyes followed his, there was a shuffling of feet and a marked difference in the atmosphere. For the woman was no other than Ivy Thompson, the neighbourhood troublemaker. The only person in the shop who didn't cringe was Ada.

Ivy Thompson was a big woman in every way. Her mountainous breasts were allowed to move freely, never having been contained in a brassiere. Her stomach was huge, but not flabby. It was as hard as a rock, as many people had found out to their sorrow. If she was engaged in a fight, which was often, then although she made use of her fists, it was her tummy which was the battering ram. Even the men in the street steered clear of Ivy Thompson.

Ada watched as Ivy swaggered in and pushed the two now silent customers out of the way to reach the counter. 'Six beef sausage and make it snappy, I'm in a hurry.'

Ronnie was trying to muster the courage to tell her to wait her turn. He didn't relish clashing swords with her, but he had found over the years that the best way to deal with Ivy was not to let her see you were afraid of her. Look timid or frightened, then she'd give you something to be frightened of. But his bravado wasn't needed, for Ada came to his rescue.

'Well, I'll be blowed! Talk of the devil and he's bound to appear,' Ada said in a loud voice. 'It's not ten minutes since me and Hetty were talking about you, Ivy.'

Ivy's hair was dishevelled and she was wearing a dirty pinny that showed signs of food stains, grease and other unmentionables. 'It's a pity yer've got nothing better to do,' she snarled. 'Anyway, I've no time to stand yapping.' But curiosity got the better of her before she once again faced Ronnie. 'What were you two jangling about me for? If yer were slagging me off to someone I'll break yer bleeding necks.'

'Oh, I don't think yer'd do that, Ivy.' Ada's voice was deceptively calm. 'Not unless yer tied me hands behind me back before yer started. Anyway, it was only me and Hetty talking about yer, no one else would be interested in what you get up to.'

'What was it yer wanted, Mrs Thompson?' Ronnie asked, while in his head there were visions of his glass counter being smashed to smithereens by two women trying to kill each other. 'Was it beef sausages?'

'I'll tell yer in me own good time, lad, so don't be trying to rush me.' Ivy turned back to Ada. 'What would you two be talking about me for? The two of yer are as thick as thieves, yer don't usually have anything to say to anyone else in the street.'

'Oh, go on, Ivy, me and Hetty talk to all the neighbours. Except you, of course, 'cos it's impossible to talk to you without getting into a fight. And when I said me and Hetty were talking about yer just minutes before yer walked in here, that didn't mean we were jangling about yer. That's your bad mind, that is.'

'Will yer stop bleeding nattering, and tell me what yer were talking about then? I haven't got all day, like you two, and these two nosy buggers standing here with their ears cocked.'

Ada let her head drop back and roared with laughter, much to the surprise of all present. They weren't to know she was goading the woman who didn't have a kind word for anyone. Nor would Ivy offer a crumb to someone who was starving. She thrived on the fact that most people were in fear of her. 'Ye're a hero, you are, Ivy Thompson. Yer don't half love throwing yer weight about. And all this because I was telling Hetty I'm going to have me living room papered. I was saying I'd be scraping the paper off the walls, to save my husband and son doing all the donkey work. And I happened to say I'd like a bit of help, like, and I mentioned I might ask you 'cos ye're good with yer hands.'

Hetty took stock of the layout before daring to say what was in her mind. Ada stood between her and Ivy Thompson, and her mate would take care she didn't come to any harm. So, taking her courage, and her life, in her hands, Hetty put a smile on her face. 'Yeah, we didn't half have a laugh over that. When Ada told me she was thinking of asking you to help scrape the walls, I nearly burst a blood vessel. I told her there wouldn't be a wall left standing if she let you loose in there.'

The sound that came from Ivy's mouth was like a raging bull. She made a dive for Hetty, but Ada stood in her path. 'What's the matter, Ivy, haven't yer got no sense of humour? If yer can't laugh at yerself, then it's God help yer. Even though I've never seen yer with a smile on yer face, I didn't think anyone was so miserable they couldn't take a joke.' Ada put her face close to the bully's. 'It was all said in fun, Ivy,' she said through gritted teeth. 'But if yer don't believe me, and yer want to make something out of it, then yer'll never have a better chance than now. I couldn't be any nearer to yer, so go on, I'm not going anywhere.'

To the surprise of the onlookers, Ivy snorted and turned back to the counter. 'I couldn't be arsed, I've got more to do.' She jerked her head at the butcher. 'Don't stand there like a bleeding fool with yer mouth open as though ye're catching flies. Get those bleeding six beef sausage and be quick about it.'

Nobody spoke until she was out of the shop, and then everyone started to speak at the same time. 'I thought we were in for a battle,' Ronnie said. 'I had visions of me glass counter being smashed. It's the first time I've seen that woman walk away from a fight.'

'She gets away with murder because people show her they are afraid of her. She's like a dog, she can smell fear. Stand up to her and she'll back down.' Ada grinned. 'Mind you, lad, tread carefully, and always have in yer mind the cost of a new glass counter.'

Chapter Five

'When yer've got the money for the wallpaper,' Ada said, looking across the table at her son, 'I'll start stripping the walls. Hetty said she'd give me a hand.'

'I can let yer have it on Saturday when I get paid.' Danny had a piece of potato speared on the end of his fork, and he popped it into his mouth before asking, 'How much d'yer think it will come to?'

Ada glanced at her husband. 'Was it four or five rolls, sunshine? It's so long since it was last done, I can't remember.'

'Five to be on the safe side,' Jimmy told her. 'We had nearly a roll over last time, but as they don't sell oddments, yer'll have to get the five.' He looked down at his plate. 'I'm not half enjoying this dinner, love. It's a long time since yer made dumplings and they're a real treat.'

Monica rubbed her tummy. 'Dumplings are me favourite, I'd rather have them than anything else. Yer should have made more, Mam, 'cos one isn't enough.'

'It's going to have to be enough 'cos we all like them, and me pan isn't big enough to take ten dumplings. So thank God for small mercies and get the stew down yer. The vegetables and barley will stick to yer tummy and do yer good.'

Danny stood his knife and fork up like soldiers standing to attention. 'The dinner is nice, Mam, and I'm really enjoying it. But can we get back to the price of the wallpaper?'

'I went to the wallpaper shop in Westminster Road today, and the paper I liked was a shilling a roll. They had some for ninepence, but it wasn't a patch on the one I liked. And after waiting years to have me room decorated, I think I deserve to be spoilt.' Ada ran the back of a hand across her mouth before pushing her plate away so she could lean her elbows on the table. 'Even though I say it as shouldn't, that was bloody lovely.'

'I can manage the five shillings on Saturday, Mam,' Danny told her, after a quick count in his head of the money he had in his pocket now, and what he'd have left of his wages at the weekend after he'd paid over the five bob. 'Yer could order it tomorrow in case they sell out of the one yer've got yer eye on.'

'It won't leave yer skint, will it, sunshine? It wouldn't hurt me to wait another week if it means leaving yer short.'

A smile crossed Danny's handsome face. 'I won't be rolling in dough, Mam, but I'll manage. I can walk to Blair Hall a couple of times to save the tram fare.'

Jimmy put his knife and fork down, and licking his lips he winked at his wife. 'That was a treat, love, a meal fit for a king.'

Paul chuckled. 'If you were a king, Dad, that would make me a prince. And we would have servants to wait on us hand and foot.'

Ada raised her brows. 'What d'yer mean, yer would have? I'm yer blinking servant what waits on yer hand and foot. And I don't get a penny wages for me trouble.'

Paul digested the words thoroughly before saying, 'Me dad gives yer his wages every week, so yer do get paid.'

Danny was quick to put his kid brother straight. 'Me mam doesn't keep the wages for herself, soft lad. Where d'yer think the money comes from for food, coal, clothes, and the rent man who wants his money every week?'

Paul tutted and jerked his head back. 'Sorry, Mam, I forgot yer had to pay all the money out again. But just wait until me and Monica are working. Yer'll be able to buy all the food and everything, and have money over to go to the pictures.'

Jimmy held his hand up. 'Before our Danny starts getting ready for his nightly hop, can we get back to discussing the decoration of this room? It's no good putting the wallpaper up before the ceiling and frieze have been whitewashed, and the woodwork painted. I'll try and get them done over the weekend, but the place certainly won't be ready for papering until the middle of next week.'

'I'll help yer with the painting, Dad,' Danny said, 'on Saturday afternoon and Sunday. It won't take long if the two of us get stuck in.'

'I'll buy the paper and the rest of the stuff we need on Saturday, and then we'll just take things as they come, eh?' Ada tried not to sound too eager. The men were working all week; she couldn't expect too much from them. But she couldn't help feeling a little impatient. She wouldn't mind having a go at hanging the paper herself, but was afraid of putting Jimmy and Danny's noses out of joint. Besides, she couldn't paint the ceiling, she didn't have a ladder big enough. Jimmy would stand on the table to do it, but Ada didn't fancy that. No, she'd leave it to the men of the house. After all, if she had to wait an extra week to see her living room bright and cheerful, it wouldn't hurt her.

'I'll give yer a shilling towards the paint, sunshine,' she told her husband. 'It's not much, but as they say, every little helps.'

'There's no need to, love. I've already asked one of the blokes in work to get it for me. He knows where he can get it cheap. Two bob for a tin big enough to do all the woodwork in this room. It might even stretch to the hall and kitchen.'

Ada began to feel excited. 'Oh, that sounds marvellous! Ay, we won't know ourselves, will we? I'll be telling me mate to wipe her feet before she comes in.'

Danny chortled. 'Don't tell me Auntie Hetty walks on the ceiling? I know you talk to the walls, 'cos I've heard yer, but I didn't think yer mate was a bit loopy as well.'

'Ay, Mam,' Monica said. 'When the new wallpaper is put up, perhaps the walls will think they're too posh to listen to you.'

'I'll soon put them in their place, sunshine, don't worry about that. All I need to do is stop passing the street gossip on to them and they'd be on their knees to me in no time. Yer see, they enjoy a bit of gossip 'cos it brightens up their day. There's many a time I've made stories up, just to put a bit of sparkle into their lives.'

Jimmy had a smile of affection on his face as he listened to his wife. Any stranger listening would think she was as crazy as a coot, but he loved her just the way she was. Warm, loving and humorous. 'Have yer ever considered that yer might be sorry to see the old paper go, Ada? Yer never know, the new paper might not be so friendly.'

'The thought had crossed me mind, sunshine,' Ada told him with a chuckle. 'That's why I had a talk to the paper in the shop. But it assured me it would be very happy to be out of the shop and on someone's walls. Especially someone who would talk to it. Apparently the man behind the counter is a miserable beggar. He hasn't spoken one word to the paper the whole time it's been rolled up on the shelf.'

'I should have known it was a daft question to ask, that yer'd have an answer. I'm getting to be as crazy as you are.'

'My old ma used to say that if yer lived with a person long enough, yer grew to be like them,' Ada told him. 'Mind you, she used to have a lot of funny sayings.'

'I remember one yer told me about yer mam,' Danny said. 'Yer said she was taking yer to the shops one day, and yer passed a woman with a dog. And she said, "Did yer notice that the dog what just passed, girl, had a face like its owner? She's had it since it was a pup, and every time I see them, they get more alike." '

'That was a saying she made up on the spur of the moment, son. She was good at making things up quickly. She hated dogs, and she said that to put me off. Not that she needed to, for I wouldn't dream of having a dog. These houses are too small to keep an animal in, it wouldn't be fair to the poor thing.'

'We could have a cat, though, Mam,' Monica said hopefully. 'They're only small, and a little kitten wouldn't take up any room. It wouldn't eat much, and it wouldn't need to be taken for a walk.'

Ada looked surprised. 'What brought this on? Yer seem to have it all sorted out in yer head, but yer've never mentioned it before.'

'My friend at school has got a little kitten,' her daughter informed her. 'It's black and white, and she said it's lovely and very playful.'

'The only time I drool over a cat is when I see one on the lid of a box of chocolates. They look very cuddly and sweet, but they leave hairs everywhere and scratch at the paintwork on the door when they want to go out or come in. So yer can forget it, sunshine, 'cos there's five people living in this small house, and that's more than enough for me to see to.'

Monica wasn't going to give in so easily. 'Ah, go on, Mam, don't be so mean. I bet yer'd love it when yer got used to it.'

Danny shook his head at his sister. 'I'd save yer breath if I were you, sis, 'cos there's no way we're having a cat in here. Even if our mam said yer could, then yer'd have me to deal with. I don't want to be going out at night covered in cat hair, it would put the girls off.'

Paul wrinkled his nose. 'They smell, too, and they don't use a toilet.' He grinned at the picture which had come into his head. 'Yer could always carry it down the yard, I suppose, and hold it over the lavvy.'

His little joke brought a sharp response from his sister, in the form of a kick on his shin. 'Yer think ye're funny, our Paul, but ye're not. So there!'

'That's enough now,' Jimmy said. 'There's nothing wrong with yer sister wanting a pet. But I agree with yer mam that it wouldn't be practical in this house. What would happen to it at night when we went to bed? It would have to sleep in the yard, or in here on the couch. And believe me, kittens have long claws. They'd ruin the furniture in no time.'

'We could find a box for it to sleep in.' Monica wasn't going to go down without a fight. 'That's what my friend did for her kitten, and she said it's as good as gold.'

Ada wasn't without sympathy, but there was no way they could have an animal in the house. They got under each other's feet as it was. 'Look, sunshine, when yer get married and have a house of yer own, then yer can please yerself what yer have in it. There'd be no one to say yer couldn't have half a dozen kittens if yer wanted.'

'That's if she marries a bloke with no brains,' Danny said. 'One who didn't mind having hairs on his clothes and all over the furniture.' His face broke into a smile when he saw his sister's woebegone expression. 'When ye're old enough to start going out with boys, always ask them if they like cats. Anyone what pulls a face, send him packing. If yer find one what says he loves cats, then tell him yer'll marry him.'

'Okay,' Ada said, 'I think we've exhausted the subject of cats, so can we talk about something else?' She eyed her eldest son. 'Aren't yer going dancing tonight, Danny? Or are we going to have the pleasure of your company for the entire evening? If yer tell me ye're staying in, I'll send for the doctor, 'cos yer must be sickening for something.'

Danny looked at the clock and stood up so quickly he nearly sent his chair flying. 'Just look at the time! It's all your fault, our Monica, you and yer ruddy cats. By the time I get there me three favourite partners will have been snapped up.'

'Yer don't know, son, yer might be lucky,' Jimmy said, feeling good inside because he had thought of something funny. 'One of them might have turned a bloke down because his clothes were covered in cat hairs.'

Danny slapped his father on his back as he passed the back of his chair. 'Nice one, Dad, ye're in form tonight.'

Monica's head gave a little shake. 'Yer all think ye're funny, but ye're not. My friend said there's something wrong with people who don't like animals.'

Danny's head appeared round the kitchen door. 'Is this the same friend who has the little kitten that's lovely and playful, and as good as gold?'

Monica glared at him. 'Yes, it is. Why?'

'I thought there was method in her madness. How long has she had this sweet little cat?'

'A week.'

Danny nodded knowingly. 'I thought as much. I bet yer any money that tomorrow she'll ask yer if yer want a lovely cuddly kitten. She's probably been told to get rid of it, and she saw you as a likely sucker.' With that his head disappeared.

Ada saw the colour rise on her daughter's face. 'Is our Danny right? Has this so-called friend asked yer to have the kitten?'

Monica lowered her head. 'Yeah. Her mam won't let her keep it.'

Danny's head appeared again, this time with shaving foam on his chin. 'Ay, this friend of yours will go far in life. I wouldn't be surprised if she ended up being a managing director in a big factory.'

Ada winked at Monica and was glad to see a smile appear. 'I don't think the girl will end up in a factory, sunshine. My money would be on her working in a pet shop. With her gift of the gab, if someone came in to buy a rabbit, she'd talk them into taking a rat, saying it was a baby rabbit what hadn't started to grow yet.'

'I don't know this school friend of yours, Monica,' Jimmy said, 'but she's been the topic of conversation here for the last fifteen minutes. And that's pretty clever, seeing as we've never set eyes on her.'

Monica quickly saw the chance of getting her own back. Not that she wanted the kitten now, for she'd been put right off it with all the talk of hairs and sharp claws. And if it made puddles on the floor, she'd be the one who had to clean it up, and she certainly didn't fancy that! 'Yer'll see her tomorrow night, Dad, 'cos she's bringing the kitten here. And she said we can have the box it sleeps in, and the blanket.'

The hot retort on Ada's lips died when she saw the sparkle in her daughter's eyes. 'That's very generous of her, sunshine, and yer can tell her I said so. But explain that we can't take her up on her offer as there's no room at the inn.'

When Ada opened the door to Hetty on the Monday morning, she asked, 'Will yer give me a hand with scraping the walls today, sunshine? I've moved all the furniture into the middle of the room and covered it over with old sheets.'

Hetty looked up with raised brows. 'Is that why ye're barring me from coming in? If I say I won't help I won't be allowed in? Yer know I'll help without asking, and I don't care whether the room's in a mess or not! So can I come in now?'

'Well, I was going to suggest we go straight out, sunshine, so we can get our shopping over with before we get stuck in. I only need to put me coat on, so shall we be on our way?'

'Are yer asking me or telling me, girl? Since ye're blocking me entrance, I'd say ye're telling me and I don't have any choice. So I'll stay here while yer put yer coat on, and then we'll be off.'

Ada turned her head to take a coat from a hook behind the door. She slipped her arms into the sleeves and stepped down on to the pavement. 'I had me coat ready for when yer knocked, and I've got me purse in me pocket. All ready, so I wouldn't keep yer waiting.'

'Aren't yer forgetting something? What about yer basket?'

After pulling the door shut, Ada said, 'I don't need me basket today. I can carry what few groceries I need.'

'Who are yer kidding, girl?' Hetty linked her arm through her mate's and fell into step beside her. 'Ten to one all yer shopping will be going into my basket, and, soft girl that I am, I'll be the one carrying the lot.'

'Stop yer moaning, sunshine, and count yer blessings. After all, I've invited yer into my house to help me scrape the walls, and yer should show some gratitude. It's not everyone I'd ask to do that.'

'Shall I tell yer something, girl, before yer heart bursts with yer generosity? It's not everyone who would be soft enough to help yer out. I'm the only sucker in our street.'

'And a lovely sucker yer are, sunshine. I'm really proud to have yer for a friend.' Ada quickened her step, causing her neighbour to do a hop and a jump to keep up with her. 'If we make a real effort, we can have all the shopping done and be back home in half an hour.'

Hetty groaned. 'I was really happy for yer when yer told me yer were having yer room decorated, but I'm starting to regret I ever said I'd help yer out. Little did I know it was going to disrupt my life so much.'

'Don't exaggerate, sunshine, yer life isn't going to be disrupted for more than a few hours. Surely yer don't begrudge giving me a hand for a few hours, do yer? Me, what's supposed to be yer best mate?'

'It's been disrupted already, and it's not ten minutes since I left me house and knocked on your door! First off, there's been no morning cup of tea, and I always look forward to that, with our little natter. Second, ye're rushing me so much I'm out of breath. And to add insult to injury, I'm going to have to carry yer shopping!'

'No yer won't, sunshine.' Ada thought quickly that a bit of soft soap was needed. 'When I was rushing to get me housework done, then move all the heavy furniture so we could get to the walls, it was you I was thinking of. I said to meself that as I didn't need much shopping it wasn't worth me taking my basket, I could put me stuff in yours, and I'd carry it. Never in a million years would I expect you to carry my things. Yer should know me better by now. I'm not ruddy hard-faced.'

'Ada, how many years are in a million?' Hetty asked, a sly look on her face. 'Do yer know? Would yer be able to write it down?'

'I don't know, sunshine.' Ada was well aware she was having her leg pulled, but she wouldn't have cared if her two legs had bells on and they both got pulled. Just as long as the ruddy wallpaper came off her living room walls before the men came home from work. 'I know it's a lot, so I suppose it's about a hundred.'

Hetty knew her friend inside out, and she certainly wasn't as soft as she made out. She pretended to be as thick as two short planks, but she was far from it. Most of the time she acted daft to give people a laugh, for she liked nothing better than to see people happy. But in a serious conversation she'd soon show herself to be knowledgeable in every subject. 'Oh, I think more than a hundred, girl, but why worry! My mam used to say, "Yer die if yer worry, and yer die if yer don't, so why worry at all?" '

'Then all I can say, sunshine, is that it's a pity yer don't take after yer mam. I know we all worry sometimes, it's only natural. We can't have a life that's all milk and honey. But you've made a career out of it. You worry over the least little thing.'

'No, I don't, Ada Fenwick, where did yer get that idea from? I worry about me family, but that's all. And don't tell me yer don't worry about yours, 'cos I know yer do.'

'Ooh, ay, talking about families, I knew there was something I had to tell yer.' And as they walked towards the Maypole, Ada told her mate the saga about Monica and the kitten. It wasn't all word for word strictly true, for she always added her own version of events to any story to make it more interesting. And she was in fine form, having Hetty doubled up with laughter. Her mate thought it was hilarious and there were tears of laughter running down her cheeks. In fact, it tickled her fancy so much, she was still chuckling as they walked back from the shops. It wasn't until they reached Ada's front door that Hetty realised why her arm was aching. She'd carried her mate's groceries all the way home in her basket.

Ada stood back and surveyed the wall she'd finished stripping, and there was a look of satisfaction on her face. 'That's one wall done, sunshine, so if we carry on at this rate we'll be finished about three o'clock.'

'I've almost finished this wall,' Hetty said, 'and I think we should have a break now, 'cos I'm gasping for a drink. By the time the kettle's boiled, I'll have it all stripped and we can take a breather.'

'Ye're right, sunshine, we deserve it. It's hard going getting this paper off. I think it's been on so long it doesn't want to be disturbed. I wonder if wallpaper has feelings, same as us?'

'Oh, don't be daft, yer silly nit.' Hetty tutted. 'Go and put the kettle on before I die of thirst.'

'Don't you dare die in this room before we've finished the job, Hetty Watson, it would be really inconsiderate of yer. Just think of the extra work yer'd put me through, with sending for a doctor, and then the undertaker. On top of that, I'd have the dinner to get ready for the family. I know Jimmy is easy-going, but he wouldn't be too happy if he came home and there was no dinner ready for him.'

A smile came to Hetty's lips as she said dryly, 'I don't think he'd worry so much about his dinner not being ready for him as he would about me being laid out cold on the floor.'

60

'Ay, sunshine, we shouldn't be talking about death, 'cos there's many a true word spoken in jest.'

'It's you what's always saying that God has a sense of humour, girl, so I bet He's having a good laugh.'

'That's what I'm afraid of, sunshine! He has got a sense of humour, but He'll only get a laugh out of people who are funny. And if there's no one in heaven at the moment who can make Him laugh, then the chances are He'll be looking down to see if there's any likely candidates down here. I hope to meet Him one day, when I'm old and feeble, so I can thank Him for the good life I've had. But I'm not ready yet. I'm far too young to want to join Him in heaven.'

'Yer might not be ready for heaven, girl, but are yer ready to throw that ruddy scraper down and put the kettle on? I told yer ages ago I was thirsty, but yer talk too much.'

'You cheeky article! If we counted the words we've used since yer asked for a drink, I bet you've used as many if not more than I have.'

Hetty sighed. 'I'd be better off going home and making meself a cup of tea there.'

Ada moved quickly towards the kitchen. 'In five minutes there'll be two cups and saucers on the table, two biscuits and a pot of tea. And by that time yer should have the rest of the paper off that wall.' As her friend moved out of sight, Hetty grinned when she heard her adding, 'God knows, she's been at it long enough.'

'Yer've done very well, love,' Jimmy said, casting his eyes over the bare walls. 'I see yer've washed the paintwork down, as well.' When he bent to kiss her cheek, there was a twinkle in his eye. 'Not bad for someone of your age.'

'Go 'way, yer cheeky beggar! I'm two years younger than you, don't forget. So if I'm old, what does that make you?' Ada clipped his ear playfully. 'Anyway, I can't take all the praise for the work. Hetty was a great help. I'd only be halfway through if it wasn't for her.'

Danny came in at that moment, and he whistled. 'I was expecting yer to have one wall done, Mam, but yer must have put in a full day's hard labour to have finished the whole room.' Then he sniffed up, his dimples deepening when he smiled. 'And if the smell is anything to go by, yer've managed a delicious dinner into the bargain.'

Monica and Paul stood quietly listening. Then Paul decided to air the grievance he shared with his sister. 'Me and Monica had to do without the jam butty we get every day, and now me tummy's rumbling 'cos I'm starving.'

'Ah, yer poor thing.' Danny clicked his tongue on the roof of his mouth. 'Didn't yer have yer dummy to suck on while yer were waiting?'

'Don't be starting any shenanigans, for heaven's sake,' Ada said. 'I'm not in the mood, 'cos every bone in me body is aching. Even bones I didn't know I had are sore.'

'Then sit down, love. I'll put the dinner out,' Jimmy said, pressing his wife down gently on to the couch. 'Me and Danny will see to it.'

Ada let out a deep sigh. 'I'm not going to argue with yer, I'm too weary. You and Danny can do it between yer, ye're both old and ugly enough. All yer have to do is put five plates out and whatever is in the pan on the stove, share between the plates. Not equal shares, like, 'cos me and the kids don't eat as much as you two.'

While she was talking, Ada's mind was working. And as soon as the two men disappeared into the kitchen, she beckoned Monica over. Keeping her voice low, so it wouldn't be heard in the kitchen, she said, 'Keep quiet, sunshine, don't say a word. I want yer to get a pencil and a piece of paper out of the drawer in the sideboard. There's something I want Auntie Hetty to know, so I'll write it down and yer can take the message to her.' When the pencil and paper were in, her hand, Ada scribbled quickly. Then she folded the paper and gave it to her daughter. 'Not a word, sunshine, just make sure yer give that to Auntie Hetty.'

'But what if Uncle Arthur opens the door, or one of the girls? What shall I say to them?'

'Uncle Arthur and the girls aren't in from work yet. I've been watching for them passing the window. So off yer go, and remember, not a word to anyone.'

Hetty looked surprised when she opened the front door and Monica pushed a piece of paper in her hand before running back home. Filled with curiosity, she walked back to the living room and sat down before unfolding the sheet of paper. Her eyes moved quickly along the lines, and her tittering turned to laughter. For Ada had written that she was being waited on hand and foot because she'd told Jimmy her whole body was aching with working so hard. She suggested her friend did the same. Lay the agony on thick, sunshine, Ada had written, and sit back and be waited on for once in your life.

Hetty threw the piece of paper on the fire and watched the flames eat it up. Then she sat on the edge of the couch and swung her legs over the side. When she was settled, she rehearsed a few groans. That should do the trick, she told herself. If she was going to tell a few white lies, she may as well do it in comfort.

Chapter Six

Ada nearly tripped over herself as she hastened to open the door to Hetty the next morning. 'How did yer get on? Did yer do what I told yer?'

'I certainly did, and it worked a treat.' Hetty was grinning as she followed her friend into the living room. 'I've got to admit I felt a bit guilty at first, knowing Arthur and the girls had put in a long day at work. Still, my pleasure at being fussed over soon outweighed any guilt I may have felt.'

'The kettle's been boiled, so sit yerself down and we'll have a cuppa before we go shopping.' Ada stood with her hand on the kitchen door. 'I cut off me nose to spite me face in one way, sunshine, 'cos when we were in bed, and Jimmy started feeling frisky, I had to fob him off. I was cursing meself, for I was feeling romantic too! But I could hardly start being active after playing the wounded soldier all night.'

'It won't hurt either of yer to go without for one night,' Hetty said, then sat back and waited for the reaction. And she didn't have to wait very long.

'What d'yer mean, Hetty Watson? Anyone listening to you would think me and Jimmy were sex maniacs! And you and Arthur must have your moments, unless ye're both made of stone. Or flipping icebergs.' Ada disappeared just long enough to higher the gas under the kettle. 'We're still young enough to enjoy ourselves in bed, and speaking for meself it's the only entertainment I get! It costs money to go to the pictures, and once the picture ends yer don't get an encore. In bed, though, I can have as many encores as I like, 'cos Jimmy is always ready, willing and able. We're good in bed together, and it doesn't cost a cent.'

Hetty was quiet as she digested her mate's words. Was there an implication there, that her Arthur wasn't as able as Jimmy? She'd better put the record straight on that. 'Don't be bragging, Ada Fenwick, 'cos Jimmy would have to go a long way to beat my Arthur. And another thing, I let him have his way with me in bed last night. I pretended I was still sore, and let out a groan every now and then, but we both enjoyed ourselves.'

The kettle began to whistle and Ada pushed her chair back. 'The water's boiling, sunshine, so we'll resume the conversation when we've got our tea in front of us.' Five minutes later she was facing her friend across the table, her hands around the cup of hot tea. And she explained to Hetty why there was a smile on her face. 'I promised Jimmy I'd make it up to him tonight, so we're having an early night.'

'What time d'yer call early?' Hetty asked. 'Six o'clock, as soon as yer've finished yer dinner, or will yer be able to hang out until the kids go to bed?'

'I think I can hold out, sunshine, but I'm not sure about Jimmy. I might have to tie him to his chair for a couple of hours.' Ada drained her cup and put it in the saucer. 'Drink up, Hetty, and let's make a move.' After pushing her chair back under the table, she put her hand on the back-rest. 'It's our day for seeing to Eliza, and I wondered if yer'd have any objection to me telling her about us scraping the wallpaper off, and then kidding our husbands into waiting on us? It would give her a laugh, don't yer agree?'

'Oh, yeah, she'd certainly see the funny side.' Then a doubt entered Hetty's mind. 'Yer wouldn't tell her everything, would yer? Like what happened after we went up the stairs? I'd be dead embarrassed if yer did, 'cos Eliza is of the old school, and in her day, what happened in the bedroom was never talked about.'

'Of course I wouldn't tell her about our nocturnal activities, yer daft nit! I've too much respect for Eliza to embarrass her. Anyway, I wouldn't talk to anyone about me private life, only you. So give us that cup so I can rinse it out with mine. I can't abide coming in to dirty dishes, it makes me feel as though I'm an untidy housewife, too lazy to keep the place nice.'

Hetty passed the cup over. 'If you're a lazy housewife, I feel sorry for meself.' Her eyes travelled over the grate and the polished sideboard. 'Yer keep yer house like a little palace. Yer might have a dirty mind, but yer home is spotless. Yer could eat off the floor.'

Eliza smiled when she opened the door. 'You're on duty today, are yer?' She stood aside to let them pass, then closed the door. 'I've lit the fire because I was feeling the cold.'

'Oh, yer should have left that for us to do, sunshine! Yer shouldn't be lugging coal around at your age.'

'I didn't have to carry the coal, Ada, 'cos John came last night and he filled the scuttle for me. And he rolled the newspaper up ready, and laid the firewood out on the hearth. So all I had to do this morning was rake the ashes out and set the fire. I had it roaring up the chimney in no time. Just looking at the fire makes yer feel warm and the room cheery.'

'Everywhere looks nice and cosy,' Hetty said. 'And there's nothing like a fire for cheering yer up on a cold day. And it is cold out; the winter will soon be upon us.'

Ada held her hands in front of the flames before rubbing them together and sitting down. 'What would yer like for yer dinner today, sunshine? Have yer anything in mind?'

'I've got me dinner in, sweetheart,' Eliza told her. 'Vera had made a big pan of stew, and John brought some up for me in a bowl. All I need to do is put it in the oven to heat up.'

'That was thoughtful of him,' Ada said. 'Him and Vera have been very good to yer over the years. They never miss a week without a visit.'

Eliza bent her head and was quiet for a few seconds. Then she looked up, and in a soft voice told them, 'There was a purpose to his visit last night. He asked me to go and live with him and Vera. He said he worries about me being on me own, especially with winter approaching. And there's plenty of room in their house, now there's only the two of them. I'd have me own sitting room and bedroom, so I could have as much privacy as I wanted. And they've got a bathroom, so I wouldn't have to go down the yard to the lavatory.'

Ada met Hetty's eyes, and each knew what the other was thinking. They'd be sad to see this gentle old lady go, for they were very fond of her. The street wouldn't be the same without her; she'd be missed by all the neighbours.

The first to find her voice was Ada. 'And have yer made up yer mind to go, sunshine?'

'I told John to give me time to think about it. It's not something which yer can make up yer mind about right away. I've lived in this house for the best part of me life. I moved in on the day I got married, and that's nigh on sixty years ago. It would be a wrench to leave it, for there's so many memories here. I can still see my beloved husband sitting in the rocking chair at the side of the fireplace, puffing away on his pipe after a hard day's work. That's when he had a few coppers to buy some baccy. And I can still see his face on the day John was born. There wasn't a prouder man in the whole of Liverpool.' There was a catch in Eliza's voice now, brought about by the memories. 'He was a wonderful husband and I loved him dearly. And I still miss him, to this very day.'

'I bet he adored you, sunshine,' Ada said, ' 'cos yer can tell yer've been a real beauty when yer were younger. Ye're still a fine-looking woman now. We all love the bones of yer, yer know that. And we'd be very sorry to see you go, we really would. Everyone in the street likes and respects yer. You would be much missed, Eliza, and I can't imagine this house without yer. It wouldn't be the same with strangers living here.'

'And I'd be sorry to go, sweetheart, 'cos I'd miss all me friends and neighbours. Particularly you and Hetty, and Edith and Jean. You've all been so good to me, always there when I needed yer, and I'll never forget that.'

Ada looked into the tear-filled, faded blue eyes, and knew her old friend's heart was being torn in two. And they shouldn't be making her miserable by saying they'd miss her, they should be cheering her on her way. 'Me and Hetty will be very sad to see yer go, sunshine, but that's because we're being selfish, and only thinking of ourselves. We should be happy for yer, 'cos yer'll live the life of Riley with John and Vera. With yer own living room and bedroom, and a proper bathroom, yer'll be better off than any of us.' She forced a grin. 'Every time I go down the yard on a cold winter's night, with me backside freezing, I'll think of you in yer posh bathroom. And I don't mind telling yer I'll be dead jealous. I know this house holds a lot of memories for yer, but don't forget the house is only bricks, while yer can take yer memories with yer. No matter where yer go, they'll always be with yer.'

Hetty carried on where her friend left off. 'Ada's right, Eliza, yer'd be mad not to take John up on his offer. If you won't, then I'll gladly swap places with yer. If I had the chance to be fussed over and mollycoddled, I'd jump at it. And it isn't as though yer'd be getting rid of me and Ada, 'cos we can come and visit yer in yer fine house.'

'Would yer really come and visit me?' Eliza started to show interest. 'That would be something for me to look forward to. And Vera makes lovely cakes, so I can offer yer some refreshment.'

'Too blinking true we'd come and visit yer,' Ada said. 'Yer don't think yer could get away from us that easy, do yer? Not now we know Vera makes nice cakes.'

'Do yer really believe I'd be doing the right thing? I couldn't sleep last night, with it going round and round in me head. What would I do if I went, then regretted it, and wished I was back in me little house?'

'Yer'll not do that, sunshine, I promise yer. Yer've got yer son with yer, who yer can talk about the old days with. Him and Vera are yer family, and they really want yer with them. It's not as though ye're going to live with strangers, and I bet yer'll be able to take some of yer belongings with yer. If ye're to have yer own sitting room, then yer'll have all these things around yer, just as they are now.'

Eliza nodded. 'John went all through that with me. And as they've had two empty bedrooms since Pat got her own house, I can take all me bedroom furniture with me as well. John has a friend with a van, so everything would be done for me. He said all I had to do was get meself there and sit with Pat in their living room while the men sort it out.' She smiled as her son's words came back to her, and when she spoke her voice was stronger. 'He even said all me furniture would be put in exactly the same position it's in here, so I won't even know I'm in a different house.'

'Well, yer can't ask for more than that, sunshine, and yer'd be crazy to turn it down. Don't you agree with me, Hetty?'

'Yer'd want yer bumps feeling, Eliza, 'cos from the sound of things ye're going to be much better off there than yer are here. We come in to see yer, and so do Edith and Jean, but for the best part of the day ye're on yer own. And yer must get lonely sometimes. So just think, yer'd never be lonely again, 'cos Vera would be there with yer.'

The old lady nodded. 'Me and Vera get on like a house on fire, always have done. She's a good wife, mother and daughter-in-law. And of course she's a good grandmother to Pat's children.'

'Ay, just think what a difference it will be for yer at Christmas,' Ada said. 'Knowing John, I bet the house will be decorated and they'll have a big tree with presents on, and Christmas dinner with yer whole family around yer. Ye're lucky, sunshine, and if I were you I wouldn't hesitate to tell John that ye're ready when he is.'

'Me and Ada will give yer a hand with any packing yer want doing, Eliza,' Hetty told her. 'Don't you be trying to do it on yer own. I can ask at the shops for any empty cardboard boxes, and we'll keep our newspapers for wrapping your ornaments in.'

'That's kind of yer, and I'll be glad of your help. What I must do as soon as you've gone is knock for Edith and Jean. I want them to know before the rest of the street find out, 'cos like yerselves, they've been very good to me. I don't want them to hear the news from anyone else.'

'So it sounds as though yer've definitely made up yer mind, sunshine.' Ada left her chair to plant a noisy kiss on the old lady's cheek. 'Good on yer, 'cos ye're doing the right thing.'

'It's listening to you two that's done the trick. I'll miss all me friends, and I'll miss me little house, but what yer've told me makes sense. I'd be a fool to turn John down, and selfish, 'cos I know he worries a lot about me. And I remember last winter, when the snow was thick on the ground, he trudged all the way through it to get here. Well, he won't have to do it this winter, because I'll be living with him and Vera.'

'Would yer like us to tell Edith and Jean? We're going shopping now, we could give them a knock.' Ada knew her offer would be turned down, for Eliza would want to tell her next-door neighbours the news herself. 'I know yer won't, but just thought I'd ask.'

'No, sweetheart, I wouldn't like them to hear it second hand. Not after they've been so good to me. After yer've gone I'll give a knock on each wall. They'll get a shock, I should imagine. I know you two did 'cos I could see it on yer faces.'

'Well, it came as such a surprise,' Ada told her. 'We knocked to see what yer wanted for yer dinner, and got told ye're leaving! It was certainly a shock, but the more I thought about it, the more I realised how much better off yer'd be.' Her chuckle brought a smile to the old lady's face, even before a word was spoken. 'I can make a joke of it now, and ask if our cooking has anything to do with yer wanting to leave home. I know Hetty's Lancashire hotpot leaves a lot to be desired, but I don't think mine's that bad.'

'You cheeky beggar! My cooking's as good as yours any day! My family all smack their lips after they've had their dinner, 'cos they've enjoyed it so much.'

Ada gave Eliza a sly wink before telling her friend, 'I've always said your family were good actors, sunshine, and that proves it. Even if the food yer served was terrible, they'd keep their faces straight because they wouldn't want to hurt yer feelings.'

Hetty showed she could give as good as she got. 'Ay, girl, I think yer've solved a mystery for me. Now I know why they queue up every night to go to the lavatory, it's me cooking what does it.'

'Don't worry about it, sunshine, yer haven't killed them off yet. I wouldn't lose any sleep over it if I were you.'

'Oh, it won't worry me, girl, but I have often wondered about it. And it's not something yer can ask about, is it? I mean going to the lavatory is quite a private thing, don't yer think?'

Her face straight, and her lips pursed, Ada nodded. 'Oh, definitely a subject that would go in the personal and private file.'

Eliza looked from one to the other. 'I'm going to miss you two. Yer never fail to give me a laugh, even though it might be at the expense of some poor unfortunate creature.'

'Oh, don't think of Hetty some poor unfortunate creature, Eliza, 'cos believe me, she can hold her own with anyone. She keeps me on me toes, I can tell yer.'

Hetty nodded. 'And I'm going to get yer on yer toes, now, girl, for it's time we were on our way to the shops. I'm getting a sheet of ribs for tonight, and they'll need steeping for a couple of hours to get the salt out. So move yerself off that chair and let's get cracking.'

Ada curled her fists to push herself up. 'See what I mean, Eliza? She's a wolf in sheep's clothing is my mate. Soft as putty on the outside, but as hard as nails inside. I might be bigger than her, but she's proved to me that there's good stuff in little parcels.' She bent and kissed the old lady's cheek. 'We'll love yer and leave yer for now, sunshine, but we'll be over tomorrow to see yer. In the meanwhile don't do anything Hetty wouldn't do.'

Hetty's jaw dropped. 'What did yer say that for? Honestly, if anyone but Eliza heard yer say that, they'd get the impression I was some fast floozy.'

Tongue in cheek, Ada asked, 'What's a floozy?'

Eliza showed she wasn't without humour when she said, 'A floozy is a woman who sells flowers, sweetheart, and fast floozy means she's quick at selling her wares.'

'Oh, is that all? I got the impression, from Hetty's face, that floozy meant someone who sells her wares, but they definitely ain't flowers.'

'Ah, well, that's what comes from having a bad mind, yer see, girl,' Hetty said. 'All is pure to the pure.'

'There speaks a woman whose mind is as pure as the driven snow,' Ada said. 'She's like the three wise monkeys, who hear no evil, speak no evil, and see no evil. There's a word to describe my mate, Eliza, and I think it's pronounced sanctimonious. Don't ask me to spell it, though, 'cos I wouldn't know where to start.'

'I know what it means, Ada Fenwick, even though I can't spell it,' Hetty said, trying to look hurt. 'And I'm cut to the quick that my best mate can say that about me. Just wait until I get home and get me dictionary out. If it takes me hours, I'll find a word what suits you.'

'Don't go to all that trouble, sunshine, I think I can help yer out. I know yer'll be looking for a big word, so would ignoramus satisfy yer? If it does, then it means yer think I'm as thick as two short planks.'

'While it suits the purpose, girl, it hasn't got as many letters in as sanctimonious, so it doesn't really satisfy my hurt feelings.'

'Oh dear, I can't have yer walking round with hurt feelings all day, sunshine, so how about stupid ignoramus? Yer get twice as much for yer money there.'

'As long as yer admit to being that, then yeah, it'll satisfy me.'

'Right now I'll agree to anything, 'cos yer've kept me standing here like a lemon for so long, me corns are giving me gyp. So while I might argue the point with yer tomorrow, I'll give in now. We'll say goodbye to Eliza and be on our way.' Ada bent and kissed the old lady who was smiling at their exchange. 'See yer tomorrow, sunshine. Ta-ra for now.'

* * *

When the friends called at Eliza's the next day they were surprised when Edith opened the door. She grinned at the look on their faces. 'I hope you two have got yer pinafores on under yer coats, 'cos there's work going on here, and it's all hands to the pumps.'

Ada brushed past her, followed by Hetty, who asked, 'What's going on? I haven't got me pinny on, but I don't mind getting me hands dirty in a good cause.'

Standing in the living room doorway, Ada was amazed at the state of the room. For there were cardboard boxes on the couch and on the table, and Jean Bowers was on her knees in front of the sideboard cupboards, passing crockery into Eliza's waiting hands. 'In the name of God, sunshine, ye're not moving out today, are yer?'

'No, sweetheart, we're just packing a few things into the boxes John brought with him last night. He thought if the small things were out of the way, there wouldn't be so much to do on Saturday when the van comes.'

'Are yer moving out on Saturday? I didn't think it would be so soon.'

'Neither did I,' Eliza told her. 'John came last night to tell me the friend of his who drives a van had asked his boss if he could borrow it to do a favour for an elderly lady. And the boss was very kind, and said the man could have it for a few hours as long as it wasn't in working time. So Saturday afternoon it is. And John reckons if I can get the small items out of the way, him and his friend can finish the job in a couple of hours.'

Jean had her head turned towards Ada, and with a grin on her face, she jerked her thumb. 'Get yer coat off, Mrs Woman, and take over from Eliza. As yer can see, she's wrapping the crockery in paper as I pass it to her, and putting it carefully into the boxes. She must be getting tired now, though, so yer could do the job and give her a break.'

As Ada was taking her coat off, Hetty asked, 'What can I do to help?'

'Yer can be my assistant,' Edith said. 'I'm emptying the drawers in the dressing table. And there's a tea chest upstairs to put all the bedding in, and the clothes Eliza won't be wanting to wear before she moves. Only the bare necessities are being left, to save time.'

When Hetty followed Edith up the stairs, Ada waved Eliza to a chair. 'Sit down and let us do the work. And if John comes before Saturday, yer can tell him there'll be plenty of men to give a hand. Jimmy and Danny will be glad to help, and so will Arthur.'

Jean passed over six small china plates, with the words, 'Be careful, girl, they're real china. Eliza's had them about fifty years, so I'd hate to see them get broken, or even cracked.' She watched as Ada spread out the sheets of newspaper on the table and wrapped each plate separately.

'Gordon and Joe are going to help as well, so everything should go smoothly. But it won't half take some getting used to when it's all over. We're so used to Eliza, it won't be the same with new neighbours.'

Ada had a thought. 'Ay, sunshine, what about the rent man? Yer know ye're supposed to give a full week's notice?'

The old lady nodded. 'John's calling to the office today in his dinner break. He's going to pay the rent up to the end of next week. He'll be handing the keys in on Monday.'

'He doesn't stand around, your John, does he?' Ada said, smiling at the old lady whom she was really going to miss. Always quiet and polite, never a shout and never a swear word crossed her lips. 'Organised and efficient, that's him.'

'He's always been tidy and organised,' Eliza told her with pride in her voice. 'Even as a boy, everything in his bedroom was exactly where it should be. And always thoughtful. He's sending a taxi here on Friday to take me to his house, so I won't get flustered with all the goings-on. At least that's what he said, but I think he's afraid of me getting upset when the time comes to walk out of the front door for the last time.'

'Are yer going in the taxi on yer own?' Jean asked, thinking Eliza shouldn't be left alone at any time on Friday, for it was bound to be a sad day for her.

'No, I'll not be on me own. Vera is coming with the taxi.'

Jean passed over a small china sugar basin and milk jug, a match to the plates which were already wrapped and in the box. 'That's this cupboard empty, Eliza.' She used her fists to push herself to her feet. 'Where shall we start next?'

'There's only the cupboard next to the fireplace now. The things in the kitchen are not worth taking, they're very old and Vera would have no use for them. Perhaps if the rag and bone man comes in the street, they could be given to him. Better for him to make a few coppers than putting everything in the bin.'

'We'll keep our eyes open for him,' Ada promised, 'and I'll tell Ronnie in the butcher's as well. If he sees the cart in the road he can tell him to call here.'

'What about the drawers in the sideboard, Eliza?' Jean asked. 'D'yer want me to empty them or not?'

The old lady shook her head. 'I'm going to sit and go through them tonight, sweetheart, 'cos although there's mostly junk in them, there's also old cards and letters which I'd like to keep for sentimental reasons.'

'Right, then me and Ada will start on the cupboard, and there's not much more after that. It hasn't taken long, has it?'

'What about yer clothes, sunshine?' Ada asked. 'Yer'll need to take yer dresses and that nice warm coat of yours.'

'Apart from a few pair of bloomers, which I'll need over the next few days, the rest of me clothes are going in the tea chest on top of the bedding.'

Ada was full of admiration for the old lady. 'I'll tell yer what, sunshine, if I ever move house I'll ask you and John to organise the proceedings. This is running like clockwork.'

'Don't you think of moving, Ada,' Jean said, pulling a face. 'We don't want a lot of strangers in the street. I hope whoever takes this house over will be as good a neighbour as Eliza's been. I'll go mad if Mr Stone lets it to a noisy, rowdy family.'

'Oh, Mr Stone won't hand the keys over to a family like that, he's very fussy who he takes on as tenants.' Ada nodded knowingly. 'He's got his head screwed on the right way, and he's a shrewd judge of character.' Then she began to chuckle. 'Mind you, he slipped up when he took Ivy Thompson on as a tenant. She's noisy and rowdy if ever anyone was.'

'Ooh, ay, ye're right there, Ada,' Jean said. 'She's a real big-mouthed bully. I was behind her in the Maypole the other day, and her language was so bad I didn't know where to put meself. I was ashamed of me own sex. And I felt sorry for the young girl who was serving her, she was shaking like a leaf. Ivy had asked her for two ounces of tea . . . no, she didn't ask, she demanded. All the customers in the shop were watching the poor girl as she weighed the tea on the scale, and the woman standing next to me said the manager should have come, not left the girl to it. Anyway, the tea was weighed and put in a bag which was handed to Ivy, and then the girl held her hand out for tuppence. And that was when Ivy took off and started banging on the counter, yelling that she'd been watching the girl weighing the tea and there wasn't a full two ounces.'

Ada sighed. 'She'd cause trouble in an empty house, that one. She doesn't worry me, I give her back as good as she gives, but that young girl in the Maypole must have been terrified. I know when they get the job they are told to be pleasant, and that the customer is always right. But they shouldn't have to put up with the likes of Ivy Thompson.'

'Well, it ended up with the manager having to show his face. He didn't stand up to Ivy, though, much to the disgust of all the women. Instead, he weighed the tea, then, the coward that he was, he added a little more to satisfy Ivy. And she walked out of that shop with her head in the air and a sneer on her face.'

Eliza had been listening intently. Then she voiced her feelings. 'The Ivys of this world may seem to come off best because people are afraid of them. But, really, they don't have a happy life because no one likes them and they don't have any real friends. They are to be pitied, for they'll never know how precious true friendship is.'

'That's right, sunshine,' Ada agreed. 'Ivy hasn't got any friends. There's a couple of women who hang around and pretend to be her friend, but only because they're frightened of her.'

There were footsteps on the stairs, then Hetty appeared. 'Edith sent me down to tell you we're just about finished, and what time is tea break? She also told me to say that even prisoners in Walton jail get a tea break, but I won't say that because it sounds cheeky.'

'We wouldn't like yer to be cheeky, sunshine,' Ada winked at her friend, 'so we'll pretend yer didn't say it. Just go and tell Edith I'm putting the kettle on now, so tea won't be long. And while the kettle's boiling, I'm slipping home to see if I can rustle up some biscuits so we can have a little tea party while we have the chance. We might not all be here at the same time again, so let's go mad and enjoy ourselves.'

Eliza sat back in her chair, and, before anyone noticed, she wiped away a tear which was rolling down her cheek. It was the end of an era. But as Ada had told her, her memories were the most precious thing she had left, and she'd be taking those with her.

Chapter Seven

The news spread like wildfire in the street on the Friday morning. The taxi was coming to pick Eliza up at one o'clock, and women were leaving their houses from half twelve so they wouldn't miss saying goodbye to the woman who was held in such great esteem by everyone. They hadn't seen much of her in the last year or so, but when she was more agile she had been out every morning scrubbing her step, cleaning the window ledge and brushing the pavement in front of her house. She always had a smile and a good word for everyone who passed. And now they stood in groups, waiting to say goodbye and wish her well.

Inside the house, Ada and Hetty, with Jean and Edith, kept the conversation going to take Eliza's mind off what was happening. She was nervous, and couldn't keep her hands still as the fingers on the clock moved towards the hour. Her four neighbours were also nervous, and sad, but Ada did her best by telling of funny incidents which brought quiet laughter from her friends and a shaky smile from the old lady. Most of the tales were made up as she went along, but they were welcome for they helped to pass the time.

It was exactly one o'clock when the taxi turned into the street, and when Vera saw the groups of women standing on the pavement outside and opposite her mother-in-law's house, her tummy turned over with fear, for she thought something dreadful must have happened. When she stepped from the taxi to be greeted by friendly smiles, she gave a sigh of relief. But what were all these women standing around for?

Jean opened the door with a smile. 'Right on time, Vera,' she said. 'Punctual as ever.'

Vera kept her voice low as she stood in the tiny hall. 'What are all the neighbours outside for? I got a fright when I saw them, thinking something had happened to Eliza.'

'They've come to wave her off,' Jean told her. 'She's very well thought of in this street, Vera, and everyone wanted to let her know she'll be missed by her neighbours.'

'But there must be about fifty women out there, probably more, and surely they can't all know her.'

'Of course they do!' Jean nodded. 'Don't forget she's lived in this street longer than anyone. And I bet she's the one person who has never had a cross word with anyone.'

Ada came to join them in the cramped space. 'What are you two whispering about? We don't allow secrets here, so out with it.'

Vera smiled at her before making her way over to Eliza and kissing her. 'I was just asking why all the neighbours are out in the street, even those who live at the top end. And Jean tells me they've come to wave you off in style.'

The old lady looked puzzled. 'Are some of the neighbours outside? If I'd known that I'd have asked them in.'

'Ye're in for a big surprise, Mam,' Vera told her. 'There's at least fifty women. I didn't have time to count them.'

Eliza gasped. 'Oh, no!'

'Oh, yes, sunshine.' Ada smiled at the look of astonishment on the lined face. 'Ye're a celebrity today, like a famous film star what yer see on the pictures. Ye're getting a real send-off with all the trimmings. They're women who've been yer neighbours for many years, and they want to see yer before yer go.'

'Can't I slip out of the back door?' Eliza was near to tears now, so what would she be like saying goodbye to women she'd lived amongst for so long? 'Yer could always explain to them that it would be hard for me, too emotional.'

'Will I heckerslike make excuses for yer!' Ada was very definite. 'They're standing outside in the cold, women who have a very high regard for yer, and the least yer can do is say goodbye to them.' Then Ada sought to soften what would be a very emotional time for Eliza. 'Anyway, yer won't be saying goodbye for good, will yer? Vera has promised to bring yer back to see us, so yer can tell them it won't be the last they'll see of yer. It's not goodbye for ever.'

'Of course I'll be bringing yer back,' Vera told her. 'Ada, Hetty, Jean and Edth, they're friends of mine, too, don't forget. I won't be losing touch with them.' She tutted and shook her head. 'It's not the end of the world, Mam, ye're not moving hundreds of miles away.'

Eliza squared her shoulders. 'Oh, all right, but if I do burst out crying, don't say I didn't warn yer. I'm going to miss this street, and everyone in it. And I'm going to miss every inch of this house. That's the truth, and I can't change the way I'm made.'

'Mam, we wouldn't want yer to be any different. Anyone who walked out of a house they'd lived in for sixty years, and didn't feel sad about it, wouldn't be normal.'

'They wouldn't have a heart,' Edith said, 'or if they did it would be made of stone.'

'A swinging brick, that's what they'd have in place of a heart.' Jean voiced her thoughts. 'And they wouldn't know the meaning of love or friendship.'

Eliza sighed. 'I'm daft, I know, but I do hope whoever the next tenants are, they'll be as happy here as I've been.' She put a hand on each of the chair arms and pushed herself up. 'I only need to put me coat on and pick up me purse and basket. Then we'd better go, 'cos we can't keep those women standing in the cold. Not after they've been kind enough to come and see me off.'

With her coat on, and the basket over her arm, Eliza waved the others to go ahead. 'Just give me a minute on me own to have a last look round. And don't worry, I won't upset meself. I just want to say a last goodbye.'

'There were over fifty women there to see her off,' Ada told her family as they sat down to dinner. 'And I don't think there was a dry eye amongst them. I shed a few tears, and I had a lump in me throat big enough to choke me.'

'Fancy the women from the top of the street coming down,' Jimmy said. 'That was good of them, considering they can't have known her very well.'

Ada tutted in disgust. 'Jimmy, Eliza Porter hasn't always been in her eighties, yer soft nit. When we first came to live here she was a real live wire, always on the go. She'd meet neighbours in the street, or at the shops, and she always had five minutes to spare to talk, and listen. And her house was the neatest in the street. And I'm happy to say we haven't seen the last of her, for me and Hetty have promised to visit her, and Vera said she'd bring her down to see us when the weather permits.'

'She is a nice woman,' Danny said. 'What I would call a real lady.'

'I'll miss her,' Ada admitted. 'Every time I look out of the window and see number twenty-two, it will be a constant reminder of her.'

'It'll be interesting to find out what the new people are like.' Jimmy had a smile on his face when he lifted his arm in self-defence before saying, 'That should keep you and Hetty busy for the next few weeks, love, getting the lowdown on the new neighbours.'

Ada pretended to aim a blow. 'You cheeky beggar! Anyone would think me and Hetty had nothing better to do than stick our noses in. I'm going to tell me mate what yer said about us being the street's nosy parkers.'

'I wonder who will get the house,' Danny mused. 'What sort of people they'll be?'

'A nice clean, friendly family, I hope,' Ada told him. 'And not some troublemaker like Ivy Thompson. If they put someone like her in, I'd be asking for a transfer.'

'I hope there's a girl in the family about my age,' Monica said. 'Someone I can make friends with.' Her legs began to swing under the chair as visions of a new friend filled her head. 'And if she goes to St James school it would be smashing, we could go together.'

Paul groaned. 'Well, I don't hope there's a girl, not if she was as soppy as you. They'd be better off with a boy about my age, 'cos boys are not as much trouble as girls.'

'Yer won't be thinking that in seven or eight years' time,' Danny told him. 'Girls will be more to yer liking than blokes.'

'Can we forget about who's going to get Mrs Porter's house, and whether boys are better than girls?' Jimmy's eyes sent a message to his two youngest children that they would be well advised to heed what he said. 'There's more important issues to be discussed, like what's happening tomorrow, love, with the removal van? What time is it supposed to get here?'

'I couldn't tell yer the exact time, sunshine, 'cos John doesn't know himself. He's got to rely on a mate who's doing it as a favour, so he can hardly give orders.'

'No one is saying he should give orders, love, so don't be flying off the handle. I'm only asking because I was hoping to get cracking with the wallpapering. If I can get a couple of hours in, with Danny's help, we could get two walls done and finish off on Sunday.'

'Once the van comes yer won't be long over the road, 'cos everything is ready to be loaded on. There'll be six of yer, counting the driver, so I'd say two hours should see it all wrapped up.'

'I'll cut the paper tonight.' Jimmy nodded to show his mind agreed with his words. 'That will save time tomorrow.'

'I've already trimmed the edges of the four rolls, so that's one job done.' Ada was feeling proud of herself. 'Once yer've measured and cut them to size, I'll give a hand to paste them and pass them to yer when ye're ready.'

Danny pulled a face. 'Haven't yer forgotten something, Dad?'

'What's that, son?'

'The ceiling and the frieze. If they're not whitewashed, it'll spoil the whole room. It'll be one thing laughing at another.'

Jimmy closed his eyes and gritted his teeth. 'Blast, I'd forgotten the ruddy ceiling!'

Ada touched his arm. 'Look, sunshine, it's no good trying to break eggs with a big stick. If yer can't finish the room off over the weekend, then yer can't, and that's all there is to it. Another few days, even a week, won't hurt us. Just wait and see how yer get on, and for heaven's sake, stop worrying.'

'Here's me thinking it was all going to be done over the weekend,' Jimmy said, looking and sounding disappointed. 'That's what I get for counting me chickens before they're hatched. Me ma was always telling me off for that. "Have a little patience," she used to say. "Things get done much quicker if yer take yer time and don't rush it."'

Paul screwed his eyes up to figure that out. Then he said, 'How can things get done quicker if yer take yer time? That doesn't make sense.'

'Everything me ma said made sense, son, she wasn't soft. She might have had a queer way with words, but whatever she said always turned out to be right in the end.'

'Then pretend yer take after yer ma, sunshine,' Ada said, reaching for the empty dinner plates. 'And tomorrow will pass smoothly, without a hitch. The ceiling will be done, and most of the papering, you'll see.'

'Right now I'll take your word for it, love, but don't blame me if it all goes haywire. It's you I'm thinking of, 'cos you'll have to put up with the mess for a week.'

'My shoulders are broad. I can take it.' Ada tossed her head. 'I've been waiting for two years to have this room decorated, so another week is neither here nor there. At least I'll have something to look forward to, and that will keep me going.'

'I don't think yer'll have to wait a week, Mam,' Danny told her. 'I've got a feeling the ceiling and the papering will be finished over the weekend. And with a bit of luck, me and me dad will have made a start on the paintwork.'

Jimmy raised his brows. 'Brave words, son, brave words.'

Ada watched through the window as Eliza's furniture was carried out to the van. The men had paired off, with John working with Jeff, his mate from work, Jimmy with Danny, and Gordon Bowers with Joe Benson. Hetty's husband, Arthur, was there too, and his job was to stand in the van and help arrange the furniture in a position that took up the least room. There were a few groups of children watching, but they were only there out of curiosity and were well behaved. After all, if children weren't curious they'd never learn anything.

'I wonder if they'd like a cup of tea?' Ada asked herself. 'It must be thirsty work lugging heavy pieces of furniture.' With no more ado, she opened the front door. 'Would yer like me to bring a pot of tea over, John?' she shouted. 'It won't take me a minute.'

John didn't answer until the iron bedstead was safely on the van. Then he lifted a hand in acknowledgement. 'No thanks, Ada, this is a bit of a rush job. Jeff has to have the van back by four, so we've no time to stop. But thanks for the offer. I wish we could take yer up on it.'

Ada waved back. 'See yer again, then, John!'

He nodded. 'Yer certainly will, Ada, me ma will see to that.'

His mate pulled on his arm. 'No time to waste, John, let's get it over and done with.'

Ada went back into the house and made her way through to the kitchen where she had a conversation with herself. 'I may as well peel the spuds ready for tomorrow's dinner, that'll be a job off me head.' Taking down a pan from the shelf that ran along the back wall, she agreed with herself. 'Good thinking, girl, it's better than standing gawping out of the window. And I might as well do the carrots while I'm at it.'

When there were no more jobs for her in the kitchen, Ada picked up her aspidistra plant from its spot in the living room. 'I don't want yer getting whitewash all over yer, sunshine, and yer'll be out of harm's way out here. Yer won't be lonely 'cos I'm bringing out all the things from the top of me sideboard, and yer know them.' She had her back to the door and didn't see Danny come in. So when he put an arm round her waist, she gave a start. 'In the name of God, son, I nearly jumped out of me skin, yer gave me such a fright.'

'I did call out to yer, Mam, but yer didn't hear me 'cos yer were deep in conversation with the aspidistra.' Affection and laughter danced in Danny's eyes. 'If ye're not careful, Mam, yer'll have the neighbours talking.'

'If I end up in the loony bin, sunshine, it'll be because of people like you frightening the living daylights out of me. Anyway, what are yer doing here?'

'The job's finished, Mam. Mrs Porter's house is empty and the van will be away in about five minutes.'

Over her son's shoulder, Ada saw her husband come in from the hall, and she called, 'That didn't take long, sunshine. Sixty years wiped out in less than an hour.'

Jimmy came through to the kitchen and turned on the tap. 'I'm surprised meself that we got it over so quick.' He swilled his hands in the cold water. 'Mind you, the men worked well together, they were a smashing crew.'

Ada winked at her son. 'He's very modest, your dad, and shy with it. Most men who thought they'd done a good job, they wouldn't be backward in coming forward. And now he's had a taste of success, I bet he'll work like the clappers and surprise us all by having the ceiling whitewashed before I've had time to make us a cup of tea.'

Drying his hands on the towel, Jimmy grinned. 'Don't go overboard, love, 'cos I haven't mixed the whitewash yet. And when I do it's got to stand for a few hours to settle. Otherwise it'll be like water and the ceiling won't look as though it's been painted.'

Ada pinched his cheek. 'Ah, I'm sorry to disappoint yer, sunshine, but in this house there's no rest for the wicked. Yer can start on the ceiling right away, for the whitewash is ready to use. As soon as yer'd left for work this morning, I got the bucket out, half filled it with water, then added the whitewash. I was stirring all the time I was putting it in, so it wouldn't go lumpy. And if yer look at it now, yer'll see I'm right when I tell yer it's ready to use.'

'Ye're a ruddy slave driver, that's what you are. Me and Danny have worked like demons to get the van filled in time, and yer can't expect us to get stuck into the ceiling without a sit down and a cup of tea.'

Danny nodded in agreement. 'That's cruelty, that is, Mam. It puts me in mind of James Cagney in that picture where he was in prison, and he had to work in the chain gang every day without food or drink.'

'Oh, now, come off it, sunshine, and take yer mind back to that picture. If my memory serves me right, James Cagney was a gangster in it, and he was in prison for murdering several people. So he should have considered himself lucky to be alive, never mind only getting bread and water.'

Jimmy put his hands on his hips and stared from his wife to his son. 'How the hell have yer managed to take the conversation from a bucket of whitewash to a gangster in a chain gang in America?'

'Don't yer be glaring at me like that, Jimmy Fenwick, it was yer eldest son what brought James Cagney's name up, I wouldn't have thought of him. Or bread and water, for that matter. So if yer take that look off yer face, and ask me in a proper manner, I'll consider making yer a ruddy cup of tea.' She pushed him playfully but firmly away from the stove. 'When someone asks me how many children I've got, I usually say three without giving it any thought. In future, though, if I'm asked, I'll say four, because you two are just as childish as Monica and Paul.'

Jimmy jerked his head towards the living room. 'I think we'd better move ourselves, son, before yer mam can think of any more insults. I'm not going to take it lying down though, not this time. I've been too soft with yer mam ever since the day we got married. But that's going to change, and she won't know what's hit her.'

Ada popped her head round the door. 'D'yer want a couple of biscuits with yer tea?'

Jimmy winked at her. 'That would go down very nicely, love, and don't forget it's two sugars for me and one for Danny.'

'Go on, Dad, what were yer saying about not being so soft with me mam,' Danny asked, 'and how yer were going to put yer foot down with her?'

'Well, it's like this, son.' Jimmy lifted one of the dining chairs which Ada had stacked on the couch out of the way. 'I had been thinking of trading her in for a newer model, but I've had second thoughts on that. I mean, would I get one with a sense of humour like yer mam? That's what I have to ask meself. Women as funny as yer mother are hard to come by. And although she can be bossy at times, yer have to admit she does look after us well.'

Danny took a chair down and placed it next to his father. 'It's a problem, all right, Dad, and I can see yer point. But if yer ever did decide to trade her in for a younger model, I can't see yer getting away with it. Yer'd have a mutiny on yer hands, with Paul, Monica and meself. We'd all follow me mam wherever she went, 'cos we know which side our bread's buttered on. If she went, we'd all go. And that would leave yer swinging with a new model who liked to lounge around all day, looking pretty but not doing a hand's turn in case she broke a nail. And yer could forget coming home to a pan of stew with lovely light dumplings on top. She probably wouldn't even know what a dumpling was. Then there'd be no laughter over the dinner table with our mam having us in stitches telling us about the shenanigans her and her mate get up to.' The gleam in Danny's eyes, and the deepening of his dimples, told of laughter being held back. 'No, Dad, yer'd definitely be on a loser.' Then a make-believe frown creased Danny's forehead. 'It has just occurred to me that if I help yer with decorating this room, I could be wasting me energy. Why should I work meself to a standstill for some young bird to reap the benefit?' He shook his head. 'No, Dad, I'm afraid ye're on yer own.'

At that moment Ada came through carrying a cup of hot tea in each hand, and in each saucer there were two ginger snaps. 'There you are, lads, that should cheer yer up before yer start grafting.' Taking a stand between the two chairs, Ada put her hands on her hips. She looked down at Danny. 'They say women gossip about anything under the sun, but you two are worse than any woman I've ever known. But I'll tell yer something, Danny, and that is yer dad may be many things, but daft he ain't. He's been promising me for years that he was going to run off with a young bit of stuff. He keeps building me hopes up, but it never amounts to anything. Which doesn't really surprise me, for who in their right senses would have him?'

'Ay, yer'd be surprised how many young girls fancy me.' Jimmy nodded so vigorously to stress his point, he spilt tea into the saucer. But it didn't put him off saying what he wanted to. 'There's a young girl works in the office, and every time she passes she makes glad eyes at me. And on pay day, when she's giving the packets out, she always takes longer to hand mine over. All the men have noticed, and they pull me leg soft over it. She wouldn't need much encouragement.'

'She's welcome to yer, and she'd have my blessings. But when yer came crawling home two days after yer left, I'd tell yer to get lost.'

Jimmy was enjoying himself. 'What makes yer think I'd come crawling back?'

'If I was a betting woman, and I had the wherewithal to bet with, I'd have five bob on yer coming home on the third day.'

'Why pick on the third day?' Jimmy asked. 'Why not the second or fourth?'

Danny wanted to know, 'Why don't yer think he'd last out a week, Mam?'

'Because of his socks, sunshine, that's why. If he leaves in the winter it won't be so bad, but he stands no chance in the hot weather. His feet sweat, yer see, and for the life of me I can't see a young flighty girl staying with a man who has sweaty socks. She'd wrinkle her nose up and head back to her mother.'

'I didn't know yer had sweaty feet, Dad,' Danny said. 'Everyone says I'm the spitting image of you, but I'm glad I haven't inherited that off yer.'

'Take no notice of yer mam, son, she's pulling yer leg.' Jimmy wasn't laughing, but he could see the joke. 'Me feet do not smell, and seeing as they're on the end of me legs, I should know.'

Ada was chuckling as she reached for her coat off the hook. 'If yer did have sweaty feet, sunshine, yer'd be sharing Danny's bed.'

Jimmy watched as his wife slipped her coat on. 'Where are yer off to? I thought yer were going to give us a hand.'

'Me and me mates are going to take over where you left off. We promised Eliza faithfully that we'd clean the house right through. So we're going to mop the floors, and wash and dust everywhere, so the place is spotless for whoever comes to live there.'

Danny's brows shot up. 'That's daft, that is! Why can't the new people clean it up themselves? They'll probably go over it all again, so ye're only wasting yer time.'

'Oh, I know that as well as you do, son, but I've made a promise and I'm going to keep it. Eliza was very fussy, and she kept that house spotless for sixty years. It was so clean yer could eat yer dinner off the floor. And that's how the new tenants will see it.' She wrapped her coat closely round her body, because she could smell the cold air when she opened the door. 'It won't take long with the four of us, just an hour or so. And it's not much to make an old lady happy.' She quickly closed the door to when she felt the cold wind. 'The kids are all right, they're playing with their mates. I've told them to be home for six, and there'll be some sandwiches made for tea. And while I'm over the road, working hard, I expect you to be doing the same. So step on it, and show us what yer can do.'

As soon as he heard the door bang behind his mother, Danny hurried through to the kitchen with his cup and saucer. 'Come on, Dad, drink up and let's get cracking. I'd like to have the ceiling done by the time me mam gets home, to show her what we're made of. With Auntie Hetty lending us that brush, I'll start at one end of the frieze and you can start the other. If we make an effort, we could have it done in no time, then we can start on the ceiling.' He stood in front of Jimmy with his hand out. 'Come on, Dad, drink up and give us yer cup.'

'Yer take after yer mother for being bossy,' Jimmy said before draining his cup and passing it over. 'Yer take after me in looks, but yer've definitely inherited yer mother's ways.'

'That can't be a bad thing, can it, Dad?' Danny said as he took the cup out and stood it in the sink. 'I've got the best bits of both of yer, so it gives me the right balance.'

'Then balance yerself on that ladder, son, and I'll stand on a chair. And I suggest we don't speak one word until the frieze is finished. Yer know what yer mam's like, she'll be going at it hell for leather. She's so quick, yer eyes can't keep up with her.'

'Shut up, Dad, and let's get on with it. I'll meet up with yer in the middle in fifteen minutes.'

In Eliza's house, the four neighbours stood in the kitchen, leaning on brushes and mops and having a little natter. 'It hasn't taken long,' Jean said. 'There's only out here to do, and the yard to brush. We'll be on our way home in no time.'

'I'm in no hurry to go home,' Ada told them. 'The longer I stay out, the more Jimmy and Danny will have done. Once I put in an appearance, they'll down tools and be wanting another pot of tea. Right now they'll be working harder without me, so I'd be cutting me nose off to spite me face if I go home now.'

'I've got an idea yer might like,' Jean said. 'Let's go next door to mine and I'll make us something to drink. Gordon's taken David to Anfield to see Liverpool play, and Jane's gone into town with a friend. We'd have the house to ourselves.'

'That sounds smashing, sunshine.' Ada chuckled. 'My feller would have a duck egg if he knew I'd been invited out for afternoon tea.' She glanced at Hetty. 'How about you, sunshine, are yer all right for another hour or so?'

Hetty was all for it. 'I've always wanted to be invited out to afternoon tea. And we may as well make the most of it and do the job properly. So while yer finish off here, I'll nip down to the corner shop for some biscuits.'

'I'll come with yer,' Edith said. 'I've got a few coppers in me pinny pocket, so I'll put it towards the biscuits.'

'Don't go the front way, girls,' Ada said, pulling a face. 'If Jimmy or Danny see yer, they'll think we've finished and they'll expect me home.'

'Okay, girl,' Hetty said. 'Me and Edith will go out the back and down the entry, while you two finish off here. Have yer any preference for biscuits? Custard creams, digestive, ginger snaps, or arrowroot?'

The voting was tied. Two for ginger snaps and two for custard creams. 'I'm not going to mess around,' Hetty told them. 'I'll get Sally to mix them, then it's every man for himself. It's not as though we've been invited to Buckingham Palace.'

Chapter Eight

When Ada opened the door on the Monday morning, she had her wraparound pinny on and her hair was hidden under an old mobcap. She grinned down at the rent collector as she handed her rent book and money over. 'Not a very glamorous sight to see early in the morning, am I, Bob? I know I must look a wreck, but I'm up to my neck in work. And much as I love yer, I didn't see much point in titivating meself up just for the few minutes yer honour me with yer presence.'

'It's not like you to greet me looking like a charlady, Ada. Ye're usually ready to go to the shops, looking very glamorous, if yer don't mind me saying so.'

'Mind yer saying so? Bob, it's not very often I get compliments, so carry on. I've got the time to listen, if you can keep the compliments coming.' Ada took the rent book back after it had been marked and tucked it under her arm. 'I've had me living room decorated, by me husband and son, and I was on me hands and knees cleaning the floor when yer knocked. There's splashes of paste and whitewash all over, and I want to get the room back to normal before I go to the shops. Me nerves would be shattered while I was out, with visions of the mess I had to come back to.'

'Did they do the whole room over the weekend?' Bob asked. 'They must have gone like the clappers, 'cos that took some doing.'

Ada shook her head. 'They did the ceiling and the wallpapering, but there's still the paintwork to be done. Jimmy said he'd have that done in two nights. The room looks lovely and bright now, and I'm chuffed with me little self. It'll be a pleasure coming down in the mornings to be greeted by wallpaper yer can see the pattern on.'

Bob Pritchard turned the page of the ledger to his next call, which was the house next door, and closed the book with his pen inside. 'Did Mrs Porter get away all right? I was shocked when Mr Stone said she was leaving. We're both sorry to lose her 'cos she was our oldest tenant. She'd been in the house forty years when Vincent Stone took over from his father.'

'I hope he's careful who he puts in there, Bob. I'd hate to see Eliza's house go to a family of ruffians.'

'I don't think yer need worry about that, Ada. He vets everyone who puts their name down for one of his properties. As yer know, he owns half the houses in this street, and dozens more besides. There's a list as long as me arm of people waiting for houses.'

Ada stepped back, remembering the work waiting for her. 'Well, you tell him from me that I'll have his guts for garters if he puts a rowdy family in the house opposite me. And for good measure, yer can tell him it won't only be me complaining, it'll be the Watsons, the Bowers and the Bensons. And remind him that all the men are over six foot.'

Bob chuckled. 'D'yer want me to tell him word for word, or can I tell him in me own way?'

'Any way yer like, sunshine, as long as the message gets through.' Ada began to close the door. 'See yer next week, Bob, ta-ra for now.'

The collector was smiling as the covered the few yards to the house next door, and when Hetty appeared, he had his greeting ready. 'Good morning, Mrs Watson, I hope you are well?' He took the book and money Hetty was holding out, and marked the rent book and ledger. 'I've heard all the news from Ada, and I've got the message.' Lifting his trilby, he told a startled Hetty, 'I'll have to be on me way, 'cos I'm running late. Good day to yer.'

Ada was on her hands and knees with a bucket of water beside her, rubbing the marks off the lino, when one of the panes of glass in the front window rattled. She looked up, couldn't see anyone, and put it down to the wind. However, a loud banging on her door soon followed, and a gale force wind wouldn't have been able to lift the heavy brass knocker. She sat back on her heels and rubbed a hand across her brow. 'Who the hell can this be? It won't be Hetty, 'cos I've warned her not to come until eleven o'clock. She knows I want to get this place shipshape before I go out.'

Hetty waited for a few seconds, then, when there was no response, she bent down and lifted the letter box. 'Ada, will yer open the door, please?'

Muttering that her friend was in for a mouthful, Ada threw the floorcloth into the bucket, wiped her wet hands down her pinny, and scrambled to her feet. 'What d'yer want, Hetty? I told yer I'd be busy until eleven. I was on me hands and knees when yer knocked, so whatever it is yer want, it had better be good, or I'll ruddy marmalise yer.'

'It was Bob telling me that yer'd told him all the news, and that he'd got the message. That's what he said, girl, but he couldn't get away quick enough. He practically snatched the money out of me hand and scarpered. What news did yer have to tell him, that's what I want to know?'

Ada put a hand to her forehead and rubbed hard, saying, 'God give me patience, don't let me lose me temper.' She looked down at her mate. 'Have you got me off me knees to ask me that? Couldn't yer have hung out until eleven? I mean, there hasn't been an earthquake, or a thunderstorm, has there?' Again she gave her forehead a vigorous rub. 'If I was a woman who used bad language, sunshine, I'd say I felt like breaking yer bleeding neck.'

Hetty's pursed lips gave her the appearance of being prim and proper. 'Well, Ada Fenwick, there's no need for that sort of language. I'm not used to it, and I strongly object to hearing it from a woman who is supposed to be me best friend.'

Ada let out a deep sigh. 'What were yer doing when the rent man called, sunshine?'

'I was just combing me hair,' said a puzzled Hetty. 'Me jobs were all done, so I was going to sit down and listen to the wireless until it was time to call for you.'

Waving a hand from her head to her feet, Ada said, 'I was like this when he called here. I was nowhere near ready to comb me hair, or listen to the wireless. I had other things on me mind. Like scrubbing the floor to get all the sticky paste off. After that I was going to put as much of me furniture back in place as I could, and then polish it until I could see me face in it. Yer see, sunshine, Jimmy and Danny didn't finish decorating until eleven o'clock last night, and the place was a mess. We were all too tired to clean up at that time of night, so I was met with it this morning.'

Hetty looked very uncomfortable as she shifted from one foot to the other. 'I wasn't to know, was I? I can't see through ruddy walls, or I'd have come in and given yer a hand. It wouldn't have hurt yer to shout over the yard wall and let me know yer were up to yer neck with all the jobs needing to be done.'

Ada's irritation was beginning to evaporate. She shouldn't be talking like this to her friend, who would be the first to roll up her sleeves and get stuck in if she was asked. So when she spoke, her voice was calm. 'I'm sorry, sunshine, I shouldn't let things get on top of me. Even though I do have a lot to do today, and me head is splitting, that's no excuse for taking it out on you. You weren't to know all this, and come what may, I will be ready to go to the shops with yer at eleven o'clock. And as for the rent man, he was being funny with yer 'cos I told him to tell Mr Stone that he better hadn't put a rowdy family in Eliza's house. That's all it was, and he had no right to get narky with yer for that.'

'Just wait until he calls next week, he'll get a piece of my mind,' Hetty said. 'And if yer want a hand now, girl, I'd be only too willing.'

'I know yer would, sunshine, but I'll manage. We'd only be under each other's feet. I'll be ready for yer at eleven, even if I haven't finished all the jobs. I can do a bit when we come back.'

Hetty couldn't wait until eleven. 'Did they finish the whole room off, girl? They must have worked really hard.'

'The room's not finished yet, there's still some paintwork to do. Jimmy's going to do the skirting board tonight, and the picture rail. The whole lot will be finished for the weekend.'

'Ooh, I'm dying to see it, girl, I bet the room looks lovely. Are yer happy with it?'

Ada knew what her friend was angling for, but she was determined no one would see the room until she'd cleaned up. First impressions were important. 'Yer'll see it soon enough, sunshine, it won't hurt yer to wait another hour. So will yer go home now, and let me get on with what I've got to do.' She smiled to soften her words. 'I'd have got the worst of it over if yer hadn't been so nosy. So off yer pop, and I'll see yer at eleven, not a minute before.'

'All right, girl, I can take a hint, I don't need a house to fall in on me.' Hetty turned towards her own front door, saying, 'It wouldn't have hurt yer to let me have a little peek.'

'Eleven o'clock,' Ada said, shutting the door very firmly. She'd have to move like lightning to restore the room to some sort of order, and get herself washed and changed to look respectable.

Hetty's eyes were wide as she gazed around the room. 'Oh, Ada, it's beautiful. I feel as though I've walked into the wrong house. They've certainly made a good job of it.'

Ada's chest swelled with pride. 'They worked hard. I bet they're aching all over today. I was really surprised at Danny, 'cos he's never decorated anything in his life before, only himself. But he kept up with Jimmy, and worked a treat. And don't yer think the paper looks better now it's on the wall than it did in the shop? And the place will look better still when the woodwork has been painted.'

The pale beige paper, patterned with soft green leaves, was a definite winner with Hetty. 'Yer've got me dead jealous now, girl. My room will look miserable compared to this. I'll have to get round Arthur to do our living room.'

A grin came over Ada's face. 'Well, use yer head for once, sunshine, and pick the right moment. If yer want a favour off yer husband, always ask in bed. The minute his arm comes round yer waist, and yer know he's feeling amorous, then that's the time to ask him. Sweet-talk him first, of course, to get his temperature to rise, then nibble his ear and whisper what yer have in mind. He may regret it the next morning, and try to wriggle out of it, but there's one way to shame him into keeping his promise.'

'Oh, aye, and what's that, girl? Come on, out with it. Yer know I'm not as crafty as you, and I need all the help I can get.'

Ada was silent for a while, until she had the scene set in her mind. Then she described it in detail to her mate. 'One night, when ye're having yer dinner, just say casually to Sally and Kitty that their dad has promised to decorate the living room, and ye're going to buy the wallpaper the next day. And if Arthur starts to choke on a piece of potato, and yer know he's about to say he never promised any such thing, then get in there quick and don't let him. Back him into a corner by praising him to the girls, and saying how nice the room will look when it's decorated. Don't look him in the eye when ye're saying all this, 'cos if yer do, he'll be giving yer looks to kill, and ye're soft enough to feel sorry for him.'

On Hetty's face there was a look of incredulity. 'Does your Jimmy know how devious his wife is?'

'Oh, yeah, and so do the kids.' Ada chuckled. 'They take that into consideration every time I tell them anything. It's part of the fun in this house. For instance, on the day Eliza hurt her ankle and couldn't move off the bed, I told them what I told the butcher, that I'd climbed a ladder to get into her bedroom. But to make it sound more exciting, I told them I got one leg through the window and the ladder fell down, leaving me with one leg in and the other dangling in space outside.' She chuckled again at the memory. 'I didn't tell them like I'm telling you, of course, I did all the actions and made it like a Charlie Chase comedy.'

'I bet they didn't fall for it though,' Hetty said with a huff. 'They're not that daft.'

'They believed me until I brought the ladder on the scene, then the penny dropped. But by the time I'd finished they were all doubled up with laughter. Yer see, sunshine, yer don't need money to have a happy home and family. A good laugh doesn't cost yer a cent.'

'I haven't got the gift for telling tales like you have, girl, I'm sorry to say. My humour only stretches to laughing at another person's jokes. The only thing I've had a talent for was singing. I was a really good singer when I was young, and in the school choir.'

'Yer've never told me that before.' Ada was surprised. 'We've been mates for twenty years, and yer've kept yer secret hidden under a bushel.'

'There didn't seem any point in telling yer, girl, 'cos I haven't sung in those twenty years. And if I'd said anything, it would have sounded as though I was bragging.'

'I would never have thought that about yer, sunshine, 'cos ye're the last person in the world I'd expect that from.' Ada glanced at the clock and told herself it was time they were making a move to get their shopping in, instead of standing gabbing. But it wasn't often her friend opened up and talked about herself. 'Were yer really good at singing, then, sunshine? On yer own, I mean, not in a choir?'

'There was nowhere for me to sing when I left school, because leaving school meant I had to leave the choir as well.' Hetty's eyes became bright when she said, 'I used to sing at home with me dad. He had a wonderful voice, did me dad, and he used to get me to join in with him when he was singing. He used to love all the old Irish songs, and with his lovely clear voice he could reach all the high notes. I can still remember the words to all those songs, but never have occasion to sing them.'

Ada shook her head, amazed at what she was hearing. 'Just think, it's taken us twenty years to find this out. D'yer know what, sunshine, my granny was Irish, and she taught me all the songs she remembered from the old country. A lot of them are sad, and I used to sit and cry me eyes out.' Once again she shook her head. 'I bet I know all the songs you know, but I haven't got a singing voice.'

'Oh, I don't know, Ada, yer haven't got a bad voice. Not the best in the world, like, but not the worst, either.'

'Now how would you know that, sunshine, or are yer just saying it to be nice to me?'

'Sod off, Ada Fenwick! Why would I say something just to be nice to yer? I might be frightened of Ivy Thompson, but I'm certainly not frightened of you. No, I know yer can sing 'cos I hear yer when ye're raking the grate out. I've even heard yer singing in the kitchen on wash days, when yer've got the door open to let the condensation out.' A smile played around Hetty's mouth. 'I've even heard yer singing in the yard, when ye're on yer way to the lavvy.'

'In the name of God,' Ada gasped. 'Can't I even go to spend a penny without the neighbours knowing?' She jerked her head towards the house on the other side of her. 'I suppose Annie Fields knows every time I go to the lavvy, too! But how come you two know that, yet I don't know when you or Annie go?'

'There's a simple explanation to that, girl, if yer think about it. You advertise the fact, while me and Annie keep quiet about it.'

Once again Ada looked at the clock, and this time she took notice. 'Shall we discuss this later, sunshine, 'cos if we don't get out now, the shops will be closed for dinner.'

Hetty's eyes went to the mantelpiece and she gasped. 'Ooh, I didn't realise it was that time, girl. I've been here over half an hour now.'

Ada buttoned her coat. 'They say time passes quickly when ye're having fun. To prove that right, you and me should be doubled up with laughter.' She felt in her pocket to make sure her purse and keys were there, then pushed Hetty ahead of her. 'When we get back, I'll make a pot of tea and then we can have a little sing-song. Just you, me, and the new wallpaper.'

Ronnie Atwill waved through the window of his butcher's shop when he saw the friends crossing the road, causing Hetty to remark, 'Ronnie's feeling in a friendly mood, girl. It's not often we get a wave from him.'

'He's probably glad to see us, sunshine, 'cos Monday isn't a busy day for him. A lot of people have a fry-up on a Monday, using the leftovers from the weekend. I've done it meself many a time, before Danny started work.'

'Good morning, ladies, or should I say good afternoon, seeing as it's twelve o'clock? Ye're late today.'

'I don't give a bugger whether it's morning, noon or night,' Ada said. 'It doesn't make any difference to me; as long as I've got food in to feed the family I'm quite happy. So I'll have six pork sausage and five slices of streaky bacon, please, Ronnie.'

'Are yer having mashed potatoes with them, girl,' Hetty asked, 'or are yer giving them fried bread?'

'I'm giving them mash, sunshine, it's more filling for the men. I love fried bread meself, and I can feel me mouth watering at the thought of it, but the men need something more substantial after a day's work.'

Hetty smiled at Barry, the young assistant. 'I'll have the same as me friend, love.'

When Ronnie was taking Ada's money, he said, 'There seems to be a lot of interest in Mrs Porter's house, Ada. Several women have mentioned it this morning, and apparently there's a few going down to the landlord's office to put their name down for it. So from the sound of things, it won't be long before yer have new neighbours.'

'That's just idle gossip, Ronnie, 'cos only the people in the street know Eliza has left. Anyway, she's paid up until next Saturday, so really it's still her house. Whoever's been talking to yer have been talking through their hat.'

'I don't know so much,' the butcher said. 'A couple of the women are noted for being gossips, but two of them are very respectable. I won't tell yer their names 'cos I don't want to start a war, but they were saying their landlord doesn't look after their property, and they've heard Mr Stone is a

91

good landlord. Anyway, we'll find out soon enough, 'cos let's face it, Ada, he's not going to let the house stand empty for long when he can be earning money from it.'

'As yer say, Ronnie, we'll find out soon enough. But if the ladies ye're talking about have gone down to the rent office, I think they'll be disappointed, for I know for a fact that Mr Stone has a very long waiting list. And now, Hetty, let's get cracking. I've got loads to do.'

'Hang on a minute, girl, I haven't paid yet.' Hetty handed some coins over to the young assistant. 'I think yer'll find that's exactly the right money, son.' She linked Ada's arm. 'Ta-ra for now.'

Outside the shop, Ada said, 'Yer wouldn't believe the things people dream up, would yer? It's a pity they haven't got better things to do.'

'What makes yer so sure they're not true, girl? They might be, for all you know. Anyone who knew Eliza would know she kept her house like a little palace. And yer wouldn't blame them for wanting a house that was ready to walk into.'

'I don't care one way or another who gets the keys to the house, sunshine, as long as they don't interfere with me or my family. We'll know soon enough who we'll have as neighbours, so can we change the subject now?'

'Yeah, ye're right, girl, we've got more to worry about. We'll know for sure in a couple of weeks, so best forget it until then.'

On the Wednesday morning, Ada went to the front door to see the children off to school. There was a nip in the air and she rubbed her arms as she told Monica and Paul to pull their collars up to cover their ears. 'Run all the way, and that'll keep yer warm.'

The children dallied. 'It was lovely coming down to the living room this morning, Mam,' Monica said. 'And it'll be nice to come home to.'

Paul nodded. 'Yeah, I bet our house is the best in the street now.'

Ada ruffled his hair. 'Don't let me hear yer saying that to any of yer mates, sunshine, d'yer hear me? That's bragging, and I can't stand snobs. Now get going, the pair of yer, or yer'll be getting the cane for being late.' Ada watched them running down the street, pushing each other playfully. Then she went indoors, shivering and rubbing her arms. And when her eyes lit on the teapot on the table, she hurried over to feel if it was still hot. 'Mmm, not as hot as I'd like. Still, it would be a waste to pour it down the sink, when it would do more good being poured down my throat.' So after pulling a chair out, Ada sat down and poured herself a cup of tepid tea. 'I'll have a ten-minute break, then wash the dishes before I start in here,' she told the new wallpaper. She felt a sense of pride and well-being as she gazed at the bright walls and gleaming paintwork. Jimmy had worked really hard the last two nights, painting the skirting boards, picture rail and two doors. 'I take me hat off to him,' she told one of the green leaves on the wallpaper. 'To do a full day's work, then come home and do another couple of hours, it's a wonder he's not dead on his feet. I'll make it up to him tonight, though, by cooking his favourite meal of liver and onions. That'll buck him up no end, when he walks through the door and the aroma reaches his nose.'

Ada drained her cup and pushed herself up. 'Much as I'd like to, I can't sit all day admiring the decoration. I'll rinse the dishes through, then start on this room.' As she was passing the kitchen door, she stood to admire the lovely white gloss. 'I'll not be laying a finger on you, sunshine, 'cos yer'll show every mark. And I'll warn the rest of the family, too! If I see a dirty or jammy fingermark, there'll be ructions.'

Singing 'We Ain't Got a Barrel of Money', Ada felt on top of the world as she washed the dishes in warm water and placed them upside down on the draining board. 'Who cares about money when they've got a living room fit for the Queen?'

As she walked back into the living room, Ada noticed the sideboard was a few inches away from the wall, and she instinctively put her hands on it to put it back in place. Then just in time she remembered Jimmy's warning about the paint not being dry yet, and pulled her hands back. He'd have her guts for garters if she blotched his paintwork. But those few extra inches the sideboard was taking up made less space between it and the dining chairs. 'Ye're in the way now,' Ada told it, 'but yer'll have to stay there until my feller comes home from work. The paint should be well dry by the time we go to bed, 'cos when I light the fire it will make the room nice and warm. So yer'll be back in yer own speck then.'

The beds were made, the fire ready for lighting, and it was still only ten o'clock. And one thing Ada wasn't good at was hanging around with nothing to do. It was an hour before Hetty was due, and there was nothing that needed doing to fill the hour in. 'I'm not sitting twiddling me ruddy thumbs,' Ada told the hearth. 'I can't abide sitting doing sweet Fanny Adams. I'll give me mate a knock, see if she'll come to the shops earlier. I know I bit her head off on Monday for coming here early, but me mate's not as bad-tempered as me. Besides, she'd never get me head in her mouth.'

Taking her shoe off, Ada used the heel to knock on the dividing wall. And within seconds Hetty was knocking back. Ada scratched her head. 'She's not supposed to knock back, the silly nit, she's supposed to come and see what I want. I mean, we could spend the day knocking on the wall, all to no avail! I'll give one more knock, and if she isn't at me door in a few minutes, I'll light a fire in the yard and make smoke signals like the Indians do. If that fails, I'll buy a drum and do a war dance.'

However, Ada's weird and wonderful ideas were not required, for soon Hetty was rapping on the window and peering through the net curtains. 'Are yer all right?' she asked, when Ada opened the door. 'Yer gave me a fright, 'cos I thought it must be something serious if yer were knocking on the wall when it's just been papered.'

Ada's jaw dropped and she flew back into the living room to examine the wall. 'Oh, my God, Jimmy will kill me! How stupid can yer get?'

Hetty, being smaller than Ada, had to bend to see under her mate's arm. 'Have yer marked, it, girl?'

'I don't think so.' Ada blew out her breath. 'I can't see anything, and Jimmy won't be going round with a magnifying glass.'

'It was a silly thing to do, though, girl, 'cos yer could have torn the paper, or even knocked some plaster off the wall. What did yer want me for, anyway?'

'Tell the truth and shame the devil, me ma used to say,' Ada told her. 'And even though yer'll think I've got a screw loose, I'm going to tell yer the truth. I had nothing to do, so I thought we could go to the shops early. All this kerfuffle just for that. There must be something wrong with me, when I can't sit quietly for an hour and enjoy the peace. I've got to be on the go the whole time, or me nerves go to pot.' She pulled a sorrowful face. 'That was God paying me back for the way I treated you the morning yer came early. I called yer all the names under the sun when yer knocked that day, so if yer want to have a go at me, sunshine, then be my guest, for it's what I deserve.'

'Don't be daft, girl, yer didn't call me all the names under the sun. At least yer might have done under yer breath, but yer didn't to me face. And anyway, the only reason I did knock that day was because I was nosy. So let's call it quits, eh? And if yer want to go out early I've only got the dishes to wash, then I'll be ready. So give me ten minutes to make meself look presentable.'

When Hetty stepped down on to the pavement, she heard the sound of a car coming up the street. It was an unusual sight and sound, for cars were seldom seen in those narrow streets. So after pulling the door closed, Hetty stood and watched as the car drew nearer, and when she recognised the driver, she quickly covered the few steps to Ada's. 'Look who's in Eliza's house,' she said as soon as she was standing in the tiny hall. 'It's

Mr Stone. I saw the car coming up the street, but I didn't know it was his until he got close.'

Ada was looking through the living room window before Hetty had finished speaking. 'He hasn't wasted any time, has he? I bet he's checking to make sure everything's been left as it should be. Well, he won't see many houses left as clean as Eliza's.' She turned to face her friend. 'I think I'll go over and see if I can get anything out of him.'

'Ooh, d'yer think yer should?' A million pounds wouldn't have tempted Hetty to walk across and speak to her landlord. She wouldn't know what to say to him. 'You can go if yer want to, but I'm not.'

'I'll put me coat on, and we can go out together. But you needn't come in Eliza's with me if yer don't want to. Yer can wait outside.'

'It's cold out there, girl, and I'll look a right lemon standing doing nothing.'

'Yer would only be there for a few minutes, sunshine. Mr Stone isn't likely to stand gassing to me for any length of time. I'll just pretend to be passing the time of day with him, he wouldn't see anything strange in that.'

'If that's what yer want to do, girl, then do it. Yer'll only moan all day if I talk yer out of it. But don't bring me in, I'm not as forward as you.'

Ada chuckled. 'In a nice way, sunshine, ye're trying to say ye're not as brazen as me, aren't yer?'

'If you say so.' Hetty waved a hand. 'Go on, get it over with so we can go about our business. But don't take it out on me if he sends yer away with a flea in yer ear.'

Ada knocked on the door, which had been left ajar by the landlord. 'Mr Stone, it's only Ada Fenwick from thirty-five.'

'Come in, Mrs Fenwick. It's a long time since we met.'

Ada found him standing in the middle of the living room, which looked stark without the furnture and Eliza sitting in her rocking chair. She shook her head. 'I'm sorry I came in now, 'cos seeing it like this makes me feel sad. Her close neighbours are going to miss Eliza, Mr Stone. We all loved the bones of her.'

'That wouldn't be hard to do, Mrs Fenwick, for she was a lovely person. One of a dying breed, unfortunately. I've just come to look round, see if any work is needed on the house before it's let again.'

'Yer'll not find anything needs doing here, Mr Stone,' Ada said, her hackles rising at the very thought. 'Eliza kept this house spotless all the years I've known her. The day she left she was worried in case the removal men left any rubbish around. So me and the neighbours either side, we all got stuck in and cleaned it from top to bottom.'

Vincent Stone grinned. 'I thought it must have been something like that, for you can smell the cleanliness as soon as you open the door. You were lucky to have known Mrs Porter for so long, but she in turn was lucky with her neighbours. I keep tabs on all my tenants, and I know she was well looked after in the last few years. You are all to be admired for that. Please pass on my gratitude to all her friends. I was sorry when I heard she was leaving, but understand her son's reasons for wanting her with them.'

Ada thought, here goes, it's now or never. 'I hope the tenants yer put in will be as good to have as neighbours as Eliza was, Mr Stone. All the near neighbours are hoping the new tenants will be clean, respectable and friendly.'

Once again Vincent Stone grinned. 'Are you the messenger for your neighbours, Mrs Fenwick?'

She chuckled. 'No, they're not as cheeky as me. They'd die if they knew I was mentioning them, even if what I'm saying is true. All the neighbours on both sides of this end of the street get on fine. There's never any trouble.' She couldn't keep back another chuckle. 'Unless Ivy Thompson decides to pay one of us a visit. That doesn't happen very often, though, and there's enough of us to deal with her. In fact, she breaks the monotony 'cos she's so over the top yer can't help laughing at her.'

'I take it you're not afraid of the Ivy Thompsons of this world?'

'Certainly not! She's a bully, and if yer don't show that ye're not frightened of her, she'd make yer life a misery. My mate, who's standing outside in the cold because she's too shy to come in, well, she's terrified of Ivy. Unless she's with me, when she puts on a brave face 'cos she knows Ivy won't tangle with me.'

'I understand that your best friends are Mrs Watson, Mrs Bowers and Mrs Benson? Am I correct?'

'Good grief, Mr Stone, yer are well informed. We used to be five good mates, but with Eliza leaving us, we're down to four. We look out for each other, always have done since the day we became neighbours. But how did you know? Does Bob keep yer informed?'

'He does. And he passed the message on about you hoping for decent neighbours in this house. Well, I do have a family at the top of my list who appear to be what you're hoping for. I have never seen the husband, but the wife, Mrs Phillips, is a very quietly spoken woman who I'm sure you would get on with. The reason I have never met the husband is because he's at work every day, but I know they have two children, a girl and a boy, both working. That is as much as I can tell you, Mrs Fenwick, but it may be enough to put your fears to rest.'

96

'Did yer say their name's Phillips, Mr Stone? I only want to know so I can say hello to them when they move in. Make them feel welcome, like.' Ada turned towards the door. 'It's been nice talking to yer, it's not very often we see yer. Now I better get out to my mate, she'll be calling me fit to burn.'

Hetty was indeed calling her mate names, for her feet were getting cold standing in the one spot. And when Ada came out of the house, Hetty had her mouth ready to tell her off. But the conspiratorial wink that came her way changed her annoyance to anticipation. 'Well, how did yer get on? Yer've been in there long enough to get his life story.'

Ada linked her arm and they walked quickly down the street. 'I wasn't after his life story, sunshine, but I did get what I was after. Our new neighbours are the Phillips family. Mother, father, and two children who are both working.'

Hetty was flabbergasted, and only managed, 'Ooh, er, go 'way!'

Chapter Nine

'Is that you, Ada?' Hetty kept her voice low, for what she had to say was for her friend's ears only. 'Ada, are yer there?'

Ada took the two wooden pegs from her mouth and pegged a towel on the line. 'If I'm not here, sunshine, ye're going to feel daft when yer find out yer've been talking to yerself. Of course I'm here, I'm pegging me washing out. There's not much chance of it drying, but at least it'll get the wet out.' She suddenly remembered it was Hetty who had called to her. 'Did yer want something, sunshine?'

'I wouldn't have called yer if I didn't want yer for something, would I?'

'What the heck are yer whispering for? I can barely hear yer.'

'Because I don't want the whole neighbourhood hearing what I've got to say. Open yer entry door and I'll come round.'

'I've got me dolly tub out, sunshine, yer can't move in me kitchen. Whatever it is, can't it wait for an hour, until I've got meself sorted out?'

'If I waited that long, it wouldn't be worth telling yer, 'cos it would be over. There'd be nothing to see, and yer'd have a cob on with me for not telling yer.'

Ada scurried down the yard to draw the bolt back on the door. If it was a choice between getting her washing done or hearing a bit of news, then the washing would lose every time.

Hetty slipped through the half-open door. 'Hurry up, girl, put a move on if yer don't want to miss anything.'

'Hold yer horses, sunshine, give me a chance to bolt me door. I don't want to look out of the window later to find some kind person has waltzed off with me washing.'

'I'm sorry I bothered to call yer,' Hetty said, her feet moving quickly over the uneven tiles on the ground. 'I thought I was doing you a favour, and now I've probably missed all the excitement meself.'

Ada hastened after her. 'What's all the fuss about, sunshine, have the King and Queen come to visit us?' She reached the living room to find Hetty moving the aspidistra plant from the little table under the window to the dining table. 'What are yer doing, missus? Talk about making yerself at home isn't in it. I know ye're me best mate, but aren't yer carrying things a bit too far?'

Hetty beckoned her over to the window. 'Will yer shut up, girl, and take a look. Our new neighbours are moving in.'

'Oh, yeah! Move over, sunshine, and give someone else a look in. Don't be hogging the whole window for yerself.' The two mates jostled for the best speck. 'Have yer forgotten yer live next door, Hetty Watson, and this is my house? Now shove over, or go home and have yer own window all to yerself.'

'I don't want to watch on me own, it wouldn't be the same. Besides, Ada Fenwick, have yer forgotten that yer wouldn't even know this was going on if I hadn't told yer? Yer'd still be hanging yer washing out, with yer mouth full of pegs.'

The net curtain was moved slightly, to give Ada a clearer view. 'Come this side, sunshine, and if yer sit on the arm of the chair, I'll be able to see over yer head. Pretend ye're sitting in the stalls at the Atlas, and I'm in the dress circle.'

'I haven't seen anyone that looks as though they belong to the family yet,' Hetty said. 'There's only the two removal men so far.'

'The family are probably inside, directing the men where to put the furniture. If the men were left to themselves they'd plonk it anywhere for the easiest.'

'The husband will be at work, and yer can't blame him. He'd lose a day's pay, and that would put a dinge in his wage packet.' Hetty took her eyes from the house opposite to ask, 'Didn't yer say Mr Stone told yer the two children work as well?'

As Ada nodded, she gave her friend a nudge. 'Ay, look over to Jean's house, and yer'll see her curtain twitch. And I bet Edith's watching, too. They've got more interest in what the new family are like than we have. They're the ones who have to live next door to them.'

'I hope we can be friends with them, like we were with Eliza.' Hetty turned her head to add, 'It makes life worth living when yer've got friendly neighbours. A smiling face never fails to cheer me up.'

'I must be a godsend to yer, then, sunshine,' Ada chuckled, ' 'cos I've always got a smile on me face.' She saw a movement opposite and moved forward quickly, knocking Hetty's head sideways, 'Look, there's a young girl come to the door to talk to one of the removal men. Mr Stone said there was a daughter, but he didn't mention her age. I'd say she was about seventeen, what d'yer think?'

'I think that if yer knock me head sideways again, like yer just did, yer could end up breaking me flipping neck.'

'Ah, yer poor thing,' Ada said, giving Hetty's neck a quick rub. 'There now, I've made it better. Can yer move it?'

Hetty's nostrils flared. 'Of course I can move it, yer daft thing. But if yer decide to lunge forward again, without any warning, I might not be so lucky. And I'll tell yer now, girl, that if yer break me neck I'll never speak to yer again.'

Ada screwed up her eyes, wondering whether she should leave well alone. But no, she couldn't resist a joke. 'Yer do realise that if yer were to break yer neck, it would bring an end to our friendship, don't yer? For yer'd have to spend the rest of yer life in bed, lying flat on yer back. And me being the good mate I am, I'd feel obligated to visit yer every day. But I couldn't cope with that, and I'd have to put sentiment behind me, 'cos if I had to stand looking down at yer, hour after hour, day after day, then I'd be doing me own ruddy neck in. And much as I love yer, sunshine, I don't fancy spending the rest of me life lying next to yer in bed.'

But Hetty missed half of what was said, for she was too busy watching the goings-on in the house opposite. 'Ay, girl, that must be the mother. She's got the same colour hair as the girl, except she's going grey.'

'She's not half thin,' Ada said, fingering the curtain. 'There's nothing of her, she's as thin as a rake.'

'Some people are naturally thin, girl, it doesn't mean she doesn't eat enough.'

'I'm not criticising her, sunshine, I'm just jealous 'cos I'd like to be nice and slim. I used to be, until I had our Danny. I piled the weight on when I was carrying him, and I've never lost it.' Ada pointed a finger. 'There's the girl again. She's very pretty, isn't she?'

Hetty nodded. 'She looks it from here. And their furniture looked all right, too. It seems as though we've hopped in lucky with the family who have taken over Eliza's house.'

'Don't speak too soon, sunshine, 'cos it's bad luck. We'll find out what they're like when we get to know them.'

'Ooh, ay, look!' Hetty pulled on Ada's skirt. 'Edith's just come out of her house and she's walking towards them. I bet she's asking if they'd like her to make a pot of tea for them. She's like that, Edith, very thoughtful.'

'If she was offering, sunshine, then her offer's been turned down. Look, the woman is shaking her head.' Ada watched Edith walk back to her own house with her head lowered and arms folded. 'Perhaps they'd already made themselves a drink. And they wouldn't ask Edith in, 'cos they'll be up to their necks, trying to get the place into some sort of order. It'll take them at least a week to know where everything is. It's twenty years since we moved in here, and I can still remember being in a mess for weeks.'

'I'd go over and ask Edith what that was about,' Hetty said, 'but it might look too obvious. What d'yer think?'

'It would look obvious, sunshine, and it would give the new people the impression we're nosy pokes.' Ada grinned. 'And we're not, are we? I'd say we were interested, curious even, but never nosy.'

Hetty frowned. 'What are we sitting here for, girl, if it's not to nose? We wanted to know what the furniture was like – whether it was in good nick or falling to pieces. And we wanted to know what the family were like.'

Ada feigned an expression that showed both hurt and surprise. 'Excuse me, sunshine, but if my memory serves me right, I was hanging me washing out, minding me own business, when you came on the scene. I only came along with yer because ye're me mate and I didn't want to hurt yer feelings, or disappoint yer. If it hadn't been for you, I wouldn't have wasted me time peeping through a window to spy on new neighbours moving in.'

Ada was a very clever actress when she put her mind to it, and Hetty stared at her in amazement. 'Well, pardon me for breathing, I'm sure.' She got to her feet, squared her shoulders and huffed. She wasn't in the same league as Ada when it came to acting, but right now she was putting on a very passable performance. 'I know when I'm not wanted, Ada Fenwick, and I won't be bothering yer again after today. If yer'll kindly let me pass, I'll go home and get meself ready to go to the shops. Seeing as I'll be on me own, just getting me own shopping, then I'll be there and back in no time.'

'To show I was brought up proper, and know my manners, I'll escort yer to the door. As it so happens, I have a very important call to make when I've finished my washing, so I'll be doing my shopping later in the day.'

'Oh, ay! And may I be so bold as to ask where this important call is to?'

'It's none of your business, really, but to satisfy yer curiosity, I'll tell yer anyway. I'm going to walk down the street, cross over to the other side, and go up the entry to Edith's house.'

'Ooh, er, shall I come with yer, girl?'

'Yeah, yer can if yer like, sunshine. I don't like going out on me lonesome. I'm always afraid some man will come along and run off with me.'

The two friends grinned when their eyes met, and soon their laughter was so hearty, they had to cling to each other in the tiny hall. 'That was good, wasn't it, girl? We both played our parts very well.'

'I'll have to watch you, sunshine, ye're getting too good.' Ada ran the back of a hand across her eyes. 'Pretty soon yer'll be outshining me if I'm not careful.'

'I've still got a long way to go before I catch up with you, girl. But I am learning, and that's because ye're such a good teacher. The advice yer gave me on how to go about getting me living room decorated, well it worked a treat. Arthur has promised to make a start at the weekend. Sally and Kitty are paying for the paper if they're allowed to choose it, and I've offered to buy the paint. The girls are really looking forward to seeing the room as bright as I've told them yours is. So, all in all, being as devious as you has taught me a lesson.'

'Ye're a dark horse, Hetty Watson. When did all this happen?'

'Only the night before last. It wasn't easy, 'cos I'm not like you, I'm shy and blush at the least thing. But when the time came, I remembered what yer'd said, pictured your nice bright living room in me mind, and plucked up the courage. Arthur agreed without even giving it any thought, for he was too busy with the job in hand. I don't think he even heard properly what I was asking, 'cos he agreed right away.'

Ada wore a sly look when she said, 'So, the night before last was a night of passion in the Watson household, eh? And was a good time had by all?'

Hetty blushed. 'If ye're waiting to hear all the details, girl, then yer can forget it. Suffice to say it worked and I'm getting me room decorated. I'm very grateful to yer for that, but apart from my thanks, ye're not getting anything else.'

'Then yer've still got a lot to learn, sunshine, that's all I can say. Getting what yer want is fine, and I'm delighted ye're getting yer room decorated – as long as it's not nicer than mine, that is. But forget the ruddy decorating, 'cos if that's all yer got out of a night of passion, then there's something radically wrong with yer. Somewhere along the line, you are not doing the right thing and ye're missing the best part.' Ada knew it was naughty of her to make her best friend wriggle with discomfort, but she couldn't resist. After all, she'd be doing her a favour by introducing her to the delights to be had in the bedroom. 'Me now, I always get two bites of the cherry. When Jimmy has agreed to whatever favour I've asked of him, I then go on to enjoy meself. After all, why should he have all the fun? Then, when I come down off the cloud, I go to sleep with a smile on me face.'

Hetty's head quivered with indignation. She couldn't stand by and let that pass, not without sticking up for herself. 'I'm not exactly made of stone, Ada Fenwick. Seeing as I have two children, I must have my moments, the same as every other wife. I just don't think they're a subject for discussion outside of the house.'

'In that case I'm not going to give yer any more hints or advice on how to improve yer love life. What's the use of me giving yer good, sound advice, if I never find out whether the advice was taken, or whether it was successful? If yer went to a doctor or a dentist for advice, they'd charge yer a lot of money. Now I don't want money, but the least yer can do is let me in on the pleasure and success my advice has given. I don't think that's too much to ask, in fact I think my fee is very reasonable.'

The two friends were standing in the tiny hall, and they jumped with fright when there came a loud knock on the door. Ada's body was almost touching the door, and such was the start she got, her heart began to pound. 'My God, that was enough to give me a heart attack.' She opened the door with a hand pressed to her breast.

'Did I give yer a fright, Ada?' Edith Benson looked up from the pavement. 'I didn't think I knocked hard.'

'It wasn't your fault, sunshine, it was me standing right next to the door. I was seeing Hetty out, yer see, that's why.'

'Can I come in a minute?' Edith asked. 'I won't keep yer long 'cos I know, like meself, yer'll have work to do.'

Ada stepped back. 'Of course yer can come in, sunshine, I don't charge.' As she closed the door, she said, 'Me and Hetty were having a laugh before we go back to our dolly tubs. But go in, we're not in that much of a hurry. We've been watching the new neighbours moving in. That's how nosy me and me mate are.' She waved to a chair. 'Sit down and take the weight off yer feet. I don't charge for that, either.'

Edith didn't move from the doorway as her eyes took in the newly decorated room. 'Ooh, it's lovely, Ada. I know yer told me yer were made up with it, but I wasn't expecting it to be so nice and bright. I like the paper, and the white paintwork doesn't half make a difference.'

'Yeah, I am pleased with it, but right now I'd like yer to sit down and pretend ye're at yer granny's. I may as well tell yer that me and Hetty were going to call over to yours later, to see what yer first impression of yer new neighbours was. Yer see, we saw yer talking to the woman who we thought was the mother.'

'That's why I'm here,' Edith told them. 'Jean isn't in, so I'll see her when she gets back from the shops. The truth is, I don't know what to make of the new people. At least the two I've seen. The girl is very pretty, and I did manage to get a half-smile from her. But not the mother, she didn't want me at the door, and she made it plain. She only spoke about half a dozen words, and that was because she had to. I'd gone to ask if they'd like a pot of tea, but the woman couldn't get me away from the door quick enough.'

'She was probably flustered, sunshine,' Ada said. 'Moving house is no joke, especially if yer husband isn't there. And it could be that she's a shy person.'

'I've thought, and I've made excuses for her being so unfriendly, and that's why I wanted to talk to one of the gang, to see what they thought. I could understand her not wanting to be bothered when she was up to her neck, but most people would have thanked me and explained they were too busy. But she kept looking down the street as though she didn't want anyone to see me talking to her. If it is because she's shy, and I hope so, then she is the most shy person I've ever seen in me life. The word I'd use to describe her is timid. She kept clasping and unclasping her hands, as though she was frightened.'

'Didn't the young girl say anything?' Hetty asked. 'Not even to thank you for offering to make them a pot of tea?'

'There was no conversation at all. I said why I was there, the mother said they'd already made tea, and while I was telling them I hoped they'd be happy there, there were just nods and a few low grunts in reply. Oh, when I was walking away, the young girl did thank me. But to tell the truth I was sorry I bothered.'

'If I were you, sunshine,' Ada said, leaning forward, 'I'd give them the benefit of the doubt. It wouldn't be fair to condemn them on one brief meeting. When they are settled in, they may turn out to be smashing neighbours. Let's hope so, anyway, for all our sakes.'

Ada didn't mention the new family to Jimmy because she knew he didn't understand why she was interested in what went on outside the house. He thought the family was the main concern, not strangers. Not that he classed their close neighbours as strangers, but anyone outside their little circle of friends was of no interest to him. However, he was the first to bring up the subject.

'I saw the bloke that lives in Eliza's house this morning. And a young boy, who must be the son. The father was wearing overalls, but the lad had his rolled up under his arm.'

Ada was careful not to show too much interest. 'Oh, ay, did they have anything to say to yer?'

'I shouted "good morning" and he waved back. No one's in the mood for talking at that time of the morning, they just want to get to work on time.'

'I haven't seen sight nor light of anyone since the day they moved in. And then it was only a glimpse of the mother and a girl of about seventeen.' Ada chose her words carefully. 'Mind you, they're probably still at sixes and sevens. It'll be a while before they settle in and get their bearings.'

'The girl sounds interesting, Mam.' Danny's eyes danced. 'What's she like to look at, and does she seem the type who likes to dance?'

Ada's eyes went to the ceiling. 'Is that all yer ever think about, son? Well, I'm sorry I can't answer yer question, but if I see the girl I'll make it me business to ask if she can dance. I'll ask which is her favourite dance if yer like, and does she have a boyfriend? Any more yer'd like to know about her, before I draw a line under the list?'

'Well, a name would be useful. She'd think I wasn't brought up properly if I said, ay, you with the long blonde hair.'

'She wouldn't only think yer were ignorant, sunshine, she'd think yer were colour-blind as well. Yer see, she's got auburn-coloured hair.'

'Thanks, Mam, that's a start.' There was laughter in Danny's eyes. 'Perhaps yer noticed whether she was tall and slim, or small and tubby?'

'No, I didn't, son, 'cos I only saw her for a few seconds, and she had her back to me. One thing I did notice, though, was that she had hazel eyes.'

Young Paul didn't see his dad's shoulders shaking with laughter, for he was too busy wanting to know, 'If yer only saw her back, Mam, how could yer tell what colour her eyes are?'

It was Danny who answered. 'Because our mam has got special powers, that's how. She can see over rooftops, and round corners, places where no one else can see.'

Paul grunted in disgust. 'Ye're crazy, you are. All yer ever think about is girls and dancing. I don't know why yer have to go chasing girls when yer've got Sally next door. She's better than any other girl, and yer can't see it 'cos ye're too daft.'

'All right, let's not have any squabbles at the dinner table. And Paul, what makes yer think Sally would want to go out with Danny, even if he asked her? She'd probably tell him she'd rather live to be an old maid than go out with him.'

Paul was bouncing up and down on the chair seat, wishing he'd thought of saying that. He wasn't quick-thinking enough to get the better of his big brother, but his mam was, she had an answer for everything. 'Yeah, like me mam said, Sally would tell yer to get lost.'

Danny didn't mind being the butt of a joke, he quite enjoyed it. 'There's only one thing wrong with that ever happening, our Paul.'

'What's that?'

'She'd have to find me first, and I'm pretty nifty on me feet.'

Ada tutted. 'If Sally could hear you two talking about her like that, she'd be really upset. And for your information, yer Auntie Hetty thinks Sally has already got a boyfriend. She hasn't brought him home to meet the family yet, though, as she says she wants to get to know him better first. She thinks she's too young to court seriously, as well. Which I think is very sensible of her. And Jane Bowers has got a boyfriend as well. She's been to his house, but hasn't brought him home to meet Jean and Gordon. She's waiting until she's sure he's Mr Right.'

Jimmy nodded his agreement. 'Two sensible girls, they are. They'll know when the right one comes along, like yer mam did with me. She knew I was a good catch, and she snapped me up before one of me other admirers got their claws into me. She's got her head screwed on, has yer mam. She knew she'd never get another as good as me.'

There was tenderness mixed with humour in Ada's eyes when she retorted, 'Don't let yer head get too big, sunshine, or yer'll never get through the door. And just to set the record straight, I gave you one hell of a run for yer money.'

'Yer did that, love. I had quite a fight on me hands. There were a couple of blokes I had to fight before I won your hand. And they weren't midgets, either, they were hefty blokes. But it paid off in the end, and the seven and six I had to pay for the marriage licence was well worth it.'

The laughter round the table in the Fenwick house was echoed by that of the Bowers family living opposite. The evening meal was always a happy affair, with tales of the day's events being exchanged. They were a close family, with Jean and Gordon being good parents to daughter Jane, who was seventeen and working in an office in the city, and fifteen-year-old David, who had a job as an apprentice with a building firm. Gordon was telling them about a mate at work who had come in that morning with a black eye. Apparently he'd gone out for a pint the night before, met a bloke he hadn't seen since they were at school together, and failed to notice the hands on the clock moving round. So he was in the pub until closing time, and not quite steady on his feet. In fact it was fair to say he'd had a couple more pints than he was used to, and couldn't even find the keyhole to let himself in.

'He was fumbling to find the keyhole when his wife opened the door,' Gordon told them, his laughter hearty. 'Apparently she took one look at him, and called him everything she could lay her tongue to. Her hand must have been very steady, for her fist had no trouble finding its target. She put some force behind it, as well, 'cos he had a real shiner. He tried the old lame excuse that he'd walked into the door, but the lads wouldn't buy that, and they pulled his leg so much, he ended up telling them the truth just to shut them up.'

'I suppose you were one of the lads making his life a misery, were yer?' Jean asked.

'Of course I was, love. He looked so sorry for himself we all thought it was hilarious. He'd have laughed his head off if it had happened to one of us.'

'It better hadn't happen to you,' Jean said, her bonny face having trouble with a smile that wanted to show itself. 'If you ever come home the worse for wear, rolling down the street blind drunk, I'll give yer more than a black eye.'

Jane, the image of her mother, asked, 'Would it be two black eyes, Mam? Or would yer take the door off its hinges and hit him over the head with it?'

They were never to hear Jean's reply, for a heavy crash against their wall had them sitting up straight in their chairs. The crash had been so loud, they thought the ceiling or wall was about to cave in.

'What was that?' Jean gasped, her eyes wide with fright. 'Did it come from in here?'

Gordon shook his head. 'It came from next door, love. They must have knocked a chair against the wall. Or dropped something heavy.'

'But it was against our wall, Dad,' David said. 'If they'd dropped something, it wouldn't have made that noise. Not against our wall, anyway.'

Jane's hand had gone to her mouth when the crash happened. Now she took it away to say, 'Something heavy was thrown against that wall. If they'd just knocked a chair over, it wouldn't have been so loud. I thought the wall was coming down.'

'I wonder if I should knock and ask if everything's all right?' Jean asked her husband. 'I haven't had a chance to talk to them since they moved in, 'cos I've never seen any of them around. This might be a good chance to introduce meself.'

'I don't know about that, love, it may not be the best time. They might think ye're complaining about them making a noise, and that wouldn't be a good way to try and make friends with them. Perhaps tomorrow yer could give a knock and introduce yerself.' Gordon shrugged his shoulders. 'It's up to you, love, if yer want to go now.'

Jean was pushing her chair back when they heard a loud, male voice shout, 'Get that bleeding thing out of me sight before I belt yer.'

Then a softer female voice, 'Leave him alone, he's not doing you any harm.' Whoever the voices belonged to, they must have moved away from the wall, for their words became fainter and no longer clear.

'Forget it, Jean,' Gordon said. 'This is not a good time to come face to face with our new neighbours.'

'I wouldn't dream of going!' Jean felt shaken. 'I hope to goodness there's a good reason for what we've just heard. I'd go mad if I had to put up with that very often. I've been looking forward to meeting the people who'll be our neighbours, but from the sound of things I'd be best keeping away.'

'Now don't start that, love,' Gordon told her. 'Yer don't know the circumstances, it could be a one-off. Give them a break, for they haven't had time to settle down and feel at home. Wait a few days, then call and introduce yerself. Or, if yer'd rather I broke the ice, I'll pay them a visit.'

'We'll leave well alone for now, see how things go,' Jean said, pulling a face. 'I'm glad I'd finished me dinner, or it would have put me off. I hate rows and loud voices, and I can feel a headache starting now. I'll be going to bed early tonight, give meself some time to say a special prayer that our new neighbours don't turn out to be bad 'uns.'

Chapter Ten

'I'm starting me Christmas clubs today, sunshine,' Ada said as she bent her arm for Hetty to link. 'Butcher's, greengrocer's and sweet shop.'

'It's funny yer should say that, girl. I think yer must be a mind-reader.' Hetty snuggled her hand in her mate's arm. 'I was going to mention it meself, 'cos we've usually started well before now.'

'That's because we had other things to do with our money. We've both got posh living rooms now, and yer can't have yer cake and eat it. We'll make it up by putting a few extra coppers in each shop. It soon mounts up, and every little helps.'

'How much are yer putting in each shop, girl, and I'll put the same.'

'I've got it all sorted out in me head, sunshine, so I won't be running around like someone demented on Christmas Eve 'cos I've forgotten something, or run out of money. I'm putting a shilling in the butcher's, and that should cover me meat. Sixpence in the greengrocer's will cover potatoes, veg, and fruit. And I'm putting sixpence in the sweetshop. I'm not joining the club at the baker's this year, I'm going to make me own cakes. Which just leaves having to buy something to wear. Danny said he'll give me an extra sixpence every week to help with that. He's nineteen in a few weeks, and he'll be getting a rise in pay.'

'He's very good is your Danny. There's not many lads would fork over more than they have to. My two girls wouldn't think of giving me extra.'

'There's a big difference in your circumstances and mine, sunshine, which yer seem to forget. I've got two children still at school, while yours are working and handing over part of their wages. Not that I begrudge yer getting more than me, 'cos I don't, I'm just pointing it out.'

'Yeah, I know, girl, and I understand how lucky I am. Have yer brought the money with yer to open the clubs today?'

Ada stopped in her tracks. 'Oh, I'm sorry, sunshine, I should have mentioned it before we left the house, to make sure yer had enough money on yer.'

'Don't worry, I've got enough with me. If I run short, I can always cadge a few coppers off you until we get home.'

'Yer'd have a hard job to borrow off me, Hetty, 'cos I've got me money sorted out to the last penny. If Ronnie's scale goes an ounce over three-quarters of a pound of stew, he'll be told to take it off, I can't afford it.' Ada chuckled. 'Unless he takes pity on me, and I can't see that happening, somehow, can you, sunshine?'

Hetty shook her head. 'If it hasn't happened in the twenty years we've been dealing with him, then it's not going to now. He's not exactly generous, is Ronnie. He'd rather err on his side than the customer's. Not once in all these years has he given us anything for nothing. He even cuts a bit off a sausage, rather than giving a customer the benefit. I've often wondered what he does with those bits, 'cos if he tried to palm them off on a shopper they'd soon tell him what to do with it. There'd be blue murder.'

'He wouldn't get away with it if he tried it on me,' Ada said, 'I'd hit him with it. And when I open the club today, I'll make sure I get a card with the payment marked on it.'

'Are yer having a turkey this Christmas, or a large chicken like we had last year?'

'If there's sufficient money for a turkey I'll get one. There'd be enough meat on it to last three days. I was weighing it up in me head last night, when I was in bed. And I've decided to put a penny away every day through the week, and I'll have an extra sixpence which I'll put in my club. I'd love to see a big turkey, roasted to a nice golden brown, sitting in the middle of the table on Christmas Day, and Jimmy carving slices off it.'

Hetty caught her friend's eye. 'Yer did all that in bed last night, eh, girl? That's not like you to waste time like that. Yer've usually got far more important things to occupy yer mind when ye're in bed.'

'Well, well, well!' Ada said. 'Life is full of surprises! Only a few weeks ago yer used to blush if I even mentioned going up the stairs to make the ruddy bed! Ye're certainly coming out of yer shell, sunshine, yer'll be swearing next.'

'That's your fault,' Hetty told her, cursing herself for saying what she had. She should have known not to give her mate the ammunition to fire a shot. 'It's you what's given me a bad mind. Before yer started sharing yer bedroom antics with me, whether I wanted them or not I must add, the only time my thoughts were in the bedroom was when I was making the bed. So there, Ada Fenwick!'

'Ay, sunshine, yer should be showing me gratitude, not laying the blame at my door. Before we became mates, yer didn't know what life was all about. Oh, I know yer've had two children, which means yer don't still believe the old fairy tale about babies being delivered by a stork, or being found under a cabbage patch. But did it never occur to yer that men and women were made different for a reason? And I don't mean just to produce children, but to give pleasure. And that, sunshine, is what life is all about.'

'Oh, and I suppose I'm supposed to get down on me hands and knees to thank yer for giving me a bad mind, am I?'

'No, not a bad mind, sunshine, but a mind that sees and enjoys the good things life has to offer without feeling guilty.'

A voice over their shoulders made them jump, before turning to see Edith standing behind them.

'You two seemed to be so deep in conversation, yer didn't hear me calling yer.' Their neighbour grinned. 'What plan are yer hatching up now?'

Hetty's eyes were sending daggers to Ada, in a bid to tell her not to dare repeat what they'd been talking about. And Ada got the message. 'I don't know about hatching a plot, Edith, but it sounds more exciting than talking about joining a Christmas club, which is what we've been doing. We've had a long discussion about how much we need to put in the butcher's shop if we want a turkey for our Christmas dinner. We're late starting the clubs this year, we haven't put anything away up to now, but we're starting in earnest today. And first on the list is the butcher.'

Hetty thought they were on safe ground now, and found her voice. 'After the butcher's, we're off to the baker's and the candlestick-makers.'

'Don't be going overboard now, sunshine, 'cos we don't need to save up for cakes, and the chandler's sells candles at two for a penny.'

'I wasn't being serious, Ada Fenwick, and you know it. So don't be making fun of me.'

'I wouldn't dream of making fun of yer, not when ye're me best mate.' Ada jerked her head at Edith. 'Don't take no notice of her, she often has spells of insanity like that. I put it down to her age. I think she's in the early stages of the change.'

There was a loud gasp from Hetty. 'I am thirty-eight years of age, Ada Fenwick, nowhere near the change of life.' Her eyes became slits as she added, 'And with the difference in our ages, that should be six months after you.'

'Blimey! We're not having a race, are we, sunshine? A competition, like, to see who goes first? And is there a prize to be won?'

'Well, you started it, not me.'

Edith thought it time to interrupt. 'If I listen to you two for much longer, yer'll have me feeling old before me time. I'm over a year younger than either of yer, but ye're putting years on me!'

'Ye're right,' Ada agreed. 'In the last ten minutes every one of me bones has started to complain. Particularly the soles of me feet. From what they're telling me, they don't like being stood on for too long. So seeing as yer seem to be going in the same direction as me and me mate, we'll walk along with yer, and yer can tell us how ye're getting on with yer new neighbours.'

Edith snorted. 'Sorry to disappoint yer, Ada, but that would take me all of ten seconds. I can't say how we're getting on with them 'cos I know no more about them than I did the day they moved in. If you hadn't got their name off Mr Stone, Ada, I wouldn't even know that. I was coming back from the corner shop yesterday morning – we'd run out of milk, and I ran down the entry to save time. I'd just reached our back door when she came out of theirs. I thought it was a good chance to introduce meself properly. So I said, "Good morning, Mrs Phillips, I was hoping to meet yer again. My name's Edith Benson, and I'm yer neighbour." And she looked at me with a blank expression on her face. "I'm in a hurry, I've no time to stand talking," she said. And she was gone in a flash. When we were having our dinner, I told Joe that it had all happened so fast I thought I'd imagined it. And I still can't believe that knowing I was a neighbour, she couldn't spare a few seconds to talk, or even give me a smile.'

Ada pulled a face. 'Not a very good start, eh? Yer'd think with them being new in the street she'd be anxious to make friends of her neighbours. Me and Hetty were only saying this morning that we hadn't laid eyes on any of the family since the day they moved in. And that was only a glimpse of the mother and daughter. Jimmy saw the father coming out of their house one morning, at the same time as he was leaving for work, and he passed the time of day with him. I asked Jimmy if they'd talked, but he said the bloke just waved back. I left it at that, 'cos men don't think the same as women, do they? Anyway, it's better to have neighbours yer don't see or hear than having a rowdy bunch living next door.'

'Oh, we hear them all right. There's not a sound all day, it's like a ghost house, but the husband makes up for it at night. He doesn't just speak, he yells. Sounds to me like a bad-tempered bugger. There's not a whisper from the other three, they're as quiet as mice.'

'Is this late at night yer hear him?' Ada asked. 'When the pubs are shut and he comes in the worse for drink?'

'I might be maligning the man, he may be harmless. It's only happened twice, both times around half seven to eight. So yer could hardly put it down to him being drunk.' Edith shook her head as though shaking her thoughts away. 'No, we've probably got a bad-tempered neighbour and there's not much yer can do about it. And if they don't want to be friendly, then that's their loss. I just wish Eliza had never left.'

'It might not be as bad as yer think,' Hetty said. 'Perhaps they've not settled in proper, still trying to find where things were put on the day they moved in. Removal men are noted for dumping boxes and crates anywhere that is the least trouble to them.'

'Hetty's right, sunshine, yer'll have to make allowances for a couple of weeks. Then, if things don't calm down, get Joe to have a word with the husband.'

'Yeah, we'll keep our fingers crossed and see how it goes. And this is where I love yer and leave yer, 'cos I'm going to see me mam. I can see a tram coming, so I'll make a dash. Ta-ra for now, and don't spend all yer money in the one shop.'

As Edith took to her heels, Ada shouted after her. 'Don't forget we're always there if yer ever need any help, or someone to talk to.'

Edith swung herself on board the tram, and gripping the post in the centre of the platform, she stayed there until it trundled past her neighbours. After giving them a wave and a smile, she swayed down the aisle to a seat by the window, where her thoughts turned to the pleasant prospect of seeing her beloved mother.

Ada spread her three Christmas club cards out on the table. 'Doesn't look much, does it? A shilling in the butcher's, and a tanner in the greengrocer's and the sweet shop. But it'll soon mount up, especially if I can manage the extra tanner in the butcher's.'

'I'm a bit better off than you, girl, because Sally and Kitty are buying their own dresses. I'll buy them a small present, 'cos it wouldn't be the same on Christmas morning if they didn't get a surprise present. I'll buy them a necklace or a bangle from Woolworth's, they'd be made up with either. And Arthur will be happy with a new shirt. I'm not worried about meself, a cheap dress from TJ's or the market will do me. It's not as though we're going anywhere special, no one is going to see us. The girls will be going out to one of their friends, I suppose. I can't see them staying in on Christmas night.'

'Well, there's no need for you and Arthur to sit in the house on yer own, sunshine. Ye're welcome to come in here. The men can get a few pints in, and we'll mug ourselves to a bottle of port between us. Christmas comes but once a year, so we may as well make the most of it.' Ada chuckled. 'It would be a good chance to show off yer singing voice, except I couldn't listen to someone singing a song I know the words to without joining in. And that would have to be after we'd had half the bottle of port each. I'd

113

have to be half plastered to let anyone hear the foghorn I've got for a voice.'

'Wouldn't yer mind if me and Arthur came on Christmas night, then, girl? It would be better than the two of us sitting looking at each other. And we'd only stay a few hours, we wouldn't outstay our welcome.'

'I don't know why ye're making such a big fuss, sunshine. Yer don't have to make out that I'm doing yer a favour, because if the truth were known I'd be glad of yer company. Besides, it wouldn't be anything new, 'cos yer came last year, remember?'

'Yes I know, and it should be our turn to have you. So shall we swap round this year, and you come to us?'

'No, we couldn't do that 'cos I've got the two kids to think of. I wouldn't leave them alone on Christmas night.'

'Won't they mind me and Arthur coming here?'

'By the time you get here, they'll be dead tired and ready for bed. That's the two young ones I'm talking about. I can't tell yer what Danny's doing, for I haven't a clue. He may have a girlfriend he's keeping quiet about, I honestly don't know. He talks about three dancing partners, but I never know whether he's telling the truth or not. But no matter what Danny does, it won't make any difference to you and Arthur coming.'

'That's good. Arthur will be pleased when I tell him. He gets on well with Jimmy, they're good mates.'

'Yeah, the life and soul of the party, both of them. While you and me are singing our heads off, with a glass of wine in our hand, they'll be deep in conversation. And what will the topic be that interests them so much? It'll be about Liverpool's chances of winning the cup next year.'

'I thought Danny was an Evertonian?'

'He is, a red hot Evertonian. And he could be our only hope of a bit of jollity on Christmas night. For if he hasn't got anything planned with a girl, and he stays in, then our two husbands won't get a look in. Much as he loves his dad, there's no way our Danny would sit quietly by and listen to anyone singing the praises of Liverpool Football Club. It's a wonder yer've never heard them arguing. If Everton are playing at home, and Liverpool have a home match as well, then when they both start, no one else can get a word in edgeways. They're like a couple of kids, and I have a hell of a time trying to quieten them down. I'm really surprised that yer've never heard them, 'cos these walls are very thin.'

Hetty shook her head. 'Well, I can't say I have, girl, and that's no lie. And talking of being able to hear through walls, what did yer make of what Edith told us about the new family living opposite?'

'I couldn't say, sunshine, 'cos I'd have to have been there meself when it happened for me to form an opinion. One thing I can say about them is that they are conspicuous by their absence, if yer know what I mean.' Ada leaned forward on the table and cupped her chin in her hand. 'There's one way of finding out, we could knock on the door and make ourselves known to the mother. It can't do any harm, and most people moving to a new house would be pleased to see a friendly face. Anyway, the worst that can happen is that she tells us to sod off. And I've got a thick skin, it wouldn't worry me.'

'Ooh, I don't know about that, girl, we might let ourselves in for a load of trouble.'

'Don't let's start thinking badly of them until we get to know them. We should give them the benefit of the doubt until we know different. If we call with the best intention of wanting to be friends, and we're not made welcome, then that's their loss. For I would never again knock on their door, or offer a hand of friendship.'

'My mother used to say, "Never trouble trouble, till trouble troubles you." ' Hetty informed her. 'And she was never far wrong in what she said, either.'

Ada repeated, 'Never trouble trouble, till trouble troubles you.' Then her eyes slid sideways. 'Did your mother have false teeth?'

Looking perplexed, Hetty nodded. 'Yes, she did as a matter of fact, but what's that got to do with anything?'

'I bet she had to take her false teeth out before she came out with that mouthful. I had to say it very slowly, and I've got all me own teeth.'

There was resignation on the face Hetty turned to her mate. 'Yer never cease to amaze me, Ada. I don't know another person who could, in half a minute, go from the Christmas festivities to my mother's false teeth. I mean, yer've got to admit it takes some doing.'

'I'm disappointed in yer, sunshine,' Ada said lightly. 'Yer don't do me no justice at all. If yer'd been paying attention, yer would have remembered I started off with Christmas, then went on to suggest we knocked on the door of the new neighbours opposite. It was after that that yer mother's false teeth came into the scheme of things, and quite frankly I can't imagine how that came about.'

'Don't be trying to pull a fast one, girl, 'cos I know yer too well. You act daft at times, but it's only put on, 'cos yer know exactly what yer say, and what anybody else says. Yer don't miss a blinking trick.'

Ada pretended to go all coy. 'Ah, I'm not as clever as yer make me out to be, sunshine, and yer've got me blushing now.'

'Blushing!' Hetty's voice was shrill. 'Yer don't know the meaning of the word. The day I see you blush will be the day I think the end of the world is not far off.'

'Ay, your mother wasn't the only one who had a saying for everything under the sun, my ma was the same. And if she'd heard what yer've just said about the end of the world, she'd have pointed a finger at yer, and warned, "There's many a true word spoken in jest, girl, so just you take heed." '

Hetty giggled. 'Did yer mother have her false teeth in when she said that to yer? Or was she gummy, like mine?'

'My ma had a routine,' Ada told her with a chuckle. 'If she wasn't expecting visitors she didn't have a tooth in her head. But if a knock came to the door, she wouldn't answer it until the false teeth came out of the glass and into her mouth. Then she would open the front door with a beaming smile on her face. She had some funny ideas, though, that I loved her for but couldn't understand. She had no objection to the coalman seeing her without her teeth in, but she'd have died if the landlord had caught her out.'

'I can understand that,' Hetty said. 'Yer mother was a proud woman. Like you and me will be when we get to that age. I bet neither of us would face our landlord if we didn't have a tooth in our heads.'

Ada clicked her tongue. 'I'm going to change the subject again, sunshine, just in case ye're taking notes. Yer see, talking about landlords brought Mr Stone to mind, and what he said about the Phillipses being a decent family. Which brings me back to where we were earlier, and how it might be a good idea to make the acquaintance of Mrs Phillips.'

'That's your idea, girl, and if I'm honest, I have to say I'm not keen on it. Yer know what I'm like, I run a mile if I smell trouble.'

'So yer'd rather I went on me own, would yer, sunshine? I will if yer feel so strongly about it, but for the life of me I can't see what ye're afraid of. There's nothing out of the ordinary about calling on new neighbours and making them feel welcome. And if Mrs Phillips doesn't want to fit in with the people she's come to live among, then that's fine by me. I'll just walk away and get on with me own life.'

'Are yer thinking of going now, girl?'

Ada nodded. 'There's no time like the present, Hetty. If we keep on putting it off, we'll end up leaving it too late. I'll go over on me own if yer don't feel right about it. You can stay here until I come back.'

Hetty's chair was quickly vacated. 'No, ye're me best mate and we'll stick together. Put yer coat back on, and let's get it over with.'

Ada slipped her arms into her sleeves. 'Ye're acting as though we're off to witness a public hanging. Put a smile on yer face, even if it kills yer.'

116

When Annie Phillips heard the knock on the door, her hand flew to her throat. She stood in the middle of the room like a statue, hoping whoever had knocked would go away. There was no reason for anyone to call, for she didn't know a soul in the area. And none of their old neighbours were told where they were moving to, she'd made sure of that. And she knew the children wouldn't have let it slip, they knew better.

Her mouth dry, and her tummy turning over, Annie told herself this was no way to live. But this was the life she'd been forced into by her bully of a husband. And she had long ago lost the strength to fight him. Sighing deeply, she waited to see if the knock was repeated. Seconds ticked by, without a sound, and she told herself that whoever it was must have gone away. So she moved across to the window and lifted the end of the lace curtain, only to find herself looking into the face of the woman she knew lived in the house opposite.

Ada smiled, and mouthed the words. 'Open the door, Mrs Phillips, please.'

Annie stared at her for a few seconds, trying to think what to do. The last thing she wanted to do was open the door, but what else could she do? She couldn't ignore the woman, that would be downright rude. Her pride and dignity had been knocked out of her over the years, but she still knew her manners. Nodding briefly, she let the curtain fall back into place and walked towards the front door.

Ada nudged Hetty when she heard the bolt being drawn. 'Smile,' she hissed, 'for heaven's sake, smile.'

Annie heard what was said as she was bending down to unbolt the door, and something unusual happened. She felt her lips stretch into a smile. But it didn't last, for it was many a long day since a smile sat comfortably on her face. She'd had more reason to cry than laugh.

'Hello, Mrs Phillips. We've called to say we hope ye're settled in yer new home, and to welcome yer family as neighbours. My name's Ada Fenwick, and this is me mate, Hetty Watson. We live across the street in thirty-three and thirty-five.'

'Yes, I've seen yer through the window, going to the shops together. I haven't found me bearings yet, I've been too busy getting boxes and chests sorted out.' Annie hated telling lies, but she'd had to tell many over the years, as excuses. And now she was going to tell another. 'I was busy emptying one of the tea chests when yer knocked. So I hope yer'll understand when I say I won't be able to stand and talk for long. But I really appreciate your calling, it was very thoughtful of yer.'

'We won't keep yer, sunshine, we'll let yer get on with what ye're doing. Besides, it's time we were getting the dinner ready for our families. But if yer ever need a helping hand, yer know yer can knock on either my door or Hetty's. Or yer can rap on the window if yer like, we don't stand on ceremony.'

'Thank you, yer've both been very kind.' Annie was stepping back as she spoke, and the door was closed very quietly.

The two friends looked at each other, then without a word they crossed the cobbles to Ada's house. Their silence lasted until they were seated facing each other across the table. 'Well, what did yer make of that?' Hetty asked.

Leaning her elbows on the table, Ada said, 'I don't know what to make of it, sunshine, except we didn't have the door slammed in our faces. I'll go over it again tonight, in bed, when everyone else is asleep and it's nice and quiet. If I was to tell yer now what my first impression was, without giving it any deep thought, then I'd say I believe she's a woman who wants to be friendly, but something is holding her back.'

'That doesn't make sense to me,' Hetty said. 'All I could think of was that at one time she'd been a really good-looking woman. But now she looks tired and weary.'

'Don't we all, at some time in our lives?' Ada slapped a palm on the table. 'It's going to be a rush now, getting the dinner ready for the family. So, instead of being chased by Mrs Phillips, yer're being chased by yer best mate. I'll see yer in the morning, sunshine, same time as usual, and we'll be able to see things more clearly in the light of day. But if yer fancy some biscuits with yer cup of tea, then yer'll have to bring some with yer, 'cos I haven't got any, the cupboard is bare.'

'Oh, so I'm invited if I bring me own biscuits, eh?' With a good-natured laugh, Hetty punched her mate on the shoulder. 'And as I couldn't sit and dunk me biscuits in front of yer without offering yer one, I'd better nip down to the corner shop before I come, and buy a packet. What would yer prefer, girl, arrowroot or ginger snaps?'

'Ask Sally to give yer half a pound of mixed. She won't mind.'

'Oh, I think I can rise to the occasion, girl, and buy a full packet.'

'Yer can rise to the occasion now, sunshine, and scarper. Jimmy likes his dinner on the table when he comes home.'

'I'm on me way, girl, and I'll see yer in the morning. I'll close the front door after meself, save yer bothering. Sweet dreams! Ta-ra.'

Chapter Eleven

It was five weeks now since the Phillips family had moved into Eliza's old house, and Annie had worked hard to make it into a bright and comfortable home. She was a methodical woman, believing there was a place for everything, and everything should be in its place. And she had a strict routine when it came to housework. Once the family had left for work, she didn't sit down and have a quiet break with a cup of tea, she'd set to and work non-stop until everything was done to her satisfaction. Even though it meant a long, lonely day ahead for her, by ten o'clock every morning her house would be like a little palace. No one would see it, for there would be no visitors. But it gave Annie peace of mind. And only then would she make herself a pot of tea and relax with her thoughts. That was until ten to eleven, when she would leave her chair and move to stand at the front window. And she would wait there until Ada and Hetty came out of the house opposite. She wasn't being nosy, and knew that people would think it was a pity she didn't have something better to do with her time. They wouldn't understand that she didn't have anything better to do. There were no friends she could go shopping with, or share a joke. She didn't seek to make friends, for she had learned the hard way that neighbours didn't stay friendly with her once they found out her husband was a foul-mouthed drunkard who was fond of lashing out with his fists. And the only time she would see a smiling face, during the long, lonely day, was when she stood behind the net curtains of her living room, and watched the neighbours opposite. They always came out of the house happy and laughing. And seeing their smiles as they linked arms, and pushed each other in a good-natured way, made a lonely woman feel better.

Annie was so wrapped up in her thoughts, she didn't notice the time passing. It was the noise of a door banging that brought her to her feet. 'I was miles away,' she told the empty room. 'I've probably missed them now.' But she was in time to see Ada stepping down on to the pavement. And whatever she was saying had Hetty bent over with laughter. And the sight brought a faint smile to Annie's face. Her life

119

could have been as happy and carefree as theirs, if she hadn't married the wrong man.

The two women on the pavement opposite began to walk down the street, arms linked and still laughing. And after letting out a deep sigh, Annie was turning away from the window when, out of the corner of her eye, she saw an object fall to the pavement. It seemed to have fallen from Hetty's pocket, but when the two friends didn't stop to pick it up, Annie thought she must have imagined it. For surely Hetty would have felt, or heard, if she'd dropped something. 'Me eyes must have been deceiving me,' she muttered. Then, just to satisfy herself, she moved the net curtain and pressed her face to the window. And sure enough, she could see something lying on the opposite pavement, and it looked like a small purse. She wondered what to do, for there was no point in knocking on the window, the friends would be halfway down the street by now.

After shaking her head to clear her thoughts, Annie said to herself, 'I can't stand here gawping, someone might come along and pick it up. And not everyone is honest.' She rubbed her chin. 'The least I can do is make sure it goes back to its rightful owner.' Without giving herself time to change her mind, Annie took her coat down from a hook near the front door. She slipped it on, then picked up the key from the sideboard. 'If I hurry, I should catch them up before they get too far away. I'll only be out five minutes.'

When Hetty felt a tap on her shoulder, she pulled her arm free and spun round. A hand to her breast, she said, 'Oh, Mrs Phillips, yer frightened the life out of me!'

Ada didn't let her surprise at seeing their new neighbour show. But she really was surprised, for they hadn't seen hide nor hair of her since the day they'd knocked on her door and received a very cool welcome. 'Take no notice of her, Mrs Phillips, it wasn't a fright yer gave her, it was a big disappointment. For one heavenly moment, she thought it was a bloke trying to cop off. In the blink of an eye, her whole life flashed before her eyes. She saw herself being whisked out of her two-up-two-down house and taken to a mansion in the country. This knight in shining armour has fallen madly and passionately in love with her, and he gives her anything her little heart desires. She forgets her poor husband, what has worked his fingers to the bone for her, and she turns her back on her two lovely children. All for the sake of living happily ever after with Prince Charming.'

Hetty looked at Annie and shook her head. 'She is as mad as a hatter,

Mrs Phillips, but not dangerous. Really, she's as tame as a pussy cat when yer get to know her. And I'm sure she'll behave herself long enough for yer to tell me what yer wanted me for.'

'It was to ask if yer've lost anything?'

Hetty looked at Ada and pulled a face, before lifting her shoulders in surprise. 'I haven't lost anything, Mrs Phillips. What makes yer ask?'

Annie held up the purse. 'Is this yours?'

Hetty gasped before putting a hand to her mouth. Then she moved her hand to her pocket. 'Oh, my God, I've got a ruddy big hole in me pocket! Me purse must have fallen out. Where did yer find it, Mrs Phillips, and how did yer know it was mine?'

Annie handed over the purse. She couldn't tell the two friends she watched them every morning, they'd think she was queer. 'I happened to be cleaning the inside of me front window, and saw yer coming out of Mrs Fenwick's house. Then, by sheer luck, I saw it falling. I did knock on the window to try and attract yer attention, but yer obviously didn't hear. I didn't know it was a purse then, but I thought whatever it was I'd better get it before someone else came along and picked it up.'

'Oh, thank God yer've got sharp eyes, Mrs Phillips, 'cos all me money is in it. And with Christmas so near, I need every penny I can get. I'd have been in Queer Street if it hadn't been for you.'

'The first thing yer do when yer get home, sunshine,' Ada said, 'is sew that ruddy pocket up. If it hadn't been for Mrs Phillips, yer'd have been up the creek without a paddle. Someone else could have come along, picked it up and thought it was their lucky day. And that would have been the last yer'd seen of it. At least yer family will eat tonight now.'

'Oh, for heaven's sake, don't be so ruddy dramatic, girl. The family wouldn't have starved, I'd have borrowed off you.'

'Some hope, sunshine, 'cos I've only got about four bob on me.'

Annie looked around, feeling very uncomfortable. 'I'll leave yer to it now. I'm glad I was of help, but don't forget to sew yer pocket up.'

'Ay, hang on, don't go running off.' It wasn't often Hetty put her foot down as hard as she did now. Her tummy was still turning over at the very thought of the consequences if she had lost her purse. It didn't bear thinking about. 'The least I can do is treat yer to some cakes, or chocolate, to show my appreciation. Come to the shops with me and Ada, and let me buy yer something.'

Ada had been watching Annie's face closely, and the flicker of fear she saw in the woman's eyes told her Hetty's request would be turned down. And because the Phillips family remained a mystery she would like to unravel, she came up with a suggestion. 'Why not let Mrs Phillips get back to what she was doing, sunshine, and invite her this afternoon for a cup of tea and a cake?'

'Call me Annie, please. And although it's kind of yer, I only did what any decent person would do. I don't want rewarding for it.'

'Ay, Annie, don't be so miserable,' Ada said. 'You might not want to be a guest for afternoon tea, but what about me? I rather fancy a nice cream slice, but I won't get one if yer turn down the invitation. It'll only be for an hour, say from two to three, and surely yer can put up with us for an hour? And I can assure and guarantee yer that yer won't catch any fleas in Hetty's house. She doesn't allow them in.'

Annie was on the point of refusing when a little voice in her head told her not to be so stupid. An hour in the company of two women who were friendly and funny . . . what harm could that do? And she deserved to have a little happiness in her life; she craved it. Besides, her husband would never know. 'I'd like to come, thank you.'

Hetty's face lit up. 'Oh, I'm so glad. Shall we say two o'clock at Ada's? She makes a better cup of tea than I do. She tells me it's the way I hold me mouth.'

Annie smiled. Her heart felt lighter than it had done for ages. 'I'll look forward to it. And a cream slice would be very nice.' She turned to walk away. 'I'll come over at two o'clock.'

At a quarter to two, Hetty walked up Ada's back yard with a plate in each hand. She wasn't in a position to knock on the kitchen door, so she raised a foot and kicked it. 'Come on, Ada, look sharp and open up.'

When the door opened, Ada eyed the plates while saying, 'What's the idea of kicking me door? It's manners to knock.'

'I'd have a job, wouldn't I, with me two hands full.'

'Why have yer got two plates, and what's on them under the tea towels?'

'If yer let me in, I'll tell yer. It's ruddy cold standing here answering questions about something yer'll find out soon enough.'

Ada grinned as she stood aside to let her mate pass. 'I hope there's something nice hidden under there, to make up for nearly kicking me door in.'

'Yer don't half exaggerate, girl.' Hetty put the plates down on the draining board. 'I barely touched yer ruddy door, never mind kicking it in.' She deliberately stood in front of the plates so Ada couldn't get to them. Unless she knocked her over, that is. 'Now, have yer got a nice clean tablecloth on for yer visitor?'

'Let's get things right, sunshine, before we go any further. She is not my visitor, she's yours. I am just letting yer have the use of me room 'cos ye're me mate. And do yer really think I'd put a dirty cloth on the table, whether the visitor was yours or mine?'

Ada moved so quickly then, Hetty didn't stand a chance of being able to keep her feet on the ground. And before she knew it, she was standing in front of the sink while Ada whipped the cloths off the plates. 'Ooh, yer've made sandwiches, sunshine! I wasn't expecting that. I'd have been quite happy with a cake, but I wouldn't refuse a butty.' Then Ada's eyes narrowed. 'What have yer put in the sandwiches? I didn't see yer buying any boiled ham.'

'No, yer saw me buying corned beef for Arthur's carry-out. And I've pinched two slices of that to make the sandwiches. I thought it looked mean to just have a cake to offer Mrs Phillips. Not after what she did for me.'

'Does that mean poor Arthur is suffering because of your generosity? He'll not be getting much corned beef on his sandwiches if yer've pinched half of it. Are yer going to tell him why he'll need his glasses to see the meat?'

Hetty huffed. 'Am I heckerslike! If I told him I nearly lost all me money because I had a hole in me pocket, I'd never hear the last of it. I'd be called all the stupid nits under the sun, by Arthur, and the girls. So I've decided the best course of action is to buy a slice of corned beef from the corner shop. Then no one will be any the wiser.'

Ada chuckled. 'Except me, of course. I could blow the whistle on yer if I choose to. So, what'll yer give to buy my silence?'

'The same as I'm giving Mrs Phillips, and it's not to buy her silence 'cos she's not as crafty or greedy as you. She got me out of a real scrape, and she's not bragging about it, or expecting to get something in return.'

Ada held her hands up in surrender. 'Okay, sunshine, I'll give in before yer have me in tears. I've only been pulling yer leg, anyway. I agree yer owe a debt of gratitude to Mrs Phillips, 'cos if she hadn't picked it up, someone else would have done. And if they were skint, as most people round here are, then the sight of a lot of money would have been very tempting.'

'I know, I've been very lucky. Now, as it's just on two o'clock, can we take the plates in? And would yer do me proud and put yer best cups and saucers out?' Without waiting for a reply, Hetty picked the plates up and made her way into the living room. And as she passed Ada, she said, 'Thanks, girl, I knew I could count on you.'

The kettle began to whistle at the same time as the knock came to the door. 'I'll answer it, sunshine,' Ada said, 'seeing as it is my house.'

Annie had been having doubts about becoming friendly with the two women because of past experiences, and she was nervously clasping her hands when the door opened. 'I really don't think Mrs Watson need go to any trouble on my account. She's probably got other things to do with her time. So I won't bother coming in, Mrs Fenwick, but would yer thank her for me, and tell her I was glad I was able to help.'

Ada bent forward and got a tight grip on Annie's elbow, and she pulled the startled woman up the two steps. 'In yer come, sunshine, whether yer like it or not. Hetty would be upset if yer cried off, and I can't bear to see me mate cry.' And herding Annie forward, Ada added, 'Let's start as we mean to go on, Annie. My name is Ada, and my mate is Hetty.'

Annie was so taken aback by the brightness of the room, she forgot her nerves. 'Oh, this room looks lovely! Someone has been very busy, and they've made a good job of it. My room looks really dark compared to this.'

'Give yerself a chance, Annie, yer've only just moved into the house.' Ada pulled a chair out for their guest. 'The person who had the house before was a lovely lady called Eliza Porter. She's eighty-two years old, and had gone past being able to decorate. But she kept her house like a little palace. She'd lived there for sixty years, and everyone in the street loved her. She's with her son now, being well looked after. But me and Hetty don't half miss her. And so do the neighbours either side of yer. Their names are Bowers on yer right, and the Bensons on yer left. I won't give yer a headache by telling yer all their first names, 'cos there's too many for yer to remember. But they're both smashing families, very friendly and very respectable.'

Hetty put her hands on her hips, tilted her head, and said, 'Don't I get a look-in here? Far be it from me to interrupt, Annie, but now and again I have to make meself heard, or me mate would hog the whole conversation.'

'I'll button me lip now, sunshine, and you can take over as hostess. Go on, show Annie what ye're made of, while I make the tea and get the cups ready.' Ada got as far as the kitchen door, then turned. 'I could only find two cups without a chip, sunshine, so I'll have the one with a ruddy big chip out of the rim. After all, if I do catch a germ, I'll have the satisfaction of knowing it's one of me own.'

Hetty saw a smile flicker on Annie's face. 'She's like that all the time, yer know. There's never a dull moment where my mate is. I think we spend more time laughing than doing housework. But it would be a dull life if we had nothing to laugh at.'

Ada carried the tea in, and soon the ladies were enjoying a sandwich with their first cup of tea, and a cream slice when the second pot came up.

'How are yer family liking the new house, Annie?' Ada asked. 'Have they settled in?'

'Yes, everywhere is straight now, and feels more like home. The living room looks dull compared to this, though. Did yer husband decorate it, Ada, or did yer do it yerself?'

'Ooh, I couldn't decorate to save me life, Annie. I did try it once, not long after we moved in here, but I got meself all tangled up in the paper after I'd pasted it. I've got no patience, yer see, and instead of taking me time, I tried to be clever and climb a ladder after I'd pasted the paper. I made a right mess of it. Every sheet of paper got torn, and I had more paste in me hair and on the floor than on the walls. So I gave it up as a bad job, and I've never tried since.' Ada took a sip of her tea. Over the rim of the cup, she asked, 'Wouldn't your feller do it for yer, if yer asked him nicely?'

Annie shook her head. 'No, he's hopeless. I've done all the decorating since we got married. I won't say I'm good at it, but it's a case of having a go, or leaving the old paper on until it drops off.'

'Yer've got a teenage daughter, haven't yer?' Ada ignored the cow eyes she was getting from Hetty. If they didn't ask questions, they'd never get to know their new neighbours. Besides, Ada was of the opinion that all was not well in the Phillips household. 'I've only seen the back of her, and that was the day yer moved in.'

'That's Jenny, she's seventeen. And I've got a son, Ben, he's fifteen. They're both good kids, never caused me any trouble.'

'I've got three,' Ada said. 'And I love the bones of them. Danny's me eldest, he's nineteen in a few days, and he's dance mad. Me other two are still at school. There's Monica, she's twelve, and Paul, who's ten.'

'I've got two girls,' Hetty told her. 'Both working. Kitty is seventeen, and works at the British American tobacco factory. Sally works at Irwin's, the grocer's shop in Stanley Road.'

'What does your husband do, Annie?' Ada asked. 'I see him going out in the morning with yer son. I'm not spying on yer, it's just that they happen to leave the house the same time as my husband and son.'

'Tom, me husband, he works on the docks. Ben only left school last year, he's an apprentice to a decorator. He said he's the can-lad really, just making pots of tea for the men. But I've told him, he can't expect anything else yet. Like every job, decorating has to be learned, but the young are very impatient. They can't wait to grow up.'

'I know what yer mean,' Ada said. 'Our Danny works with his dad in the building trade, and he can't wait to be twenty-one and earning full pay. I keep telling him he's wishing his life away, but when I think back, me and me mates were the same. We couldn't wait to grow up so we could go out with boys. And I'll say this for our Danny, he's very generous with his wages. Any overtime he gets, he gives me half of the money.'

'He's more generous than my two girls,' Hetty said. 'They spend every penny on clothes, lipstick and powder, and stockings. They're usually on the borrow by the middle of the week. Heaven help them when they get married, they won't know what's hit them.'

'Well, you don't do them any favours by lending them the money,' Ada said. 'I'm not saying yer should be mean with them, but they should learn that money is hard to come by, it doesn't grow on trees.' She chuckled. 'Worse luck. If it did grow on trees, I'd be at the park every day, shinning up the trees like I used to when I was a little girl.'

'See, Annie.' Hetty nodded her head knowingly. 'She must have been a holy terror when she was a kid. And she hasn't changed at all, 'cos she's still a holy terror. There's times when I don't know where to put meself, the things she comes out with.'

'I don't like people calling me for everything to me face, so can we change the subject?' Ada winked at Annie. 'Have another cup of tea, sunshine, and sit back and listen while I turn the tables on me best mate. To look at, she seems holier than thou, as though butter wouldn't melt in her mouth. But wait until I spill the beans on her.'

Annie was enjoying herself. To be with women of her own age, who were good company, was indeed a treat. But she'd been keeping her eye on the clock, and she really should be going home to see to the dinner. Jenny and Ben got in about the same time, six o'clock each night, and she always had their dinner ready for them to sit down to. But it could be eight o'clock before her husband rolled home, after spending a couple of hours in the pub with his pals from work. She never knew when to expect him, but it was woe betide her if his dinner wasn't ready to put in front of him. And if it was dried up through being in the oven to keep warm, he would either throw it on the fire or aim it at one of the walls. Then he would rant and rave in anger, his language foul as he lashed out at her. The children would always try to protect her, but they were no match for a man who was violent in drink. Annie would have left him years ago, but where would she go with the two children? Where would she get the money from to put a roof over their heads and feed them? No, she was tied to him, even though she'd stopped loving him soon after they got married. Tom Phillips didn't take long to show his true colours. And then it was too late.

'I won't stay, thank you. It's been really nice having someone to talk to, but I must go and get started on the dinner.' She stood up and pushed the chair back under the table. 'Thank you again.'

The two friends walked to the door with her. 'Annie,' Ada said, 'if ever yer decide to decorate yer living room, me and Hetty will give yer a hand. Even if it's only cutting the lengths of paper, or handing it up to yer, it would all be a help.'

'I won't be doing it just yet. I want to settle into the house first. But thanks for the offer, and I'll let yer know.' She began to cross the cobbles. 'Thanks again.'

The mates called back in unison, 'Ye're welcome.' Then Ada closed the door and they walked back into the living room.

'I don't know why, sunshine, but from the first time I saw Annie, I felt there was a sadness about her. I can't explain, but I felt it stronger than ever today.'

'Ye're imagining things, girl,' Hetty said. 'She seems all right to me.'

'Yeah, ye're probably right.' Ada pointed to the table. 'Will the tea in that pot be warm enough to drink, I wonder?'

'Ye're a proper tea-tank, you are, Ada Fenwick. I reckon yer must go through about twelve cups a day.'

'It could be worse, sunshine. It could be twelve bottles of milk stout, and then yer'd have something to say.' Ada chuckled. 'Mind you, that wouldn't worry me, 'cos I'd be far too drunk to hear yer.'

'I hope that nice smell is coming from a pan of hotpot, Mam, 'cos I'm cold right through to me bones.' Jenny closed the kitchen door behind her. After kissing her mother, she unwound the scarf from her neck. 'I'm glad of this scarf, it keeps me neck and ears warm.' She was a very pretty girl, with a mass of auburn hair framing her face, and deep brown eyes. And she slipped her coat off to reveal a slim, shapely figure. 'I'll hang me coat up, then stand by the fire to get warmed through.'

'I've put dumplings in the hotpot, sweetheart,' Annie said. 'As soon as yer brother comes in, I'll put the dinner out. That will warm yer up.'

Jenny had just left the kitchen when the door was opened again, and Ben came in, bringing a blast of cold air with him. He quickly closed the door and grinned at his mother. 'It's not fit for man nor beast out there, Mam.' His nose and cheeks were bright red, as were the lobes of his ears. 'I tried to catch up with our Jenny, but she legged it up the entry as though she was being chased.'

Jenny left the fire to pop her head round the kitchen door. 'I was being chased. The wind practically lifted me off me feet and carried me along.'

'Go in by the fire and I'll put yer dinner out.' Annie ruffled her son's mousy hair. He took after his father in colouring and features, but his

127

nature was entirely different. Unlike his father, he had a good sense of humour, and a smile came easily to him.

Annie put two plates of dinner on the table, and Jenny and Ben quickly took their seats. 'I'm ready for this, Mam,' Ben said. 'Me tummy's been rumbling with hunger.'

'Then tuck in, son, while I fetch mine. Then I've got something to tell yer.' Annie's heart was feeling lighter than it had for ages. And it was down to the neighbours across the street. They had made her feel welcome, and given her two hours free from worry. And she wanted to share this with her children. She sat down and picked up her knife and fork, but made no attempt to use them. 'I want to tell yer about the nice afternoon I've had. I'll be as quick as I can, but if yer dad comes in before I've finished, then I'll have to leave the rest for another time.'

Jenny and Ben leaned forward in their chairs. It wasn't often they saw their mother's eyes so bright, or her voice so animated as she told them about the dropped purse, and having afternoon tea with the neighbours opposite. 'I really enjoyed meself. They are very funny, and it was a change for me to be with nice people and have a laugh. Ada, that's Mrs Fenwick, she's just had her living room decorated and it's lovely. Her and Hetty even offered to help me if I decided to do this room. I couldn't let them, of course, not with yer dad being the way he is. But it was nice of them to offer.'

'It's about time yer had some friends, Mam,' Ben said. 'If me dad doesn't know, then he can't stop yer. Me and Jenny won't say nothing.'

Jenny laid down her knife and fork. 'Mam, if the two ladies are as nice as yer say, then it would be great if yer could make friends with them. Yer can't go through life being worried about what me dad will do. I know what he's like, and I don't care who hears me say it. He's a cruel, bad-tempered, foul-mouthed villain. He's not fit to be a husband, or a father. All he's fit for is getting blind drunk and using his family as punch bags. When me and Ben are older, and earning more money, we aren't staying here. We'll be off like a shot, and we'll be taking you with us. But as that's a few years off yet, can I tell yer what I'd do if I was in your position?'

Annie nodded. There was affection in her eyes for the daughter who reminded her of herself at that age. 'Go on, sweetheart, tell me what yer would do in my position.'

'I'd confide in the women. Tell them what a brute yer husband is. They'll find out some time, anyway, 'cos although me dad's only taken off once or twice since we moved in here, we all know it won't last. This is the lull before the storm, Mam, and you know it. One night he'll come home rotten drunk and the neighbours will get a taste of what an animal he really is. So, if these women want to be friends with yer, grab their friendship with both hands. But empty yer heart to them first. Tell them the truth. It's not your fault that the man yer married turned out to be a lousy husband. You shouldn't have to go through life looking over yer shoulder, as though it's you who's in the wrong. They may turn out to be real friends, Mam, and heaven knows, the day might come when yer need friends. Me and Ben are out at work every day, and we'd both feel better if we knew yer were getting some pleasure out of life. And that there'd be someone there for yer if yer ever needed help.'

Ben loved his sister, but he was more proud of her now than he'd ever been. He agreed with every word she'd said, but he would never have been able to put the words together himself. 'Yeah, our Jenny's right, Mam. Yer should do that.'

Annie heard the key turn in the front door, and she held her hand up for silence. Then she pushed her chair back and hurried to the kitchen to put her husband's dinner out. She didn't want her day spoiled by him being in one of his bad moods.

Tom Phillips was a big man, six feet tall and very well made. He would have been quite handsome if it wasn't for his flabby beer belly, and the florid complexion common in men who liked their beer. He flung the living room door open so hard, it banged against the end of the couch. Then he stood looking at his son and daughter, a sneer distorting his face. Suddenly, without warning, he lunged forward and grabbed Ben by the scruff of his neck, and dragged him off his chair. The young lad's breathing was cut off and he started gasping for air.

Jenny rounded the table with a fork in her hand. 'Let go of him.'

With his free hand, Tom pushed her away. 'Sod off, or you'll be the next.'

Jenny looked down and saw the fear in her kid brother's eyes. Then she pressed the prongs of the fork against her father's cheek. She was shaking inside, for she knew only too well how violent he could be. But she was now more concerned for her brother than herself.

'Let him go now, or I'll stab yer with this. And don't think I won't.' She pressed the prongs into his fleshy cheeks. 'Leave go now!'

Annie came rushing through from the kitchen. She was carrying her husband's dinner in her hand. But she didn't put the plate down on the table, she held it in front of his face. 'Take yer hands off my son, or yer'll get this plate broken over yer head.'

Tom relaxed his grip on the boy's neck and flung him on to the couch. It wasn't his wife's threat that worried him, it was the look of hatred on his daughter's face. And he knew she wouldn't hesitate to stab him. So, like the Artful Dodger, he pretended he was only fooling. 'Put me dinner down, yer silly cow. Can't yez take a bleeding joke?'

Jenny wouldn't have let him get away with it, but when she saw her mother's face drained of colour she held her temper and hatred in. She hadn't finished her dinner, and though she had no appetite for it now, she sat at the table. Patting the chair next to her, she said, 'Sit here, Ben, and eat yer dinner. Me mam's having hers in the kitchen. Eat it all up after she went to the trouble of making it for us.'

They were silent as they ate their meal, the only sound being the occasional loud belch coming from the man facing them. He never put a hand over his mouth, or excused himself, and the sound sickened Jenny. She waited until Ben had finished his meal, then she put her plate on top of his. 'I'll take them out, our kid. Are yer going round to yer mate's?'

Ben was still shaking inside from fear. He really had thought he was going to choke to death. 'I told Billy I'd go round to his for a game of cards, but I'm not fussy now.'

'You go, Ben, 'cos he might be waiting for yer. Yer don't want to let a mate down. I'll give yer a couple of coppers to buy some sweets to share between yer.'

Tom's top lip curled. 'That's all he's fit for. Sucking sweets like a baby.'

Jenny was walking towards the kitchen when she turned her head to say, 'It's better than propping a bar up, spending all yer money on beer and making a show of yerself.' She didn't hear the obscenities following her, as she was speaking softly to her mother. 'Mam, I want yer to promise yer'll invite Ada and Hetty over for tea tomorrow afternoon. I'll look forward to yer telling me and Ben how much yer've enjoyed yerself.' She kissed her mother's cheek. 'Promise?'

Annie kissed her back. 'I promise, sweetheart.'

Chapter Twelve

Annie stood by the window with her coat on and a woollen scarf round her neck. She was watching for Ada's door to open, then she intended to open her door at the same time, and act as though it was a coincidence. She had butterflies in her tummy, but she'd made a promise to her daughter and wasn't going to back out. Jenny's words that morning, as she'd left for work, had been, 'Don't let me down, Mam. Remember yer promise.'

When Ada's door opened, Annie moved like streaked lightning, so fast she banged her shin on the leg of the small table. Another time she would have rubbed at the pain, but she couldn't spare the time right now.

'Hello, Annie,' Ada shouted. 'Going to the shops, are yer?'

Annie waved and nodded simultaneously. 'I'm late today. I've usually been there and back by now.'

'Yer may as well walk down with us,' Hetty called. 'Yer can keep me and Ada company.'

Annie picked her way over the cobbles. 'I'm afraid I'm not very exciting company, Hetty. I've got no jokes up me sleeve. In fact I couldn't tell a joke to save me life.'

The women walked three abreast down the street, which was a regular experience for the two mates, but a new one for Annie.

'Hetty will tell yer some jokes, Annie,' Ada said, a smile on her face. 'As long as yer don't mind dirty ones. She makes me blush sometimes when she's telling them to the man in the butcher's. And his face goes as red as the blood in the meat he's got on the chopping block.'

Hetty gasped. 'Ada Fenwick, I've never told a dirty joke in me life. I don't know any, and I don't want to, either! If you told one, I wouldn't listen.'

Ada's head went back when she chuckled. 'Yer'd have to listen to know whether it was a smutty joke or not, sunshine. And by then it would be too late. The damage would have been done, and your mind sullied for ever.'

'Trust you to think of that.' Hetty jerked her head at Annie. 'She's got an answer for everything. I've never known her lost for words in twenty years.'

'I'm often lost for words,' Annie told them. 'I think it's being on me own too much. I don't know what to say to people.'

'Surely yer have the children to talk to? Mine never stop. Except when they're asleep.' Ada glanced sideways to where Annie was walking on the other side of Hetty. 'When we're sitting round the table having our dinner, it's hard to get a word in sideways. They've all got something to say, and they're all talking at once. And my feller is as bad as the kids, he won't be left out.'

'Oh, my husband doesn't talk very much.' Annie decided to drop a hint, and gradually build up to the truth about her husband. 'When he does, it's usually to find fault. He's not the easiest person in the world to live with.'

'Then yer haven't got him house-trained, Annie,' Ada said. 'I started with Jimmy on the day we got wed, and he's well trained.'

'Take no notice of her, Annie, 'cos Jimmy can stick up for himself,' Hetty said. 'To hear my mate talk, anyone would think her husband was henpecked. But I can tell yer, he's far from it. He's got a smashing sense of humour, and always good for a laugh. And Danny takes after him.'

Ada narrowed her eyes. 'How come yer know so much about my husband, Hetty Watson? Yer must stand with yer ear glued to the wall.'

'I don't need to, girl, 'cos yer've all got loud voices,' Hetty told her. 'We'd have to put cotton wool in our ears if we didn't want to hear yer. But we do want to hear yer, especially the laughter. Even though we don't know what ye're laughing at, we all laugh with yer.'

'It's funny how laughter can be contagious, isn't it?' Annie said. 'If I hear anyone laugh, it always brings a smile to my face.'

They were walking along the main shopping street by this time, and Annie still hadn't plucked up the courage to invite her two neighbours over for afternoon tea. She was telling herself if she didn't speak how it would be too late. They'd be parting company soon, for the butcher's would be the first call for the two mates, and Annie didn't want to ask in front of strangers. Then the problem was solved for her.

'It's my turn to buy the cakes today, Annie,' Ada said. 'So, unless yer have a more pressing engagement, then it's two o'clock at my place.'

Annie pulled on Hetty's arm and they came to a halt. 'Oh, I was going to ask yer over to mine this afternoon. To repay yer kindness, like. My living room isn't as posh as yours, but I'm sure neither of you are the type to lift me rug to see if I've brushed the dirt under it. Me house may be humble, but it is clean.'

'I'm sure it is, sunshine, I wouldn't expect anything else.' Ada told her. She was surprised by the invitation, and beginning to wonder if she was wrong in her judgement of the Phillips family. But she and Hetty had a routine, and for today they'd stick with it. 'Would yer mind if we swapped round, Annie? You come to me today, and tomorrow me and Hetty will come to you? I know it sounds daft, but I'm a creature of habit, and I go all funny if I don't stick to me normal routine. Yer don't mind, do yer?'

'Of course Annie won't mind, will yer, girl?' Hetty asked, raising her brows. 'A cake is a cake, no matter which house it's eaten in.'

'That's fine with me.' Annie nodded. 'Ada's today, and mine tomorrow.' She was feeling light-hearted now. It was something to look forward to, and Jenny would be pleased that she was to have company on two afternoons.

As soon as Jenny closed the kitchen door behind her, she asked, 'Well, did yer have yer visitors today, Mam?'

'I didn't have visitors here, sweetheart, I went visiting instead.' Annie held her cheek for her daughter's kiss. 'Ada and Hetty take it in turns to share a pot of tea every afternoon, and today was Ada's turn. So we settled for me going over there today, and tomorrow they come over here.'

Jenny took her coat off and folded it over her arm. 'That's good, Mam. Did yer enjoy yerself?'

'It was fantastic, sweetheart. I feel like a new woman. Ada and Hetty are so funny I never stopped laughing. Me sides were sore with it. Ada is the one for making up tales, and Hetty falls for them. They pretend to have rows, shouting at each other, but they're really the best of friends.'

Jenny studied her mother's face. 'Yer don't only feel like a new woman, Mam, yer look like one. I've never seen yer eyes sparkle like that before, and yer look years younger.'

Annie smiled. 'That praise will be giving me such a big head, Jenny, I won't be able to get through the door. Now, go and hang yer coat up. Ben will be here soon, and I'll put the dinner out. I've made barley broth with dumplings, and if the smell is anything to go by, it's delicious.'

'What's delicious, Mam?' Ben slipped into the kitchen, then closed the door with his bottom. 'Apart from yourself, that is.'

'Oh, dear, the compliments are flying tonight! Yer sister reckons me eyes are sparkling, and I look a lot younger.' Annie shivered when Ben pressed his cheek to hers in a kiss. 'Go and get a warm, son, yer face is like a block of ice.'

Although Annie kept an ear cocked for the sound of a key in the door, the meal was a happy one. She had Jenny and Ben laughing at some of the comical sayings of Ada, and how she wound Hetty up to tantalise her. 'It was only for two hours, but they really cheered me up. and I'm looking forward to having them here tomorrow.'

Then the mood changed when they heard the front door open. Smiles faded from faces, and silence reigned. Before his father entered the room, Ben picked his plate up and moved to sit in the chair at the end of the table. This would put him out of reach of his father's temper.

'What are yez all sitting like stuffed dummies for?' Tom's eyes darted round the room, looking for something to pick on. 'I heard yer laughing when I passed the window. What were yer laughing at?'

Jenny sensed her mother's body stiffen in fear, and this saddened the girl. They shouldn't have to live like this. They could be a happy family, if it wasn't for the rotter eyeing them with a sneer on his face. 'I was telling them about a girl I work with, if yer must know. But it wouldn't be of any interest to you.'

Tom Phillips ignored his daughter and jerked his head at his wife. 'Get off yer fat backside and get my dinner on this table. Make it snappy.'

'Me mam hasn't finished her dinner yet,' Jenny said. 'It won't hurt yer to wait five minutes, yer've only just walked through the door.'

'I'm talking to the organ grinder, not the monkey. So you keep yer bleeding trap shut, or I'll shut it for yer.'

Annie pushed her chair back and stood up. 'It's in the oven. I'll get it.'

But Jenny pulled on her mother's arm. 'Sit down, Mam, and finish yer dinner. Ye're not his slave. Let him wait, it won't kill him.'

Tom growled in anger. As he walked towards his wife, he was undoing the buckle of his belt. 'Get off yer backside, I said. Now move!' He pulled the leather belt free of his trousers, and began to wind it round his hand. He stopped winding when there was about twelve inches of leather dangling, with the steel buckle at the end. He laughed as he raised the belt to let his wife see what he was going to beat her into submission with. He licked his lips in anticipation, thinking he wasn't going to let her get the better of him. He was the boss in this house, and he'd teach her not to forget. But he hadn't reckoned on the hatred his daughter felt for him.

Jenny jumped from her chair and put herself between the belt and her mother. 'Don't you dare use that on my mother. If yer must fight, pick on one of yer drunken cronies, someone yer own size.' She snorted in scorn. 'But yer wouldn't do that, 'cos ye're too much of a coward.'

The sound that came from Tom Phillips's mouth was more animal than human. 'You stuck up bitch, I'll have yer for that. Yer'll be on yer knees begging for mercy by the time I'm finished with yer.'

Ben watched in horror as his father raised his arm, the belt buckle danging, and the steel glinting in the gaslight. The boy was paralysed for a brief second, as his brain took in the scene that was unfolding. Then he jumped to his feet and made a dive for the upraised arm. He managed to push it sideways, so the blow landed on the sideboard, and not on his sister.

Annie had watched, horrified and racked with guilt. She loved her children dearly, every bone of them, and it tore her apart to have to witness them grapple with their father to protect her from his blows. They didn't know, for she would never tell them, that the man she had married made her suffer every time something happened to upset him. He was crafty, as well as violent. He always belted her where the bruises wouldn't be seen. Never a night went by when he didn't shame her in bed. And if she didn't do his bidding, her punishment would be a blow in the small of her back, on her tummy or between her shoulder blades. And he did it knowing she was too ashamed to tell anyone. All these years she had suffered in silence for the sake of the children. And watching them now, standing between her and a madman, she felt her fear turn to anger.

Without saying a word, she made her way to the kitchen. Opening a drawer, she took out a wooden rolling pin. Fear had numbed her brain, and she felt calm as she walked back into the living room with her arm down by her side, and her hand gripping the rolling pin.

'Sit down, Jenny, sweetheart, and you, Ben. Leave this to me.'

'That's right, yer little bastards, sit down and watch while I teach yer mother a lesson.'

Everything happened so quickly after that, the children didn't have time to protest. For as Tom Phillips's arm came down with the belt, Annie used all her strength to bring the rolling pin up, to deflect his aim. And when he yelped with pain, she brought it down again with full force. Her upward swing had caught his wrist, her downward, his fingers.

'You bleeding cow! You stupid bleeding cow!' The belt was thrown to the floor as Tom nursed his hand. 'Yer've broken me fingers, yer bleeding cracked mare.' Pacing the floor with his hand cradled, he swore, 'Yer'll pay for this. Oh, yeah, yer'll pay for this all right. If yer've broken one of me fingers, I'll break every one of yours. I'll have yer on yer knees, pleading for bloody mercy.' He kicked a chair out of the way. 'Yer'll get no mercy from me, though. What yer will get is the hiding of yer bleeding life. When I've finished with yer, yer'll be sorry yer were ever born.'

'That's how I felt the day after we got married.' Annie was churning up inside, but she spoke calmly. 'That's the day yer showed yer true colours, and I realised I'd married a bully. That day I was sorry I'd ever been born. And I've been sorry every day since. The only good thing that came out of our marriage was the children. I love them dearly, but regret that it is through me they have to suffer having you as a father.'

When Tom made a move towards her, anger and hatred in his eyes, Annie lifted the rolling pin and shook it in his face. 'Yer would be a very stupid man to try. I wouldn't think twice about hitting you over the head with this.'

Tom was seething, his face contorted as he sucked in his breath. 'Get me bleeding dinner.' He banged on the table with his good hand. 'Get it now, I'm starving.'

Jenny and Ben had been watching and listening with eyes wide. They had never known their mother stick up for herself before. They felt proud of her, but also afraid for her. This was a one-off, and they knew their father would make her suffer for what she'd done. But it wasn't over yet, for their mother had another surprise in store.

Standing in front of her husband, Annie stared at him for several seconds without even blinking. Then she said, 'If yer want any dinner, yer can get it yerself. It's in the oven keeping warm. Me and the children are going for a walk. We don't want to go for a walk on a night as cold as this, but we need some fresh air in our lungs. We're going out to rid ourselves of the nasty smell that's in this room.' She turned to the children. 'Get yer coats on, kids, and let's get out of here.'

Her children either side of her linking her arms, Annie walked quickly, as though she wanted to put distance between her and the man she'd left shouting obscenities after them. The street lamps were lit, and as the trio passed them they could see their breath floating upwards in the cold air. 'If either of yer had made plans to go out tonight, then go. Don't let that brute take away all yer pleasure.' Annie squeezed their arms. 'He's ruined my life; don't let him ruin yours. And don't worry about me, I'll be all right.'

Ben shook his head. 'Nah, it's too cold to walk to me mate's and then back home again. I'll stay in with you.'

'I wasn't going out anyway,' Jenny said, crossing her fingers. She didn't like telling lies to her mother, but this was an emergency. She had arranged to go to the pictures with two mates from work, but it couldn't be helped. She would worry herself to death all the time she was out, in case her dad took off again. She'd make an excuse to her friends at work tomorrow, they wouldn't mind. And there were two of them, it wasn't as if she was letting a girl on her own down. 'We'll have a game of cards when we get back, in front of the fire.'

They walked quickly, to get the circulation in their feet moving. And it was when they reached the corner of their street that Jenny said, 'Yer'll have to watch out, Mam, 'cos me dad will have it in for yer.'

'I'll be all right, sweetheart, I'll sleep on the couch. It'll be comfortable enough, and the room won't be cold 'cos I'll bank the fire up.'

Jenny shivered, but it wasn't with the cold. It was the thought of her father sneaking downstairs when he thought they were asleep, and beating her mother up. 'Yer can sleep with me, Mam, we'll keep each other warm. It's only a single bed, but we'll manage. We're both thin, and we can cuddle up.'

'Yeah, you do that, Mam, it's a good idea.' Ben was blessing his sister, for he knew she wouldn't let any harm come to their mam. 'Me dad won't go in Jenny's room.'

'It's too cold to stand talking, me teeth are chattering,' Annie said. 'Let's make for home. And I will come in your bed tonight, sweetheart, thank you.'

They were nearing their front door when Jenny pulled them to a halt. 'Mam, yer'll still have the neighbours over tomorrow afternoon, won't yer? It'll buck yer up, and yer'll feel better having friends in who'll make yer laugh. Even if it is only for a couple of hours, it'll make yer feel better.'

Annie felt in her pocket for the front door key. 'Yes, I'll have them over, sweetheart. I wouldn't put them off, not after they've been so kind to me. And a damn good laugh will do me the world of good.' But as she turned the key, and thought of the evil man she would have to face, she let out a sigh.

The back bedroom in the small two-up-two-down house was divided in two by a wooden partition running down the middle. Most families in the street had partitioned the room off, for as the children grew older, the girls and boys wanted privacy. But there was barely room to move, with a single bed taking up all the space. However, with Annie and Jenny cuddled up close for warmth, they didn't feel cramped. And it wasn't long before Annie could hear the gentle breathing of her daughter, and the snoring of her son through the wooden partition. She felt a sense of contentment, tinged with sadness, for this was the first time since she got married that she was lying next to someone who really loved her. And soon, her mind free of the worry of her husband's hands mauling her, or his fist in her back, she too was sleeping soundly.

Annie ran her life like clockwork, for Tom Phillips was always on the lookout for something to complain about. So every morning without fail, she was awake at six o'clock. This gave her time to clean the grate out and light a fire, before starting on the breakfast. She didn't need the help of an alarm clock to wake her, for her brain was finely tuned after a routine of twenty years. So the next morning, waking at her usual time, she lay in the dark for a few minutes, her mind going over the layout of the room. She didn't want to make a noise and disturb her daughter, not when Jenny was sleeping peacefully.

It was pitch dark outside, and not being familiar with the small room, she sat on the edge of the bed and put her hands out to feel the wall. Then she stood up and groped her way to the door, and then out to the staircase. The lino was freezing under her feet, and she shivered as she lowered herself down each of the stairs, careful to keep to the side so they wouldn't creak. Once in the living room, she closed the door softly and felt for the box of matches she kept on the sideboard behind the glass bowl. Two minutes later, the gas mantle was lit and the flickering light cast an eerie glow over the room. Annie told herself the sooner she got the fire lit the better, it would cheer the room up a bit. So she set to, raking the ashes out of the grate on to the hearth. She was on her hands and knees brushing the hearth when she heard the door behind her open, and her blood ran cold. Her first thought was that her husband had heard her coming down, and had followed with the intention of seeking revenge. She was scrambling to her feet, her mind telling her she would be more able to protect herself if she was standing up, when she heard her daughter's voice. 'I felt yer getting out of bed, Mam. What time is it?'

'It's only ten past six, sweetheart, yer've got another three-quarters of an hour before yer need to get up. Go back to bed and I'll call yer when it's time.'

Jenny shook her head. 'It's freezing up there, Mam, and the bed will be cold now. I'll stay down and help yer. Shall I bring a shovel of coal in?'

'There's no need, the scuttle is nearly full. You sit on the couch, and in ten minutes there'll be a fire blazing up the chimney. While we're waiting, I'll make us a hot drink.'

'I'll do that, Mam, while you get the fire going. I may as well make meself useful instead of sitting here watching yer.'

'That would be nice, sweetheart, but don't use a lot of milk. The milkman is usually here by seven, but if he's late and there's not enough for yer dad's breakfast, there'll be hell to pay.'

'I'll go easy on it, Mam, don't worry.'

'I heard that, sis.' Ben slid quietly into the room, closing the door behind him. 'I don't mind tea without milk, if it comes to the push. As long as it's wet and hot.'

'What's the matter with yer both this morning?' Annie asked. 'I'm usually shouting at yer for ages before yer'll get up. Ye're upsetting me whole routine now, and keeping me back.'

'No, we won't keep yer back, Mam,' Jenny said as she walked into the kitchen. 'I'll make the tea, you get about yer business. And Ben, you can take the ashes out and empty them in the midden.'

'Ooh, ye're not soft, are yer! It'll be ruddy freezing out there, and I'm not dressed properly yet.' Ben was sorry as soon as the words left his mouth. His mother must make the journey down the yard every morning, and you never heard her complain. 'Leave them, Mam, I'll put me coat on and take them out for yer.'

The three sat round the table when the tea was made, but Annie's eyes kept going to the clock and she wouldn't let them linger. The fire was burning brightly, the kettle was on the stove on a low light, and the bread was cut ready for toasting. She couldn't see anything for her husband to find fault with. 'Yer've had a swill at the sink, son, so go upstairs and get dressed. Give yer dad a shout, and keep shouting until he answers.' She turned to her daughter. 'Use some water out of the kettle to get washed, sweetheart, then fill the kettle again. Go on, while yer've got the chance.'

While Ben made for the stairs, Jenny hurried to the kitchen. If she had a quick cat's lick and a promise, she could be dressed before her father came down. She always made sure she was well covered in his presence, for she hated to feel his eyes on her. Several times he'd opened the bedroom door when she was getting dressed, and the look on his face sickened her. There was no lock on the door, and he would push it open and brazenly lean against the wall watching her. She'd never told her mother for she knew it would cause her more heartache. And God knows, she had a rotten life as it was, without her daughter making it worse for her. She'd told Ben the last time it happened, and he'd promised that if their father ever left the breakfast table saying he wanted something from his bedroom, then Ben would find an excuse to follow him. They vowed to protect each other from his violence, and to stick by their mother through thick and thin.

When Tom Phillips came downstairs, he was in a foul temper. He hadn't slept well, for two of his fingers were throbbing and painful. They weren't broken, he was well aware of that. But he was a weakling when it came to pain, and what another man would shrug off, he tended to make heavy weather of. And that morning, when he saw his two children sitting at the table and talking to each other, he was filled with ill will. He pulled a chair out from under the table and sat down. There was no greeting from him, never was. In fact if he came in with a smile on his face and a greeting on his lips, they'd think something was drastically wrong.

Annie came in from the kitchen carrying a plate of toast. She set it in front of him, then poured him a cup of tea and put sugar and milk in it.

And all the while she could feel his eyes on her. She knew he wouldn't touch her, not in front of the children. But his hatred was almost tangible and it frightened her. Somehow, sometime, he would get his revenge for last night. All she could do was be ready at all times, to fend him off.

Tom ate his toast and drank his tea in silence, using his left hand. He didn't utter one word, but his head was filled with dark thoughts.

Chapter Thirteen

Jenny watched her brother follow their father out to the front door. Ben's shoulders were slumped and his head was down. He looked a picture of dejection, and her heart went out to him. He was afraid of his father, and didn't like to be near him. And there was no reason for him to go out every morning at exactly the same time, for when they got to the bottom of the street, without a word's being exchanged, they would go in opposite directions. But if Ben dared to object, the answer he'd get would be a clip round the ear. In fact, with the mood Tom Phillips was in this morning, the punishment would be far worse than a clip round the ear. It would take a very brave person to look sideways at him. Not a word had crossed his lips since he'd come downstairs, but the venom in his eyes spoke volumes. It would only take a sideways glance, and all hell would break loose.

Jenny sighed. Her brother was only a kid, no match for a man who was six feet tall and thick-set. And violent and ruthless. What sort of life was it for a young lad, when he was afraid to speak in his own home? Jenny was about to turn away from the window when she saw the door opposite open and two men step down on to the pavement. She hadn't seen much of the neighbours, as she used the back entry to come and go. From a young girl, she'd learned friends weren't easy to come by. Oh, when they moved into a new house, which was very often, the children would be friendly with her, playing hopscotch or jumping with the skipping rope in the street. But their friendship never lasted long, after Tom Phillips's reputation as a drunkard and a bully became known. So she'd never known what it was to have a true friend she could call for, or who would knock on her door and ask if she was coming out to play. Her only interest in the men coming out of the house opposite was because her mother had become friendly with Ada Fenwick, and she was curious. And she hoped with all her heart that they were going to be true, lasting friends, for her mother needed someone in her life whom she could turn to.

'Mam, is that Mrs Fenwick's husband just come out of the house?'

Annie came to peer over her shoulder. 'Yes, that's Ada's husband and son. They're very alike, aren't they?'

141

'They look very pleasant,' Jenny said, her eyes following the figures until they were out of sight. 'It's not often yer see men smiling at this time of the morning.'

'Don't class every man with yer father, sweetheart, because they're not all the same. From what I've heard, Mr Fenwick is a happy and loving husband. And according to Ada, and Hetty, young Danny is a smashing lad.'

'He's a nice-looking boy.'

'Mad on dancing, so his mother told me. Goes jazzing every night.'

'Not every night, surely?'

'That's what his mam said. He's nineteen at the weekend, and Ada is buying him a tie. She said he spends so much time getting himself ready, she can't get near the sink. His hair is slicked back with Brylcreem and yer can see yer face in the shine on his shoes.' Annie turned and walked back to the table to collect the dirty dishes. 'Sit down, sweetheart, and I'll make a fresh pot of tea. Would yer like a slice of toast with it?'

Jenny pulled a chair out and sat down. 'Only if you're having one, Mam. Yer haven't had anything to eat yet.'

'Yer know I never eat anything until yer father's gone out. I wouldn't enjoy it, it would stick in me throat. He puts the fear of God into me, the looks I get off him.'

'Well, he's not here now, so let you and me enjoy a nice cup of tea and some toast. While you're making it, I'll get meself washed. Then we can relax for half an hour, and yer can tell me what ye're getting for yer visitors this afternoon.'

Jenny was drying her face when Annie carried the pot of tea through and put it on the chrome stand. 'Fetch the toast in with yer, sweetheart. I've done two rounds each.'

'Ooh, it looks good, Mam! Lovely golden brown. I can't wait to get me teeth into it.'

'I've gone mad this morning, and put butter on it. I usually only put butter on yer dad's, 'cos he knows the difference between that and marg. But it's a little treat for you and me.'

Jenny bit into a piece of toast and sighed with pleasure. 'Mmm, that's good, Mam. If only we were rich, then we could have butter every day.'

'It's no good hankering for something we can't have, sweetheart. Let's be thankful for what we've got.'

'I know, Mam, but there's no harm in dreaming, is there? Yer never know, I might meet a feller with pots of money, who lives in a big house. He might fall madly in love with me, and there'd be room in the house for you and Ben. I know that's an impossible dream, but it's better to look on the bright side than be dead miserable and think things will never get better.'

'I'll be happy if yer meet a good man, Jenny, never mind whether he's rich or poor. Love makes life worth living, whether it's in a two-up-two-down or a mansion.'

Jenny looked at the clock on the mantelpiece. 'I'll have to be on me way in five minutes, Mam, so hurry up and tell me what ye're getting in for yer visitors.'

'I thought of getting two ounces of boiled ham for sandwiches, and a cream cake each.'

'Have yer got enough money? I can always give yer a tanner to help out.'

Annie shook her head. 'I'm all right, sweetheart, I've got enough in me purse for what I want. I'm careful with money, 'cos Tom's never been generous. Most of his wages goes on beer, in every pub from here to Seaforth docks. But with what you and Ben turn up, I can manage.' She was thoughtful for a few seconds, then said, 'I'll let yer into a secret, sweetheart, 'cos ye're old enough to know what's going on. I've got a few pounds put by in case of emergency. Over the years I've gone without to put sixpence away each week without fail. I've always had it in the back of me mind that one day yer dad will go too far, and I'll be forced to run away with you and Ben. What I've got isn't enough for us to live on, but it's adding up each week. So if it ever gets to the stage where we were forced to flee, we wouldn't starve. It would last us until we found a roof over our heads. And I'll never touch me little nest egg, unless it's a case of life or death.'

Jenny listened in silence, but inside she was crying. Her mother deserved better than this. 'Mam, what did yer ever see in me dad to marry him? Yer could have done a lot better. I'm sure yer weren't short of boyfriends. Yer must have been very pretty when yer were younger, 'cos ye're still a fine-looking woman. Yer deserve better than him.'

'I was blind to his faults, love, and I'm paying for it now. My mother could see through him, and she tried to talk me out of marrying him. She said I'd rue the day, and by God she was right. I only wished I'd listened, and taken her advice. But I was eighteen, and I thought I knew better than me mam.' Her hand covered one of her daughter's. 'Don't make the same mistake I made, sweetheart. Make sure the man yer marry is kind and loving. And he'll look after yer and treat yer with respect.'

Jenny scraped her chair back. 'Yer need have no worries on that score, Mam, I'll make damn sure. I have no love for me dad, nor respect. But the one thing he has taught me is to make sure the man I marry is the right one for me.' She bent and kissed her mother's cheek. 'I'll have to scarper, or I'll be late clocking on. But I hope yer have a lovely afternoon with Ada and Hetty. I know I shouldn't be so familiar, using their first names, but if I ever get to meet them I'll be careful to show respect. Finish the tea off, Mam, and relax for a while. I'll see yer tonight for all yer news. Ta-ra.'

'I warned yer it wouldn't be as bright as your room, Ada, but one of these days it will be.' Annie held out her hand. 'Give me yer coats and I'll hang them up. Otherwise yer'll not feel the benefit of them when yer leave.'

Ada and Hetty gazed around the room. 'What does it remind yer of, sunshine?' Ada asked, chuckling. 'Just like ours looked a couple of weeks ago.'

Hetty grinned as she handed her coat over. 'Mine looked a damn sight worse than this. It reminded me of the black hole of Calcutta.'

Her eyes narrowed, Ada sat down. 'Where the hell is the black hole of Calcutta?'

'I dunno,' Hetty answered. 'In Calcutta, I suppose. But don't try and tell me yer've never heard the expression, Ada Fenwick, 'cos I wouldn't believe yer.'

'I went to school, sunshine, and I was good at geography. So of course I've heard of Calcutta. But I never knew it had a ruddy black hole.'

Annie had a smile on her face as she hung up the coats on hooks in the tiny hall. What a difference there was in the atmosphere since the two women had walked through the front door. She felt happier and more light-hearted, and the house didn't seem as dark. 'I've got the kettle on the stove. Tea will be up in five minutes.'

Ada raised her brows. 'Five minutes! Ye're slow, aren't yer, Mrs Phillips? When me and me mate are invited to afternoon tea, we don't expect to have to wait five minutes. Yer'll have to improve yer service if yer want us to be regular callers. Don't you agree, sunshine?'

'What was that, girl? I missed half of what yer said, 'cos I was too busy trying to remember the last time we were invited anywhere for afternoon tea. And d'yer know what? Not only can I not remember the last time we got invited out, I can't remember the first! In other words, girl, I don't think we've ever been in anyone's house except each other's.'

'That's right, make a liar of me!' Ada pretended to be put out. 'Yer've got a very short memory, sunshine, 'cos what about the day after Eliza moved out of here? You, me and Edith, we went next door to Jean's and we had a little party. Surely yer can remember that?'

Hetty nodded her head slowly. 'Yeah, I remember that, girl, 'cos we had a good laugh.'

Ada suddenly slapped a hand to her cheek. 'I'm glad we brought Eliza's name up, 'cos I might have forgotten.' She looked up at Annie, who was still standing at the end of the table. 'We've told yer about Eliza, the woman who used to live here, haven't we? And how much we all loved her. Well, I had a letter from her this morning. It was to Hetty and meself, and she told us she was settling in nicely at her son's house. Getting waited on hand and foot, so she says. She's coming to see us next spring, when the weather is fit. She still misses this house though, and it will always have a place in her heart. But she understands she couldn't live on her own much longer. Anyway, she hopes the new tenants, which is you, have settled in and are as happy here as she'd always been. And I was thinking that when she comes to see us next spring, yer could meet her for yerself. Perhaps even have her in for a cup of tea, so she can see the old house is in good hands?'

Annie couldn't meet Ada's eyes, so she began to pour the tea out. How could she pretend they were one big happy family when it was untrue? It wasn't the fault of the house, for it was as nice a house as they'd ever lived in. But their stay was never a long one, while Eliza's had been sixty years. 'She'll be welcome to come and see her old home, Ada, and I've heard so much about her, I'd like to meet her.'

The teapot was put down on the chrome stand, and Annie said, 'I'll bring the plates in.' In the space of five minutes, her happiness at having friends in her house had turned to sadness. She hated having to pretend all was right in her life, when it wasn't true. She'd been brought up by loving parents, who had taught her the difference between right and wrong. And telling lies was wrong. She might not actually be telling lies to Ada and Hetty, but she was acting a lie, which was just as bad.

Ada's eyes rolled to the ceiling when she saw the plates. 'Ooh, chocolate eclairs! They're me favourites!' She ran the back of a hand across her lips. 'Me mouth's watering now, and me teeth can't wait to bite into that chocolate and cream.' Then she suddenly sat up straight in the chair and slapped her wrist. 'Behave yerself, Ada Fenwick, and don't be so ruddy greedy. Anyone would think yer'd never had an eclair before. Just behave yerself and mind yer manners.'

Hetty saw Annie's look of bewilderment and smiled. 'Don't worry, girl, she's not dangerous. Me mate often has moments of madness. I used to worry about her when I heard her talking to the flowers on the wallpaper. But I take no notice of her now because the flowers have gone, and she doesn't seem to have befriended the leaves on the new paper. Perhaps it's because leaves don't have the same nice smell.'

Annie told herself to forget all her troubles for as long as her visitors were here, and to act as daft as them. 'Does the new moon cause it, d'yer think? I had an uncle once, and every new moon, his wife had to tie him to a chair and put a gag in his mouth.'

'Oh, and why was that?' Ada asked. 'Was he a bit loopy?'

'Not all the time, no! He was a clever man as a matter of fact, had a good job in an office. It was only when there was a new moon, he used to come over funny. He used to wail like a banshee, terrifying everyone. All the women in the street used to take their children indoors when there was a full moon.'

While Hetty sat wide-eyed and all ears, Ada was smiling. 'Ay, it didn't take you long to come out of yer shell, Annie Phillips. We're going to have to keep our eyes on you, otherwise yer'll be telling better tales than us. Yer were quick off the mark, 'cos I reckon yer made that up as yer were going along.'

Hetty stared at her mate. 'What makes yer say Annie made it up? Everyone's not like you, yer know.' She turned to Annie. 'Yer didn't make it up, did yer?'

Before Annie had time to answer, Ada said, 'Of course she made it up, soft girl! The only bit she left out was that her uncle used to turn into a werewolf.'

'That's not very nice of yer, girl, saying things like that.'

'What's not nice of me?'

'Well, yer come here as an invited guest, and turn round and tell Annie her uncle wasn't right in the head.'

'I never said no such thing!'

The banter between the two friends lifted Annie's spirits. For two hours she'd put her troubles and cares behind her, and enjoy herself in pleasant company. She lifted the plate with the sandwiches on. 'Anyone ready to eat?'

Ada didn't hesitate. 'Ooh, yeah, I am! The sooner we finish the sandwiches off, the sooner we can have our cake.' She nudged her friend in the ribs. 'D'yer know what, sunshine? If I was offered the choice between an evening of passion with my husband and a chocolate eclair, the cake would win hands down.'

Hetty huffed, and clicked her tongue on the roof of her mouth. 'Have yer forgotten ye're not in yer own house now? Perhaps Annie doesn't appreciate that kind of talk.'

'I'll shut my mouth, then, shall I? Will that make yer feel better? Right, then I'll close it in the nicest possible way.' With that, Ada leaned across the table, picked up a chocolate eclair and put it in her mouth. And the sounds of bliss were accompanied by a slowly shaking head, and screwed-up eyes.

'It doesn't take much to please her,' Hetty told Annie. 'Just listen to her.'

Ada licked the chocolate off her fingers before opening her eyes. 'D'yer know what I've just discovered, sunshine? That the sound of pleasure yer've just heard is exactly the same sound I'll be making in bed tonight when my feller gets frisky. So yer could say that all in all, it's going to be a good day for me.'

John Griffiths was a quay foreman at Seaforth docks. Known as Griff to his friends and the gang of dockers under his command, he was a good boss. Firm but fair. Having worked his way up over the years by sheer hard graft, from being a casual worker, he had little time for idlers or loafers. No one was allowed to swing the lead in his crew; he expected every man to do a fair day's work for a fair day's pay. He didn't mind getting his hands dirty, either, which earned him the respect of his crew and his bosses. If a ship was being loaded, and there was a rush to complete the work in time for the ship to sail on the evening tide, he would work as hard as any of the gang. And today was one such day. He was directing the cargo that was being winched on board in a cradle made of strong ropes, signalling to the hatch foreman who was on the deck of the ship with his crew. The men were working to orders, and the quayside was a hive of activity.

Such was the noise and bustle, Tom Phillips thought he wouldn't be missed for five minutes. So he waited until Griff's eyes were elsewhere, then sidled off to take cover behind a stack of crates. He leaned back, his flat cap pulled down over his forehead, and a Woodbine hanging out of the side of his mouth. With his eyes half closed against the smoke from the cigarette, he began to rub his two fingers. They weren't sore now, and his reason for rubbing them was to keep alive the anger he felt towards his wife. The two children came into that anger, but his main hatred was reserved for Annie. She wasn't going to get away with it, not by a long chalk. He'd make her pay, by God he would. She'd never answer him back again, or refuse to obey him.

John Griffiths came charging round the crates like a bull, his nostrils flared ready to do battle. 'I thought as much, yer lazy bugger. Standing here smoking while yer mates slog their guts out. I've a good mind to report yer and have yer suspended. Now get back to work, and I want to see yer working twice as hard as any man there.'

That frightened Tom for a brief second, for jobs were hard to come by. But crafty as he was, he decided to bluff his way out. 'There's a reason for it, Mr Griffiths.' There was a whine in his voice. 'I've worked for the last couple of hours in agony. Yer see, me son banged the front door on me fingers this morning, as we were leaving for work. The lad didn't mean it, so I'm not blaming him. But, honest to God, I thought he'd broken these two fingers.' He held up his right hand. 'Me wife told me to stay off and go to the hospital, but I knew yer needed every man today 'cos of the rush job.'

Griff's stare was unblinking, and Tom lowered his eyes. 'If yer fingers were broken, Phillips, then yer'd be crying out in agony. And why didn't yer report this when yer signed on this morning?'

'I didn't want to make a fuss. I know me two fingers aren't broken, 'cos as yer say, I'd be in agony. But they're hurting like hell, honest. Trying to pull on the ropes I was nearly crying out in pain. And that's the truth, Mr Griffiths. But as I don't want to let yer down, I'll go back to the gang and do me best.'

'Oh, no, yer won't, Phillips.' Griff didn't believe a word the man said. For some reason he couldn't take to Tom Phillips; the man gave him the creeps. You never heard him laughing like his workmates, nor talking about his family. And at times his language was foul. But he was good at his job. And until now, Griff couldn't fault his work, even though he disliked the man. 'I can't have anyone lagging behind. Go to the office and sign off for the rest of the day. Yer'll lose half a day's pay, but that's your bad luck. I'll get someone to take yer place.' There was a hint of sarcasm in his voice. 'And don't bother getting out of bed tomorrow if yer fingers are still sore. I don't carry any passengers, yer should know that by now.'

'I'll rest them tonight, Mr Griffiths, and I bet they'll be all right by tomorrow.'

The sarcasm still there, Griff said, 'Oh, I'd bet any money on them being all right for tomorrow. Yer wouldn't want to lose another day's pay, that's for sure. Think of all the pints yer'd have to go without.' He waved a hand. 'Go on, out of my sight. I've got more to do than listen to any of your moans. There's a ship to be got ready to sail with the tide. Thank goodness there's men who'll work flat out to make sure it does. Now scarper.'

Griff turned and walked away. He'd only gone a few steps when he hesitated, then spun round. 'I'll tell yer workmates yer can't be here to help them because yer've got two sore fingers. I'm sure they'll have something to say about that tomorrow. And I'm sure it won't be a vote of sympathy. Now get the hell out of here.'

Tom watched his boss walk away before flicking his cigarette on to the ground and using his foot to put it out. He didn't feel any sympathy for his workmates, or regret for letting his boss down. He'd never taken time off before, so they couldn't come down too hard on him. Anyway, he told himself, by the time I clock on tomorrow things will have calmed down. There would be no mad panic like today. A cargo ship was due in tomorrow, but not until the evening tide. So there'd be breaks for a sit down and a ciggie, or a cup of tea from the tea wagon. Oh, the men would probably have a go at him, but they'd soon find something else to talk about. He didn't care anyway. It would be like water off a duck's back to him.

But for all his bravado, Tom made sure he wasn't seen leaving by any of the blokes he worked with. He left the docks by a different exit. And once outside the gates, he pushed his flat cap up from his forehead, lit another Woodbine, and swaggered towards the nearest pub. His eyes were glinting as he thought of the look of fear he would see on his wife's face when he walked in on her. There'd be no one there to protect her this afternoon; he'd have her all to himself. And after he'd given her the hiding of her life, he'd drag her upstairs. He didn't have to worry about her crying out for help, she never did. She was too proud to let the neighbours know. He could do what he liked, and there wouldn't be a sound from her.

Tom licked his lips. Just the thought of what he intended to do with his wife was making his heartbeat quicken. And his desire was being aroused. But first he'd get his kicks from tormenting and humiliating her. She was his slave, and she would be forced to do his bidding. And when his need for revenge was satisfied, he would satisfy his lust. He would take her roughly, until she whimpered with pain, and pleaded with him to stop. But he wouldn't stop. Not until he was good and ready. There'd never be a repeat of what happened yesterday, he'd see to that. This afternoon he intended to teach her what would happen if she stepped out of line again.

The pubs weren't open yet, but Tom knew the landlord of one on the dock road. Being a good customer, he was allowed in any time. All he need do was knock on the side door. So as he lifted his curled fist to knock, Tom was feeling on top of the world. He was going to enjoy himself this afternoon, and a couple of pints would put an edge on his appetite. What awaited him at home was worth losing half a day's pay for. And any red-blooded man would feel the same. The blokes he worked with were always praising their wives, saying how well they looked after them. Tom always sneered inwardly when he heard them. They didn't know what they were missing. If only they knew how docile his wife was, and how he could do what he liked with her, how envious they'd be. Silly, henpecked buggers, that's what they were. Not a real man, like himself.

Chapter Fourteen

'Have another sandwich, Ada.' Annie handed the plate over. 'It's no good letting them go to waste.'

'Oh, they won't go to waste, sunshine, yer've no need to worry on that score. I've got a healthy regard for food, thanks to my mother.' Ada nodded as memories came back. 'She drummed it into me that it was a sin to waste good food when there were millions of people in the world who were starving. If I turned me nose up at a jam butty, I'd get a lecture on how millions would think it was their birthday if they were offered a jam butty.' She picked a sandwich from the plate and took a bite. 'When I was a kid, I came home from school one day and asked me mam if I could have a butty 'cos I was hungry.' She turned to Hetty. 'I often think of that day, sunshine, 'cos I was ashamed of meself afterwards.'

Hetty's brows shot up. 'Why would yer feel ashamed just asking for a jam butty? I used to ask my mother for one when I came home from school. Most kids do.'

'Wait until I tell yer why I was ashamed, and yer'll understand. I'd brought a mate from school with me, and I remember she was standing next to me in the kitchen while I was waiting for me butty. I was showing off, I suppose, 'cos when I saw me mam putting dripping on the bread, I wasn't very happy. So I stamped me foot and said I wanted jam on me butty and not horrible dripping.'

Hetty was taken aback. 'Yer didn't give yer mam cheek, did yer? I would never answer me mam back or give her cheek.'

'I never did after that day, I can tell yer. I learned me lesson the hard way. Yer see, I didn't get a butty after all. What I did get was a clip round the ear, and a lecture on how she hoped the day would never come when I'd be so poor I'd give anything for a dripping butty. And with that I was sent out to play with me tummy rumbling, and me mate from school telling me I was a greedy pig.'

Annie had been listening with interest. 'I often have bread fried in dripping. When the family have gone off to work in the mornings, I make meself a few rounds every day. Bread fried in dripping until it's crisp, yer can't beat it.'

'I know that now, Annie, 'cos I enjoy it meself,' Ada admitted. 'But because I had me mate from school with me that day, I wanted to show off.' She pulled a face. 'Instead of me showing off, me mam showed me up! And d'yer know what? That's one of the days in me life that I often look back on. I learned a lesson that day, and I've never wasted bread since.'

'It might have taught yer a lesson on being more careful with food, girl, but did it teach yer anything about manners?' Hetty moved sideways, out of reach of her mate's expected reaction. 'It strikes me yer've forgotten a lot of what yer mam tried to drill into yer. Yer manners can be shocking at times.'

'Yer might well move away, Hetty Watson, yer cheeky beggar.' Ada managed a soulful expression before dropping her head. 'That hurt, that did. I really thought yer were me very best mate. How could yer say those things about me?' A sob came to her voice. 'If yer'd stuck a knife in me heart, yer couldn't have hurt me more.'

'Oh dear, oh dear, oh dear! Who are we today? Is it Ethel Barrymore, or is it Bette Davis?' Hetty gave a deep sigh. 'Ethel Barrymore, I think, 'cos that's the sort of thing she would say.'

Ada's face broke into a wide smile. 'Got yer there, sunshine. It was Vivien Leigh in that picture with erm . . . erm . . . oh, what's his name? You know, sunshine, the one what yer said yer'd leave home for?'

'I think I know who yer mean,' Annie said. 'Is it Stewart Granger?'

Ada banged the table with her hand. 'That's the one, sunshine, Stewart Granger. Hetty's got a real crush on him. The only man she'd leave home for. Those were her very words.'

'You lying hound!' Hetty was really on her high horse now. 'I never said no such thing, Ada Fenwick. All I said was that he was really handsome, and a good actor into the bargain. But you have to add your twopennyworth, don't yer?'

'I'll tell yer what,' Ada said, loving every minute. 'We'll let Annie say who she thinks is telling the truth.'

'Don't be bringing me into it,' Annie said, waving her hands. 'I'm not getting involved in any argument.'

'No, I don't blame yer, Annie,' Hetty said. 'It's not fair to ask yer, 'cos yer don't know us very well. Yer've only just become a member of our gang.'

Annie was delighted, but she tried not to let it show. She was being treated like a real friend now, and it would be wonderful if she really did

152

become one of their gang. She could have a little private life of her own. Something precious her husband couldn't take away from her. With a daughter and son she loved the bones of, and two close friends to fill her days with warmth and laughter, she'd be the happiest woman on earth. 'I'll put the kettle on and make a fresh pot of tea, eh? It's only a quarter to three, we've got an hour and a quarter to go before we need to start on the dinners.'

'Good idea, sunshine,' Ada said. 'The best yer've had all day. And the day is still young yet. Just think, by six o'clock yer could have thought of an idea that'll make yer rich. Yer could invent something that no one else has thought of, and make a fortune.'

'Such as?' Hetty asked.

'How the hell do I know! If I did know, I'd invent the bloody thing meself, wouldn't I, soft girl?'

'Well, what d'yer mean by invention?' Hetty was like a dog with a bone now. 'What could Annie invent, like? Give us some idea.'

Ada's eyes rolled to the ceiling. 'Well, I can't think of anything offhand. But I do know she couldn't invent electricity, could she, 'cos someone beat her to it. Or the wireless or telephone, 'cos they've been invented already as well.'

'Oh, I see what yer mean, girl,' Hetty said, her brow furrowed. 'Can't yer think of something that hasn't been invented yet?'

Ada tutted as she slowly shook her head. Then she shouted through to the kitchen, 'I'm flogging a dead horse here, Annie. So will yer hurry up with that tea before I strangle me best mate.'

Annie was chuckling as she lit the gas under the kettle. It had certainly been her lucky day when she met these two.

The pub landlord, Jim Duncan, was pulling a pint of draught beer when across the smoke-filled room his eyes lit on Tom Phillips. The man was becoming a pain in the backside. Jim was regretting now that he'd let him in the side door at half ten, because there'd be trouble with the police if they found out he was serving out of hours. Tom had told him it was only for a sly pint, as he was on his way home to go to the doctor's. He told some cock and bull story about having his fingers caught in the door, but the landlord had the feeling he was pulling a fast one. But because he was a regular, and spent a lot of money in the pub, Jim pretended he believed him and even showed sympathy. That was at half ten, and at twelve o'clock, when the pub opened, the man had come through from the back room to the bar, and had plonked himself down at one of the tables. He'd had four pints up to now, and his tongue was becoming loose. He was making a nuisance of himself, and Jim decided enough was enough.

The landlord placed the pint glass of bitter in front of the customer. 'There yer are, Dick, look at the head on that.' He took the man's money and put it in the till. Then he heard the voice of Tom Phillips, arguing loudly with a bloke sitting near him. Time to intervene, Jim told himself, before it comes to blows.

'I thought yer'd got off work to go to the doctor's?' Jim picked up three empty pint glasses from the small round table. 'It's about time yer got moving, isn't it? Although yer don't seem to be having much trouble with yer fingers now.'

Tom looked at him through narrowed eyes, a cigarette dangling from the corner of his mouth. 'Me fingers are giving me gyp, mate, I'm in bleeding agony. But I'm not a cissy, like some blokes. I don't cry me eyes out like a baby.'

'I still think yer should head home, Tom,' the landlord said. 'When yer get into bed, and the beer wears off, that's when yer'll feel the pain. And then yer'll be too late for the doctor's. Take my advice and make yer way home.'

His eyes screwed up against the cigarette smoke wafting upwards, Tom hiccuped a few times, then asked, 'What's the bleeding time, mate?'

'Two o'clock, nearly. I'll be calling last orders any minute.'

Tom shook his head to try to clear the haze. He'd had four pints, which wasn't many for him, but he'd drunk them on an empty stomach, and it was having an effect. But his reason for going home was becoming clear to him now, and he pushed himself to his feet. He was leaning towards Jim's face when he belched, and the smell, and the lack of manners, was the last straw for the landlord. He put the glasses back on the table, and taking a tight grip on Tom's arm he pulled him to his feet and steered him towards the door. 'On yer way, pal, and good luck with the doctor.'

'Oh, I'll be going home before I go to the bleeding doctor's. I'll be paying me wife a call.' Tom hiccuped loudly three times in quick succession, but didn't think to apologise. 'She'll do me more good than any bleeding medicine. As much as I want, and all for nothing.'

Jim shook his head in disgust and pulled his hand away. This left Tom without support, and he fell back against the tiled wall of the pub. The fresh air, combined with the drink, had him swaying as he staggered away. 'I'll get me bleeding bellyful when I get home. Then I'll go to bed for a couple of hours, so I'm fit for me pint tonight.' He turned back, to add, 'She'll be glad to see me will the missus. Always ready to oblige.'

'I hope ye're fit to make it to the tram stop.' Jim was fast losing patience. 'This is a busy road, yer need to have yer senses about yer if yer don't want to get knocked down.'

'I'll be all right, mate, I can take me ale.'

'Okay, if you say so.' The landlord walked back through the pub doors, saying under his breath, 'Good riddance to bad rubbish.'

Unsteady as he was, Tom Phillips had enough wits about him to lean back against the wall. He breathed in the fresh air, and stayed there until his head felt clear enough to move. Then he made for the tram stop, a sinister smile on his face. He couldn't wait to see his wife's face when he walked in. She'd be on her own, with no kids to come to her aid.

When a tram came trundling along, he pulled himself on board and made for a seat by a window. He'd be home in twenty minutes, and then the fun would begin.

'Fares please.' The conductor came down the aisle clicking his ticket machine, and he stopped by Tom's seat. 'Fares, please.'

Tom handed over two coppers. 'Tuppenny single.' He took the ticket, put it in his overall pocket, then went back to thoughts of his wife. He could feel himself becoming excited, for the power he had over her made him feel like someone special. He was a docker at work, like all the other men. But in his bedroom, he reigned supreme. He was well aware that he wasn't popular with the blokes he worked with, they made that quite clear. But he didn't care, in fact he felt sorry for them. He often heard them talking about what good wives they had, and he felt like laughing in their faces. If they only knew.

Annie heard the sound of the latch clicking on the entry door, and a frown creased her forehead. It was far too early for any of the family to be coming home, unless there was something wrong. She pressed her face close to the kitchen window, and suddenly felt as though all her breath was leaving her body. For she could see her husband closing the door after himself, then turning to walk up the yard. For a few seconds her mind clouded over, then she dashed into the living room. 'I'm going to have to ask yer to leave. I'm sorry, but me husband's come in the back way, and he doesn't like visitors.'

Hetty, as naive as ever, smiled. 'Oh, we may as well stay and make his acquaintance.'

But Ada was quick to see the panic in Annie's eyes. 'It's too late, sunshine, he's just opened the kitchen door. We'd never make it out in time.'

155

The scene that met Tom Phillips's eyes was like a tableau. Two women sitting and one standing, all like statues. No movement, not even a blink.

'What the bleeding hell is going on here?' Tom took in the empty plates and the cups. 'Having a bloody party, are yer?' He jerked his thumb towards the front door. 'Two bleeding gasbags, with nothing else to do all day but sit on their fat backsides.' The smell of beer filled the room as he leaned over the table. 'Sod off, the pair of yer.'

Annie's face drained of colour as she wrung her hands. 'Tom, these are two of our neighbours from opposite.' She felt so ashamed, having to make excuses to a man who was the worse for drink. 'They've only been here a few minutes.'

Hetty was feeling very uncomfortable now. She wasn't used to bad language, or drunken men. She made a move to get off the chair, but saw Ada make a sign for her to stay where she was.

'Are yer both bleeding deaf, or what? I told the pair of yer to get off yer backsides.' Tom's rage was frightening. 'It's my house, and I'm telling yer to bugger off.'

As quick as the click of someone's fingers, the fog in Annie's mind cleared and she saw the scene for what it was. This had been a happy room until her husband had filled it with the smell of beer and bad language. And he was making a show of her in front of the only friends she had. Belittling her, and taking away her pride and dignity. She couldn't take it any more. Even if he took his belt to her and beat her to pulp. 'This is my home as well as yours, Tom Phillips, and these are friends of mine. They will stay until they are ready to leave.'

Ada hadn't spoken a word so far. She wanted to make sure her instinct was right before saying anything or walking out. So she sat still, her eyes going from husband to wife, then back again.

Tom Phillips was beside himself with rage. This wasn't what he'd imagined himself coming home to. 'Don't you dare answer me back, yer stupid cow. If yer know what's good for yer, yer'll get them out of here now, before I belt yer one.' He raised a curled fist to Annie's face. 'Do as I tell yer, unless yer want a taste of this.'

When Ada saw Annie cower in fear, she could no longer stay quiet. She pushed her chair back and got to her feet. Passing behind Hetty's chair, she stood in front of the man whose nostrils were flared, and whose eyes were wild with rage. 'I have never interfered between husband and wife before, because I've never had cause to. But I'll not stand by and see any woman, friend or stranger, beaten by a drunken bully.'

Tom roared like a lion, and lifted his fist. 'If yer don't want a taste of this, then get to hell out of my bleeding house, yer fat cow.'

Hetty gasped. Ooh, she said in her mind, my mate isn't going to like being called a fat cow. Why didn't they leave when Annie asked them to? If it was up to her, they'd get out now, while the going was good. Before the situation got any worse. But it wasn't up to her, and she wasn't leaving without her mate.

Ada's face was inches away from Tom Phillips's, and she found the smell sickening. 'I will willingly leave your house. In fact, I'll be delighted to leave your house. I wish I was anywhere but in yer ruddy house. And it pains me to say I'd like to leave this house, because I've been coming in here for twenty years now. I've always been happy and welcome here, because the person who lived here before was a lovely lady. Yer wouldn't hear bad language in here then, or have to put up with the stink of beer. However, I will only leave if I'm sure in me mind that Annie won't come to any harm after me and me mate have gone.'

Annie touched her arm. 'Don't get yerself upset over him, Ada, he's not worth it. He's fond of using his fists. In his tiny mind, he thinks hitting women and children makes him more of a man.'

'Tell me the truth, Annie,' Ada said. 'Are yer certain that he won't belt yer as soon as me and Hetty are out of the house?'

Annie lowered her eyes. 'I'm fed up with telling lies about my husband, but I'll not lie to yer now. The man I married, God help me, has always been a down and out rotter. And I'm ashamed to say I've never had the strength to stand up to him.' She turned to stare at Tom's face, which was distorted with rage, then looked back at Ada. 'At least I'd never stood up to him until last night. I've never ever told anyone that he beats me, not even the children. Or that he gets such a kick out of it that he's laughing as he's beating me. But last night, with the help of the children, I turned the tables on him. I actually hit him on the hand with the rolling pin. And he'll want his revenge. I'd bet every penny I've got in me purse that revenge is the reason he's taken time off work. He knew he'd find me on me own in the house. As soon as you and Hetty leave, he'll take off his leather belt and pay me back in his usual way.'

Annie wasn't watching her husband but Ada was. And out of the corner of her eye, she saw him raise his arm. She quickly pulled Annie out of the way, and Tom's heavy blow missed its target. Then he became a raving lunatic. 'This is my bleeding house,' he screamed, 'and my bleeding wife. I am master of both, and can do as I bloody well like with both. So sling yer hook if yer know what's good for yer. If yer don't get out, and take yer mate with yer, then yer'll both be kicked out on yer arse.'

Ada ignored him. 'Get yer coat on, Annie, and come over to mine until yer dear husband has sobered up.'

157

'Oh, I can't do that, Ada,' Annie told her tearfully. 'I'll have to have a meal ready for when Jenny and Ben come in from work.'

'Yer can come back then,' Ada said quietly. 'I'm sure they won't mind dinner from the chippy for once. If they're anything like mine, they'll enjoy chips and scallops for a change.'

'Don't you bleeding well be telling my wife what to do.' Tom's voice and stance were threatening as he stood in front of Ada, and the veins standing out on his temples and neck told of the rage he had bottled up inside him. 'I'm the boss in this house, and what I say goes. Now sling yer bloody hook, yer nosy biddy, I've got some unfinished business to sort out with me wife.'

That was the deciding point for Annie. She'd taken punches, even the belt, for a quiet life. But she knew her husband's unfinished business would be carried out in the bedroom, and she couldn't face being humiliated and degraded. 'I'll get me coat on the way out, Ada. Let's go.'

Tom Phillips's jaw dropped and he looked stunned. His wife had never defied him before, she didn't dare, for she knew what her punishment would be if she stepped out of line. It was all the fault of that bitch from over the road. She was egging his wife on. He grabbed Annie's arm. 'Don't you walk out on me, yer stupid cow, or yer'll be sorry. Your place is here, looking after my needs, not listening to bloody women what have got nothing better to do. What d'yer think I pay yer for?'

But Annie closed her ears to his ranting. For the first time in her married life she didn't care any more. She slipped her arms into her coat, picked up her purse and keys, and followed Ada and Hetty out of the front door. She crossed the cobbles with the two women, and never once looked back. If she had, she would have had cause for concern. Tom Phillips had his face pressed to the window, and it was distorted with anger, while his eyes blazed with rage. How dare she walk out on him. She'd suffer for it, by God she would. She'd rue the day she disobeyed him, he'd make sure of that. And as for the two bitches over the road, they'd be sorry they ever encouraged her to walk out on him.

Tom watched until the three women entered the house opposite and the door was closed behind them. Then he let the curtain fall back into place and walked to the fireside chair. He was in a dark mood, and the blame was all laid on his wife's shoulders. Oh, the two biddies from opposite had encouraged her to defy him, but he was her husband and Annie had sworn to love and obey him. As far as he was concerned, that meant she was there to do his bidding. To satisfy his needs. And he'd come home early today to have those needs satisfied. He'd been looking forward to an hour or two of fun in the bedroom. Of seeing his wife squirm as she carried out the tasks he ordered her to do. All the way home his body had been getting excited at the thought of what was ahead. It wasn't love he felt, it was lust. And now his body was crying out for release as he squirmed in the chair. He tried to comfort himself by thinking she'd be home soon, and then he'd have some fun with her. He didn't doubt she'd come back in time to make dinner for Jenny and Ben. They were the aces up his sleeve, and he knew it. She loved them, and would do anything to keep the peace in the house so they wouldn't be upset. Yeah, she'd be back home soon to start their meal, and he could satisfy his urgent needs then. He'd leave the fun until later, when they went to bed. He could take as long as he liked to get his own back on her. All night if he wanted, and she wouldn't make a sound.

With the warmth from the fire, and the four pints of beer still having an effect, he soon became drowsy. And with thoughts running through his mind of the satisfaction he was going to get by teaching his wife a lesson, he went to sleep with a smirk on his face.

Jenny walked through the factory gates with two of her mates. They were going to the Rialto dance hall that night, and were coaxing her to go with them. 'Come on,' Barbara said, 'don't be so ruddy miserable. Yer'd enjoy it once yer made the effort. Me and Pat have a whale of a time, don't we, Pat? We're never short of partners.'

'It's all right for you two, yer can go and come home together,' Jenny told them. 'I'd be by meself, and I don't fancy going home in the dark on me own.'

'Yer wouldn't be on yer own for long,' Pat said, 'not with your face and figure. There'd be no shortage of fellers to take yer home. Yer could pick and choose.'

'I'll see what I feel like when I've had me dinner,' Jenny said. 'I'll leave yer here, so I can catch an earlier tram. It would give me more time to get ready if I feel like joining yer.' She began to run. 'I might see yer later. Ta-ra.'

There was a tram at the stop when Jenny turned the corner into the main road, and she sprinted for it. 'Yer just made it, lass,' the driver said. 'Got a heavy date, have yer?'

Jenny grinned. 'Yeah, with a hot dinner. Thanks for holding the tram for me.'

The driver turned the handle and the tram moved on. 'Ye're welcome, lass. Mind you, if yer'd been twenty years older, I might not have been so obliging.'

The conductor was coming down from the top deck, and he heard. 'I'm going to tell yer missus, Bert. Does she know yer've got an eye for a pretty girl?'

'She should do, smart lad, 'cos I married her and they don't come prettier than that.'

'Oh, ay, bragging, are yer?' The conductor laughed. 'Well, if we're boasting, I may as well tell yer that my wife's got a figure like Lana Turner. And figures don't come any better than that.'

Jenny was smiling as she took a seat near the front of the tram so she could be off quickly. If she felt like it after dinner, she might surprise her mates and turn up at the Rialto. It all hinged on whether Ben was going out, though. If he was, she'd stay in and keep her mother company.

It was dark when she ran up the entry, and she was glad when she was inside the back yard. She noticed there was no light on in the kitchen, but thought her mother must have the dinner ready and be keeping herself warm by the fire until she and Ben came in. But when she opened the kitchen door it felt strange. There was no smell of cooking, and none of the gas rings were lit. She walked into the living room expecting to see her mother, but sitting in the chair in front of the fire was her father. What was he doing home at this time? There was something wrong. Her mother not here when she should be, and her father sitting there as large as life when he shouldn't be. She didn't want to talk to her father, for he filled her with disgust, but it was unavoidable. 'Where's me mam? Is she upstairs?'

'No, she's gone to the chippy,' Tom growled. 'She'll be back in a minute.'

Alarm bells were ringing in Jenny's head as she slipped off her coat and put it over her arm. 'That's not like me mam. Are yer sure she's gone to the chip shop?'

Tom eyed her blossoming figure. She was a looker all right. Slim waist and firm breasts. 'That's what she told me. Hang yer coat up, she'll be here any minute.'

Jenny didn't believe him. The whole set-up was wrong. Her mother always had a dinner ready for them, she never went to the chip shop. But Jenny knew it was pointless to ask her father; she wouldn't get the truth out of him. So she walked to the hall to hang up her coat. She was stretching up to reach the hook, when she was pushed forward with force and pinned against the wall. Then a hand was pushed under each of her armpits, and cupped her breasts. It all happened so quickly she was unprepared, and although she tried to push her father back, she was no

160

match for his weight. She could hear him groan as he pressed his body into hers, and she could smell the stale beer as he breathed over her shoulder.

'Get off me, yer dirty, filthy thing. I'll scream if yer don't take yer filthy hands off me.' Jenny put all her strength into trying to push him back, but she couldn't move him. 'I'm warning yer, I'll scream the house down if yer don't get away from me.'

'No yer won't, my girl, 'cos yer wouldn't want to upset yer mother, would yer? Besides, I'm enjoying meself too much to back off. I bet you're enjoying yerself too, on the quiet. No one else has ever had their hands on these, have they?' He caressed each breast. 'Yer can tell yer mam if yer like, she can't do nowt about it. In fact yer can tell the whole street if yer like, it's no skin off my nose. My house, and my daughter. Who's to say yer didn't encourage me, eh?' His cackle sent shivers down Jenny's spine. 'Yeah, I'll tell them I was asleep in the chair and yer came and sat on me knee and put yer hand down me trousers.'

When Jenny felt the saliva from his mouth trickle on to her neck, she thought she was going to vomit. She'd always disliked the man who had fathered her, but right now she hated him with every fibre of her being. And her hatred spurred her into action. She managed to wriggle one of her arms free, and she bent her elbow so she could reach back and claw his face. She heard his cry of pain at the same time as the kitchen door opened, and she heard Ben's voice, followed by her mother's. 'Jenny, are yer upstairs, sweetheart?'

Tom Phillips moved back, a hand held to his cheek where Jenny had clawed it. 'Tell yer mother, and yer'll live to regret it,' he hissed. Then he fled silently up the stairs.

Jenny was trembling with shock, but she tried to pull herself together before walking into the living room. She wouldn't tell her mother because she knew how upset and hurt she'd be. And God knows, she had enough on her plate as it was. So pulling her jumper down, and forcing a smile to her face, Jenny walked into the living room. 'I was just hanging me coat up.' She kissed her mother's cheek. 'What's going on, Mam? I was worried to death when I came home and there was no sign of any dinner on the go, and no sign of you. Me dad was sitting in the chair, and when I asked him where yer were, he said yer'd gone to the chippy. Then he took himself off upstairs.'

'Is that all yer've seen of him?' Annie asked. 'Didn't he say anything to yer?'

Jenny shook her head. 'Only that yer'd gone to the chippy. What is going on, Mam? Has he been at yer again?'

161

Annie crossed the room to close the living room door. 'I'm sorry there's no dinner ready for yer. I've been standing at the bottom of the entry waiting to explain everything to yer, but yer must have been early getting home. Ben said he'd hang on and wait a bit longer, but it was cold for him to stand around, so I made him come with me. Which was lucky, for he could still be standing there.'

'Mam, what happened?' Jenny asked. 'It must have been something bad for yer to come and meet me and Ben. What's me dad been up to, and why is he home so early?'

'Sweetheart, today has been a nightmare. The worst day of me life.' Tears threatened and Annie's voice was husky. 'I'll tell yer the worst part quickly, then I'll explain the rest when we're walking down to the chippy. It's going to have to be fish and chips tonight, there's nothing else ready. And yer've got to have something to eat, yer must be starving.'

'What about me dad?' Ben asked. 'Are we bringing some back for him?'

'No, sweetheart, we're not. If yer dad is hungry, he can go out and get his own. I'll not be at yer father's beck and call any more. Just sit down and listen, while I tell yer what he did to me today.'

Chapter Fifteen

'I couldn't tell yer while Annie was here,' Ada told her husband as the family sat down to their dinner. 'It would have embarrassed her.'

'Why was she crying when we came in from school, Mam?' Paul asked. 'Had she hurt herself or something?'

'No, sunshine, she hadn't hurt herself.' Ada tried to tread carefully, reminding herself that little pigs have big ears, and Monica and Paul couldn't be trusted not to repeat to their friends what they'd heard. 'Her pride was hurt, that's all. She'd had a row with her husband and was a bit upset.'

Paul jerked his head back and his eyes went to the ceiling. 'That's daft that. A grown woman crying 'cos she fell out with her husband.'

Monica gave him a dig in the ribs. 'You don't have no sympathy for anyone, you don't. I felt sorry for Mrs Phillips, and I think she's a nice woman.'

'Had she been crying, love?' Jimmy asked, looking puzzled. 'I must admit I was little surprised to see her here, 'cos I didn't know yer were so friendly with her. Certainly not pally enough for her to come to you for a shoulder to cry on.'

'Me and Hetty are the only ones in the street she knows,' Ada told him. 'And I didn't mind her coming, she's a good, respectable woman.'

'Yes, she seems nice, Mam,' Danny said. 'But I thought she had a grown-up son and daughter? It's a wonder she wasn't home getting their dinner ready. After all, the row with her husband was probably no more than a slight difference of opinion. I bet as soon as she got in they kissed and made up.'

'I think it was more of a row than a spat, sunshine. The same as me and yer dad have rows now and again, but ours don't last long and are soon forgotten.' She raised her brows to her husband, and then her eldest son. And the look told them there was more to it, but she was not prepared to tell them in front of the children. 'Every family have the odd tiff, they wouldn't be normal if they didn't. And I don't want anything heard in this house to be broadcast in the street. Monica and Paul, did yer hear what I said?'

There was a look of disgust on Paul's face. 'Me and me mates have got more to talk about than some woman crying over nothing. But yer'd better tell our Monica to keep her trap shut. She's like all women, loves to gossip.'

Monica didn't answer with words, she answered with action. Paul yelped when she delivered a sharp jab in his ribs. 'You are the one with the big mouth, our Paul. It's so big, yer could get a football in it.'

Paul frowned as he sought to find an answer to that, but he couldn't think of one that would beat it. 'I've finished me dinner, Mam. Can I go out now? I promised me mate I'd go round for a game of snakes and ladders.'

'After yer've taken yer plate out and washed yer hands, then yer can go out.' Ada turned her eyes on her daughter. 'Are you going to Audrey's, sunshine?'

'I said I might, but I don't think I will 'cos it's freezing out.'

'If yer got well wrapped up yer wouldn't feel the cold.' Ada had been hoping both children would be going out so she could tell Jimmy and Danny the real story about what had happened in the house opposite. 'You and Paul take yer plates out, and I'll follow yer to the kitchen 'cos I want to have a word with yer.'

Paul was standing with his plate in his hand 'What about, Mam?'

'If I wanted yer dad and Danny to know what I have to say, then I wouldn't be wanting to do it in a freezing kitchen, would I, soft lad? Go on, on yer way. I'll follow yer out when I've finished eating me dinner.'

After waiting until she could hear the children squabbling about who should be first at the sink, Ada said in soft tones, 'There was murder over the road this afternoon, but I don't want the kids to hear, 'cos yer know what they're like for repeating things. I'll tell yer the tale when they've gone out.' She pushed her chair back and stood up. 'And what a tale it is, too! It'll make yer hair stand on end.'

As she walked towards the kitchen, Ada heard her husband's chortle as he said to Danny, 'Yer mam doesn't half like to exaggerate. Cut everything she says in half, and yer'll probably get somewhere near the truth.'

Ada turned. 'In that case I'd better make everything out to be twice as bad as it really was, so when yer cut it in half, yer'll end up with the truth.'

Paul was drying his hands on the piece of towelling hanging on a hook behind the kitchen door. 'The truth about what, Mam?'

Ada told him, 'That's for me to know, sunshine, and you to find out.' She closed the kitchen door before putting a finger to her lips. 'Keep yer voices down. Now, have yer forgotten it's Danny's birthday tomorrow?'

'We haven't forgotten, Mam,' Monica said. 'Me and Paul were talking about it last night. We've kept a penny of our pocket money to buy him a card, but we can't buy him a present 'cos we've no more money.'

'When ye're going out tonight, I'll come to the door with yer. I'll give yer sixpence each, that's all I can afford. But it's enough to buy him a little something to go with the card. Hankies, perhaps, a comb, or even a slab of chocolate. He'd be happy with any of those.'

The children were delighted, feeling very grown up. 'I'll get something on the way home from school tomorrow, Mam,' Monica said. 'And I'll ask the shop to put it in a nice bag.'

'We could club the money together,' Paul said, 'and that way we could buy him all three things. That would be good, wouldn't it, Mam?'

'Smashing idea, son. He'd be so happy he'd think it was his birthday.'

Paul opened his mouth to speak, then closed it quickly before he made a fool of himself. His mother was always quick off the mark with a joke. 'I'm ready to go out now, Mam, so yer won't forget to come to the door with me, will yer?'

'I've only got to dry me hands,' Monica said, 'so yer can hang on and wait for me. While we're walking down the street, we can decide what to buy Danny. And I hope ye're not going to be awkward, like yer usually are.'

'Well, I like that!' Paul's face was a picture of injured innocence. 'Just listen to Miss Goody Two-shoes.'

'Before there's any argument, let me tell yer that the money only comes if yer behave yerselves. So it's up to you.'

Monica jerked her head at her brother. 'Come on, Paul, let's put our coats on and get out before you say anything that costs me a tanner.'

Paul had his head bent as he followed his sister out of the kitchen, but under his breath he muttered, 'She's a right pain in the neck.'

Ada was behind him and heard. She tapped him on the shoulder. 'Yer must have been sitting in a draught, sunshine.'

Paul turned his head. 'What makes yer say that, Mam?'

'I heard yer saying yer had a pain in the neck.' Ada chuckled silently when her son went the colour of beetroot. 'Yer see, sunshine, yer never know who's walking behind yer, listening to what ye're saying.'

'It was only in fun, Mam. I didn't mean it.'

Ada bent to whisper in his ear. 'A certain person wouldn't have liked it. She'd have clocked yer one.'

Paul grinned up at her. 'I know that, Mam! What did yer think I whispered it for?'

Monica was standing by the front door with her coat on. 'Come on, slowcoach, it'll be time to come home before we get out.'

'Don't forget ye're to be in by half eight, Paul, no later.' Ada followed the two children to the door. 'And nine o'clock for you, Monica. I don't like you out on these dark nights.'

Both children promised to be in on time, and after seeing them off Ada returned to the living room rubbing her arms briskly. 'The best place is at home in front of the fire tonight. It's freezing out there.' She eyed Danny. 'If you go out, yer want yer bumps feeling.'

'Don't feel the cold when I'm dancing, Mam.' Danny's dimples deepened. 'I'd bc colder sitting in by the fire than I will be doing the quickstep.'

'Never mind the weather,' Jimmy said. 'What's this tale ye're going to tell us which will make our hair stand on end?'

Ada pulled her chair closer to the table and leaned her elbows on it. 'Before I start, Jimmy, I want yer to know this is not one of me make-up tales. If I never move off this chair, I swear every word out of me mouth will be true.'

'Before yer tell us what happened this afternoon, love,' Jimmy said, 'tell us first how yer came to be so friendly with Mrs Phillips.'

Ada glared at him. 'Who's telling this story, sunshine, you or me?'

'You are, love, but I like to get the full picture in me mind. Like how well did yer know her before today?'

Danny butted in. 'And I hope it's not going to be a long story, Mam, or I'll be late getting to Blair Hall.'

Ada took her elbows off the table and sat back in the chair. 'Sod the story! I've gone off telling yer now, so forget it.'

'Ah, ay, Mam, don't be like that,' Danny said. 'It was only a joke.'

'There's nothing bleeding funny about standing between a drunken man and his wife!' Ada sat forward again. 'Or being called a gasbag and told to get off me fat backside. Not only me, but Hetty as well. And he raised his fist to me face and said if I didn't want a taste of it, I should get me fat backside out of his bleeding house.'

The smile faded from Danny's face, while Jimmy put his knife and fork down. 'Is this Mrs Phillips's husband ye're talking about? Did he really swear at you and Hetty, and threaten yer with his fist?'

'He swore at both of us, but he didn't threaten to hit Hetty. Yer see, she didn't open her mouth, she was petrified when he started bawling and cursing at Annie. Yer should have heard the way he talks to his wife, he treats her like a piece of dirt. And I wasn't going to sit there and let any man hit a defenceless woman. Especially one as nice as Annie. So I stood up to him, and that's when he threatened to hit me.' Ada sighed as the memory came back. 'Anyway, I'll start from the beginning, and tell yer

166

what he's like.' Then she glanced at Danny. 'You don't have to stay in, sunshine, get yerself ready and go to the dance. Yer'll enjoy yerself more than listening to what I have to say about our new neighbour. I won't call him a man, it would be an insult to all the good men. He's an animal. So go ahead, Danny, get yerself washed and ready to go out and have some pleasure.'

'Not on your life! I'm not having some drunken bully threatening you! I'll listen to what yer've got to say, then I'll go over with me dad and have words with the blighter.'

Jimmy shook his head. 'No, I'll go over on me own, son. It wouldn't look good if the two of us went over.'

'Neither of yer are going over,' Ada told them firmly. 'Tom Phillips wouldn't take a blind bit of notice of yer. He'd been boozing, and was in a drunken rage. I'm not making excuses for him, 'cos I think he's pathetic. And a good beating is what he needs. But whatever yer did, Annie is the one who would suffer. Her and the two children.' Ada went on to tell them the whole story, and explained why Annie was there when they came home from work. She left nothing out, telling of the daily beatings and humiliation Tom Phillips put his wife through. And how she'd suffered in silence because of the two children. When she told how Jenny and Ben had saved Annie from a beating with his belt buckle, she heard both men gasp. Their tight faces told of their disgust and anger.

'He wants sorting out for once and for all. And it needs a man to do it. By the sound of things he's only a bully with his wife and children. Easy targets for him.' Jimmy snorted in anger. 'What sort of a life is it for two young people, who should be enjoying themselves?'

'A life of hell, that's what it is,' Ada answered. 'The boy, Ben, hasn't long left school, and his father gives him a dog's life. The poor kid only has to look sideways and he gets a belt. And according to Annie, life in the house would be ten times worse if it wasn't for her daughter, Jenny, who is beginning to face up to her father.'

She rubbed a finger over the pattern on the tablecloth. 'I feel heartily sorry for them, and Annie. She's a really nice person, and she deserves a damn sight better than to be living with a head case like Tom Phillips.' She looked up to say, 'D'yer know, Annie has had to up sticks every couple of years and move to another district? They've never stayed in one house for very long because of the queer feller. He picks fights with neighbours when he's been drinking, then they're hounded out of the street. He doesn't care, 'cos he knows Annie will find another house they can live in for a year or two. Neither Annie nor the children know what it is to have a proper home, with friends and neighbours. And Annie has never told a living soul, until today, what a hell their lives have been. Not even her parents or sisters, for she's too ashamed. Today was the first time she's opened up to anyone, and once I'd coaxed her a little, it all came tumbling out. She told us about the way Tom Phillips has treated her since the day they got married. And once she started getting it off her chest, she poured her heart out to me and Hetty. I don't know how I stopped meself from crying, but I kept telling meself it would make Annie worse if she thought I felt sorry for her.'

'Anyone that didn't feel sorry for her would have to be made of stone, love,' Jimmy said. 'I don't know the woman, or the kids, but I know that's no life for them. The man doesn't seem to have any feelings of love, or pride, for his family.'

Danny nodded his head. 'I know how yer feel, Mam, 'cos my blood is boiling. Like me dad said, he needs sorting out.'

'I haven't told yer the whole of it yet.' Ada sighed. 'How he punches her in bed every night, in her stomach, or the middle of her back. He seldom hits her anywhere where a bruise would show, he's too crafty for that. And he's laughing while he's doing it, 'cos he knows she won't cry out for she wouldn't want the kids to know and be upset. She's black and blue all over, from the neck down. To show she wasn't telling lies, she pulled the neck of her dress down, and there were bruises of all colours. When I saw them, I was so mad I'd have throttled him if I could have got my hands on him. I was sorry I hadn't clocked the sod when I had the chance.' Ada's nostrils were flared and her voice defiant. 'I'm really glad I made her come over here with me and Hetty. She didn't want to, I had to talk her into it. She felt she was being a nuisance, burdening us with her troubles. But if I'd left her there, he'd have battered her, I know he would. All because she was having two neighbours in for a cup of tea. Apparently he's never allowed that in all their married life. The miserable bugger doesn't think Annie should have any life of her own. She's there to look after him, be at his beck and call, not to make friends with the neighbours.'

'Why has she put up with it for so long?' Jimmy asked. 'Surely she should have gone to the police and reported him? A night in the cells might have knocked some sense into him. And the police would have ticked him off.'

Ada shook her head. 'It doesn't work like that, sunshine. Apparently some of the neighbours in several of the streets they've lived in have sent for the police when Tom Phillips has been rotten drunk and belting hell out of Annie and the kids. The police came, but they said they can't interfere between man and wife. They said it was a domestic issue, and they weren't allowed to get involved. It was against the law to interfere in a domestic row.'

'That's crazy!' Jimmy was shocked. 'If that's the case, then someone should alter the law. No man should be allowed to batter his wife and kids and get away with it.'

'I know that, love, the same as you. But, sadly, Tom Phillips knows he can do what he likes and no one will lift a finger to him.'

'If I ever meet him in a dark entry, Mam, I'll lift more than a finger to him.' Danny was really incensed that any man would hit his wife and children. He had never known any violence in his home, except for a slap on the backside when he was young and had given his mother cheek. It was the same with all his mates if they answered back. But punishment never went beyond that. 'If he was taught a lesson, it would force him to change his ways.'

Jimmy had been thoughtful while Danny was talking. Now he said, 'It's a wonder the Bowerses and the Bensons don't hear what's going on, living either side of the Phillipses. These walls are so thin yer can hear when anyone raises their voice.'

'I couldn't tell yer if they hear everything that goes on, 'cos yer know both families keep to themselves. But just after the Phillipses moved in, Edith did say she'd heard the father shouting and bawling. She said his language was terrible. Since then, though, she's never mentioned them. At the time, we put it down to the unheaval of moving house, and everything being at sixes and sevens.'

'It might be a good idea to put them wise, love, so they know what sort of man they're dealing with.'

Ada was shaking her head. 'Oh, I couldn't betray a confidence, sunshine, I'd never sleep at night if I did that. Annie would be mortified if she knew I'd been broadcasting her business. And she wouldn't think much of me as a friend.'

'Mam, I think me dad is right,' Danny said. 'If Mr Phillips is a heavy drinker, the time might come when he goes too far and really does Mrs Phillips an injury. Or even one of the children if they go to help their mam. If that happened, they'd be in need of help. And Gordon Bowers and Joe Benson are the kind of men who would want to help. They're the salt of the earth, both of them.'

Ada chuckled. 'I know this isn't the time for laughter, but I can't help it. In me mind, there's a picture of Tom Phillips's face when Gordon and Joe barge in. Especially Gordon, with him being six feet five inches in his stockinged feet. He'd put the fear of God into Annie's husband. And wouldn't I just love to be there to see that.'

'Ada,' Jimmy said, 'Gordon isn't a fighter.'

'I know that, sunshine, and you know that. But the brave Tom Phillips doesn't. And, oh, wouldn't I just love to be a fly on the wall when he's shaking in his shoes as his eyes travel the height of Gordon. Nothing would give me greater pleasure than to watch buggerlugs getting his comeuppance.' Ada tapped her fingers on the table. 'I won't mention anything to Jean or Edith until I've talked it over with Annie. I agree with yer that it would be wise to warn them in case of emergency, but it's not my place to say anything until I've had a good talk to Annie. Me and Hetty are the only friends she's got in the street, and I don't want to turn her against us. I'll just take it slowly, and mention it in the course of conversation. I won't make a big deal out of it, 'cos I don't want to frighten her off.'

She looked up at the clock on the mantelpiece. 'It's too late for yer to go dancing now, sunshine, so how about having a game of cards with me and yer dad? It's not often we have the pleasure of yer company in the evenings, so it will make a nice change. We'd get a game in before Monica and Paul come home.' She grinned across at her son. 'I'd ask yer to have a dance with me, Danny, so yer didn't have withdrawal symptoms. But I don't think I'm up to your standard. Besides, the room isn't big enough for the twirls yer keep telling me about.'

As Danny was getting the cards out of a drawer in the sideboard, he bent to kiss Ada's cheek. 'It would be my pleasure, Mam, to dance with the prettiest woman in the dance hall.'

'Flattery will get yer everywhere.' Ada smiled at him. 'Yer dad is very mean with his compliments. He never tells me I'm pretty.'

'I don't need to, love, the mirror will tell yer that. That's why I don't say much. If me and the mirror both paid yer compliments, yer'd end up big-headed. And yer don't want that to happen, do yer? So really, I'm doing yer a favour.'

'Oh, that's it, is it, sunshine? Well, I'll be eternally grateful for yer thoughtfulness.'

Danny sat down with the pack of cards in his hand. 'Is it rummy we're playing?'

'It's the only game I know,' Ada told him. 'And I'm not very good at that.'

'Are we playing for money?'

'Ay, what d'yer think I am?' Ada asked. 'I'm not made of money, and if I lost some, there'd be nowt for yer dinners tomorrow.'

Danny raised his brows. 'A penny a game, Mam? That won't skint yer, surely?'

'Oh, okay, I don't suppose that will skint me. But if I win, don't expect me to spend me winnings on cream cakes for yer.'

There was much laughter round the table as Danny tried to pass a card to his mother under the cover of the chenille cloth. Then Jimmy tried to cheat by picking two cards from the pack instead of one. Ada was the biggest cheat, though, because she pretended to be a novice at the game, when in fact she was just the opposite, since she and Hetty often had a game in the afternoon if it was raining and not fit to walk round the shops.

'Hurry up, love,' Jimmy said. 'Throw one of the cards away.'

Ada took a few seconds to take stock of the cards in her hand. Then, keeping her face straight, she threw one of the cards on the table before laying down her full hand. 'I think I've won. Will yer check for me to make sure, before yer hand me winnings over?'

The two men gaped in surprise. 'I thought yer didn't know how to play the game, Mam!' Danny said. 'How come yer won?'

'I never said I couldn't play the game, sunshine, did I? I could have put me cards down ages ago, but I was watching you and yer dad. Both of yer cheated, but I couldn't quite make out who was the best at sleight of hand. And yer dad won by a mile. He's so quick, yer can hardly see his hand move.'

Jimmy put on a hurt expression. 'Ah, that's not fair, love. And it's not true, either. For if I'm as quick as yer say I am, how come you won the game?'

'Through practice, sunshine. I'll let yer into a secret, but yer must never tell Arthur, 'cos I don't want to get Hetty into trouble. Yer see, there's a woman lives in the next street what runs a card school. And me and Hetty go there three times a week.' Ada was making it up as she went along. 'And I never come away without a few extra coppers in me purse. Hetty's getting good at it, too. She won twice last week.'

Jimmy and Danny stared, disbelief written on their faces. They were still drinking it in when Ada asked, 'D'yer know the funniest part about it? Well, it's looking at your two faces now. Yer both fell for it, hook, line and sinker.'

Jimmy was the first to recover. 'I wasn't taken in for a minute, love. I knew yer were having us on.'

'Yeah,' Danny said, 'me too! I knew right away yer were kidding, 'cos ye're not the type to waste yer money on gambling.'

Ada shook her head slowly. 'I can't quite make up me mind whether ye're better at cheating or telling fibs. But whatever it is, it doesn't make any difference to the fact my cards were down on the table, face up, first. And as I believe that makes me the winner, then kindly pass yer pennies over. And I don't want any buttons or foreign coins, either.'

While Jimmy put his hand in his trouser pocket to root a coin out, Danny passed over a silver sixpence. 'That's for you to buy three cream cakes with, Mam. For you and Auntie Hetty, and Mrs Phillips.'

Ada waved it away. 'I don't want money off yer, don't be daft. Put it back in yer pocket, sunshine. And you, Jimmy, leave the penny in yer pocket. It was only a game of cards for heaven's sake, and it was a good laugh, I enjoyed meself.'

Danny pushed the silver coin back across the table. 'I enjoyed meself, too, Mam. And that sixpence would have gone in the dance hall, so I'm no worse off.'

Ada had a smile on her face as she picked up the coin. 'Well, sunshine, if yer put it like that. And I thank yer on behalf of meself and Hetty, and Mrs Phillips. We'll toast yer with our cups of tea.'

Chapter Sixteen

There was a queue in the chip shop, but Annie and the children didn't mind, for it was nice and warm. 'I love the smell of fish and chips,' Jenny said. 'It always makes me feel hungry.' Then she thought of how much it would cost for three fish, and knew her mother couldn't afford to fork so much out. 'But me favourite are scallops, so can we have a few with our chips, Mam?'

'Of course yer can, sweetheart.' Annie's smile was forced. She was putting a brave face on for the sake of the children, but inside she was full of apprehension. Tom Phillips wouldn't let her get away with what she'd done today, and she feared what he had in store for her. But no matter what it was, she wasn't going to allow him to treat her the way he had for nearly twenty years. Blows she could cope with. But the humiliation she'd suffered in the bedroom, that was a thing of the past. She was determined that would never, ever happen again. And she'd put her foot down with him when it came to Ben. If the lad didn't want to go out at the same time as his father every morning, then she'd make sure he wasn't forced to.

Annie sighed as they moved a step nearer to the counter. Brave words were easy when they were in your head. It wasn't so easy when you had a violent drunk in front of you, determined you were going to do as he said. But she'd made a vow to herself that no longer would she be afraid of telling people that her husband was a drunkard who lashed out at his wife and children. That he used his fists instead of kind words. And he cared for no one except himself. She'd unburdened herself to Ada and Hetty, and she felt a lot better for it. They didn't back off from her like other folk had over the years. They were sympathetic and understanding. And they'd listened without laying the blame at her door for being so weak. She'd been truly blessed finding friends like Ada Fenwick and Hetty Watson.

'Only two more in front of us now, Mam,' Jenny said. 'It's a pity we can't eat them in here, where it's warm. I don't fancy eating them in front of me dad. One look at his face would put me off them.'

'We could stand in a shop doorway and eat them.' Ben thought he'd choke if he had to eat with his father glaring at them with hatred in his eyes. 'Let's eat them out of the paper. They'll be red hot, so they'd keep us warm.'

'We'll see,' Annie said, shuffling forward. 'But I think a shop doorway would be preferable to yer father's temper.'

Then it was her turn at the counter. The man behind it was the only person in the shop who didn't have a red nose from being out in the cold. He'd been run off his feet for two solid hours, and was roasting. 'Yes, missus, what can I do for yer?'

'A pennyworth of chips and a pennyworth of scallops, three times, please. And I'd be very grateful if yer would put salt and vinegar on, and wrap them up separately in two lots of paper so they'll stay hot until we get home.'

The man, whose name was Walter, was turning the chips over in the hot fat. 'Blimey, missus, yer wouldn't want me to eat them for yer as well, would yer?'

Even though Jenny knew the man didn't mean to be sarcastic, she took umbrage on behalf of her mother. 'We're quite capable of eating them ourselves,' she told him. 'We even know how to use a knife and fork.'

The man looked put out. 'It was only a joke, love.'

'I'll forgive yer,' Jenny said, 'but yer can give us an extra chip for being so cheeky.'

'Seeing as ye're a pretty girl, yer can have two.'

'Me mam is pretty, too,' Jenny said, smiling. 'And me kid brother is handsome.'

'What about yer next-door neighbours?' Walter tipped the chips from the hot fat into the next container and winked at Jenny. 'And haven't yer got a grandma what is pretty?'

A man standing behind the Phillipses shuffled his feet. 'Before yer go through all her ancestors, would yer mind serving a man who isn't pretty, but who is nearly ruddy well starving with hunger?'

Walter moved like lightning then. He shovelled fresh chips on to a piece of greaseproof paper, laid three scallops on top, then wrapped them in double sheets of newspaper. He repeated the performance twice, then passed the three parcels over and held his hand out for the sixpence Annie had ready to give him. 'Run home and eat them in front of a roaring fire, girl, and they'll taste a treat.'

Annie took the parcels and thanked him, but inside she was wishing she could do as he said. If he only knew. Outside the shop, she passed over the children's share and said, 'Well, would yer rather eat them in a shop doorway, or take a chance on yer father being home when we get there?'

The children answered as one. 'A shop doorway, Mam.'

'There's every likelihood he'll be propping the bar up in the pub,' Annie said. 'I'll kick meself for standing in a freezing cold shop doorway if I get home to find the house empty.' There was steam rising from the parcels, and the smell of chips was irresistible. 'In the chandler's doorway, kids, it's the nearest. I didn't realise I was hungry, but the smell is making me tummy rumble.'

They tore some of the newspaper to make a hole, and each of them picked out a chip. 'Oh, boy, I'm not half going to enjoy these,' Ben said. 'Chips always taste better when yer eat them out of a newspaper. He's put loads of vinegar on, too. They taste great.'

'Ye're not kidding,' Jenny said. 'They're a treat.'

'Enjoy them, sweetheart, 'cos we might be in for a rough ride when we get home. Yer father's not going to let me get away with walking out on him. Especially going against him in front of neighbours. He didn't like that one little bit. His pride was dented, and I could see by the look in his eyes he was in a blazing temper. In fact, if looks could kill, I'd have been dead before I got out of the front door.'

'It would have been far worse for yer if Mrs Fenwick and Mrs Watson hadn't been there,' Jenny said, before blowing on a chip. 'If yer'd been on yer own, heaven only knows what he'd have done to yer for hitting back at him last night. He'd have battered the daylights out of yer.'

'He'll have it in for us, as well,' Ben said, picking out a scallop from the opening in the newspaper. 'I'm dreading going out with him in the morning, 'cos I know I'll get a clip round the ear before we get to the bottom of the street.'

'No, yer won't, son,' Annie told him. 'Ye're not going out at the same time as him in the morning, or any other morning for that matter. I'd made my mind up about that earlier on. Yer leave the house fifteen minutes after him, and that's definite. If he kicks up a stink, then let him. There's three of us, and only one of him. His days of ruling the roost are over. I don't care if he knocks hell out of me, I'm going to do as I like in future. If I want to have friends in, then I'll have them in. And if I'm invited to their houses, I'll be delighted to go. Having good friends is worth a few clouts.'

'If I get a chance, I'm going over to see Mrs Fenwick, to thank her,' Jenny said, waving a long chip in the direction of her mouth. 'It was good of her and Mrs Watson to stand up to me dad. He'd have put the fear of God into most women, and they'd have run out of the house as though the devil was chasing them.'

Annie nodded. 'Ye're right, sweetheart. I expected them to do that when yer dad started on them. I thought they'd be out of the door sharpish, and I'd never set eyes on them again. And I can't say I'd have blamed them. They've made me take stock of meself, as well. The way Ada Fenwick stood in front of yer dad without a flicker of fear was a lesson to me. That's how I should have been with him since the day we got married. I should have been stronger, and stuck up for meself. That, or walked out of the door and left him swinging. I did think of that several times in the first few months of our marriage, but I never had the guts to face me parents and tell them what was going on. I know they'd have taken me back with open arms, and me dad would have gone round to sort out the rotter I'd married. But me pride wouldn't let me. I kept telling meself, like a silly nit, that I'd made me bed and now I had to lie on it.'

'It's no good raking up the last twenty years, Mam,' Jenny told her. 'It's over and done with. What yer have to concentrate on is the future. How much more are yer going to put up with from me dad?' She felt in the paper to see if there were any chips hiding in the folds, then, clicking her tongue in disappointment, she screwed it up into a ball. 'He's not right in the head, yer know, Mam. I bet Mrs Fenwick's husband doesn't treat her like a piece of dirt.'

Annie managed a smile. 'He wouldn't be allowed to, sweetheart. Ada wouldn't put up with it. But from what I've heard and seen, they're very happy together. In fact all the family are happy, and there's a lovely warm feeling in the house.'

'It's like that when I go round to me mate's,' Ben said. 'They're always laughing and joking. I go round there nearly every night, but I wouldn't ask him round to ours in case me dad took off on him. And it's not fair. I should be able to ask me friends round without having to worry about them being insulted or thrown out.'

'I can't promise yer anything, son, 'cos I won't make a promise I know I might not be able to keep. But I'll do my best to make a better life for all of us. I feel more able to stand up to Tom now, thanks to Ada Fenwick. And, please God, if her and Hetty still want me for a friend, then I won't feel so alone with them to talk to. I can honestly say, that out of all the houses we've lived in, and all the neighbours who have shunned us because of the antics of yer father, this house is going to be lucky for us.'

Jenny took her mother's chip paper and screwed it up with Ben's and her own. 'I hope ye're right, Mam. I'm seventeen years of age, and I've lived in about ten or eleven houses. I've never been in a street long enough to make a friend.' A bitter tone came into her voice. 'I don't have anything to thank my father for. I know we're supposed to love and respect our parents, but I have no love, or respect, for my father.' She shivered as she remembered the feel of his grasping hands on her breasts. She'd never forget what he did, and never forgive him. 'I love you to bits, Mam, and our Ben. But for my father I feel only disgust and anger.'

She paused and took a deep breath to calm herself down. 'When I'm lying in bed at night, waiting to drop off to sleep, my mind often goes back to when me and Ben were little. And I think of all those wasted years. We never had a normal childhood. Never knew what it was like to have a father who laughed and played with us. Never gave us a hug or a kiss, or told us he loved us. He never even gave us a ha'penny for sweets. We never looked forward to him coming home from work, didn't run to meet him like other kids in the street ran to meet theirs. We dreaded the sight of him. He wasn't like a father . . . more like a bogeyman, come to frighten us. And he did frighten us, Mam. I can remember how I used to shake with fear.'

There were tears in Annie's eyes as she opened her arms and gathered her beloved children to her. 'I am so sorry, sweethearts, so very sorry. I'm more to blame than yer dad, because I've been a coward and let him get away with his shenanigans. As yer mother, I should have done more to protect yer. I did me best, but me best wasn't good enough. I'm a pathetic excuse for a mother, and I'm ashamed.'

'No, Mam, don't blame yerself.' Jenny kissed her mother's tear-stained cheek. 'I can remember enough of my childhood to know that many's the time you stood in front of me and Ben, and took the blows aimed at us. Yer've been a good mother, we couldn't ask for better. But I have to say yer must have had yer eyes closed the first night yer met me dad and made a date with him.'

Ben was telling himself he mustn't cry, he wasn't a baby any more. And he tried hard to swallow the lump in his throat before saying, 'Yeah, yer did look after us, Mam. I can remember me dad belting yer 'cos yer wouldn't let him get near us. It's him what spoils things for us, not you.'

Giving a long drawn out sigh, Annie dropped her arms. 'Those chips and scallops were very nice, but more good will come from us getting everything off our chests. We've aired our feelings, and we'll feel better for it. From now on, with your help, we'll make life a damn sight better than it's been. If we pull together, we can do it. I know we can. I've had me eyes opened, and taken stock of meself. And that's all down to Ada Fenwick.'

Jenny hugged her mother. 'She's been good for you, Mam, 'cos yer look and sound a lot more optimistic. And if me dad's not in when we get home, I'm going across to knock on Mrs Fenwick's door and thank her.'

Annie looked a bit uncertain as the three came out of the shop doorway and turned towards home. 'Ada might not feel like a visitor at this time of night, sweetheart. Leave it for another day.'

'Never put off till tomorrow what yer can do today. That's what they say, Mam. And I wouldn't go in the house, anyway, I'll speak to her at the door. Just for a few minutes, to thank her for what she did this afternoon. And I also want her to know that the rest of the family are not like me dad.'

'What if me dad's in?' Ben asked. 'If he is, he'll be in a terrible temper knowing we've had something to eat, and he hasn't.'

'Don't worry, I'll not go out if he's in the house.'

When the knock came on the door, Danny jumped to his feet. 'I'll go, Mam, it'll only be our Monica or Paul.'

'I'll put the kettle on to make a hot drink for them,' Ada said. 'They'll probably come in shivering with the cold.'

Danny's lips were puckered in a whistle when he opened the door. He was expecting his sister or brother, and his whistle was cut off as he gazed at the young girl standing looking up at him. He was quick to note that she looked as surprised as he was.

'Is Mrs Fenwick in, please?' Jenny was wishing the ground would swallow her up. She didn't want to discuss her father in front of anyone, she'd be too ashamed. 'Could I speak to her for a minute?'

'Of course yer can.' Danny opened the door wide and the light from the living room allowed him to see that the girl he was looking at was very pretty. 'She's just putting the kettle on. Come in out of the cold.'

'No, I won't come in, thank you. I don't want to disturb Mrs Fenwick if she's busy. I'll leave it until another time.'

'Nonsense! Come on in,' Danny insisted. 'Me mam would clip me round the ear if I didn't act like a thorough gentleman and invite yer in. Besides, she's not busy really. When we heard the knock, we expected it to be either me kid brother or me sister. And because me mam thought they'd come in shivering with the cold, she wanted to make a hot drink for them.' He stepped down and took her arm. 'If yer don't want me to get a thick ear, then yer'll come in. I'm sure me mam will be happy to see yer. She's been stuck with me and me dad for the last few hours, so I'm sure she'll welcome seeing another female.'

Before Jenny could think of a good excuse not to enter the house, she found herself standing in the hall. Then Danny was closing the front door while calling through to the living room, 'Yer've got a visitor, Mam.'

Ada's voice came back. 'If it's that nuisance from next door, tell her I'm in bed asleep. I've had enough of her company for one day.'

'It's not Auntie Hetty, Mam, so wake up. I can't announce the visitor, 'cos she's a stranger to me. She wanted to have a word with yer at the front door, but I told her ye're too fragile to stand talking at the door. And I can't get her to move into the living room. I think her shoes must be stuck to the floor.'

'In the name of God, Danny, will yer stop acting daft and close the door. I'm getting blown off me ruddy feet here. It's too cold for one of yer jokes.'

Danny was chuckling as he pulled gently on Jenny's arm. 'Here she is, Mam. It wasn't one of me jokes, yer see.'

Ada was astonished to say the least. But it wasn't long before recognition dawned. 'Hello, sunshine. Ye're Jenny, aren't yer?'

Jenny nodded. 'I'm sorry to bother yer, Mrs Fenwick. I didn't want to come in, but yer son was rather insistent. He said yer'd give him a thick ear if he kept me standing on the step. I only intended to introduce meself to yer, at the door, then leave yer in peace.' She was backing out as she spoke, but Danny was standing behind her, and she trod on his foot. 'I'm sorry, I didn't know yer were behind me.'

Ada could see the girl was embarrassed and agitated. 'Don't worry about Danny, sunshine, he's used to getting his feet trodden on. But it's usually in a quickstep, waltz or fandango.' She patted the chair next to her. 'Come and sit down, love, and have a cup of tea with us. It's just been made, so it's piping hot.'

'No, thank you, I'll get back home.' Jenny was sorry she hadn't taken her mother's advice and left her visit for another night. 'It's late to be calling on people, me mam did tell me that, and I should have listened to her. So I'll leave yer to get yer cup of tea in peace, and see yer again some time.'

Jimmy had been watching with interest. He'd never seen the girl before, but as he studied her, he made the connection. It was the mass of auburn hair that did it. He clicked his thumb and forefinger. 'Ye're Annie's daughter!'

Ada clapped her hands. 'Very good, sunshine, yer can go to the top of the class. How did yer know?'

Her husband was feeling pleased with himself. 'It was the hair at first, then I could see the resemblance. Same shaped cheekbones, and nose.'

Jenny could feel herself blushing. She wouldn't have been so shy if Danny hadn't been there. But she knew he and Mr Fenwick had come home from work to find her mother there. They'd heard what a rotter her father was, how he was a drunkard who beat his wife and children. And the little voice in her head which was telling her it wasn't her fault didn't

179

stop her from being ashamed. 'I'll get back home, Mrs Fenwick. Me mam told me not to stay long.'

Ada's heart went out to the girl. What sort of life was it for her? She was a lovely-looking girl, and she should be walking tall, enjoying the good things in life. 'Never let it be said that any visitor left this house without being given a cup of tea. If word got around, I'd be the talk of the neighbourhood. So sit yerself down, sunshine, and Danny will do the honours with the teapot.' She took the girl's hand and pulled her down on to the chair next to hers. 'I always enjoy a cup of tea when our Danny pours it out. I don't know why, but it seems to have a special taste to it.'

Danny adored his mother, and usually when she asked him to do anything he would jump to it. But he was reluctant tonight, for he wanted to make friends with the girl from number twenty-two. He'd seen the outline of her through the window, but hadn't ever seen her outside the house. Now he had, and he wanted to find out more about her. 'Why can't me dad pour out for a change?' He gave his father a knowing, conspiratorial wink. 'I'm sure any tea he poured out would be twice as sweet as mine.'

Jimmy took the hint. Pushing his chair back, he grinned at Jenny. 'Even though I say it meself, I pour out a mean cup of tea. You would be very foolish to turn it down. Now, do yer take milk and sugar?'

His smile did wonders for the girl's nerves. She couldn't help but smile back. 'A little milk and one sugar, please.'

Ada was intrigued by the girl's visit, and wanted to know the reason for it. And she knew she wouldn't get much out of Jenny with Danny sitting across from her. 'Give yer dad a hand with the cups, sunshine.'

'Ah, ay, Mam! Me dad doesn't need me to hold his hand, he's a big man.'

Ada nodded. 'Yeah, yer dad is a big man, and he's a very clever man. But he's not ruddy well clever enough to carry in four cups of hot tea! He's only got two hands, and he'd be grateful for the loan of your two. So out yer go, and don't forget to take yer hands with yer.'

She waited until her son was in the kitchen, and she could hear him talking to his dad. Then she spoke softly. 'Was it anything special yer wanted to see me about, sunshine?'

Her eyes on the kitchen door, Jenny whispered back, 'Not really, Mrs Fenwick, and I'm sorry I've interrupted yer evening. I just wanted to thank yer for being so kind to me mam this afternoon. She told me what happened, and how good you and Mrs Watson were, and I want yer to know how grateful me and me brother are. We love the bones of our mam, but we can't be here all the time with her. She has a terrible life with me dad, but she never complains. He's a bully, my father. A coward, a drunkard, and a bully. I don't think I've ever seen him smile once in me whole life. He sneers and snarls, but there's never a real smile. And his language is disgusting. How me mam ever came to marry him, I'll never know. She deserves much better.' The sound of cups being placed on saucers had Jenny putting a finger to her lips. 'I won't say any more, but I thank you from the bottom of my heart. In the short time me mam's known you and Mrs Watson, she seems to be stronger. And I'm so happy knowing she has friends she can talk to – we've never lived in the same place long enough for her to make any before.'

'Don't you worry, sunshine, me and Hetty will keep an eye out for yer mam. The one thing I can't abide is a man hitting a woman. I've drummed it into Annie that if she ever needs help, then me and Hetty are here for her. And if she needs a bolt-hole, our doors are always open. That also goes for you and Ben. There'll always be a welcome here for yer.'

Jenny gripped her arm and whispered, 'Thank you,' just as Danny kicked the kitchen door open and walked through with a cup and saucer in each hand.

'I don't know, you women have an easy life.' He placed a cup of tea in front of them, his smile wide and his dimples deep. 'Waited on hand and foot.'

'And that's the way it should be, sunshine.' Ada reached up to pat his cheek, her eyes tender with love for her eldest born. 'I'll swap places with yer if yer like? I'll go out to work every morning, and you stay home and do the washing, ironing, cleaning, shopping and cooking. Would yer like to swap?'

'I'm not soft, Mam, I know when I'm on to a good thing.' Danny sat down facing Jenny. 'I couldn't find a biscuit anywhere, sorry. Me mam and her mate have got a very sweet tooth. As well as cream slices, they've always got their hand in the biscuit tin.'

Jimmy came in carrying cups of tea for himself and Danny. 'Ay, have yer seen the time, Ada? The kids are out late, aren't they? They should be well home by now.'

'They're probably in the middle of a game of ludo, or snakes and ladders. Yer can't expect them to leave off in the middle of a game. They'll be along any minute.'

'If they're not in by the time I've drunk me tea,' Danny said, 'I'll go and look for them.'

'They'll be in before yer've had time to drink yer tea,' Ada told him. 'And they won't come to any harm, they're only in the next street.'

But when there was no sign of Monica or Paul fifteen minutes later, Ada began to get worried. 'I'll break their necks for them when they get in. Worrying the life out of me like this.'

Danny was grinning as he pushed his chair back. 'I'll go and get them. I know where their friends live, so it'll only take me ten minutes.' He leaned across the table and put his face close to Ada's. 'I won't tell them they're coming home to get their necks broken, Mam, it might just put them off.'

'Go and get them, soft lad, before me hair turns white with worry.'

Jenny stood up. 'I'd better be going, too. Me mam will think I've left home.'

Danny's dimples appeared. 'I'll walk yer home.'

'I only live in the house facing. I can see meself home.'

Danny put a hand to his forehead. 'Did yer hear that, Mam? I've been turned down!'

'Serves yer right, bighead. Now get going and find my two children.'

Outside the front door, Danny cupped Jenny's elbow. 'Whether yer can see yerself home or not, I'll never let it be said that Danny Fenwick left a girl to walk home on her own.'

'You're daft, you are,' Jenny said. 'I can reach our house in ten strides.'

'Talking about strides, Jenny,' Danny said, 'can yer dance?'

She bit on her bottom lip to keep herself from laughing. 'That's a secret. Now go and look for yer brother and sister so yer can put yer mother's mind at rest.'

'Yeah, I better had. Yer can let me into yer secret next time I see yer.'

'What secret is that?'

'The one about whether yer like a slow foxtrot best, or a waltz.'

'Goodnight, Danny.' Jenny let herself into the house with a smile on her face, and calling, 'It's only me, Mam.'

Chapter Seventeen

'Me and Ben thought yer'd left home, sweetheart.' Annie smiled at her daughter. 'Yer said yer'd only be five minutes.' She saw Jenny's eyes dart to the kitchen, and was quick to put her mind at rest. 'It's all right, sweetheart, there's only me and Ben here. We haven't seen hide nor hair of yer father. He's probably in the pub, and will stay there until throwing out time. That means he'll have had a bellyful of ale and be roaring drunk. So it would be wise for us to be in bed before he gets home.'

Jenny hung her coat up and moved towards the fire, rubbing her hands. 'Are yer sleeping with me again tonight? I think yer better had. If me dad hasn't had anything to eat, he'll have been mad before he went to the pub. So yer can imagine what he'll be like after a few pints of beer. He'll be like a raging bull, and we wouldn't be able to handle him.'

Annie bent forward to put the poker between the bars of the grate. The fire was dying down, but she couldn't afford to be putting more coal on at this time of night. So she lifted the dying embers, hoping for a warm glow to cheer them up. 'We've got half an hour before the pub shuts, so tell us why yer were so long over the road. Me and Ben are curious.'

'Well, I thought Mrs Fenwick would open the door, and was just going to thank her for helping yer today. But her son, Danny, came to the door, and although I asked him if I could speak to his mam for a minute, he would have it that I went in. In fact, he said if his mam knew he was keeping someone standing on the step, she'd give him a thick ear.'

Annie chuckled. 'That sounds like Danny, from what I've heard about him. But I was led to believe he goes out dancing every night.'

'He mentioned dancing.' Jenny smiled. 'He's not half funny. He was going out to bring Mrs Fenwick's two other children home, 'cos it was getting late for them. And he insisted on walking me home! I told him he was daft, that I only lived about ten strides away, but he said he would never let a girl walk home on her own.' When she giggled at the memory, her mother and brother laughed with her. It was strange to hear the sound of laughter in the house. 'It was then he asked me if I could dance.'

'Ooh, he must have taken a fancy to yer, sweetheart, to ask that.'

Ben leaned forward with interest in his eyes. 'What did yer say to that, our Jenny?'

'I told him it was a secret, that's all.' Jenny changed the subject. 'I was shy at first, Mam, but Mr and Mrs Fenwick are so easy to get on with, I soon felt at home. And they made me have a cup of tea, which Mr Fenwick and Danny made. Not that they wanted to make it, they were ordered. They get on really well together, and yer can tell by the atmosphere that it's a warm, happy home. They're not sloppy, but yer can almost feel the love in the room. Not like here, when me dad's in. We can't laugh and joke in case it offends him, and we never know when he's going to lash out at us. You in particular, Mam, he picks on you for the least thing. I can't picture Mr Fenwick beating his wife, he's so easy-going.'

'Ada wouldn't stand for it, sweetheart. She's got more guts than me.'

'Mam, having guts doesn't come into it over there. You need them here, because me dad is a madman. But not in the house over the road. They're a loving family, and yer can feel it as soon as yer walk in the door.'

Ben lifted his hand. 'Hush, I think I can hear me dad.' There was silence for a few seconds, then the boy jumped to his feet. 'It is me dad, and he's shouting in the street.'

Annie's hand went to her throat. 'Oh, my God, he's rotten drunk. He'll make a holy show of us.' She reached to pull the chain at the side of the gas light and the room was plunged into darkness. 'Up the stairs, quick, before he comes in. We can't stop him making a show of us, but we can protect ourselves by keeping out of his way. With a bit of luck he'll be too drunk to climb the stairs. Hurry up, sweethearts, I couldn't stand another fight with yer dad.'

The three huddled together in Jenny's small bedroom, and they listened for the key turning in the lock. But the noise came from outside in the street. And it was the sound of Tom Phillips shouting at the top of his voice. What he was shouting didn't make sense, except for the obscenities. And then came the angry voices of neighbours who had been brought out by the row. It was too much for Annie, who covered her ears with her hands. 'I'll not be able to show me face in the street after this. What have I ever done to him that he makes my life a hell?'

Jenny put an arm around her mother's shoulders. 'Sit on the bed, Mam, and I'll go and bring me dad in.'

Ben was quick to side with his sister. 'Go on, Mam, me and Jenny will get him in.'

Annie shook her head. 'I'll not let me children fight me battles for me. I married him, fool that I was, and he's my burden, not yours.'

* * *

184

Across the street, Ada pulled the curtain aside. 'Just listen to the language out of him. He's got half the street out.'

Danny stood behind her. 'Is that Jenny's dad making that racket? I thought Mrs Phillips was exaggerating, but she certainly wasn't.' He turned to his father. 'Can yer hear him, Dad? He's blind drunk. It's a wonder he can stand up straight.'

'I can hear him all right. The whole neighbourhood must be able to hear him. Why doesn't he go in and sleep it off, instead of making a racket?'

Ada turned her head from the window. 'Why doesn't he do a lot of things? Like stop beating his wife and children. Why doesn't he behave like a man who appreciates he has a wonderful family? And, most of all, why doesn't he love them?'

As Ada turned back to the window, she saw the door opposite open, and Annie stepped into the street, followed by Jenny and Ben. 'Oh, my God, she can't handle him, not the state he's in. I'm going out there, and so help me I'll clock him one.'

Jimmy shook his head. 'You'll stay right where yer are, love, and me and Danny will sort the queer feller out. We'll send Annie and the kids inside, then we'll throw him in and he can sleep it off on the floor.'

But Ada wasn't having that. 'I'll come with yer to see to Annie and the kids. I won't get involved in fisticuffs, I promise.' Then, as she was slipping her coat on, she added, 'Unless he hits me, like, 'cos then I'd have to hit him back.'

When Jenny saw Danny crossing the cobbles, she felt like hiding her head in shame. And the hate she felt for her father grew. She tried to take hold of one of his arms, but he was waving them about like a madman. With tears threatening, she said, 'We can manage him.'

'Yer can't manage him.' Danny pushed her gently towards the front door. 'Go inside with yer mam and brother, we'll see to yer dad. And don't worry about the neighbours, they'll go back in their houses when Mr Phillips is inside.'

'Danny's right,' Ada said. 'Take yer mam and Ben into the house. Jimmy and Danny will soon have yer dad sorted. I'll come in after yer, to make sure yer mam's all right.' She watched Jenny leading Annie inside the house, then turned to where Tom Phillips was wrestling with Jimmy and Danny. There were a few neighbours standing near, but they weren't shouting any more, they were staying out of interest, to see what the outcome would be. It would be the talk of the street in the morning, and they wanted to be able to say they'd been there, and to add their little bit of spice to what was said. And they were glad they had stayed when Ada

185

added a piece of unexpected excitement. Standing in front of the man struggling with her husband and son, she curled her fists. Her right went to his stomach with some force, which had him gasping, and her left caught him on the jaw. Then she dusted her hands and said, 'That's for hitting a friend of mine. And now I'll go and wash me hands to take the dirt away.' With that, she smiled sweetly at her husband and made her way into number twenty-two.

Jimmy looked across at his son. 'The way we were going on, we'd have been here all night, son. We should have done what yer mam just did, and we'd have been back in our house by this time.'

'Leave him to me now, Dad. I'll put him over me shoulder and get him inside.' Tom had stopped struggling and Danny picked him up as he would have done a sack of coal. Then he grinned at his father. 'I think it was the left hook that did it, Dad. It was a belter.'

Maggie Richardson, a little woman who lived a few doors away from the Fenwicks, tapped him on his arm. 'No, Danny boy, it was the first punch what did it. Knocked the wind out of him it did. I'm glad Ada gave him what he deserved. And yer can tell her from me it was as good as going to the pictures any day.'

Danny chuckled. 'We should have sold tickets, Mrs Richardson. We'll do that next time, and we'll bring a chair out for yer so yer don't get tired standing. But this feller's a bit of a weight, so I'd better get him inside before I drop him.'

'I'll give yer a hand, son,' Jimmy said. 'We'll carry him between us.'

'No, leave it, Dad, it's no good messing around now. I can carry his weight, and once I get inside I can dump him on the couch.'

'I'm coming in anyway,' Jimmy told him. 'Just to make sure the queer feller is out for the count. He sounds a crafty bugger, and he might not be as drunk as he's making out. I don't want him taking off on Annie and the kids when we've left.'

Annie was putting a light to the gas mantle when Danny walked in with Tom over his shoulder. Her hands were shaking, and her face was as white as a sheet. She felt so humiliated she was afraid to look anyone in the face. 'Put him down on the couch, lad, and then leave him be. He'll sleep through the night, so we'll come to no harm.'

Ben was looking down at the form of his father, and he was filled with disgust. The smell of beer filled the room, and saliva was running down the chin of the man who was so drunk he didn't know what was going on. It's a good job we didn't try and bring him in on our own, the boy thought. We'd never have managed it. He looked at Danny, shrugged his shoulders and sighed. 'He's no good, my dad. He's always doing this and making a show of us. And although I'm sorry your family's been dragged into it, I'm glad yer were there. We couldn't have coped with him, he's too much for us.'

Jenny wouldn't meet Danny's eyes. He must think we're a right lot, she was thinking. He'll not be inviting me in for a cup of tea again in a hurry. 'We'll be all right now,' she said to Ada. 'He'll still be like that when it's time for us to go to work in the morning. He doesn't think about us, only himself. It wouldn't ever occur to him that he shames us in front of everyone. He's not fit to be a husband, or a father.'

'No one can blame you,' Danny said. Seeing how sad she looked, he wished it was him who'd belted Tom Phillips, and not his mother. 'None of you are responsible for his actions, so don't let it worry yer.'

Still avoiding his eyes, Jenny said with bitterness, 'You don't have to live with him. It's like living with the devil himself. In fact, the only friend me dad's got is the devil. They're both wicked.'

Ada could see the girl was tormented with shame, and she could hear it in her voice. And she hadn't failed to notice that Jenny had never once looked at Danny. I'd feel the same if I was her age and in her shoes, Ada told herself. It must be a dreadful life for a young girl, having a rotter for a father. 'Come here, sunshine.' She held the girl close. 'Just put this thought in yer head, and remember it whenever yer dad takes off. You are not responsible for him, you don't owe him anything, and you have a life of yer own to lead.'

'Ada's right, sweetheart,' Annie said. 'You and Ben are growing into adults now, and it's time to make yer own way in life. Not that I want yer to leave home, God forbid, 'cos I'd be lost and heartbroken without yer. But yer must carve out a future for yerselves. If yer want to go out with friends, then go out. Yer don't have to stay in every night because ye're afraid I might bear the brunt of yer father's bad temper. I'm going to make a stand, and not be browbeaten by a man who isn't worth worrying about. And you and Ben must do the same.'

Jimmy watched and listened in silence. He'd often heard of men who beat up their wives and kids, but he'd never seen it close at hand before. And he was horrified. His eyes went from Annie to her two children. Nice, friendly woman, mother of two lovely, polite children. What more could anyone ask for? Then he looked down at Tom Phillips, and felt sick from the stench and the grunts coming from the man. He deserved to be locked up in a cell, and the key thrown away.

'I'll get back over the road, love,' Jimmy said. 'Just in case Monica or Paul are awake and wondering where we are.' He smiled at Annie. 'Any problems, Annie, yer know where to knock. Any time, night or day.'

'Thank you, Jimmy. I'm sorry we're being such a nuisance to you and yer family. I'm not attempting to make excuses for tonight's performance, for me and the kids are used to it. And we know that after a few repetitions of tonight, there'll be so many complaints from the neighbours, we'll be forced to move on once again.'

'Don't even think about it, sunshine,' Ada said, her nostrils flared in temper. 'If anyone leaves this house, it won't be you or the kids, take my word for it. Me and Hetty, and the neighbours either side of here, have a soft spot for this house. It means a lot to us for it holds happy memories. And I'm blowed if a drunken rotter is going to be allowed to ruin those memories.'

Jimmy nodded. 'I agree with the wife on that. But I think it's best if we all call it a day now, for I'm sure Annie and the kids must be tired. We'll talk about it when our heads are clear and tempers calmed down. Come home with me, love, and let Annie and the children go to bed and have a good night's sleep.'

'I'll stay for a while,' Danny said, 'just to make sure Mr Phillips doesn't come round. But I'll be over before yer go to bed, Mam, so leave a cup of tea in the pot for me.'

Ada saw the dismay on Jenny's face, and quickly said, 'No, sunshine, yer can come with me and yer dad. Let's leave these good people to do as they wish. I'm sure a cup of sweet tea would go down a treat, Annie, and then up the stairs to dreamland.'

Annie walked to the door with them. 'There's not enough words to thank you. But yer'll be in my prayers tonight, I can promise yer that.'

Ada gave her a kiss. 'Good night and God bless, sunshine. I'll see yer in the morning.'

After Ada waved the children off to school the next morning, she began to clear the table. But her mind wasn't on what she was doing, it was on the events of the night before. Pictures kept flicking into her head, of the fear and shame on the faces of Annie and her children. And of the state of Tom Phillips as he swayed, with stream after stream of obscenities leaving his mouth.

'Fancy having to live with the likes of that,' Ada told the kitchen window as she put the breakfast dishes in the sink. 'He should have been drowned at birth.' She half filled the kettle and put a light under it. 'I'll have a nice cup of tea, then nip over and see how Annie got on. It wouldn't surprise me in the least if Tom Phillips is still on the couch, out for the count. I can't see him being fit for work, not the state he was in last night.'

When the tea was made, Ada carried a cup through to the living room.

She'd have a quiet ten minutes, then get cracking. She lifted the cup from the saucer, and it was halfway to her lips when there was a loud knock on the door. In her haste, some of the tea left the cup and landed on her knees. 'Blast it! Is there no ruddy rest for the wicked? If it's a canvasser, I'll break their flaming neck.'

However, Ada's disappointment at being robbed of her quiet spell soon disappeared when she opened the door and found Jean Bowers and Edith Benson standing on the pavement. And the look of expectation on their faces told her they were here about the kerfuffle last night. 'Come in, girls. I've just made meself a cup of tea, and there's enough in the pot for another two cups.' Ada's eyes closed when she heard the door of the next house being pulled shut, and she added, 'It will have to run to three cups, 'cos here's me mate.'

Hetty hurried forward and joined Jean and Edith on the pavement. 'I know yer don't like to have visitors so early in the morning, girl, but I couldn't wait any longer. Especially when I saw these two crossing over. I wasn't going to have them hearing the news before me. And I knew yer wouldn't tell the three of us to get lost. Yer can be very outspoken when yer feel like it, but not even you would be that outspoken.'

'Don't bank on it, sunshine, 'cos I'm not in the best of tempers. I only got about an hour's sleep last night.' A resigned sigh left Ada's lips as she jerked her head. 'Come in, but don't all speak at once 'cos me head is debating whether to have an ache or not.'

The three neighbours pulled chairs out for themselves and sat down. It was Hetty who spoke first, and she did it quietly. 'We won't open our mouths, girl, we'll leave the talking to you. Just tell us, in yer own time, what the hell was going on last night?'

'I'm not letting this cup of tea go cold, so get off yer backside, Hetty, and pour another three cups out. There should be enough in the pot to go round.'

Hetty put her hands on the table and pushed herself up. 'I'll go on the understanding that not one word is to be spoken before I'm back with the tea, and sitting comfortably.'

Jean Bowers nodded. 'Honest to God, not one word, I promise.'

Ada called through to the kitchen, 'Is it all right if I ask what the weather's like out? Oh, and can I break the news that it's Danny's birthday today? Is that allowed, Mrs Watson?'

'Don't be sarky, girl, or yer head will ache, just for spite. Anyway, I'm on me way.' Hetty came through with a cup and saucer in each hand. 'It's coming to something when yer best mate tells yer to see to her visitors and make yer own tea.'

When she was seated with her tea in front of her, Hetty said, 'To answer yer question, girl, it is very cold out. And I hadn't forgotten it's Danny's birthday. I've got a nice card for him in me bag.'

Jean couldn't wait any longer, and she leaned forward. 'Ada, what on earth went on last night? The noise was enough to wake the dead. We were watching through the window, and couldn't believe our eyes or ears. That neighbour of ours was rotten drunk, and his language had me blushing. Gordon was all set for going out and telling him off, but when we saw you coming out of your house with Jimmy and Danny, I told him not to get involved. But what a to-do it was! I've never seen anything like it, in all the years I've lived in the street.'

Edith nodded. 'The language out of him was disgusting, and I felt ashamed in front of Elsie and Vincent. They're not used to that. Their dad comes out with the odd "bloody" now and again, but that's as far as it goes. And to think that man is living next door to us. If it happens again, I'm going to complain to the landlord. We don't want the likes of him in the street, never mind right next door.'

'Drink yer tea before it goes cold, girls, and then I'm going to tell yer a little story. And Hetty will tell yer whether I'm telling yer the truth or not.' Ada picked up her cup, took a sip and pulled a face. 'Mine's only lukewarm, so drink up. I'll make a fresh pot after I've told yer all there is to know about yer neighbours.'

'I don't know what to say.' Jean looked from one to the other. 'I'm stunned.'

'Yeah, me too.' Edith shook her head. 'If I'd known the full story, I'd have gone out meself and hit him where it hurt most. I'm glad you belted him, Ada, it was what he deserved. In fact he deserved a lot more.'

'I knew yer'd both be sympathetic when yer heard the truth,' Ada told them. 'Annie Phillips and the two children have a dog's life with him. They've lived in about a dozen houses, because his behaviour has the neighbours complaining and they have to move on. And Hetty will vouch for what I say when I tell yer there isn't a nicer woman breathing than Annie. And the two children are lovely. They're well brought up, and they're very protective of their mother.'

Hetty nodded in agreement. 'Annie's a lovely woman, and how she puts up with him I'll never know. She's very shy, and doesn't like talking about the dreadful life she has. But Ada got it out of her, and both of us were nearly in tears when she showed us some of the bruises he'd given her. It's not often I swear, but he is one bad bugger.'

Jean tutted. 'It just goes to show that yer shouldn't be quick to judge anyone, unless yer know the truth. I was calling the whole family fit to

190

burn last night. They all got the blame for the antics of the father. But we weren't to know any better. Mrs Phillips hasn't exchanged more than half a dozen words with me or Edith.'

Ada leaned back in the chair and folded her arms. 'Me and Hetty have made friends with her, for she has no one to talk to. Her bully of a husband doesn't allow her to have friends or visitors. Me mate and I have offered her a helping hand, and according to her daughter, Jenny, she's started to stick up for herself. But she needs to have a lot more confidence in herself. She's been under his thumb for twenty years, and it's taken all her pride away.'

'He must be a right sod,' Jean said. 'What he needs is a man to put the fear of God into him. I've always said that any man who hits his wife is a coward. They wouldn't try it on with a man, they'd be frightened of getting hurt.'

'D'yer know what really got through to me yesterday? The saddest thing of all, which I could cry over? Well, young Jenny came over last night to thank me and Hetty for helping her mam yesterday. She said she was glad her mother had found friends, 'cos she's never had any with having to move house so often. And that young, seventeen-year-old girl had come to thank me. Me and Hetty had only been in her company three times, and we'd only shared a cup of tea and a cream slice. Not much to thank us for, yet it shows how much Annie is loved by her children. A sod of a husband, but wonderful children.'

'It makes yer think, doesn't it?' Edith said. 'We don't know how lucky we are with our husbands. My feller will get a big hug and kiss when he comes home tonight, just to show how much I appreciate him.'

'If I see Mrs Phillips, I'll make a point of speaking to her,' Jean said. 'After all, she can't help it if the man she married has turned out to be a rotter.'

'I was hoping you and Edith would be sympathetic and understanding,' Ada said. 'And I'd like yer to get to know her. So if I invite her over for a cup of tea this afternoon, would yer both come over? Yer would have to pretend it was just a chance call, for if she thought it was all arranged she'd be embarrassed. I would like yer to meet her, though, and yer could see for yerselves what a smashing person she is. And with a bit of luck Annie will end up with two friends opposite, and one either side of her.'

Jean's nod was enthusiastic. 'Yeah, I'd like that.'

'Me too,' Edith said. 'I don't like to think of any woman being badly treated. We should all help each other.'

Ada smiled. 'That's settled then. She'll be coming over about two o'clock, so if yer keep watch out of yer windows, yer could time it to come ten minutes after her.' Ada turned to her mate. 'Isn't it your turn to buy the cream cakes, sunshine?'

Hetty's jaw dropped and Jean giggled. She leaned across Ada to say, 'It's our turn tomorrow, Hetty. Me and Edith will buy the cakes and make the sandwiches. We'll bring them up the back entry and hand them in here. If we're going to join your afternoon click of friends, we'll put our names on your rota system. That means us tomorrow, then we'll take turns as yer normally do.'

Ada sat back with a smile on her face. This was the outcome she'd been hoping for. The more friends Annie had in the street, the sooner Tom Phillips would be cut down to size.

Chapter Eighteen

Ada and Hetty were coming out of Irwin's later that morning when they bumped into Jean and Edith. There was a cake bag being carried very carefully on an open palm by Edith, and Ada smiled as she pointed to it. 'Cream slices, I hope?'

'I've bought the cakes, and Jean's got the bread and ham for sandwiches. We'll bring them up to yours about half one, is that all right?'

'That's fine, sunshine. It'll be very tempting having the cakes in the house, 'cos I have a very sweet tooth. Sometimes the craving for chocolate is so bad I have to give meself a good talking to. But seeing as this afternoon is an important occasion, then I'll be very strict with meself.'

Hetty gave her mate a dig. 'We'd better make a move, girl, if we want to get our dinner on the way. Otherwise it will be one mad dash, and we won't be able to rclax and enjoy the afternoon.'

'It's going to be a very pleasant afternoon, sunshine, with good friends.' Ada smiled at her mate before turning to Jean and Edith. 'Don't say a word about what happened, just let things take their course. Otherwise Annie will run like a scared rabbit. Leave it to me and I'll bring it up gradually, as though it's no big deal.'

'Yer can rely on us, we'll be the soul of discretion,' Jean said. She linked her arm through Edith's, and they began to walk away. Then she remembered something and turned back. 'Oh, how's Danny enjoying his birthday?'

'He is delighted. He's got six cards, a nice blue tie, a jar of Brylcreem and a slab of chocolate.' Ada chuckled. 'He'll go out of the house tonight with a spring in his step, a perfect knot in his tie, his hair slicked back with the Brylcreem the kids bought him, and a broad grin on his face. And from next week, he'll have an extra half a crown in his wage packet. As far as Danny is concerned, life couldn't be better.'

'That's the way it should be at his age,' Hetty said, pulling on Ada's arm. 'We haven't got all day, girl, so come on. We'll have plenty of time for small talk this afternoon.'

'Your word is my command, sunshine. You lead and I'll follow.'

Annie stood on the pavement looking up at Ada. 'I didn't know whether to come or not, Ada. I thought after last night yer might not want to have anything to do with me.'

Ada tutted. 'Don't be so daft, yer silly nit, of course I wanted yer to come. What happened last night wasn't of your making. Besides, no one got killed, did they? Come in before yer catch yer death of cold. Hetty's inside. She'll tell yer a few jokes, and that'll warm yer up.'

Hetty grinned when the two women walked in. 'That's a joke in itself, girl. I'm not exactly known for me sense of humour. Me mate's the one with the wit, I'm not in the meg specks.'

'Ah, don't be putting yerself down, sunshine, 'cos yer do have yer moments.' Ada turned her head a little to give a sly wink to Annie. 'I've got a very good memory, and I can remember yer telling a cracking joke once.' She cupped her chin with a hand, and while using the first finger to tap her chin, she frowned in concentration. Then she muttered, 'When was it now? It'll come to me in a minute. Oh, yeah, I've got it now, I can remember it as clear as daylight.' She dropped her hand and bent down to face her mate. 'It was a couple of days before Christmas and we were run off our feet. Then yer came out with this belting joke, and it was so funny, we finished our shopping in a very happy frame of mind.'

There was a smile on Hetty's face. 'I can't say I remember, girl. Was this last Christmas?'

Ada shook her head. 'No, sunshine, it was the second Christmas after we moved into this street and became neighbours.'

'But that was eighteen years ago!'

'Yes, I know, sunshine. But it goes to show what a good joke it was if I can remember yer telling it after all that time.'

Hetty had a look of expectancy on her face as she leaned forward. When a few seconds had passed and there was nothing forthcoming from her mate, she asked, 'Well, come on, tell us the joke and give us a laugh.'

Ada's eyes flew open in surprise. 'Yer don't think I can remember a joke after eighteen years, do yer? I've got a good memory, but not that ruddy good.'

Hetty took a leaf out of her mate's book and put on a show. 'Oh, yer can remember it was a couple of days before Christmas eighteen years ago, but yer've conveniently forgotten what the ruddy joke was! Pull the other one, girl, it's got bells on.'

'The trouble with you, sunshine, is that yer believe everything I say. Yer should know by now to take most things with a pinch of salt.'

'Oh, so ye're telling me I shouldn't believe a word me best mate says 'cos she's a liar?'

Ada moved her head slowly from side to side. 'I wouldn't go as far as to say I'm a liar, sunshine. I'm just a teller of fairy tales. They don't hurt no one, and if they give people a laugh, well, what harm is that?'

Hetty gave in. 'No harm at all, girl, no harm at all.'

'Right, well now we've got that settled, let's get down to discussing something that isn't in the least bit funny.' Ada looked at Annie. 'How did yer get on after we left yer last night, sunshine?'

Her neighbour gave a deep sigh. 'Me and the kids went straight up to bed, so whether Tom slept all night, I don't know. When I came down this morning he was getting washed in the kitchen and I just went about making his breakfast as usual. There wasn't one word out of his mouth. Not to me, or the children. And the only time I spoke to him was to tell him Ben wouldn't be going out at the same time as him any more. He didn't answer, just walked out of the house and banged the door behind him.'

Ada's face showed her amazement. 'Yer mean he was capable of going to work this morning, after being so rotten drunk last night he could barely stand?'

'You don't know Tom, Ada. He could drink a pub dry and still find his way home. He gets drunk and causes a scene, but it never stops him from going to work the next day.'

'I don't know how he does it, then,' Ada said. 'Two pints and that's the lot for my Jimmy. He couldn't take any more, even if he could afford it.'

'I'm just worried about what the neighbours thought last night.' Annie was wringing her hands. 'I've been ashamed of showing me face this morning. I was at the shops before they opened and was back before any of the neighbours came out. They must wonder what sort of a family they've got living in their midst.'

'Things are not as black as yer think, sunshine, so stop fretting. The neighbours either side of yer are really nice people, and they're the only ones yer need worry about. There were a few out last night, but it was mostly out of curiosity. In fact, there's some who would have enjoyed a bit of excitement to brighten up their lives. Gives them something to think about.' Ada chose her words carefully when she spoke again. 'We were talking to the neighbours either side of yer this morning at the shops, weren't we, Hetty?'

'Yes, girl, we were. Jean Bowers and Edith Watson, they're lovely people. Yer'd get on like a house on fire with them, if yer had the chance to get to know them.' Hetty decided it would be best to leave the rest of the

195

talking to her mate. Ada seemed to have a knack of using the right words, while she'd most likely put her foot in it.

Annie let out a sigh. 'I've forgotten what it's like to be friends with me neighbours, Hetty. I'm not allowed to live a normal life, Tom won't let me. He's beaten me into submission over the years and I haven't had the strength to fight back. And I bet me neighbours were calling us for everything, were they? I wouldn't blame them if they did, 'cos no decent family would want us living next door.'

'Well, I'm not going to lie to yer, Annie, 'cos I know yer wouldn't believe me anyway. Jean and Edith weren't very happy about the commotion last night. They've both got teenage children, and they objected to the bad language as well as the noise. But I don't think you should take the blame, or be punished because yer've got a lousy husband. So I tried to put the record straight with them. Yer don't mind my doing that, do yer, sunshine? Yer need to have friends in the street if ye're ever going to settle down here. And let's face it, yer can't be moving to a different house every year. That's not the answer to yer problem, is it? The answer lies in bringing Tom Phillips to heel.'

'I've given up all hope of that happening, sweetheart,' Annie said. 'I've seen him getting many a good hiding off neighbours twice his size, who were fed up with his carryings-on. He's often been knocked out, and left on the pavement for me and the kids to drag into the house.' She shook her head. 'It's been going on too long for him to change. It would take a miracle, and yer don't hear of many of them, do yer?'

'I didn't have a miracle in mind, sunshine,' Ada told her. 'Yer could say a prayer, or wish on a star, but that wouldn't do yer any good, either. What might do the trick is having enough friends in the street on your side. If we could bring that about, it may get through Tom Phillips's thick skull that his days of ruling the roost are over. For even he wouldn't be stupid enough to try and take the street on.'

'D'yer think I haven't tried to make friends over the years, sweetheart? Believe me, I've had women who I thought were tough enough to forget Tom and take me on as a mate. But no one has ever stuck it out, and I've had me heart broken a few times. There's not many will stand by me once they've found out what sort of a husband I've got.'

'Me and Ada have, girl, and we'll not be walking away from yer,' Hetty said quite emotionally. 'And there's many more like us.'

Ada gave her mate a smile of thanks before facing Annie again. 'What Hetty just said is true, sunshine. And I'm going to introduce yer to Jean and Edith, to prove it to yer.'

A look of alarm crossed Annie's face. 'Oh, no, Ada, I couldn't meet them. They must think I'm the lowest of the low after last night, and I couldn't look them in the face.'

In for a penny, in for a pound, Ada told herself. If it didn't happen now, it would never happen. 'You can look anyone in the face, Annie, for yer've done nothing wrong. And don't fly off the handle when I tell yer that Jean and Edith will be over any minute now. They want to meet yer, so I invited them. There's no need to be afraid, sunshine, and any time yer feel uncomfortable, then all yer have to do is make an excuse and leave. That won't happen, I know. And I also know that before the afternoon is over, yer'll have four friends in the street, not two. And yer'll find yerself getting along with them as well as yer do with me and Hetty.'

'Ooh, I don't know, sweetheart, I don't think I can do it. I'll nip out the back way, and leave you to enjoy the company of yer friends.'

Just then there came a knock on the door, and Ada pushed Annie back down on her chair. 'It's too late now, sunshine, they're here. And let's see a nice smile on yer face when I introduce yer to two women who are the salt of the earth. I promise yer won't regret it.'

Annie was a bag of nerves when she shook hands with her next-door neighbours, and her smile was shaky. But their returning smiles were so friendly, and their faces so open, her heartbeat began to slow down. 'I'm glad to meet yer, so I can apologise for the rumpus my husband caused last night. I'm sorry yer had to put up with it. I only wish I could put yer minds at rest and say it won't happen again. But I'm afraid that is something I can't promise. My husband is a law unto himself.'

'We'll be prepared for it next time, and we'll shut him up before he starts,' Jean said. 'I'll have the rolling pin ready to hand, and Edith said she'll lift me up so I can hit him on the head with it.' She smiled to show she wasn't in earnest. 'Anyway, let's talk about it over a cup of tea. It's not the end of the world, girl, so don't look so worried.'

'Is that a hint for me to put the kettle on, by any chance, Mrs Bowers?' Ada was feeling relieved that things seemed to be going well. 'Ye're not backward in coming forward, even if yer pretty face makes yer look shy and retiring, as though butter wouldn't melt in yer mouth. It goes to show yer can't take people at face value.'

Hetty jumped to her feet. 'I'll help yer with the tea, girl, or it'll be time to go home before we get one.' She followed Ada out to the kitchen. 'I'm starving, and me tummy is beginning to rumble. Don't forget I didn't have any lunch.'

'Ye're not on yer own, sunshine, 'cos I've had nothing to eat since me breakfast. So ye're not likely to get any sympathy off me.'

197

Edith called through from the living room. 'We're a chair short, girl, so can I fetch the one over from by the window?'

'Of course yer can, sunshine! Make yerselves at home and pretend ye're at yer granny's. Me and Hetty will see to the tea while you and Jean get acquainted with Annie.'

Hetty mouthed the words, 'It seems to be going well, girl, don't yer think?'

'Like clockwork, sunshine, like clockwork. And even though it sounds as though I'm bragging, I've got to say I'm feeling pleased with me little self.'

'I'm glad for Annie,' Hetty said, taking the cloth off the plate covering the sandwiches. 'It would be nice if the five of us got together once or twice a week for afternoon tea.' She giggled. 'Doesn't afternoon tea sound posh?'

'It does that, sunshine.' Ada put three teaspoonsful of tea into the earthenware pot. 'Yer'll soon be getting ideas above yer station. It wouldn't surprise me if one of these days yer don't suggest we go to the Adelphi Hotel for our afternoon tea.'

'Ooh, I don't think so, girl. Someone told me it's half a crown to get in, and all yer get for that is a paper-thin sandwich and one scone. Oh, and yer get a cup of tea of course. And it's served in a china cup.'

'I know it sounds a lot of money, sunshine, but don't forget yer get music with it. And, so I'm told, they've got palm trees as well.'

'Go 'way! Ooh, the woman didn't say nothing about music or palm trees. Where did yer hear that, girl?'

'I think it was our Danny who told me. He hasn't been himself, it was only what he heard.'

Hetty was tickled by her thoughts. 'Ay, girl, can yer just see us sitting in the Adelphi, under a palm tree, nibbling a wafer-thin cucumber sandwich?'

Ada was picking up the full tray when she chuckled. 'We'd have to remember to curl our little finger, like the posh people do.'

Jean's voice reached them. 'Ay, are you two having a party of yer own out there? Here's us, yer visitors, with mouths as dry as bones, gasping for a drink, while the only noise coming from the kichen is laughter.'

Ada walked through with the tray, and Hetty followed with the plates. 'Keep yer hair on, sunshine,' she said, 'it's all ready now.'

'What were yer laughing at, sweetheart?' Annie asked, feeling much more relaxed now she'd faced her next-door neighbours. 'Won't yer let us in on the joke?'

'Yeah,' Jean said. 'Don't be so miserable, keeping the jokes to yerself. We enjoy a good laugh as well, yer know.'

Ada set down the tray carefully before answering. 'We haven't been telling jokes, Jean, we've been laughing at what our imagination conjured up. If yer'll wait until the tea's poured out, and yer've got a sarnie in yer hand, I'll explain what tickled our fancy.'

A few minutes later, Jean said, 'Well, go on, girl, we're all settled.'

Never one to miss an opportunity, Ada decided that plenty of laughter was called for today. She wanted her three neighbours from opposite to go out of her house together. And she wanted them to be laughing, having forged friendships which would endure through hardships and ups and downs. So she sat back in her chair, with her fingers curled round a cup of tea, and an eye on the sandwiches and cream slices. 'Are yer sure yer wouldn't like to eat before I start?'

There was a chorus of protests, so she shrugged her shoulders and set off on one of her fairy tales. 'Me and Hetty were saying we wouldn't mind going to the Adelphi one day for afternoon tea. We could see ourselves dressed up to the nines, our hair marcel-waved, nails coloured, and wearing bright red lipstick. They've got palm trees there, yer know, and we can see ourselves sitting under one. And while eating a wafer-thin sandwich, with our little finger curled, like the toffs do, we sit entranced by the music being played by the four musicians on the stage. There are couples dancing, and the huge crystal chandeliers hanging from the high ceiling are shining on the jewellery worn by the young women.'

Ada put a hand to her mouth and coughed behind it several times. She did this to stop herself from bursting with laughter. Her four friends were drinking in every word, as though they were seeing the scene as she told it. But it was Hetty who was bringing Ada to a point where she wouldn't be able to keep the laughter back for much longer. For Hetty, who was the one who started all this off, was listening as though she believed what Ada was telling them, and she could almost hear the music being played. She was hunched over the table with her arms crossed and her eyes fixed on her mate's mouth. And she was getting impatient. 'Well, go on, girl, tell us some more.'

But Ada's hunger got the better of her, and she decided she'd better cut it short or she'd starve to death. 'You're the one that can finish it off, sunshine, 'cos you were the one who caught the eye of a very handsome toff. He came over, and acting like a knight of old, he bowed down from the waist, then held his hand out and asked if he could have the pleasure of dancing the waltz with yer. Well, I got fed up sitting there like a wallflower, all on me own. So after watching you and yer partner gazing into each other's eyes, and him lifting yer hand to his lips every few minutes, I decided to call it a day. And I came home on the tram, all on me lonesome.'

There was a burst of applause, the loudest being from Hetty. She was over the moon to have been the heroine in one of the best fairy tales her mate had ever told. 'Yer might have gone on a bit further, girl, I was enjoying that.'

'Yeah, me rumbling tummy told me yer were enjoying it so much, yer'd have kept me at it until bedtime. Anyway, sunshine, how much further did yer want me to go?'

'Well, he could have wooed me. Even asked for me hand in marriage.'

'Let me have a cup of tea and something to eat first, sunshine, then I might feel more like it. At the moment me tummy thinks me throat's cut.'

'You've had your turn, Hetty, anyway,' Jean told her. 'When Ada's refreshed, she can start with it being me who has attracted the knight in shining armour. I could tell Gordon about it in bed tonight, and it would put some spice back in our lives.'

'That's an idea,' Edith said. 'Ye're good at making things up, Ada, so couldn't there have been two knights, instead of one? Then I could have one.'

Annie, who was by now completely relaxed with her neighbours, thought she'd join in the fun. God knows, she'd had little of it in her life up to now. 'Excuse me, ladies, but didn't the knights of old travel in threes?'

'No, yer've got yer wires crossed, Annie,' Jean said. 'It was the musketeers what travelled in threes.'

'Well, one of them would do,' Annie said, feeling very daring. 'Yer must all admit that if anyone needs to be carried away by a good man, then it's me.'

Ada bit into her cream slice, a look of bliss on her face. What a wonderful afternoon it had turned out to be. She couldn't get a knight in shining armour for Annie, or even a musketeer, but she had been able to get her two more very good friends.

'D'yer know, I feel on top of the world,' Ada told the family while they were having their meal. 'Jean and Edith were marvellous with Annie. They didn't look down on her or anything. They did mention the fuss her husband caused, and said if it happened again they'd be out to him with a rolling pin. But they said it jokingly, so Annie wouldn't get upset or embarrassed. She did look nervous at first, and if she'd had her way she'd have been off down the entry before they came. But I managed to talk her into staying. And believe me, after the first half-hour, she looked like a different woman. She joined in the laughter, and even took part in the little fantasy tale I'd made up. When the three of them left here at four o'clock, she was as happy as Larry. Anyone would think they'd been mates for years.'

200

The fork was halfway to Jimmy's mouth when he said, 'Yer said three of them, love. Wasn't Hetty here?'

'Oh, yeah, me mate was here. It wouldn't be a show without Punch. But she didn't leave with them, she stayed behind for a little natter. Only to say how well things had gone, and how glad we are that Annie's next-door neighbours now know what the score is. If Tom Phillips starts any shenanigans, they'll hear him and either knock on the wall, or get the men to go to the front door and confront him. So Annie and the kids have friends watching out for them now, and I feel more contented knowing that.'

'Mam, what did yer mean when yer said yer made up a fantasy tale?' Monica asked. 'D'yer mean like the Three Bears, or Cinderella?'

'I was going to ask yer that, Mam,' Danny said, his eyes shining with laughter. 'What weird and wonderful gem did yer come up with this time? Yer must have a brilliant imagination to dream up these tales of yours. Yer should write a book.'

Ada chuckled. 'There's one drawback, sunshine. I've got a good mouth for telling stories, it comes easy to me. But if I was asked to write them down I'd be stumped. Ruddy hopeless at spelling, son, and that's my downfall.'

'Tell us what yer told yer mates this afternoon, Mam,' Paul pleaded. 'Go on, it's ages since yer told me and our Monica a story.'

'Ye're too grown-up for fairy stories, son. If I told yer the one about Dick Whittington and his cat, yer'd be bored stiff.'

But her son persisted. 'Tell us the one yer made up today, then. Yer said it made the ladies laugh, so it must have been funny.'

'I thought it was funny, sunshine, and so did they. But we are all the same age, three or four times your age. You might not find it a bit funny.'

'Ah, go on, Mam,' Monica coaxed. 'If yer told yer friends, why can't yer tell us? Don't be a meanie.'

'Eat yer dinner before it gets cold, and then I'll tell yer.' Ada turned to where her eldest son was sitting. 'I think you'd be better finishing yer dinner quick, Danny, and start getting yerself ready for going out. Once yer start to listen to me, yer'll make yerself late for the dance. And I'd hate to get the blame for making yer miss a slow foxtrot.'

'How long is this tale?' her son asked. 'Surely it didn't last for the whole two hours yer mates were here for?'

'Of course it didn't, soft lad. I started it in the kitchen with me and Hetty having a laugh. Then it sort of carried on when we got back in the living room, and took on a life of its own. One thing led to another and I found meself inventing things in me head. The ladies were enjoying it, and adding their own ideas. We all had a good laugh and it was a really nice afternoon.'

'Go on, Mam,' Danny said. 'If I don't listen to it, I'll be filled with curiosity all night and won't enjoy the dances. I wouldn't be able to concentrate, and I'd be treading on me partner's toes.'

'While I'd hate to be responsible for yer standing on a girl's toes, I still think yer should skip my little tale for tonight, and hear it another time. It's yer birthday and all yer partners will wonder what's happened to yer.' Ada's eyes went to the ceiling. 'I have to say I was glad yer were here last night, though, sunshine, to give yer dad a hand. He'd have had a struggle on his own.'

'I was glad I was here, Mam, 'cos think what I would have missed. I've never seen a performance like that in me life. It shows what a sheltered life we've led. We don't know how lucky we are to have a mother and father who have shown us nothing but love and laughter.' Danny's dimples appeared when he added, 'Except the odd clip round the ear when I've put a ball through someone's window, or sagged school to go to the park with me mates.'

Monica was taken aback. 'I never knew yer sagged school, our Danny.'

'He's pulling yer leg, sunshine,' Ada said quickly. 'He'd have got more than a clip round the ear if he'd ever sagged school. That's something he wouldn't have got away with.'

Danny leaned across the table to pick up the now empty dinner plates. 'I'll take these out, Mam, and then I'm staying to listen while yer tell us what made yer afternoon so enjoyable. It won't kill me to miss the first dance.'

Ten minutes later, in the house next door, Hetty lifted her hand for silence. 'Just listen to the screams of laughter from next door. I bet Ada's been telling them about this afternoon, and even adding a bit more to it. How she dreams all these things up I'll never know. But I'm glad she's got a good imagination, and I'm glad she's me mate. My life would be really dull if it wasn't for her.'

'So would ours be, Mam,' Sally said. 'What would we talk about over the dinner table if it wasn't for Auntie Ada and her tales?' Just then a loud burst of laughter could be heard, and Sally raised her brows. 'See what I mean? We've all got a smile on our face, and yet we haven't got a joke between us. Long live Auntie Ada, that's what I say.'

Chapter Nineteen

When Jenny and Ben came home that night from work, they were met by a very animated mother. Annie couldn't wait for them to hang their coats up before she was telling them about the wonderful day she'd had. The words poured from her mouth as she told how Ada had introduced her to their next-door neighbours, and how she'd got on with them like a house on fire. Her face was aglow, and her happiness brought a smile to her children's faces.

'I was afraid of meeting Jean and Edith, in case they looked down their noses at me after the way yer father behaved last night. In fact, I was so ashamed, I would have run for me life. But Ada wouldn't let me run, she made me stick it out. And I thank God she did, for Jean and Edith are two of the nicest people yer could wish to meet. They soon put me at me ease, and it wasn't long before I thought I'd known them all me life.'

'What did they have to say about the way me dad was last night?' Jenny asked. 'They must have seen or heard him.'

'Oh, they did! But Ada had told them a bit about how things are here, and they were sympathetic. Towards us, like, not yer father. They said if he takes off again, like he did last night, they'd be out like a shot with a rolling pin.'

'I hope me dad doesn't make a habit of getting drunk and being rowdy in the street, though, Mam,' Ben said. 'Even the best of friends would find that hard to take.'

'Yer don't need to tell me that, sweetheart, haven't I had twenty years of it? And haven't I had mates who turned out to be fine weather friends? At the first sign of trouble, they couldn't walk away quick enough. But I'm as sure as I'll ever be of anything that Ada and Hetty will be good mates. And although I've only really met Jean and Edith today, I'd say they were from the same mould. Don't forget, the day we moved in, Edith came to the door and offered to make us a pot of tea. And didn't I throw her kindness back in her face because I knew it wouldn't be long before she found out what yer father was like?'

'Did she mention that today, Mam?' Jenny asked. 'She must have felt terrible when yer sent her packing that day.'

'No, she never mentioned it, sweetheart.' Annie glanced at the clock. 'The dinner is ready in the oven, I'll see to it now. I want to have our meal over before yer father comes in. After the show he made of us, and himself, last night, I don't think I could sit at the same table as him. The food would stick in me throat.'

'Would it be all right if I went out tonight, Mam?' Jenny asked. 'I promised two of the girls in work I'd go to a dance with them.'

'Ah, I've promised me mate I'd go round to his tonight,' Ben said. 'I let him down last time I was supposed to go, I don't want to let him down again.'

'We can't both go out and leave me mam in here on her own,' Jenny told him. 'Yer know what me dad's like. He'd take off on her if she was here alone.'

Annie turned at the kitchen door. 'Don't worry about me, I'll be all right. Yer can't let yer mates down, and I wouldn't want yer to. At your age, yer should both be out enjoying yerselves, and I'm not going to stand in yer way.'

'No, I don't like the idea of yer being in here on yer own with me dad.' Jenny had a determined expression on her face. 'I'd never forgive meself if I came home and saw he'd given yer a black eye.'

While Annie was opening the oven door, she called through to the living room, 'There's a very easy solution to the problem, sweet-heart.'

Jenny got up from her chair and made her way to the kitchen, with Ben close on her heels. 'What solution is that, Mam?'

'I'll go out somewhere. Yer father could get his own dinner out of the oven for once. He's going to have to learn that I'm not waiting on him hand and foot any longer.'

Ben asked, 'But where would yer go, Mam?'

'I could go to the pictures. If I'd thought of it before, I'd have prepared meself to go to first house, but it's too late for that. So I'll go to the last house.'

Jenny bustled into the kitchen and took the two plates her mother had in her hands. 'Mam, yer wouldn't miss much of the first house if yer ate yer dinner quick and went straight out. I'd see to our Ben, yer don't need to worry about that. And by the time yer came in from the pictures, me dad would have had his dinner and gone out to the pub. He won't come home till closing time, and Ben will be back by then. I won't stay until the last dance, so I won't be home late, either.'

'I'll not let yer spoil yer night because of me, sweetheart. It's not often yer go out, so make the most of it.'

'Don't argue, Mam! Go and sit at the table and I'll carry yer dinner in.' Jenny jerked her head at her brother. 'You too, Ben. Sit down and get stuck in.'

Annie picked up her knife and fork, but she looked uncertain. 'If Ben goes out after his meal, it could mean yer'd be on yer own with yer father for a while. Have yer thought of that, sweetheart?'

'He doesn't usually come in until half seven, and he's out again as soon as he's had his dinner. Anyway, I might be gone before he gets in from work, and I won't set eyes on him.' And to put her mother's mind at ease, Jenny added, 'Even if he came in, I'd ignore him. I wouldn't even acknowledge his presence. So get that dinner down yer, and go and see a nice romantic film. Anything would be better than staying in the house on yer own. And Mam, how long have yer been saying ye're going to put yer foot down with me dad? Talking about it isn't going to get yer anywhere, so stop the talking and begin the action. Start now, right this minute. And if yer feel yerself weakening, then just think of yer new friends. Yer don't want to lose them, do yer?'

Annie was smiling when she shook her head. 'I certainly don't, sweetheart, and I shouldn't need me daughter to remind me. It just shows how pathetic I've been. But I give yer me solemn promise that I'll stand up to Tom Phillips no matter what he says or threatens me with. I can't fight him, for I'm no match for him. But I can beat him in other ways, you'll see.'

'I believe yer, Mam,' Jenny said, 'but will yer get that dinner down yer, and be off before the terror comes in.'

'I've finished me dinner,' Ben said. 'So hurry up with yours, Mam, and we can go out together. If we see me dad, we'll pretend we haven't and walk past him.'

It wasn't long before Jenny was seeing them off. 'I'll clear the table, Mam, and wash the dishes, so that's one thing yer don't have to worry about. You enjoy the film, and yer first taste of freedom.'

Annie blew her a kiss before linking her arm through Ben's. 'This is the man in me life, and I couldn't ask for better. And although I say it as shouldn't, I think we make a very handsome couple.'

'Ay, Mam,' Jenny said, 'I told yer to get tough, not big-headed.' She was smiling as she closed the door. It was such a change to see her mother looking almost carefree, with not a frown on her forehead, nor anxiety in her eyes. Let's hope it keeps up, Jenny thought as she began to collect the dinner dishes. She'd wash them first, then get herself ready for the dance.

Her workmates would be dressed to the nines, and she didn't want to turn up looking dowdy.

When she heard the key in the door, Jenny ground her teeth together. The dishes were washed and put away, and she'd shaken the tablecloth in the yard. All she had to do now was see to herself, and she'd hoped to do that before her father came home.

Tom Phillips stood in the kitchen doorway, his usual scowl on his face. 'Where the hell's yer mother? She should be here, waiting to put me dinner down in front of me.'

'Me mam's gone out, and yer dinner is in the oven. Surely ye're capable of lifting a plate out of the oven?'

'That's yer bleeding mother's job, not mine. What does she think I pay her for?' His lip curled as he growled, 'You get me dinner out, I've been bleeding working all day. Wait till yer ma gets in, it's a hiding she's asking for.' He swayed into the living room and fell back into the fireside chair. 'Where the hell's she gone, anyway?'

Jenny's mind was ticking over. She felt like telling him to get off his backside and see to his own dinner. Anyone would think he was the only one working all day. But her common sense told her that to cross him would be asking for trouble. Best to give him his dinner, and while he was eating she could get herself ready to go out. It would be less trouble all round to do it that way. So, using a tea towel to shield her hands against the heat, she opened the oven and carefully removed the plate that was covering the dinner so it wouldn't dry up.

'Here's yer dinner.' The plate was put down in front of Tom Phillips, and the look he gave his daughter showed he was in a raging temper and ready to flare. 'I asked yer a question, yer stupid mare. Where's yer mother gone?'

'How do I know? I'm not me mother's keeper, she doesn't have to tell me where she's going. Or you, for that matter. Anyway, there's yer dinner, so stop yer moaning. I'm going to get washed. I'm going out, too.' With that she turned on her heel and walked back to the kitchen. A quick wash, clean her teeth, change her dress, apply a little lipstick and comb her hair. Ten minutes at the most, then she'd be on her way. Thank goodness. She didn't fancy spending any time with a man who had no control over his violent temper.

Tom Phillips pushed himself out of the fireside chair and reached for the table to support him and hold him steady while he pulled out a dining chair and sat down. He stared at the plate of sausage and mash in front of him, and snorted. He wasn't really hungry, for he'd stopped at a pub on the way home for a few pints. But it wasn't hunger that was fuelling his temper, it was the fact his bitch of a wife had the nerve to be out when he got in from work. Adding to that, was her absence from his bed for the last two nights. He didn't love his wife, but in his mind she was there to gratify his lust whenever he felt the urge. It was her duty to see he was satisfied in that quarter. That was what she'd promised to do when they got married, wasn't it? In his fuddled mind, he was telling himself she'd stood in front of the priest and made these promises, so she should be made to keep them. And, by God, when she got in, he'd make sure she did her duty by him. She'd get a good hiding first, to remind her who was boss, then it would be back to the way things used to be, where he told her what he wanted her to do to please him, and she would oblige. He knew she did it out of fear, not a wish to please him, but it was seeing the fear in her eyes that thrilled him and heightened his desire. And the fact that she was frightened didn't worry him. He didn't care what she thought or felt. All he could think of now was that she would be back in his bed tonight or he'd beat the living daylights out of her.

Tom pushed the plate away in disgust. It wasn't the food he objected to, it was the absence of a wife who should be there to do his bidding. Then his lip curled in a smile that was more of a grimace. His wife wasn't there, but her daughter was.

In the kitchen, Jenny had swilled her face and reached for the towel she'd placed within easy reach on the draining board. She was holding it to her face, and didn't see the figure standing in the doorway, saliva running from the side of his mouth as he eyed her young figure with desire stirring in his loins. The first she knew was a hand on the back of her neck, and her head being pushed down into the sink. She could sense her father's heavy breathing on her neck, and the foul smell of beer. Her heartbeat began to race, but it was all happening so fast she couldn't think clearly. Instinct made her push back, to try to move his body away from hers. But his full weight was leaning on her, and she couldn't budge him. And the pressure on her head was such that she had visions of him breaking her neck. Then a cry left her lips as she felt a hand on her leg. 'Leave me alone,' she snapped, 'and take yer dirty hand off me.'

Tom's coarse laugh sent a chill down her spine, and his words filled her with terror. 'Yer ma's not here to give me what I want, so you can stand in for her. Now keep still, yer stupid cow, or it'll be worse for yer.'

Jenny felt his hand moving up her leg, over the bare flesh at the top of her stocking, and into the leg of her knickers. Fear gripped her, and she had to stop herself from screaming. All she could think of was that the neighbours mustn't know what was going on. No one must know. Then her fear turned to anger when she felt a finger moving inside her knickers. It galvanised her into action, and she began to kick backwards, using both feet. She heard her father laugh, for she was missing his legs, and the sound spurred her on. He wasn't going to do what he liked with her, she'd kill him first. So she bent her arms, and with her elbows and feet she began digging and kicking like a mad woman. Then she heard him yelp with pain as one of her kicks caught him on the shin. He loosened his grip on her for a second as he rubbed his leg, and Jenny took advantage and pushed him away. She fled into the living room, leaving Tom Phillips hopping on one foot and swearing. He hobbled after her, but Jenny was quick, being driven by fear and loathing. She grabbed her handbag from the sideboard as she passed, and her coat from the hook by the front door. A moment later she was outside, and banging the door behind her.

Leaning back against the wall, Jenny breathed in the night air as tears ran down her cheeks. She thought of what her father had done, and could feel the bile rising to her throat. She felt dirty, and wanted to be sick. How could her father do that to her? He wasn't a real father, he was a madman. If her mother found out what he'd done, it would kill her. She'd be so ashamed, and blame herself. But she would never find out, no one would. Not from her anyway. The hatred she felt for her father now was so overwhelming, she never wanted to see his face ever again. He'd made her feel cheap and dirty. The very thought of him made her skin crawl. And she swore that she'd get even with him one day.

Jenny shivered as the cold penetrated her clothes. She didn't have a scarf or gloves, there hadn't been time to pick them up. Her only thought had been to get out of the house and away from the roving hands and the filthy mouth of the beast who was her father. She didn't know what to do. She couldn't go to the dance, not the way she felt. So once again she'd not only let her mates down, she'd have to lie to them. Make some sort of excuse. One thing was certain, they'd never ask her again. And she couldn't stay where she was, leaning against the wall of the house. Any minute now the man who had degraded her would be coming out and strolling up to the pub as though he didn't have a care in the world. He'd treated her like trash, belittled her and made her feel unclean, but that wouldn't bother him. He wouldn't even give it a second thought. And her mother had put up with him for twenty years.

In her mind's eye, Jenny could see her mother as she was earlier. She was smiling, and you could see there was hope in her heart for a better future. But there was no bright future for any of them, not while Tom

Phillips ruled the roost. The thought brought tears to Jenny's eyes, for she loved her mother dearly. She was a wonderful mother, loving and caring. And she was a good woman, who deserved better than to spend the rest of her life with a drunken rotter.

Tears blurred Jenny's vision, and although she heard a door bang, she didn't know where the sound came from. But she told herself she'd have to move, or anyone passing would think she was crazy for standing out in the cold. She'd walk to the bottom of the street and hang around until her mother came home from the pictures. Then she'd make an excuse and say she hadn't felt like going to the dance after all.

Danny Fenwick banged the door behind him and stepped down on to the pavement. He had a smile on his face after listening to the antics of his mam and her mates. Then as he turned to walk down the street, he caught sight of Jenny leaning against the wall outside her house. As he made to cross the cobbles, she began to walk away, so he called to her. 'Hey, Jenny, are yer running away from me? I won't eat yer, yer know, because I've just had me dinner and I'm full up.'

Jenny quickened her pace. She couldn't face anyone now, not with tears rolling down her cheeks and her whole body shaking. The only face she would welcome now was that of her mother or Ben. She could tell them she'd run out of the house because she couldn't stand her father's bad language. And they'd believe her because they knew what he was like. At least they thought they did. But it would never even enter their heads that he was wicked enough to molest his own daughter.

Danny caught up with her and pulled on her arm. 'What's the hurry, Jenny? Ye're walking so fast anyone would think the devil was after yer.' He was quick to note how she drew her arm back, and cringed as she moved away from him. They were nearing the end of the street now, and by the light from the gas lamp he could see her red, tear-stained face. 'What's the matter, Jenny? Has yer father been up to his tricks again? There must be some reason for yer walking the street in this cold weather without a scarf or gloves on.'

He had given her an excuse, and a reason, although he would never know it. And Jenny was grateful, and quick to take advantage. 'I ran out of the house like this, 'cos I couldn't listen to me dad's moaning and complaints any longer. And his language makes me sick.'

'Is yer mam in?'

Jenny shook her head. 'No, me mam went to first house pictures. That's where I'm going now, to meet her coming out. And our Ben is at his mate's.'

Danny narrowed his eyes. The words didn't ring true. There was far more involved than Jenny was saying, for he felt sure no amount of bad language would have her running down the street crying. It was obvious she'd been upset, for apart from the red-rimmed eyes, she was trembling like a leaf. He wasn't going to probe, though, that would upset her more. 'Did yer mam go to the pictures on her own, then?'

Jenny nodded. She was praying he would go away and leave her alone. He was a nice boy, but right now she was wishing him miles away. She dreaded him putting his hand on her arm again, for she didn't want a man's hands on her. 'She'll be along soon, so yer've no need to stay with me. I suppose ye're off to a dance?'

'I am, yeah! Must have me nightly dose or I won't sleep properly. But there's no hurry. I can walk with yer to meet yer mam, keep yer company. It won't kill me to miss a dance. As long as it isn't a slow foxtrot, like, 'cos that's me favourite.'

'Yer don't have to miss a dance on my behalf,' Jenny said. 'The first house pictures will be coming out soon, so I'm going to meet me mam.'

'Why not come to the dance with me, Jenny?' Danny asked. For some reason he didn't want to leave her on her own. She looked so vulnerable. 'Then I might find out the secret of yer favourite dance. Yer wouldn't tell me, remember?'

'What? Go to a dance looking like this?' Jenny opened her arms wide and looked down at herself. 'I'd make a holy show of yer, Danny. Yer mates would wonder where yer picked me up.'

'I'm not a snob, Jenny. I'd never be ashamed of a friend.'

'Well, I'd be ashamed, if you weren't.' Jenny was hoping he would just go away. She was still feeling sick, and her tummy felt as though it was filled with butterflies. And she felt dirty. As soon as she got home, she was going to scrub herself from top to bottom. A little voice in her head was telling her she had done nothing to be ashamed of, but that didn't make her feel any better. And her biggest worry was that every day she would be reminded of the horror her father had put her through, for she couldn't avoid seeing him. Unless she left home. But as soon as the thought entered her head, Jenny discarded it. She would never leave home while her mother and brother were still there.

It was the sound of a tram trundling along that brought Jenny out of her thoughts. 'Go to the dance, Danny, or I'll be kicking meself all night because I made yer miss it. Go on, or yer'll miss the tram.'

'On one condition, Jenny.'

'What's that?'

'That I can call and see yer tomorrow night, so yer can tell me the truth about why ye're walking the streets on yer own. I can't believe it was only because of yer dad's bad language.'

'Danny, the tram is starting to leave, but yer could jump on if yer hurry.'

'I can get the next one. They're along every few minutes.' Danny thought fleetingly of his dancing partners, Janet, Dorothy and Betsy. He didn't go to the dance last night, and if he missed again they'd wonder what was wrong with him. 'Yer mam might be along by then, and I'd feel better. But I'd still be curious.'

'Curious about what?' Jenny was getting agitated. She didn't want him to be with her when her mother came along. 'I don't know why ye're so bothered, Danny, 'cos yer don't even know me! Me mam has made a friend of your mam, which I'm very grateful for, but you don't know me from Adam.'

'No, that is correct. But I do know when a damsel is in distress. Also, we are neighbours, our parents are friends, and we are roughly in the same age group. So I would like to get to know you much more than I would like to get to know Adam.'

Upset as she was, Jenny couldn't stop a glimmer of a smile crossing her face. It would be hard to fall out with this boy. Like his mother, he was kind and caring. And he had the deepest dimples she'd ever seen. She would like to get to know him better, but there was a big obstacle in the way. A father from hell.

Jenny heard a tram in the distance. 'Don't miss this tram, Danny, please. I'm going to start walking towards the picture house, to meet me mam. Yer don't need to worry about me, I'm fine. I admit I was upset by me father, and I admit I can't stand the sight of him. But that is not your problem. So please get on the tram that's coming towards us.'

Danny nodded. 'Okay, you win. But tell me one thing first. Did your father hit you tonight? Is that why yer were upset?'

It was easier to lie than tell the truth. 'We got into an argument over me mam not being there to give him his dinner. He thinks she shouldn't have any life of her own. So when I was putting his dinner in front of him, I told him what I thought of him. It ended up with us shouting at one another, and as he doesn't like being answered back, he lifted his hand to hit me. But I got out of his way quick. Hence the coat, with no scarf or gloves. He was in a fighting mood and I wasn't going to stick around. There you have it, so, now yer curiosity has been satisfied, run and catch that tram.'

For a while Danny had been under the impression that, for one reason or another, Jenny didn't want her mother to see them together. And as he didn't want to upset her again, he pretended to believe her version of what had happened in number twenty-two. 'Okay, I'll make a dash for it.' He looked down into her face and grinned. 'Yer've got a lousy dad. But yer mam more than makes up for him. I'll see yer.' As he sprinted away, he waved his hand. The last Jenny saw of him, he was swinging on to the tram platform.

Annie's eyes flew open when she saw her daughter standing outside the picture house. Her heartbeat quickened, and she was sure something terrible had happened. For wasn't Jenny supposed to be meeting friends to go dancing? 'What's wrong, sweetheart? Why are yer standing here? I thought yer were going out with friends.' Without giving Jenny time to answer, she went on, 'It's yer dad, isn't it? He's been up to his tricks again. I knew I should never have come out.'

'Mam, will yer give me a chance to get a word in?' Jenny felt even worse now, seeing the worry on her mother's face. She just hoped she could lie convincingly. 'There's nothing wrong. Except for me dad, of course, but yer should be used to his shenanigans.'

Annie sighed wearily. She'd enjoyed the Robert Donat film, but she should have known her husband would do something to take the pleasure out of it. 'What's he been up to now? Making a show of us again, in front of the neighbours?'

Jenny shook her head. 'No, nothing to do with the neighbours, so don't look so upset. It was me and me dad, we had a slanging match. He was in a terrible temper because you weren't there to put his dinner down in front of him. He thinks you're his slave. Put on this earth for the sole purpose of waiting on him. He had nothing to moan about, because I took his dinner out of the oven and put it on the table. But then he started to rant and rave, yer know how he does. And I got fed up and began to answer him back. He got in a right rage, and his language would have turned the air blue. So I thought me best bet was to get out of the way, and I grabbed me bag and coat and scarpered.'

'Oh, sweetheart, yer missed meeting yer friends and going to the dance. I am so sorry, I should never have come out. He's determined to spoil my life. I'm not allowed any happiness or freedom. But I shouldn't let him spoil yours, or Ben's. I won't go out again, sweetheart, I'll make sure ye're never left alone with him.'

Jenny had to lower her eyes, she couldn't face her mother. For if she was to tell the truth, her real reason for fleeing the house, her mother wouldn't be able to cope with the knowledge. She'd go out of her mind. 'It comes to something, Mam, when three people are having their lives ruined for the sake of just one, pathetic man. When three people have to dance to his tune. It can't carry on. We have to do something about it.'

'What can we do, sweetheart?'

'I don't know, but I'm not prepared to let him ruin my life, as he has yours. I should have been meeting me friends tonight, Mam, but instead I had to get out of the house to escape a man who is neither a good husband nor a real father. He uses you as a doormat, and I'm fed up seeing you being put down by a man who isn't fit to be in the same room as yer. And I'm fed up with me and Ben being used as punch bags.' Jenny took hold of her mother's hand. 'Come on, we can talk as we walk. But I don't want yer to say anything to our Ben, 'cos I feel more sorry for him than I do for you or meself. He's a fifteen-year-old boy, just got his first job and bringing a wage packet home. He should be walking tall, and be able to have his mates calling for him. But what sort of man is he going to grow up to be, when the only example he's got is me dad! When I was in the Fenwicks' house last night, the difference in the atmosphere hit me in the face. Yer can actually feel the warmth, and the love they have for one another. We have never known that, and I hate me dad for not loving us as he should. I can't remember ever having been kissed or hugged by him, or even being smiled at. All the love, hugs and kisses me and Ben ever had came from you. And we both love the bones of yer. We'd do anything to make yer happy, but we're not allowed to. By order of our father, there is to be no love, laughter, kisses or hugs in our house. Or should I say houses, seeing as we've lived in so many?'

'I've let you and Ben down badly, haven't I, sweetheart? May God forgive me for being so weak, but I can't even promise yer that life will get better in the future. You and Ben are going to have to forge a life for yerselves. At your age yer should have a boyfriend, sweetheart, and be out enjoying yerself. Ye're very pretty, yer could have half a dozen boyfriends if yer went to the right places to meet them. They'd be fighting each other for yer. Like tonight, if yer father hadn't spoilt things, as usual, yer could be on the dance floor now, with a handsome partner.'

There was no humour in Jenny's voice when she spoke. 'I don't doubt I could find a boyfriend, Mam, 'cos there's a couple of lads at work who are always asking me out. And I'd very much like to go out with them. But what would happen if they insisted on walking me home? Would me dad behave himself and welcome them with open arms? No, we both know he wouldn't even pass them the time of day. Chances are, he'd be too drunk to even stand up.'

At that moment, Annie felt so bitter against her husband, she was wishing he would meet with an accident that would cost him his life.

She'd even be grateful to any woman who would take him off her hands. It would be good riddance to bad rubbish. 'I hope the neighbours didn't hear him bawling tonight.'

'No, they wouldn't have heard him, Mam.'

'Thanks goodness for that! I was beginning to think I'd made two friends today and lost them tonight.'

Jenny shook her head while gathering her thoughts together. 'No, the neighbours wouldn't have heard anything. But Danny Fenwick saw me. He came out of his door at the same time as me. I'd been having a cry, 'cos I was mad at me father for taking his temper out on me, and also 'cos I'd let me mates down.'

Annie pulled her to a halt. 'Yer were crying, sweetheart? That's not like you. Yer father didn't hit yer, did he?'

'No, mam, me dad didn't hit me. But he did manage to spoil everything I was looking forward to. And I suppose I was feeling sorry for meself. Anyway, Danny could see I'd been crying, and I had to tell him it was because I was fed up with being bawled at. He was very nice, was Danny, and wanted to stay with me until you came. But I wouldn't let him, 'cos he was on his way to a dance. In the end he hopped on a tram, and by this time he'll be waltzing a girl around the dance floor.'

'Perhaps yer can go with him one night. I'm sure he wouldn't mind. He's a nice lad, and yer'd have someone to bring yer home.'

'Mam, with his looks, he's probably got girls falling at his feet. And he most likely takes a different one home each night. He's lucky. Good home and family, and out dancing every night. Yer can't beat it. I don't begrudge him having a good time, I envy him.'

Chapter Twenty

'What happened to you last night?' Dorothy asked as Danny twirled her expertly out of the way of another dancing couple. 'It's not like you to miss a night.'

'Some friends arrived unexpectedly, and me mam said it would be very rude of me to go out. Yer see, it isn't very often we see these old friends of hers, and I had to agree it would be very bad manners to say I preferred a slow foxtrot to their company.'

'Well, don't let it happen again, Danny, 'cos Betsy and Janet missed yer as well. We spent the night watching the door every time it was pushed open.'

'Me heart would bleed for the three of yer if I thought yer were telling the truth. But I bet yer never missed a dance.' Danny's eyes were smiling down at Dorothy, but it was from habit. In his mind he was seeing the red-rimmed eyes of the girl from number twenty-two. He should have brushed aside her objections and stayed with her. The more he thought about it, the more odd it seemed. If her father was shouting at her, and was about to hit her, then yes, she was right to walk out. But was it bad enough to make her cry?

The music came to an end, and after leading his partner back to her friends, Danny joined the group of boys standing near the door. He never stayed with the girls he danced with, for that would give them the wrong impression. He liked them, they were smashing girls and good dancers. But at just nineteen, he had no intention of settling down for a good few years yet. Twenty-three was a good age to get married, he thought, and at the moment that seemed ages away. And that was only if he'd met a girl he wanted to spend his life with.

Danny's thoughts were interrupted when a bloke standing next to him said, 'I had a good night last night 'cos you weren't here, mate. I had every dance with yer three girlfriends. Usually no one gets a look in with Dorothy or Betsy when ye're here.'

Danny grinned. 'Yer danced every dance with me three girlfriends, did yer, Spike? That must have been uncomfortable for them. And I bet yer got a few dirty looks for taking up the whole of the dance floor.'

Spike had gained his nickname because his hair refused to stay flat, and stood up like spikes on a railing. He now looked very puzzled. 'What are yer talking about? I'm as good a dancer as you, mate, any day.'

'Oh, I don't doubt that. In fact yer must be better, 'cos I don't think I could manage to dance with three partners at the same time.'

Spike looked blank for a second, then squared his shoulders. 'Are you being funny? Who said I danced with three girls at the same time?'

'You did, mate! And I think Tommy will back me up on this, 'cos I know he was listening.' Danny turned his head to wink at a bloke standing beside him. 'Didn't Spike say he had every dance with me three girl-friends?'

Tommy nodded. 'That's what he said. I heard him with me own ears.'

Spike was getting mad now. 'Well, yer'd have had a job to hear me with someone else's ruddy ears, wouldn't yer? And I'm blowed if I know what the pair of yer are getting at. Unless yer don't understand plain English? Shall I say it slowly, then perhaps it'll sink in?'

'Instead of telling us, why don't yer show us? Then we'd all be happy.'

Once again Spike squared his shoulders. They were making fun of him, but he'd show them. He'd have the last laugh. 'Okay, smart lad, which one shall I ask first?'

'The three of them.' Danny was chuckling inside. 'It was you what said yer danced with the three of them, so go on, I can't wait! I've never seen a bloke dancing with three girls at the same time. Yer must be good, Spike, so go on.'

'Yer think ye're funny, don't yer?' He curled his fist and held it up. 'For two pins I'd let yer have this.'

'That's very kind of yer, Spike, but I've got two of me own. I appreciate the offer, though, and I may take yer up on it some time.' The three-piece band struck up with a slow foxtrot and Danny said, 'I'm asking Janet, if it's all right with you.'

Spike rubbed his hands. He still didn't understand what all that had been about, but whatever it was, it looked as though he'd won. 'I'll ask Dorothy. And I'd better hurry up, 'cos I can see another bloke making his way towards her.'

Danny looked at Tommy. 'He still doesn't get it, does he? I bet he has a sleepless night, tossing and turning, trying to figure out what it was he said wrong. Or whether we've just been pulling his leg.'

Tommy raised his hand to a blonde girl who was watching him with expectation in her eyes. 'His mam will put him right. Anyway, I've got more to do right now than worry me head over Spike. He's a nice enough lad, but I wish someone would tell him about Brylcreem. His ruddy hair gets on me nerves.'

Janet was tapping her foot impatiently when Danny approached. 'About time, Danny Fenwick. Are yer playing hard to get or something?'

'Yeah, something like that,' Danny said, leading her on to the dance floor. 'Just 'cos I miss one night, I get the rounds of the kitchen off you and Dorothy. It's worse than being flipping well married.'

'Oh, no, it's not worse than being married, Danny, take it from me.' Janet's dancing was smooth and seamless. 'If yer heard the way my mam and dad argue, yer'd wonder why they ever bothered. They must have been in love once upon a time, but the novelty seems to have worn off quickly for them.'

'No marriage is perfect,' Danny said. 'Although I've got to say the marriage of my mam and dad must have been made in heaven. They get on brilliantly together, and there's no such thing as sulking. My mam says she doesn't have time to sulk, she's too busy looking after her three children and her husband. But she's only kidding, 'cos she has a better social life than I do. It's only having mates in for a cuppa, but they don't half know how to enjoy themselves.'

'I was only joking before, yer know,' Janet told him. 'My mam and dad get on really well. They act like a courting couple sometimes.'

'Then you and me are lucky, 'cos it's not all milk and honey behind every closed front door. I used to think every family was as happy as ours, but that's not the case. Some kids have a dog's life.'

'Ye're getting very serious all of a sudden, Danny.' Janet leaned back in his arms to look into his face. 'What brought this on? Where is the sparkle, and the jokes? Taking last night off didn't do you any good. Did yer miss us that much?'

'I'd like to say I did, but to be frank with yer, there was so much going on I didn't even think about the dance.'

'Oh, ay, and what was that, then? I'm cut to the quick because yer didn't miss me, and to make up for it I think yer should tell me what yer got up to.'

'I'm sorry to disappoint yer, but there was no excitement.' Danny went on to tell her the same tale he had told Dorothy. 'So yer see, it was more dull than exciting. Not that me mam's friends are dull, like, but they spent the night going on about the old days, and it was a little bit before my time.' As he was talking, Danny was thinking he was getting to be like his mam for making stories up. As she'd once said to him, 'I don't tell lies, sunshine, I just make things up to make people laugh and be happy.' Then Danny changed the subject. 'I believe Spike had yer up a few times last night. He seemed dead chuffed about it.'

217

'Yeah, he's not a bad lad, Spike. Not the brainiest person in the world, but he means well. Wouldn't hurt a fly.'

Danny was about to tell her about the curled fist, when the music stopped and the interval was announced. He walked Janet back to her friends, then joined the bunch of lads by the door. He was laughing and joking with them as usual, but inside he was feeling restless. And against his will, he kept thinking about Jenny. Did she meet her mother, and what happened when they got home? If Tom Phillips had taken off once because his wife wasn't home to serve him his meal, then there was every possibility he would take off again when she came in. And ten to one Jenny wouldn't stand by and see her mother hurt, she'd put up a fight.

When the short interval was over, and the band started off with a waltz, Danny looked for Betsy. Soon he was waltzing her around the floor, their bodies and steps in perfect harmony. They were watched with envy by other couples, some of whom left the floor so they could enjoy seeing what one said was poetry in motion. Betsy didn't like to talk when she was dancing, so there was no conversation, only pleasure. 'I enjoyed that, Danny,' she said as he walked her off the floor. 'I missed yer last night. Not that ye're God's gift to women, but because no one does a waltz as well as you.'

'What, not even Spike?'

She chuckled. 'He's a trier, but not quite up to your standard. He's coming on, though, and pretty soon yer'll be having some competition from that quarter.'

'Well, a bit of competition won't do me any harm. Take me down a peg or two.' Danny was walking away from her, when he suddenly turned back. Before he'd given it any thought, the words were leaving his lips. 'Oh, I'll be leaving early tonight. I promised me mam I'd take a message to one of her mates. But I'll see yer tomorrow, without fail. Will yer tell Dorothy and Janet for me, in case they think I'm deserting them?' He spun round, strode out of the hall, checked his overcoat out of the cloakroom, and five minutes later found himself standing at the tram stop with no clear intention in his mind.

Annie put the key in the door very carefully, so it didn't make a sound. Then she turned to Jenny and put a finger to her lips before stepping up into the hall. She cocked an ear for any sign of life in the living room, and after a few seconds she jerked her head. 'Come in, there's no one here. Yer father must have gone to the pub.'

Jenny was so cold her teeth were chattering. She went straight to the fireplace and held out her hands, even though there was barely a flicker from the few coals in the grate. 'I'm going to put a few pieces of coal on, Mam, 'cos I need to get warmed through before I go to bed. Me feet are like ice, and so are my ears and nose. It was stupid of me to rush out without taking me scarf and gloves. I should have had more sense because I knew how cold it was out. But me dad was in such a rage, I wasn't thinking straight. All that was running through my head was that I had to get out, and quick.'

'There's some coal in the scuttle, sweetheart, so you pick a few cobs out while I put the kettle on. While I'm waiting for the water to boil, I'll put a page from the newspaper in front of the fire and the draught from underneath will have the fire going in no time. We'll soon have a hot cup of tea in our hands, and a nice bright fire to cheer us up.'

Jenny shivered, both from the cold and from nerves that were frayed. She dreaded her father coming home. What if he tried to maul her in front of her mother? She wouldn't put it past him, for he didn't care what he did when he'd got a few pints down him. He'd take a delight in humiliating the pair of them. She could see him now, in her mind's eye, taunting them with that horrible smirk on his face, while slobbering at the mouth. 'Mam, when our Ben comes in, I'm going straight up to bed. I couldn't bear to face me dad.'

'There's the kettle whistling, sweetheart. Yer'll feel better when yer've had a hot drink. And when yer go to bed, I'll come with yer. We can keep each other warm.'

It was nine o'clock when Ben came home, and Annie poured him out a cup of tea. She'd made a fresh pot, for she'd known he'd be home soon, and that he'd be glad of a warm drink. As she handed him the cup, she said, 'Yer father's been up to his tricks again. In a temper because I wasn't here to put his dinner in front of him, he took off on Jenny.'

'What did he do, Jen?' her brother asked, 'Shout, or hit yer?'

Jenny told him the same tale she'd told her mother. 'And I went to meet me mam coming out of the pictures. I was like a block of ice, 'cos I didn't have enough clothes on.'

'I got the fright of me life when I came out of the pictures and saw her waiting for me,' Annie said. 'It was me first time out at night, and it'll be me last. I'll never leave either of yer alone with him again.'

'I made a right fool of meself through him,' Jenny told her brother. 'He'd got to me so much, I was crying me eyes out when I ran into the street. I'd banged the door shut and was leaning against the wall when Danny from over the road came out. He was on his way to a dance, and I tried to get away from him, 'cos I felt stupid for crying like a baby. But Danny was really nice, and he wanted to wait with me till me mam came home from the pictures. I wouldn't let him, though, for I felt really awful. A seventeen-year-old, crying like a baby. All because I've got a lousy, bullying father. Honestly, I know yer shouldn't say yer hate anyone, but I'm afraid I hate me dad.'

'Had he been drinking, sis?' Ben asked. 'Or was it just his bad temper?'

'It was both.' Jenny sighed. 'He stank of beer, and I'd say he'd had quite a few on the way home. That, on top of me mam not being in, well, yer don't need me to draw a picture for yer. Both of yer know what he's like.'

'And he's in the pub now, is he?' Ben asked.

'There's nowhere else he can be,' Annie said. 'It's not as though he's got any friends he could have called on. I don't think he's ever had a friend in his life. Even the bloke who was his best man when we got married, I've never seen sight nor light of since that day.'

'If he'd had drinks earlier, and he's propping the bar up again now, he'll be in a right state by throwing out time.' Ben pulled a face. 'And he'll either make a fool of himself in the street again, or he'll take it out on us. So I think I'll go to bed when I've finished me tea, Mam, and I think you and our Jenny would be well advised to do the same.'

'We intend to, sweetheart. We'd already decided to go to bed once you were in and had had a cuppa to warm yer up. So, if ye're ready, I think we should make ourselves scarce. The pubs start throwing out at ten, and it's ten minutes to now.' Annie dropped her head for a few seconds, so her children couldn't see the despair in her eyes. She didn't think she could put up with this life for much longer. It had been dragging her down for years, and now she felt she had reached rock bottom. With a weary sigh, she rose from the chair. 'Come on, let's go. With a bit of luck, yer father will be so drunk he'll just throw himself on the couch and spend the night there.'

'Are yer leaving the light on, Mam,' Ben asked, 'or shall I turn it off?'

'Better turn it off son, in case he sets fire to the ruddy house. If he's no matches to light a ciggie, yer know he puts a piece of newspaper to the mantel. He'll burn the house down one of these days.'

Ben pulled the chain at the side of the gas light, and plunged the room into darkness. As he followed his mother and sister upstairs, he said, 'I wouldn't care if he did burn the house down, Mam, as long as he was the only one in it.'

Ada raised her brows in surprise when Danny walked in. She looked to the clock on the mantelpiece to make sure she hadn't got the time wrong. 'What are yer doing home at this time? Are yer sickening for something?'

Danny pulled a chair out and sat down. 'When I left here tonight, Mam, there was a little incident, and I couldn't enjoy the dance because it was on me mind.'

It was Jack who asked, 'What sort of an incident, son? Did someone get run over?'

'No, nothing like that, Dad.' Danny scratched his head. 'In fact, I'm probably making a mountain out of a molehill. But I couldn't get it out of me mind, and it put me right off dancing. Even the slow foxtrot didn't seem the same.'

'In the name of God, sunshine, are yer going to keep this mystery to yerself, or are yer going to tell me and yer dad about it?'

Danny smiled, and his dimples appeared. 'I'm not having yer on, Mam, but I guess yer'll think I'm crazy when I tell yer what's been playing on me mind.'

Ada tutted and clicked her tongue. 'If yer don't hurry up and put me out of me misery, sunshine, so help me I'll clock yer one.'

Once he started, it didn't take long for Danny to explain what had happened, and what his thoughts were. 'I felt really sorry for Jenny, 'cos yer could see she was ashamed. She'd been crying and her eyes were red. She was shivering in just her working coat, with nothing round her neck and no gloves. And after seeing the antics that father of hers can get up to, I was really afraid for her. I offered to walk with her to meet her mother, but she wouldn't have it. She practically chased me off. I couldn't very well stick around when she didn't want me there, but I got the feeling there was more to it than a shouting match with her father.'

Ada left her chair and crossed to the window. She drew the curtain aside and looked out at the house opposite. 'I can't see a light. I wonder if the queer feller's in the pub, and Annie and the kids have gone to bed to keep out of his way?'

'It'll be throwing out time in the pub any time now,' Jimmy said. 'I hope he doesn't kick off like he did last night. I don't mind carrying him home once in a while, but I'm blowed if I'll do it night after night.'

'I'll keep me eye open for him,' Ada said. 'He goes to the pub at the top of the road each night, so I'll watch for him.' There was anger in her voice when she said, 'Me blood is boiling, it really is. To think that in the house opposite, a woman and two children have gone to bed early because they're frightened of a flaming, jumped-up drunkard. I've never known the likes of it before.' She turned her gaze back to number twenty-two. 'I hope he does start, 'cos I'm just in the mood for him. I've made a friend of Annie, and I'll not stand by and see a friend in trouble.'

221

Danny scraped his chair back. 'Mam, come and sit down. I'll walk up to the pub, and when he comes out I'll follow him.'

'That's if he's in there,' Jimmy said. 'He might not be.'

'He'll be there.' Ada dropped the curtain and returned to her chair. 'Apparently he has a routine that he sticks to without fail. A few pints in a pub down by the docks where he works, home to be waited on hand and foot, then up to the pub on the corner. And he stays there until the landlord throws him out.'

Danny donned the overcoat he'd taken off when he came in. 'I'll walk up now. I won't do or say anything to him, I'll just walk behind and see what he gets up to.'

'I don't like the idea of yer getting tangled up with him, sunshine, 'cos he's a bad bugger. Stay here and we'll keep a lookout through the window. If he starts anything, the three of us can deal with him.'

'I'll go with Danny, if it makes yer feel better, love,' Jimmy said. 'But if it's to be a regular occurrence, I think the police should be called. A night in the cells might just bring the man to his senses.'

'There's no need for you to come, Dad, I'll be all right on me own. I'm a big boy now, yer know, and a big sober boy can lick a drunken man any day. If he's in the state he was last night, he'll see three of me.' Danny dropped a kiss on his mother's cheek. 'I'll yell if I need any help, but it's not very likely.'

With his coat collar pulled up to protect his ears from the biting wind, Danny walked up the street. He could hear the voices of men laughing and joking as they left the pub, but they were men who could only afford one pint, and they made it last until last orders were called. When the exit of the drinkers tailed off, and there was no sign of Tom Phillips, Danny thought he'd missed him. Until he heard the landlord's voice saying, 'Out yer go, mate. And if yer make it home in the state ye're in, it'll be a bloody miracle.' And into view came the staggering figure of Jenny's father. He could hardly stand, and put his hand on the wall to support him.

Danny stood back in the shadows, watching with amazement the performance of the man from twenty-two. Backwards, forwards and sideways the body rolled, and several times Danny held his breath as it seemed the man must surely fall. But when Tom Phillips had finally got himself facing the right way, he began to sway and roll his way forward. Then he began to talk to himself in a loud voice, using words that only the lowest of the low would use. The street was deserted and quiet, but the drunken man had no thought for other people. In fact he was so drunk, Danny told himself the landlord of the pub had been right. It would be a miracle if Tom Phillips ever made it to his front door.

It was when Jenny's father began to shout his obscenities out loud that Danny decided to try to calm the man down so the family wouldn't be humiliated. Jenny had had enough of this man for one day. So when they were near enough to number twenty-two, Danny came alongside him, but stepped into the gutter to dodge the swaying figure. How the man was even on his feet was a mystery to him. 'Good evening, Mr Phillips.'

His body swaying precariously, and his eyes blinking through a drunken haze, Tom Phillips snarled, 'Who the bleeding hell are you? Bugger off before I belt yer one.'

Danny could see the funny side of the remark, but this was no time for humour. And he didn't want to antagonise the man, he just wanted to get him home before he had the neighbours out. 'I'm a friend of yer daughter, Jenny.'

Tom Phillips was far too drunk to stand upright, or to see clearly, but the words seemed to have got through to him. He tried to lean forward to get a better look at who he was talking to, but couldn't balance properly. Slobbering and burping, he got the words out. 'Oh, got herself a feller, has she? Getting what yer want off her, are yer? That's right, lad, you get in there.' His words were slurred but understandable, and Danny was stunned. Then came a feeling of revulsion and anger. What sort of man was he, who could talk like that about his own daughter? He deserved a bloody good hiding. And Danny would gladly have given him one, except for the vision in his mind of Jenny and her tears.

But Tom Phillips hadn't finished. To him it was a huge joke. In between hiccups, he said, 'Nearly had her meself tonight. Had me hand in her knickers, but the silly bitch ran away.'

Unknown to Danny, his mother and father were standing at the front door. There was no way Ada was going to sit in the house when her beloved son could be in trouble. They'd been watching their son walk alongside the drunk, but they couldn't hear what was being said. However, they did see their son raise his arm, and they did hear his fist connect with the jaw of Tom Phillips. Then they saw Tom fall backwards. 'Oh, my God,' Ada said, a hand to her mouth. 'What's going on?'

'You stay here, love.' Jimmy was across the cobbles in seconds. 'What happened, son?' He gazed down at Annie's husband, who was out for the count. 'What made yer punch him?'

'He deserved more than a punch, Dad, he got off lightly. But I'll tell yer later. Ask me mam to knock for Mrs Phillips, and let's get this feller in the house before some nosy parker comes out to see what's going on.'

* * *

223

Jenny had dropped off to sleep, but Annie was wide awake. She couldn't rest until she knew her husband was in and fast asleep. That was the only time she could relax. So when Ada's light knock came, she was down the stairs in seconds, and slipped her coat on over her nightdress.

'Don't get upset, sunshine,' Ada said, 'there's nothing to worry about. Everything is under control. Yer husband got himself plastered, and Jimmy and Danny are here with him. If yer'll move out of the way, they'll bring him in and put him on the couch.'

Annie stepped aside, thankful of the darkness for it hid the pain and shame in her eyes. Was her life going to be one of humiliation until the day she died? This was one of the times she felt she couldn't go on much longer. But she had the children to think of, and they were the only reason she kept going. 'Shall I put the light on so yer can see what ye're doing?' Annie asked, her voice shaking with nerves. 'It won't take a second to put a match to the mantle.'

'No, ye're all right, love,' Jimmy told her, as he and Danny laid Tom Phillips none too gently on the couch. 'Yer husband is well away, so if I were you I'd go back to bed and forget about him.'

'If only I could forget about him for ever,' Annie said wearily. 'My life might be worth living if it wasn't for him.'

'And what of yer children?' Danny couldn't help asking. 'They won't be having much of a life with a father who is always drunk.'

'I know that, lad, and God knows I have tried. But now I've got to the state where I haven't the strength to stand up to him. I've been given a cross to bear, and it's a heavy one.'

Ada shooed her husband and son towards the front door. 'You two go home, I'll stay for a little while with Annie. Have the kettle on so I can have a hot drink before going to bed.'

When the men had gone, Annie began to sob. 'I'm sorry, sweetheart, yer family shouldn't have to carry my burden. They'll rue the day yer ever made friends with me.'

'What a load of nonsense, Annie Phillips. Now pull yerself together, and get a grip. Instead of feeling sorry for yerself, start getting angry with that useless, good-for-nothing heap on the couch. Put yer foot down with him once and for all. Yer could stop feeding him for a start, that might bring him to his senses.'

'Easier said than done, sweetheart.' Annie's sigh was heavy and drawn out. 'I hate him with an intensity that sometimes frightens me. If it wasn't for the kids, I think I'd have killed him long before now. I'm frightened of him, I'll admit that, but the fear doesn't go as deep as my loathing for him. I cringe when I'm near him, for everything about him is dirty. His habits, the way he eats, and the filth that comes out of his mouth. And the saddest thing, the one that tears me apart, is that the children suffer for my mistakes. I should never have married him, but that is no excuse. I could have left him any time, if only I'd had the guts.'

Ada put a comforting arm across Annie's shoulders. 'Listen to me, sunshine, just for a minute, and then you can get back to bed and I can go home. Yer mightn't like what I'm going to say, but yer'd do well to listen.' It was dark in the room, with only a glimmer through the curtain from a street lamp a few doors away. It wasn't possible to see the state of Tom Phillips, she could only see an outline. 'Tomorrow morning, I want yer to stay in bed until it's time for Jenny and Ben to get up. Make them their toast and whatever, but don't offer the queer feller anything, Not even a cuppa, or the time of day. He's so drunk, he won't be fit to pick a fight with yer, so ignore him. No matter what he says, or does, ignore him. And tell the kids to do the same thing. He's giving you a dog's life, so do the same to him.'

After squeezing Annie's shoulder, Ada kissed her on the cheek. 'Think of what a rotter yer've picked for a husband, sunshine, and all the bad things about him. That way yer'll get yer dander up, and yer'll be ready for whatever he wants to throw at yer. Yer'll feel better for it, I promise. And with those words of wisdom, I'll love yer and leave yer, before my feller thinks I've run off with the milkman. Good night and God bless, sunshine, and try and get some sleep.'

Annie watched her crossing the cobbles, and called softly, 'Good night and God bless, sweetheart, and thank yer husband and son for me.'

Chapter Twenty-One

'Whatever made yer punch Mr Phillips hard enough to knock him out, sunshine?' Ada asked, her hand curled round the cup of hot tea. 'It must have been some punch to knock him senseless.'

'He was senseless before I touched him, Mam, he could hardly stand.' Danny's mind was all over the place. He still couldn't come to terms with what Jenny's father had said about her. And he certainly wasn't going to repeat it to anyone. It wouldn't be fair on the girl, and would have a devastating effect on Mrs Phillips. 'I couldn't help meself, and I'd do it again if the occasion arose. He's got a filthy mouth on him, Mam, and it's not only the bad language. If yer asked me what I thought of him, I'd say he was a dirty old man. I'm not going to repeat it, yer'll have to use yer imagination. And I don't want yer to tell Mrs Phillips what I've said. She's got enough to cope with without me adding to it.'

'Yer can say that again, son, she's got more than enough. The trouble with her is she's too good. If she hadn't let him get away with his antics when they first got married, he'd be a lot tamer than he is now.' Ada leaned over to put a hand on her husband's arm. 'You're an angel compared to the queer feller, and I want yer to know, sunshine, that I do realise how lucky I am. And having a diamond of a husband meself makes me feel more sorry for Annie. But as I've just told her, she's going to have to change, or her and the kids will never have any chance of a decent life. Whether what I told her penetrated, I don't know, but I think she's a smashing woman, and I'm going to keep on at her. She's a mate now, and me and Hetty aren't going to stand by and see her ill treated.'

'What advice have yer given her, Mam?' Danny asked, telling himself he was lucky to have a mother who was considerate, kind and loving, and had a heart as big as a week, and a wonderful sense of fun. 'What pearls of wisdom have yer passed on to her?'

Ada chuckled. 'I'd love to be a fly on their living room wall if she does what I suggested. I said she should stay in bed tomorrow morning until it was time for Jenny and Ben to get up. She shouldn't cook for the queer feller, nor should she speak to him. If he starts shouting, she should just ignore him, pretend he's not there. See to herself and the kids, and let him get on with it. If he's hungry, he can make himself a jam butty.'

'I don't know much about drunks, love,' Jimmy said. 'My dad was never a drinker, and neither am I. But if Tom Phillips wakes up in time to go to work tomorrow, then I'll eat me flaming hat.'

'We'll have to wait and see.' Ada put her cup down. 'Have yer seen the time? Yer'll be lucky if ye're up in time to go to work yerself.' She pushed her chair back. 'Leave the cups, I'll see to them in the morning.' She stood in front of her son, tenderness in her smile. 'Yer did a good job, sunshine. If Tom Phillips had managed to get home, the state he was in, God knows what havoc he'd have caused. So have a good night's sleep. God bless.'

'Good night and God bless, Mam. And let's hope yer words of wisdom work wonders with Mrs Phillips. She's the only one who can turn things round for them. We can help, but with the best will in the world, we can't be watching them twenty-four hours a day.' Danny slapped his father on the back. 'Good night, Dad. See yer in the morning.'

Annie was lying awake, her eyes on the ceiling. She'd had a restless night with very little sleep. Her mind was overactive with worry about the embarrassment and humiliation her husband was bringing down on her. She'd put up with it for twenty years, but didn't think she could stand it much longer. She was even losing the will to live. If it wasn't for the love she had for her children, she would have been long gone. She could have found herself a job, or even slept in doorways. Anything would have been better than living with a man she'd come to fear and loathe.

The shrill sound of the alarm clock jolted Annie from her thoughts, and she slipped her hand from under the bedclothes to switch the alarm off on the clock which stood on the floor at the side of the bed. She did it with speed, so the shrill sound wouldn't wake the girl sleeping beside her. And when Jenny didn't stir, Annie lay back on the pillow. The clock was set to go off at six fifteen every morning, giving her time to light the fire and start Tom's breakfast before he came down. But this morning she made no effort to leave the warmth of the bed. Ada's words about not letting Tom Phillips walk all over her had been running through her mind all night, and she was willing herself to be strong. She'd wait another fifteen minutes, then go down and light the fire and see to breakfast for Jenny and Ben. And if her husband started throwing his weight around she would do as Ada said, and ignore him. But things are easier said than done, and old habits hard to break. After five minutes Annie couldn't lie still any longer. She made excuses to herself as she slipped her legs over the side of the bed, saying the living room would be cold for the children to come down to, and it wouldn't be fair on them. Reaching for the cardigan she'd left on top of the bedclothes, she slipped her arms into the sleeves, shivering as she stood up on the cold lino-covered floor. Apart from the bed, there was no other furniture in the small room for her to bump into, so she put her hand out until she felt the wall, then followed it to the door.

Creeping down the stairs, Annie resolved to be brave, no matter what sort of mood her husband was in. She was apprehensive, of course, for hadn't she had twenty violent years when she didn't know how or when she would be attacked. But as she tried to avoid the stairs that creaked, she kept reminding herself that this time she had to be brave, otherwise she stood to lose the only friends she had. And that one thought was enough to strengthen her resolve.

Annie stood outside the living room door for a while, listening to the snores and other sounds coming from within. She was surprised, for no matter how drunk he'd been, Tom Phillips was always up in time for work. But from what she could hear, he was still asleep. She opened the door quietly, slipped inside, then quickly closed it behind her. If he woke in a rage, she didn't want the children to hear. It was dark in the room, and not wanting to wake her husband by lighting the gas, she lifted the curtain to let in some light. For several seconds she gazed down at the man she was married to. He reeked of beer, and the sounds coming from his throat were sickening, as was the saliva running out of the side of his mouth. He was her husband, but all she felt for him was contempt. And with the contempt came a question. Why had she allowed this rotter to rule, and ruin, her life? 'Never again,' Annie told the sleeping form. 'Those days are over.'

With the curtain pulled back enough to give her sufficient light to rake the ashes out of the grate, Annie set to. She glanced over to the couch several times, expecting her husband to be woken by the noise. But he never stirred. Even when Jenny and Ben came down, he seemed not to hear them as they washed in the sink before sitting down to their breakfast.

'Is me dad all right, Mam?' Ben asked, his eyes going to the couch. 'He's never slept like that before. He'll be late for work.'

'That's his worry,' Jenny said. 'He's still breathing, so there's nothing wrong with him. Even if there was I wouldn't feel sorry for him. He got himself drunk, so let him suffer for it.'

Ben was uneasy, though. 'He'll be blazing when he wakes, Mam. You'll get the blame for not waking him up.'

'Don't you worry about that, sweetheart, I can look after meself. I'm not going to back away from him ever again, I've made up me mind on that. His days of ruling the roost are over, and the sooner he realises it the better.' Annie glanced towards the couch before lowering her voice. 'I went in his pockets for the first time in me married life. And I've taken a couple of bob out. He'll have enough for his fare to work and back, but not enough to get drunk on.'

This confession caused Jenny to raise her brows. 'Mam, d'yer think that's wise? Yer could be asking for trouble, 'cos I can't see him letting yer get away with that.'

'I might be asking for trouble, sweetheart, but it'll be the first time in twenty years. Yer father's got away with murder over those years, because I've been too frightened to stop him. But when I told yer I wasn't backing away from him ever again, I meant it.'

'I'll take the day off, Mam,' Jenny said, fearful for her mother. 'I can say I was sick or something. I won't get into trouble, 'cos I'm never late clocking on, and I've never taken time off. I'd rather tell a lie than worry meself sick all day, wondering how yer are. It's all very well saying ye're not backing away from me dad ever again, but when it comes to the push, yer couldn't stand up to him, he's too strong for yer. It would be different if me and Ben were here, we could help yer. We'll always help yer, yer know that.'

'I know yer would, sweetheart, but yer don't need to take a day off on my behalf. You and Ben don't have to worry yer heads about me. Ada gave me a good talking to last night, and I've made up me mind to be strong and not be afraid of yer father ever again.' Annie lowered her eyes. 'Did yer hear the goings-on last night, sweetheart?'

Jenny shook her head. 'No, why? What happened?'

'I heard a bit of commotion,' Ben told them, 'but it didn't last long, and I soon fell asleep.'

'There wasn't much commotion, even though yer father was rotten drunk again. Danny Fenwick gave him a punch and knocked him out for the count. If he hadn't, the street would have been up again.'

Jenny gasped. 'Danny knocked me dad out? Oh, my God, what are we coming to, Mam? What are the neighbours going to think of us?' While she was speaking, Jenny was shivering inside. She could still feel her father's hands touching her, and the sensation made her feel sick. And it also made her feel dirty. Twice he'd caught her unawares, but it wouldn't happen again for she would never stay in the house alone with him. She'd never forget what he did, and she would never forgive him. 'I don't know why Danny knocked him out, but I'm glad he did. And I hope he hurt him.'

Three pair of eyes turned to the couch. The sounds were still coming, and Tom Phillips's chest was going up and down, so they knew he was still alive. But he hadn't moved an inch. 'You two get yerselves off to work, and don't give him another thought. Once yer've gone, I'll wake him up and he can please himself whether he goes back to sleep or goes to work. He'll get into trouble for being late, but that's his lookout, not ours.'

As Jenny was putting her coat on, she said, 'Yer will run over to Mrs Fenwick's if me dad starts on yer, won't yer, Mam? Promise yer won't try and tackle him on yer own? Never let him catch yer on the hop, for heaven's sake. Remember, he's wicked, and he'd think nothing of beating yer to pulp.'

'He'll not catch me out, sweetheart, yer can rest assured on that point.' Annie followed her children to the front door. 'What I can't understand is why he's still asleep. I raked the ashes out, lit the fire, made yer breakfast, and he's never so much as stirred. And I haven't tiptoed around, I've made the same noise raking the grate out as I always do. I don't know whether Danny packs a powerful punch, or whether it was the amount of beer yer father had.'

Ben, who was a few inches taller than his sister, looked down at her. 'Haven't yer noticed this is the front door, Jenny? This is the first time yer've ever come out this way.'

Jenny smiled. 'Yer've heard the expression about the worm turning? Well, if me mam can turn, so can I. No more running down the entry for me. It's the front door in future, with me head held high and a smile on me face.'

Annie patted her cheek. 'Good for you, sweetheart. If we stick together and let him see we're no longer afraid of him, perhaps he'll turn into a worm as well.'

'Mam, the worms you and me are talking about are just a figure of speech. But with me dad, well, he's a real worm. Always has been, and always will be.'

It was half past eight when Tom Phillips stirred. Annie had washed up, made the beds, dusted the living room, and had just sat down with a fresh cup of tea. She stayed in her chair and watched as he looked up at the ceiling for a few seconds before turning his head. He did it with a groan, for his whole body ached through lying in one position for so long. He seemed disorientated for a while, as though he couldn't make out where he was.

'Awake then, are yer?' Annie held the cup to her mouth and sipped the hot tea. 'I was beginning to think yer were dead.'

Tom tried to sit up, but the cramp in his back and legs was painful and he laid his head down again. 'What's the bleeding time?'

Annie couldn't believe she was so calm, but she relished the feeling. 'It's twenty-five to nine.'

The words were enough to bring Tom Phillips to a sitting position. He was so shocked, he forgot the pain and stared at his wife as though she was mental. 'I said what's the time, so don't try and be funny, yer stupid cow. What's the bleeding time?'

Amazed at her lack of fear, Annie said, 'Stupid cows can't tell the time, so why don't yer look at the clock yerself?'

The next five minutes, however, were to test Annie's new-found strength. For Tom Phillips was off the couch like a shot out of a gun. He peered at the clock to make sure he wasn't imagining things, then he turned on his wife. 'Yer stupid bleeding mare! Why the bleeding hell didn't yer wake me up? Ye're sitting there like a stuffed dummy, which yer are, while I've lost half a day's pay!' He was beside himself with rage. 'Get off that fat bleeding arse of yours, and see to me breakfast while I get washed. I'll pay yer back for this tonight, mark my words. I'll bloody skin yer alive.' And when Annie didn't move, he stood over her and ranted, 'Are yer bloody deaf as well as daft, yer stupid cow!'

Annie swivelled in her chair to face him. She was shaking inside, but kept telling herself that if she gave in now the rest of her life would be the same as the last twenty years. And she kept a picture of the two children in her mind so she wouldn't weaken. 'If yer want breakfast in this house, yer'll be down at the right time for it. If not, then yer make yer own. I've finished running round after yer, so get that through yer thick skull. And if yer don't want to lose a full day's pay, then I suggest yer get yerself moving. Don't look at me for help, 'cos yer won't get it.'

The veins on his temples standing out with anger, Tom grabbed a handful of Annie's hair and pulled her to her feet. 'Get me breakfast on, or yer'll be sorry. And keep away from that nosy cow over the road, she's filling yer head with nonsense.' He shook his hand, causing Annie to grimace with pain. She thought he was going to pull her hair out by the roots. But the mental picture of her children helped her to stand firm.

'Yer can kill me if yer like, Tom Phillips, but I'm not making yer any breakfast. I am not a slave, and I'll not be treated like one.'

Tom threw her from him with such force she pushed the table forward and fell to her knees. But her mind was clear, and when she saw the foot coming towards her she was quick to roll away and scramble to her feet. And if Tom thought he could put the fear of God into her, he'd done just the opposite. It wasn't fear Annie felt, but anger. Grinding her teeth together, she said, 'I told yer I'm not making yer any breakfast, and I mean it. If ye're hungry, then see to yerself. God knows ye're old and ugly enough.'

'I'll deal with you tonight,' Tom snarled. 'And on top of what yer've done to me this morning, there's the little matter of where yer sleep. Tonight yer get back in my bed, where yer belong. And don't pretend to be tired, for I'm going to keep yer very busy. Yer've been out of me bed for a few nights now, so yer can spend the day thinking of ways to make up for lost time. Ways to make yer husband happy.' His sinister laugh sent a cold shiver down Annie's spine. 'Pretend ye're a whore, they know how to send a man to heaven and back. But why should I pay when I've got one of me own? I've got you well trained now on what to do to please me, so why should I throw good money away when all I have to do is lift me finger and you jump?'

Annie faced him, her eyes filled with the contempt she felt for him. But that didn't worry Tom Phillips, who didn't care what anyone thought of him. He just laughed in her face before turning towards the kitchen feeling cocky. While he was having a swill, she'd make his breakfast, he was sure of that.

But he was wrong. For while he was at the sink with the tap running, Annie picked up her purse, took her coat down off the hook and left the house by the front door. She'd be back when she'd done a bit of shopping, and given him time to get ready and leave for work. She never doubted he would go to work, for he looked forward to the few pints he had every night in the pub on the dock road. He was a creature of habit, was Tom Phillips. A few pints after work put him in the right mood to go home and throw his weight around. He was a nobody at work, not even liked by the rest of the gang. But at home he was the lord and master, and this made him feel powerful.

All these things were going through Annie's mind as she stood in the doorway of the sweet shop. It was a handy spot, for she'd be able to see her husband when he turned the corner of the street and headed towards the tram stop. And once he was on the tram she could go home, make herself a hot drink and calm down. And when her head was clear, she could decide what action to take when it came to bedtime. For nothing on God's earth would make her get into Tom Phillips's bed ever again.

'Fares please.' The conductor walked down the aisle of the tram clicking his ticket machine. 'Have the right money ready if yer can.' He stopped by Tom's seat. 'If yer've got a ticket, mister, can I see it?'

Tom's mind had been miles away. He was trying to think of an excuse for being late. One his boss would believe. Without looking at the conductor, he put his hand in his pocket for the tuppence he needed for his fare. A puzzled expression crossed his face as he twisted to one side and put a hand in his other pocket. He sensed the conductor was getting impatient, and passed over a silver sixpence. 'A tuppenny one.'

The conductor jerked his head in disgust as he turned the handle on his ticket machine and caught the ticket as it came out. There are some miserable buggers in this world, he thought. Never a please, a thank you, or even a kiss me backside. So for spite, he held on to the ticket until Tom held out his hand for it, and the change from his sixpence. And because his mind was elsewhere, Tom didn't hear the muttered, 'Miserable bugger. I bet he's never the life and soul of a party.' Then came a chuckle as the conductor made his way to the front of the tram to tell the driver, 'There's a bloke back there who would be perfect as one of those professional mourners what yer see walking in front of a hearse.'

Even if he had heard, it wouldn't have penetrated Tom's brain, for he was too busy wondering what he'd done with his money. All he could find in his pocket was the sixpence and a threepenny piece. And he should have more than that. But no matter how hard he racked his brains, he couldn't remember how much he had with him when he went to the pub last night. Or how much he spent in the pub. In fact he didn't remember anything at all about last night. Not even leaving the pub, or getting home. He mustn't have gone to bed, because he was wearing his working clothes when he woke up. It was all the fault of that stupid cow he was married to. She should have made sure he was up in time to go to work, and had a breakfast ready for him. She was slipping, and he'd have to sort that out before things got out of hand. The cow what lived opposite, she was feeding his wife's mind with all sorts of rubbish, and it had to stop.

With the tram swaying from side to side, Tom pushed thoughts of his wife aside to concentrate on what was important to him. Where was he going to get the money from for the three or four pints of beer he had every night? All the money he had on him was the fourpence change out of the sixpence, and the threepenny bit. Keeping tuppence back for his tram fare home, that would leave him with the paltry sum of fivepence. That was like a drop in the ocean. He needed at least four bob to add to it, for his beer on the way home, and for going to the pub later. None of the lads would have that much money to lend him, but if he could scrounge a shilling off someone, that would see him right for a few pints on his way home. And he'd get money off his wife and kids to go to the pub with. If they didn't want to part with the money, he'd belt them until they handed it over.

* * *

233

Annie's head was splitting as she sat at the table, her fingers nervously picking at the chenille cloth. Tom's words were going round and round in her head, until she felt like screaming. She had made up her mind she would never again get into bed with him, but had known him long enough now to know that when he said something, he meant it. And if she refused point blank to go into the front bedroom, there would be holy murder. She wasn't so much afraid for herself, it was the children she worried about. Ben was fifteen, Jenny seventeen. Both far too young to hear the filth that would pour from his mouth. She didn't want them to hear words no decent man would use in front of children. Words used only by the lowest of the low.

Annie pushed her chair back so quickly, it toppled over. And as she bent to pick it up, she told the empty room, 'I've been weak, and my kids have suffered for it. But no more. For all I care, Tom Phillips can rot in hell. Let him go to the whores he likes to talk about, that's all he's fit for. They wouldn't worry about his coarse language, or filthy habits, not when they were taking his money.' She stood for a while with her hands on the chair back, her mind seeking an answer to her problem. There had to be a way, but it was finding it. She had nowhere to go, no place of safety for herself and the children, and no money. Her parents were still alive, but they were too old and frail now to take her troubles to. Besides, it was so long since she'd been to see them, she felt ashamed.

Taking a deep breath, Annie let out a long sigh. Her eyes looked through the window to the house opposite. Ada had told her she could go to her any time with her problems. But was this one problem Ada couldn't help her with? Annie knew if she was going to act, she had to do it quickly, before she lost her nerve. So she pulled her coat from the hook, slipped her arms into the sleeves, and made sure the front door key was in the pocket. Then, without giving herself time to think, she crossed the cobbles.

'In the name of God, woman, yer must have the keenest nose in the neighbourhood,' Ada said when she opened the door. 'I'm just pouring tea out for me and me mate. Come in quick, before yer let the cold in.'

Annie was wishing she hadn't come now. 'I won't bother yer if ye're just going to have a drink, sweetheart. I'll come back later.'

Ada leaned forward and pulled on her arm. 'In yer come, sunshine, there's no need to waste shoe leather by coming back later. It's only me and Hetty, we haven't got two fancy men here as well. And even if we did, we're not selfish, we'd share them with yer.'

Hetty called, 'Will yer come in and shut the flaming door! I'm getting blown off the chair here.'

Annie was losing her nerve. To face one woman with her problem was bad enough, but two she just couldn't cope with. 'No, I'll not come in, sweetheart. You and Hetty have yer cup of tea in peace, and I'll come over later.'

'Yer'll do as ye're told and come in now.' One sharp tug had Annie standing in the tiny hall, facing her neighbour. 'We're mates now, sunshine, and we never begrudge a mate a cup of tea.' Ada pushed her forward. 'Move, before Hetty starts moaning again.'

Hetty greeted Annie with a smile. 'You must be like my feller, girl. He can smell tea from a mile off.'

'We'll let you be mother, Hetty,' Ada said, 'seeing as ye're nearest to the teapot. And as I've mentioned to yer before, the tea always tastes nicer when you've poured it out.'

Her neighbour grinned. 'Don't be trying to soft-soap me, girl, I know yer too well. But if it makes yer happy, I'll pour the tea while you go to the larder for the biscuits. I never enjoy a cuppa if I haven't got a biscuit to dunk.'

While Hetty was busy pouring the tea, and complaining about how difficult it was to dry the washing in this cold weather, Ada pretended to be listening by nodding her head now and again. But out of the corner of her eye she was watching Annie, clasping and unclasping her hands, her chest heaving with sighs she tried to smother. Trouble again, Ada told herself. I couldn't live like that. I'd either leave the bugger, or poison him.

Hetty didn't notice anything amiss, and she kept the conversation going through the first cup of tea and two Nice biscuits. The fact that Annie was so quiet was lost on her. But it wasn't lost on Ada, and after she'd finished her tea, she put the cup back on the saucer and ran the back of a hand across her mouth. 'Well, sunshine, out with it. What's up?'

Annie's nerves were shattered. 'What d'yer mean, what's up?'

'I wasn't born yesterday, sunshine,' Ada told her, 'and it's sticking out a mile that all is not well with yer. I can tell by yer eyes, and yer whole body is as taut as a violin string. So come on, what's bothering yer?'

Annie sucked in her breath, then blew it out slowly. 'What's bothering me, sweetheart, is that I'm bothering you. I come to you with all me troubles, and it's not fair. Yer'll rue the day yer ever knocked on my door.'

Ada clicked her tongue and slowly shook her head. 'Listen, sunshine, when yer know me a bit better, yer'll find out I don't suffer fools gladly. If I thought yer were a moaner, who just liked the sound of their own voice and talked for the sake of talking, then I'd tell yer to yer face to hop it. But if I make a friend, then I expect them to listen to my troubles, and help me out if they can. And it works the other way round. If a mate of mine needs help, then I'll give it.' She turned to Hetty, who was listening with interest. 'Isn't that right, sunshine?'

'It certainly is, girl. We've been mates for twenty years, and we've always shared everything. Joy, sorrow, heartache, the lot.' There was affection in the smile Hetty gave her friend. 'Many's the time I'd have been lost without Ada. She's always been there for me.'

'Yes, but you've forged that friendship over the years,' Annie said. 'Yer've only known me a few weeks and I've brought yer nothing but trouble.'

Ada tried to make light of it. 'Oh, I don't know, sunshine, yer've brought us a bit of excitement, as well. And whatever it is that's bothering yer now, get it off yer chest and we'll see if there's anything we can do to help. I know it's got to be something to do with that ruddy husband of yours, so let's be having it.'

Annie closed her eyes. They knew Tom Phillips was a drunkard and a bully, they'd seen that for themselves. But how could she start to tell them of the degradation and humiliation inflicted on her behind the bedroom door? What she'd had to suffer every night since her wedding night? They'd be horrified and sickened. And perhaps they'd think less of her for putting up with it.

Ada put a hand over Annie's. 'Come on, sunshine, ye're with friends now. Whatever yer tell us, me and Hetty won't repeat to anyone. That is a solemn promise. And yer'll feel better when yer get it off yer chest.'

Annie laced her fingers and dropped her head. She would tell them. She had to clear her mind if she was to keep her sanity. But she was too embarrassed to face them. 'Yer know my husband is a bully, a drunkard who beats his wife and children. But there are things I have never told yer. Things I've never told anyone, because I'm too ashamed. So when yer hear my story, try not to think badly of me. My only sin is being too weak.'

Annie's voice was faltering at first, then it grew in strength as anger built up inside her. Several times Hetty looked so shocked Ada was afraid she was going to cry out, and she had to tap her mate's foot to warn her to keep quiet. If Annie stopped now, she may never pluck up the courage to start again. And she told it all. The humiliation, the torment, the gloating, the punches, the lot. And the more Ada heard, the more angry she became. Tom Phillips wasn't a man, he was an animal. But she didn't say a word. She waited until Annie was through and had got it all off her chest.

Hetty didn't speak when Annie had finished. She was shocked to the core. Her own life was so sheltered, with a good husband who adored her and their children. She had no idea there were men on the earth as bad as Tom Phillips.

But Ada wasn't lost for words.' And you've put up with that for twenty years, sunshine? Yer deserve a medal. I'd have done him an injury years ago. But then we're not all alike, are we? And there's no point in us sitting here going over what has been, it's too late for that. What we should be talking about is what are yer going to do tonight, Annie?'

Annie shook her head. 'I honestly don't know, sweetheart. I could say I'd rather cut me throat than be in the same bedroom as Tom Phillips, and it would be true. But I've got two children to think of. They are the only reason I have for living.'

'Ay, we'll have less of that talk, Annie Phillips,' Ada said with a look of determination on her face. 'I'm not going to sit back and let some little twerp like yer husband ruin your life or the kids'. And I'm bloody sure I'm not going to sit here tonight knowing you're over the road going through hell.'

'There's not much we can do about it, sweetheart,' Annie said. 'I'll send the children out so they don't get involved. It's all I can do.'

But Ada wasn't having that. 'It's a desperate situation, sunshine, and it calls for desperate measures.' She rolled up her sleeves. 'Put the kettle on for a fresh pot of tea, Hetty, please, while we figure out a plan of campaign. We'll put a stop to that bugger's shenanigans if it's the last thing I do. And now, Annie, let you and me put our heads together so we get the timing right.'

Chapter Twenty-Two

Annie's eyes kept going to the clock as she paced the floor. The children should be in any minute now. They'd gone out to work at the same time this morning, and agreed to meet each other off the tram after work and walk home together. Their dinners were in the oven on plates and she was on pins as she prayed this was one night they wouldn't be late. Any other night she wouldn't have worried, for Tom Phillips would be going for his usual few pints of beer, and would be home later than them. But not tonight, for she knew he had no money. In fact he'd be lucky if he had enough on him for the tram fare to work and back. Which meant he'd be in a worse temper than usual.

Two shadows passed the window and Annie flew to open the front door. 'Ooh, thank goodness ye're not late. I've been on pins waiting for yer.' She hugged Jenny and kissed her, then did the same with Ben. 'Take yer coats off and hang them up, while I put yer dinners out.'

'What's the hurry, Mam?' Jenny asked. 'Yer look all hot and bothered. I'm not going out tonight, so I'll be here with yer when me dad comes in.'

Ben looked sheepish. 'I've promised to go to me mate's, Mam, but if yer want me to stay in, I will do.'

Annie was on her way to the kitchen when she answered, 'No need to stay in, son. If yer've made arrangements, then you go out.'

Jenny followed her mother to the kitchen. 'How did it go this morning, Mam? What time did me dad wake up?'

'I think it was about half eight, sweetheart. I didn't wake him, I left him there until he came round.' Annie put a cloth over her hand to take one of the hot plates from the oven. 'As yer can imagine, I got the height of abuse off him. It was all my fault according to him. I don't think he even remembered being rotten drunk, or that he was knocked unconscious for being rowdy. None of it was his fault. I should have woken him up in time for work, and made him breakfast into the bargain.'

Ben came forward and took the plate from her. 'I'll take it in, Mam. Is this mine, or is it our Jenny's?'

'They're all the same, son. You take that in and me and Jenny will bring our own through.'

When they were seated round the table, Jenny said, 'I bet he had a right cob on, Mam. Did he have a go at yer?'

Annie raised her brows. 'He was in a real temper with being so late for work, but I just sat here and listened to him. He got very cocky, telling me what he'd do to me when he got home tonight. And when I just sat and stared him out, he got more bad-tempered than ever. In fact he ordered me to get his breakfast ready while he was getting washed. But I didn't stay to listen to any more. I took me purse and me coat, and left him to it. That'll be another black mark against me, like, but I couldn't care less.'

'I'll be here when he gets in, Mam, and if he starts, we can both take him on.'

'I'll be here, too,' Ben said. 'I won't go out.'

Annie laid down her knife and fork. 'I'm not going to tell yer everything yer dad said, 'cos yer've heard it all before and yer know what he's like. But you are going out tonight, Ben, and so is Jenny. And I don't want any arguments from yer. I want yer to eat yer dinner as quick as yer can, and be out of the house by the time yer dad comes in.'

'Mam, ye're keeping something back, and I want to know what it is,' Jenny told her. 'I'm not going out tonight because I've got nowhere to go.'

'I'll have to be brief, 'cos yer father could walk in any minute, seeing as he's no money to go boozing. I made up me mind this morning, after he'd been ranting and raving at me, that I'd taken enough off yer father over the years, and I wasn't prepared to take any more. So I called at Mrs Fenwick's, to get things off me chest, like. Yer see, I can't just run away and leave you two here, for ye're all I've got in life. And we've no money to find a place of our own. So I put me pride in me pocket and had a good talk to Ada. She's very good is Ada, very cool and sensible. And she came up with a plan which we hope will teach yer dad a lesson.'

This information was of great interest to the two children. There was nothing they wanted more than for their mother to have a good life, without the fear of violence. 'Ooh, that sounds too good to be true, Mam,' Jenny said. 'What is this plan?'

Annie shook her head. 'I can't tell yer that, sweetheart, 'cos things don't always go according to plan. I mean, I can't say for sure whether yer father will come home soon, or whether he'll have borrowed money off one of his workmates and gone for his few pints. I don't know what sort of mood he'll be in, or if he'll be going to the pub tonight. As Ada said, we'll have to play it by ear. And that's all I can tell yer, sweethearts, except I want both of yer out of this house as soon as yer've finished yer dinner.

239

And I don't want yer near the street until half past ten, when all the pubs are shut. And I want yer to promise me that.'

Jenny was shaking her head. 'Mam, I've nowhere to go! I can't walk the streets until half past ten, that's asking too much. And I'm not going to the pictures on me own.'

'Yer won't be walking the streets, sweetheart, I wouldn't allow yer to do that. I want yer to go over to Ada's, and stay there until we see if her plan works. Even if it does, it's not going to turn yer father into an angel overnight. But it will be a start. He's got to learn that in this life he can't have everything his own way. I'm not banking on it, just hoping. And I'm not telling yer any more 'cos it might all come to nothing.'

Jenny looked stunned. 'I can't go and plonk meself in Mrs Fenwick's until half ten, I hardly know the woman! Oh, I know she's a nice person, Mam, and she's being a good friend to you. But I wouldn't know what to do with meself over there. I wouldn't know what to talk about. And I can't understand why I can't stay here with you. If me dad starts his shenanigans, we could manage him between us.'

Annie averted her eyes. She knew it sounded weird, what she was asking the children to do, but it was better than telling them the truth about how depraved their father really was. They were too young to carry that burden. 'Yer could play cards with them. They have a few games every night, and it would pass the time away. Yer wouldn't feel in the way or anything, sweetheart, 'cos they're very friendly. And yer'd certainly have a good laugh.' Never very good at telling lies, Annie felt she was losing the battle. 'It is important, Jenny, or I wouldn't be asking yer. It's only for a few hours, and when it's over, and yer know why I'm being so secretive, then yer'll understand. Something might happen, something might not happen. It all depends upon yer father. It's worth a try, for we can't carry on the way we are. It's no sort of life for any of us. So please, bear with me, just for tonight.'

Jenny looked into her mother's careworn face, and her heart went out to her. 'I can't say I understand what yer hope to gain, Mam, 'cos it doesn't make sense. It'll take more than any plan yer've got to change me dad. He's had his own way for so long, he'll never change now, that's a dead cert. But as it seems to mean a lot to yer, then I'll go over to the Fenwicks'. But I'm going to change me dress first. I'm not going over in me work clothes. It's bad enough being ashamed of me dad, without feeling ashamed of meself. I'll nip upstairs and change me dress, it won't take me five minutes.'

Jenny had her pride and wanted to look her best. Especially if Danny was there. For the last two nights he'd had to carry her father home, rotten drunk, and he must wonder what sort of family they were. She didn't know much about the lad, except he was nice-looking and seemed kind. And she didn't want him to think that because her father was a rotter, it ran in the family. So with her change of dress came a quick dab of powder and a trace of lipstick. She heard Ben leaving the house, and although she knew her mother would be waiting, she allowed herself a few seconds to run the hairbrush through her thick auburn hair. Then she felt she could face anyone without feeling guilty about who she was.

Annie was waiting at the bottom of the stairs, and at the sight of her daughter looking so pretty, she could feel tears stinging the backs of her eyelids. 'Oh, yer do look bonny, sweetheart. A sight for sore eyes.' She had to turn away, for she didn't want her daughter to see her upset. But running through her mind was the thought that the only good things that had come from her marriage to Tom Phillips were her beautiful children. They were her life, and she adored them. But the man who had fathered them had no love for them, or pride in them. To him they were just figures he could vent his anger and wickedness on. Well, the day might soon come when he wasn't around to treat them like slaves, and they would have no cause to be ashamed of who they were. And that day couldn't come quick enough for Annie.

When Jenny stepped down into the street, she looked up at her mother. 'Mam, don't let me dad knock yer around, d'yer hear? Run over to Mrs Fenwick's, and I'll come back with yer. Promise me yer'll do that?'

'I'll give yer me promise, sweetheart, but I don't think it'll come to that. I won't say any more now, let's wait and see. For all we know, this might turn out to be the best day of our lives. The turning point, perhaps.'

Jenny couldn't see that happening, but she wasn't going to put a damper on her mother's spirits. 'I'll be home at half ten, then, Mam. Okay?'

Annie nodded. 'I'll be fine, don't worry.'

Tom Phillips was smirking as he walked out of the dock gates. He had two bob in his pocket that he'd scrounged off the men he worked with. Several of the men had sent him packing with a flea in his ear, because they didn't like him. But four of the gang, unknown to each other, had been talked into lending him sixpence each. They didn't know it was for beer; he'd told them he'd lost his money through a hole in his trouser pocket, and they'd believed him. And he'd promised to pay them back the next day. He'd given the same excuse to his boss for being so late clocking on. No money for the tram fare, so he'd had to walk all the way.

As he neared the pub, and the smell of beer invaded his nostrils, he was feeling on top of the world. Two shillings would see him all right for a few pints here, with a bit over. Still, it was a mystery what had happened to the money he had in his pocket last night. He must have had more to drink than he thought, or he'd lost it somewhere. Anyway, there was no point in spending time worrying about it. He could get what he wanted from that stupid cow of a wife of his.

There was a woman of about thirty leaning against the wall of the pub. With a cigarette dangling from the corner of her mouth, her face thick with powder, rouge and bright red lipstick, she looked what she was . . . one of the many prostitutes who plied their trade near the docks. She approached Tom as he neared the door of the pub. 'You look like a feller who appreciates a bit of fun. How about it? For a tanner, yer can have anything yer like.'

'I can get what I want at home for nothing.' Tom brushed her aside. 'I've got me own slave there who's very well trained. I don't need no whore.'

'I can turn tricks yer've never even thought of.' The woman sneered. 'Yer don't know what ye're missing, lad. Yer wife's an amateur. Yer should try a professional, then yer'll be a real man.'

The words brought Tom to a halt. The woman was touting for business, and he'd always looked down on the women who hung around the docks. But her words had him wondering. Was he missing out? Then he shook his head. No, he was quite happy with his wife. She wasn't enthusiastic in what she did for him, on the contrary, she hated it, and he knew it. But that was part of the thrill for him.

Tom picked his glass up off the counter and took it to one of the small tables. The whore's words stayed in his mind as he drank his way through that pint, and the next two. Perhaps he should try it some time. It wouldn't hurt. If he never tried, he'd never know and would always wonder. It seemed they only charged a tanner, so it was worth a try. He'd take the sixpence out of his wife's housekeeping. Yeah, that was a good idea, he liked that. He'd be having the time of his life at her expense. Comparing his wife with the whore reminded Tom that he'd ordered Annie to be in his bed tonight. And on that thought, he downed his third pint of beer, left the empty glass on the table and headed for home.

As an hour ticked by, Annie knew her husband must have borrowed money off someone to go for a few pints. Which meant he'd be in an excitable, but unpredictable, mood. Drinking beer seemed to have different effects on different men. Some became happy and talkative, while Tom Phillips became an abusive bully. She wasn't looking forward to hearing his key in the door, but she was not going to back down. Not this time. There were a lot of people putting themselves out to help her, and she'd rather take all the blows Tom Phillips aimed at her than let those people down. It would be throwing their kindness back in their faces. She just hoped things worked out as Ada had planned. Not only for herself, but for Jenny and Ben. They were only young once, and when they were older she wanted them to be able to look back with fond memories.

Annie's heart skipped a beat when she heard the key in the door. And she had to take a deep breath to calm her jangling nerves. She could smell the beer before her husband even entered the room, but she forced herself to sit down and remember word for word what she'd been advised to say. 'I thought yer'd be home earlier than this, because I knew yer had no money.' She picked up a half-crown from the table and held it out on her open palm. 'This must have fallen out of yer pocket when yer were asleep on the couch. I found it when I was brushing the floor.' This wasn't exactly true, but part of the plan hinged on Tom Phillips's going to the pub that night. 'Here, take it while I see to yer dinner.'

Tom grabbed the money without so much as a thank you. But he was gloating inside. He'd be able to go for his pints after all, and still have a bit of money over. And if he added that to the coppers he had in his pocket, he only needed another shilling and he could give the money back that he'd borrowed off his workmates. He threw his cap on to the sideboard before sitting down. 'I need a shilling off yer. Where's yer purse?'

Annie came in from the kitchen. 'I haven't got a shilling to give yer. It takes me all me time to manage on the pittance yer give me. I'm living from hand to mouth now.'

'I don't care if yer starve to bleeding death, yer stupid cow. When I say I want a shilling, then it's up to you to find it from somewhere. What d'yer think I give yer housekeeping money for? It's no good having a dog and barking yer bleeding self.'

The plate Annie was carrying had just been taken out of the oven, and it was very hot. And for one wild moment, she felt the urge to dump the contents of the plate on his head. But Ada's words pulled her up short. She put the plate on the table, saying, 'If I give yer the last shilling I've got, I'll have no money to buy any food for tomorrow's dinner.'

'That's your bleeding worry, not mine.' Tom let fly with a punch to her ribs, then laughed when she cried out in pain. 'That's just a taste of what yer'll get tomorrow if there's no bleeding dinner on the table when I get home from work.' He remembered the prostitute outside the pub, and threw his head back, laughing like a maniac. 'Go down Lime Street, and see how much yer can make. Ha-ha! They charge a tanner a trick, but they're good at the game. You'd be bleeding lucky if yer got one of the dirty old men in long raincoats. Yer might get one of them to take yer down an entry for a threepenny bit.'

He was deliberately taunting her, hoping to see her cringe in horror at his words. When she didn't, he picked up his knife and fork and started on his dinner. His lack of manners when eating disgusted Annie far more than his words had. This was one of the many times when she felt like killing him. She would get a lot of pleasure out of seeing him writhe in agony. He'd caused her so much pain, she wouldn't feel any pity for him if he pleaded for mercy.

'Don't stand there like a gormless idiot, yer stupid bleeding cow.' Tom Phillips jerked his head. 'Get out there and make me a cup of tea. Yer've been sitting on yer big fat arse all day, now get cracking.'

After putting a light under the kettle, Annie stood by the sink, her hands gripping the edge. She whispered softly, 'May God forgive me for me bad thoughts, but he is a bastard and I wish he was dead.' Then she closed her eyes. If things went as Ada had promised they would, then tonight he could get a taste of his own medicine. It might only happen the once, but oh how she would enjoy seeing him cower in fear, as he'd often reduced her to doing over the years.

'Get that bloody tea in here on the double, yer lazy fat cow.' The beer, as usual, was having the effect of making Tom Phillips feel powerful. It also gave him a warped sense of humour. When Annie carried his tea through, and put it down in front of him, he gripped her wrist. 'I hope yer haven't forgot the treat I promised yer this morning? I bet yer've been looking forward to it all day. Ye're in my bed tonight, so be ready for me when I get back from the pub.'

Annie kept her face straight. 'Oh, ye're going to the pub, are yer?'

'Of course I'm going to the pub, yer stupid cow. Yer don't think I'm going to sit in and look at that bloody face of yours all night, do yer?'

Annie didn't answer as she carried his dirty plate out. Everything was turning out as Ada had forecast. She'd keep her fingers crossed, and say a little prayer, that her friend from across the street had got the ending right as well.

'Take yer coat off, sunshine, and I'll hang it up,' Ada said to Jenny, a wide smile on her face. 'Then sit down and make yerself at home. The two children have gone round to their friends, so there's only me and Jimmy here, and we're not strangers to yer.'

'Take a pew, love,' Jimmy said, feeling sorry for the girl, who was looking ill at ease. 'We don't charge for the use of a chair.'

Danny, who had been getting washed in the kitchen, popped his head round the door. 'A word of warning, Jenny. They don't charge for sitting on a chair, but they do if yer break one of the legs.'

Jenny thought he looked very handsome when he smiled, and he always seemed happy, as though he enjoyed life. Heaven only knows what he thinks about me and my family, she thought, he can't have a very high opinion of us. But he was looking at her expectantly, so she put a smile on her face and answered, 'I'll try not to break a leg.'

Ada pulled a chair out and sat next to her. 'Me bold laddo is off jazzing, as per usual. If he could, he'd spend his ruddy life on the dance floor.'

'Ay, don't be talking about me behind me back.' Danny came and sat on a chair facing them. 'It's coming to something when me own mother tells people I'm a good-for-nothing.'

'Well, I can criticise yer, sunshine, seeing as I'm yer mother. But woe betide anyone else who did.' Ada winked at Jenny, before saying, 'Me first born, yer see, and he's been spoilt rotten.' Then for the next ten minutes the talk was about the cold weather, work, and how soon Christmas would be upon them. And Jenny was coming out of her shell and joining in. It was easy to feel comfortable in the warm atmosphere in the Fenwicks' house.

Then Danny looked at the clock, tutted, and pushed his chair back. 'I'd better get me skates on. Me dancing partners will think I've deserted them.'

Ada's face was the picture of innocence, and no one would have guessed it had all been rehearsed. 'Why don't yer ask Jenny to go with yer, sunshine? I'm sure she'd enjoy it more than sitting with two old fogies.'

Jenny seemed to shrink in her chair. 'Oh, no, Mrs Fenwick, I'd rather stay here with you. Danny doesn't want me hanging on to him. He's got his own friends.'

'Ay, that's a good idea, Jenny!' Danny was playing his part well. 'I've got three dancing partners, but I'm not the only one they dance with. And remember, yer never did tell me what yer favourite dance is. So, if yer come with me, I'll find out for meself. Unless yer don't want to come with me, of course. I can't make yer.'

'It's not that I don't want to come with yer, Danny, but I don't want to spoil yer night for yer. I'm not really dressed for a dance, and I haven't got me dancing shoes with me.'

'Yer look good enough to me,' Danny said. 'It's only a local hop, the girls don't wear long dresses or tiaras. And only the show-offs wear silver shoes.'

'Yer look fine to me, lass,' Jimmy told her. 'If I was your age, and I went to a dance and saw yer, I'd be across the floor before anyone else could snap yer up.'

245

'Oh, would yer now?' Ada curled a fist under his nose. 'When we're on our own, sunshine, yer can expect some sharp words from me. Fancy sweet-talking a young girl in front of yer very own wife, what yer paid seven and six to marry. I've a good mind to get meself all dolled up and go to the dance with our Danny.'

'Ah, ay, Mam!' Danny held his hands up in mock horror. Then he fell on one knee in front of Jenny. 'Please, I beg of yer. Say yer'll come with me, before me mam starts putting her lipstick on.'

Jenny couldn't help but laugh. What fun this family were. 'I'll come with yer, but I won't stay with yer. It wouldn't be fair on you or the girls yer usually dance with.'

Danny jumped to his feet. 'It's a bargain.' He stooped to kiss Ada. 'It's not that I don't love yer, Mam, 'cos yer know I love the bones of yer.'

'Be a gentleman and get Jenny's coat for her.' Ada smiled at the young girl, who was dazed by the speed everything had been arranged. 'Yer look very pretty, sunshine, and if the other boys have got eyes in their head, there'll be no shortage of partners for yer.'

'I won't stay till the end, Mrs Fenwick. I promised me mam I'd be home by half past ten.'

'Don't worry about yer mam, sunshine, I'll be keeping me eye on her. That is a promise, so you go and enjoy yerself. And tomorrow yer can tell me what these dancing partners are like. Danny talks about them, but won't say what they're like, or if he's got a favourite.'

Across the street, in number twenty-two, Annie was at the window, watching her husband walking up the street towards the pub. She was about to drop the curtain when she saw her daughter step down on to the pavement, followed by Danny. And her eyes followed them until they were out of sight. Ada's plan was working a treat so far.

'I'm paying me own tram fare, Danny, so don't argue.' Jenny had the tuppence ready in her hand. 'Don't embarrass me, just take the money.'

Danny took the coins, but wasn't happy. 'This goes against the grain, Jenny. A girl shouldn't pay for herself when she's with a bloke.'

'But I'm not yer girlfriend, Danny, I'm only a neighbour! It's bad enough yer've been talked into taking me, without yer having to fork out.'

'I wasn't talked into bringing yer, Jenny! And seeing as ye're getting all anxious about it, I'll let yer pay yer own tram fare. But let's get one thing straight before we get to the dance hall and yer start kicking up a fuss. If yer refuse to let me pay, then yer'll make me feel about two foot tall. I'd really take it as an insult. So shall we call a truce? You pay yer own fare, I pay for the dance tickets? Okay?'

When Jenny found herself looking into Danny's eyes, her heart skipped a beat and her tummy turned over. She looked away, wondering what had hit her. Then in her mind she told herself that her home life had made her wary of boys, and she'd never let one get so close to her before. She was being silly and childish. 'I'm sorry, Danny, I didn't mean to insult yer. And yeah, I'll do like yer said. I pay me tram fare, you pay for the dance ticket.'

He looked relieved. 'Yer see how easy it is when yer don't take the huff? Life's too short, so make the most of it while yer can.'

When they reached Blair Hall, Jenny left Danny buying the tickets while she went to the cloakroom. She didn't want him to think she was clinging to him, and that he had to stay with her. So when they went into the dance hall, she said, 'You go and get one of yer partners up, I'll be all right. I'll be a spy for yer mam, and report back to her what yer partners are like. In other words, I'll be a sneak.'

There was a quickstep playing, and Danny could see Dorothy waving to him. 'Stay here until the dance is over, Jenny, and I'll come back to yer.'

However, Danny had only just walked away from her when Jenny felt a hand on her arm. 'Would you care to dance?'

The blond-haired boy looked very presentable, and Jenny didn't have the heart to turn him down. 'I'm not the best dancer in the world,' she told him, 'but I'll do me best.'

'I'm no Fred Astaire meself,' the lad said, showing a fine set of white teeth when he smiled. 'But I think we can get round without tripping each other up.'

They suited each other very well, their steps matching easily and gracefully. They were halfway down the dance floor when they passed Danny and his partner. To say Danny was surprised would be an understatement. His jaw dropped and his step faltered. But he quickly pulled himself together and smiled. 'All right, Jenny?'

She smiled back at him and nodded. Her spirits were lifted, and she could actually feel her confidence growing. At least Danny would know now she wasn't going to be a drag on him all night. It would leave him free to dance with his regular partners. But, Jenny told herself, that was wishful thinking. She might not get asked up again for the rest of the night.

Her partner, however, had other plans. And when the dance was over, he walked her back to the edge of the dance floor and stood with her. 'The next dance will be a waltz. Will yer dance with me?'

'Yes, if yer want.'

The blond boy smiled. 'I'm Tony, by the way. What's your name?'

'Jenny.'

'That's a nice name. Are yer a friend of Danny's?'

'We're neighbours. We live in the same street.'

The next minute Danny was beside them. 'Hiya, Tony, I see yer've been dancing with me friend. She'll be all right now, I'll look after her. I promised her mam, yer see.'

Tony grinned. 'Get lost, Danny. I've already asked Jenny, and she's promised me the next dance.'

Danny didn't let his surprise or disappointment show. 'Okay, I'll let yer have this dance with her, but if yer stand on her toes, I'll tell her mam on yer. And the next dance is mine, whether yer like it or not.'

Tony rubbed his chin. 'Right, that means Betsy will be free for the quickstep. I'll book it in advance. Then after that I'm back with Jenny, if she'll have me.' The music started up for the waltz, and he put his arm round Jenny's waist. 'See yer later, Danny.'

Danny scratched his head. He wasn't feeling very happy about the situation, and couldn't understand why. Never mind. He'd better look for Janet before someone else did. But as he walked towards the girl, he muttered under his breath, 'The bloody cheek of him! Who does he think he is? If he thinks he's going to hog her the whole night he's mistaken. And he can forget about taking her home. She came with me, and she'll go home with me. If he starts getting funny, I'll clock him one.'

'Are you talking to yerself?' Janet asked as Danny led her on to the dance floor. 'I could swear I saw yer lips moving.'

'I was singing the words of the song,' Danny said. 'They can't lock yer up for singing, can they?'

'Ooh, er, don't bite me flipping head off,' Janet said, then stayed silent until they were dancing. Then she asked, 'Is that one of yer girlfriends dancing with Tony?'

'She's not a girlfriend, she's just a neighbour. I promised her mam I'd keep an eye on her, so I'll be having a few dances with her.'

'She's very pretty,' Janet said, 'but when it comes to dancing, she's hardly in the same class as you.'

'Perhaps it's her partner holding her back.'

'Come off it, Danny, yer know as well as I do that Tony's a good dancer.' Janet moved back to look him in the eye. 'Are yer sweet on this girl? I wouldn't blame yer if yer were 'cos she's nice-looking. I wish I had that mop of hair, it's gorgeous.'

Danny huffed. 'Look, she lives in our street, me mam's a mate of her mam's, and yes she has got nice hair. As for her dancing, I'll let yer know later, 'cos I'm having the next dance with her.'

248

'Ye're very touchy tonight, Danny. Has someone rubbed yer up the wrong way?'

'Janet, ye're beginning to sound like me mam. Will yer concentrate on yer dancing and stop the third degree? Ye're putting me off me stride.'

When the dance was over, Janet said, 'I might see yer later, then, Danny?'

'Yeah, of course yer will.' Danny lifted his hand, then went looking for Jenny. He didn't have to look far; she was standing near the door with Tony. And she was glad to see him walking towards her. For Tony was asking her for a date, and she was having trouble trying to find a believable excuse.

'Right, I'll take over now, Tony,' Danny said. 'Otherwise Jenny will tell her mam I left her on her own all night. And her mam will tell my mam, and I'll end up getting a thick ear.'

Tony was grinning as he shook his head. 'Yer can't half talk, Danny Fenwick. Ye're worse than a flipping girl. And ye're taking over for the next dance, not for the whole night. Jenny's promised me the next waltz.'

'Yer don't know Jenny like I do,' Danny told him. 'She'll tell yer one thing and mean another. Anyway, on yer way, pal, I'm taking her for this slow foxtrot. If yer move yerself, yer might be in time to nab Dorothy before someone more handsome gets to her first.'

When Danny led her on to the dance floor, Jenny said, 'Yer don't have to dance with me, yer know, Danny. I bet yer regular partners are calling me for everything.'

'I know I don't have to dance with yer, Jenny. There's a lot of things I don't have to do if I don't want to. Like walking into a bus, for instance.'

'There's no clock in here, Danny, and I haven't got a watch. Can yer tell me the time?'

Danny looked at his wristwatch. 'It's a quarter past nine, why?'

'I want to leave at ten, so will yer give me the wire just before then?'

'Why is it so important that yer leave at ten? The dance isn't over until half past.'

'I want to be home by half ten,' Jenny told him. 'Me mam will be expecting me. So don't let me down, will yer. Give me a nod just before ten.'

'I'll come home with yer. We can get the tram together.'

'You will do no such thing!' Jenny said. 'I'm quite capable of getting home on me own.'

Danny's dimples showed when he grinned. 'Ay, I've just noticed something, Jenny. Ye're a good dancer. Ye're following me as though we've been dancing together for years.'

'Don't change the subject, Danny.' But secretly Jenny was pleased with what he said. She'd been worried she wouldn't be as good as his partners. 'I'm off at ten, you're staying until the dance is over. There's something going on at home, concerning me dad, but me mam wouldn't tell me what it was. And I'm worried about her. But that's no reason to spoil your night, so do as ye're told.'

'The more anyone tells me not to do something, the more I dig me heels in. Besides, if ye're worried about yer mam, that's more reason for me to be with yer.'

'I'm going home on me own, Danny, will yer be told!'

'I'll be told, yes. But if I happen to get on the same tram as you, don't be surprised. I can be very stubborn when I want.'

And Danny did get on the same tram as Jenny. Not because he was stubborn, but because he knew of his mother's plans, and wanted to be there in case of trouble.

Chapter Twenty-Three

Tom Phillips was one of the first out of the pub when the landlord called time, and put towels over the pumps. He wasn't drunk, even though he'd had two pints and was still under the influence of the three he'd had a few hours previously. He was able to walk a straight line, and was full of bravado, congratulating himself on his cunning. He'd cut down on his drinking for one reason, which he thought was really clever. The tanner he'd saved might come in useful if the prostitute was outside the dockside pub again. He'd decided that it would be worth sixpence to see what she had to offer. Particularly when he intended to get more money from his wife. If she knew what was good for her, she'd hand it over without any trouble. And he'd have enough to pay back what he'd borrowed, pay the tart, and still have some over for a pint or two.

'Not a bad day's work,' Tom muttered as he walked home. 'And I've got the wife coming in me bed tonight. She might kick up a stink, but she'll give in eventually because she won't want to upset her two brats. So I'll get a bellyful tonight, then see what the tart has to offer tomorrow. I might learn a few tricks I can teach that stupid cow I'm married to.'

As he put the key in the door, Tom was telling himself that if the kids were there, he'd send them up to bed. But there wasn't a sound, so they were either still out, or in bed already. Not that it made any difference, because if his wife protested about sleeping with him, he'd only have her to fight, and one blow would do the trick. But while he had everything sorted out in his head to his satisfaction, he wasn't prepared for the sight that met his eyes when he threw open the living room door. For sitting round the table, all with playing cards in their hands, were his wife, the nosy cow from across the street, and two women he'd never set eyes on in his life before.

'What the bleeding hell is going on here?' Tom was about to let rip with a mouthful of obscenities when Ada beat him to it.

'You remember me, Mr Phillips, I've met yer before. And these two ladies are yer neighbours from either side. Jean Bowers, and Edith Watson.' Ada felt like roaring with laughter at the look on his face. But she kept to

251

the plan they'd worked out. 'With Annie being on her own, we thought we'd keep her company. And it's been really nice, we've enjoyed ourselves. Even though we haven't been playing for money.'

Jean and Edith both smiled, and said in unison, 'Pleased to meet yer, Mr Phillips.'

Tom's earlier good humour quickly evaporated and his temper was rising fast. These stupid bitches had upset all his plans. Not for long, though, because he was the master here, and he wanted them out. 'Well, yer've had yer fun and games now, so pack up and bugger off. This is my house and I don't want bleeding strangers in it.'

'We might be strangers to you, Mr Phillips,' Ada said calmly, 'but not to yer wife. We're all friends of Annie's. But I can understand yer wanting a bit of peace after a day's work, so when we've finished this hand we'll vamoose and leave yer in peace.'

'Oh, yer'll just finish yer game of cards, will yer, yer cheeky cow?' Tom's voice was shrill with anger. He wasn't going to have a bleeding woman talking to him like that in his own house. 'Some hopes yer've got, 'cos if yer don't leave of yer own accord, I'll throw yer out on yer backsides. So move yerselves, and be quick about it.'

Jean had been told how rude their neighbour was, but she had never dreamed any man would talk like that to women. 'If my husband heard yer calling me a cow, he wouldn't take very kindly to it.'

'Nor mine, either.' Edith glared at him. 'What a rude man you are.'

Tom's lip curled in a sneer, as he imitated Edith's voice. 'Oh, what a rude man yer are.' He thumbed his wife. 'Get them out, or I'll throw them out. I was going to say I'd throw you out with them, but I've got a job for yer to do here. You stay, they go.'

Tom had his back to the front door, and didn't see two figures hovering behind him. 'Don't sit there like stuffed bleeding dummies, get those fat arses off my chairs and scram, before I take me belt to yer.'

A quiet voice behind him asked, 'Are you threatening my wife?'

Tom spun round, and found himself looking into a man's chest. He let his eyes travel upwards, angry words ready to spill from his mouth. But when he'd reached the top of Gordon Bowers's six foot five frame, he swallowed hard. The man was a bloody giant! But he couldn't lose face in front of the women. 'Who the bleeding hell are you, and how did yer get in my house?'

'You didn't close the front door properly.' Gordon was fibbing, for he had been given a key by Annie. He now moved aside to allow Joe Benson to step forward. 'This is Mr Benson. He lives next door in number twenty, and I live the other side in twenty-four. The lovely lady with dark curly hair is Mrs Benson, and the pretty, fair-haired lady is my wife. Lucky for you Mr Fenwick is not here, for like myself and Mr Benson, he would be very angry to hear his wife spoken to in such a manner. And like ourselves, he would expect you to apologise for your rudeness.'

This was too much for Tom. In his mind, women were slaves, put on this earth solely for the purpose of keeping men happy. 'I didn't invite them into my house, so why should I bleeding well apologise? It's them what should apologise for putting ideas into my wife's head. So, now, I'd like yer all to leave. And I don't want to see any of yer here again, filling me wife's head with a load of nonsense.'

Gordon had to bend down to look Tom Phillips in the face. 'We are going nowhere until you say you're sorry to the ladies. My wife, and the other ladies, are not used to being spoken to in that way. Except for your wife, of course, who deserves a medal for putting up with your behaviour.'

Joe Benson took over then. Like Gordon, he'd been told how this coward treated his family, and was disgusted. 'Can I have my say now? I've heard the way yer talk to yer wife and children, 'cos these walls are very thin. Many's the night I've wanted to come in and give yer a piece of me mind. Ye're not a man, ye're a disgrace. A foul-mouthed bully who would run a mile from a real man. And I'll warn yer now that if I ever again hear yer even raise yer voice to Annie, or the kids, I'll come and boot yer door in. Then I'll give yer the chance to fight someone yer own size. It would be my pleasure to knock the stuffing out of yer.'

'If Joe doesn't, then I will,' Gordon said in a deceptively quiet voice. He couldn't abide a man who beat his wife and was cruel to his kids. 'In front of you, I am going to tell Annie that if you so much as threaten her, or raise your hand to her or the children, then all she has to do is shout out, or knock on the wall either side.'

'Yer can't come booting yer way in here,' Tom blustered. 'What goes on between man and wife, in their own home, has nothing to do with no one. And if yer try and interfere, I'll have the police on to yer.'

'Oh, I don't think you will, Mr Phillips. At least you won't have the police on to us,' Gordon said. 'More likely they'd be on to you. Yer see, the sergeant at the police station is a friend of mine, and I was talking to him only yesterday. I mentioned you to him, as it happens. How you get drunk, cause a disturbance in the street which upsets the neighbours. I mentioned that you get so drunk, you've had to be carried home on a couple of occasions. I also told him you beat your wife and children, and he was very concerned about that. In fact, the sergeant was so interested, he said the next time you caused a disturbance, we should send for the police. He reckoned a night in the cells would teach you a lesson.'

Tom Phillips ran his tongue over lips that were dry with fright. He looked towards his wife, hoping she would stick up for him. But Annie's eyes showed no sympathy whatsoever. Nor did they show any fear. There was a deadly silence for about twenty seconds, broken when Ada thought they'd achieved what they'd set out to do. 'Come on, let's all go home. There's no point in waiting for an apology which has to be forced.' She reached over and touched Annie's arm. 'Yer can come home with me if yer like, sunshine?'

Annie shook her head. 'No, thank you, sweetheart, I'll be all right. The children will be in any minute now, and I want to be here for them.'

Chairs were pushed back as the ladies got to their feet. They donned their coats and headed for the door without saying a word. There was nothing left to say. But Gordon and Joe hung back. 'Will you be all right, Annie?' Gordon asked. 'We can wait with you until the children come in.'

'I'll be fine, Gordon,' Annie told him. 'I'll put the kettle on so there's a hot drink ready for them when they come.' She walked to the door with the two men. 'I can't thank you enough. I'm a stranger to yer, yet yer came to help me. That is something I'll never forget.'

'All you have to do, day or night, is shout or knock,' Gordon said. 'I really mean that, and I know the same goes for Joe. Any time at all. And now we'll wish you good night.'

Annie closed the door and made her way back to the living room, where she faced a man seething with anger. Tom Phillips was sat in the fireside chair, and it was only fear that stopped him from leaping from his seat. 'You bitch.' He ground the words out. 'Yer sat on yer fat backside and let them make a fool of me in me own house.'

'No, Tom, I didn't let them make a fool of yer.' Annie was surprised she felt so calm. 'Yer did that yerself. And yer made a good job of it. Yer see, when it comes to hitting a woman and children, that makes yer think ye're a real big he-man. But when it comes to facing another man, well, that's a different kettle of fish. It cuts yer down to size. Shows yer up for what yer really are. And that's a coward. An ignorant one at that. Yer really showed yerself in yer true colours tonight to our neighbours, and I'm glad they know yer for what yer are now. I won't need to feel ashamed any more, or make excuses, and that's a relief.'

But Tom wasn't going to let her get away with that. 'This is my house, and don't yer forget it. I pay the rent, and I can chuck you and the kids out in the street whenever I want. And I will do if yer ever let those bleeding la-di-da bleeding neighbours in again. They don't come over the doorstep, d'yer hear me?'

'Oh, I can hear yer, I'm not deaf. But it doesn't mean I'm going to do as you say. If I want to invite me friends in, then I will. Throw me and the kids out if yer think yer can get away with it. We'll find somewhere to go, don't worry. You're the one what would suffer, with no one to have yer dinner ready every night, or keep the house clean. I've put up with yer shenanigans, but yer'll not find another sucker like me. And while I'm getting things off me chest, yer may as well get the lot. The pittance I get off you for housekeeping wouldn't be enough to put a good dinner on the table every night. It's the coppers I get from Jenny and Ben that help out.' Annie threw her hands in the air. 'I don't know why I'm wasting me breath talking to yer. For as long as yer can go to the pub twice a day, and drink yerself paralytic, you don't give a toss for anyone else. As long as yer belly's full of food or drink, that's all yer live for.'

'It's those bloody neighbours filling yer head,' Tom said. 'Well, keep away from them if yer know what's good for yer. And if they're here again when I come home, then I'll be showing them the door.' He snorted. 'Don't you be getting big ideas, or I'll knock them out of yer. And I hope yer haven't forgot I need a shilling to go to work tomorrow. Pass it over now, before I forget.'

There came a pounding on the front door, and Annie threw her husband a look of contempt before she went to let Jenny and Ben in. And such was their relief to see she was all right, she found herself being pressed against the wall as they both flung their arms round her. 'How are yer, Mam?' Jenny asked. 'What's been going on?'

'Yeah,' Ben told her, 'Danny was watching for me coming up the street, and he called me in there. But neither him nor Mr Fenwick would tell us why we couldn't come home.'

'As yer can see, sweethearts, I'm fine.' Annie removed their arms from her neck. 'I had some of the neighbours in for a game of cards.' She winked, nodded to the living room and whispered, 'Yer dad's in there, but not very happy.'

Jenny pulled a face. 'That's nothing new, he's never happy.'

Annie put a finger to her lips. 'Less said the better, sweetheart. I'll tell you and Ben all about it in the morning.'

'Don't be bleeding whispering out there.' Tom's voice came through to them, but it wasn't as loud as usual. 'Get in here and make me a cup of tea.' When the trio entered the room, he curled his lip in a sneer. 'You two can get up the bleeding stairs, it's time yer were in bed. I want to have words with yer lazy good-for-nothing mother.'

'Oh, no.' Annie shook her head, and waved her hand to the chairs round the table. 'Hang yer coats up, then sit yerselves down. I'll make us all a cup of tea.' Her eyes dared her husband to argue. 'And I'll be going up to bed when they go. I'm sleeping in Jenny's bed.'

Tom had to salvage some pride, and there was only one way he could think of. 'Then before yer bugger off, give me the shilling I need for tomorrow. Don't tell me yer'll give it to me in the morning, I want it now.'

'I haven't got a shilling to spare,' Annie told him, 'and yer know that 'cos I've already told yer. If I give yer a shilling, I won't be able to buy any food for the dinner.'

Tom sat forward and pointed a finger at Jenny. 'I'll have it off you then, buggerlugs.'

'I haven't got a shilling!' Jenny's voice was shrill. 'Where d'yer think I'd get that from? By the time I've given me mam her housekeeping, I don't have much over. Don't forget I've got tram fare to pay.'

'I don't give a bugger whether yer have to walk to work or not.' Tom was in his element now, having someone to boss around who was still afraid of him. 'Pass yer handbag over and I can see for meself.'

'Some hope you've got!' Jenny was determined. 'Yer'll not get yer filthy hands in my bag. Why can't yer go without one of yer pints of beer if ye're short of money?'

Tom made a growling sound as he put a hand on each of the chair arms and pushed himself up. 'That does it! I'll not have a bleeding chit of a girl talk to me like that.' He grabbed a handful of Jenny's hair and pulled it tight. 'Get the money out of yer bag before I pull this patch of hair out.'

Annie looked on in horror. What was it going to take to teach her husband a lesson? She remembered Gordon's words about knocking for him or Joe any time she was in trouble. But she couldn't do it five minutes after they'd left. 'Take yer hand off her or yer'll get the teapot on yer head.'

'I can give yer sixpence,' Ben said, hoping to stop what looked like trouble brewing. 'Will that do yer?'

'You keep yer nose out of it, yer little sod.' Tom began to pull on Jenny's hair. 'If I say I need a shilling, then that's what I want.'

'Let go of her hair, and we'll see what we can scrounge together,' Annie said, as her daughter screwed up her eyes in pain. 'Do it right now, or I'll make sure you suffer for it.' She lifted a heavy glass vase from the sideboard and raised it above her head. 'Let go now, or so help me I'll smash this on yer head.'

Tom relaxed his grip on Jenny's hair, but didn't let go. He knew he'd get what he wanted in the end. Annie would do anything to stop her children being hurt. 'Get the money on the table, where I can see it.'

'Here's my sixpence.' Ben placed the silver coin on the table. 'I can't give any more, Mam, 'cos I need to pay me fare to work.'

Annie opened a drawer in the sideboard and brought out her purse. 'I'll put the other sixpence down, but ye're cutting off yer nose to spite yer face. Don't come moaning to me when tomorrow's dinner isn't to yer liking. I can't produce money out of the air.'

'I'll let yer have threepence, Mam,' Jenny said. 'It's not much, but it might help.'

With the coins in his hand, Tom Phillips felt he'd won a victory. Those two fellers from next door, they thought themselves better than him. The silly buggers. Wait until tomorrow, when he was enjoying himself, he'd be the one having the last laugh.

Across the street, in the Fenwick house, Ada, Jimmy and Danny were sitting round the table, a cup of tea in front of them. The two children were in bed, so there was no need for Ada to think before she spoke. 'I honestly think the man's got a screw loose. He's definitely not right in the head.' She chuckled, then pulled a face. 'I know it's nothing to laugh about, but I can't help meself. Yer should have seen the looks on Jean's and Edith's faces when Tom Phillips told them to "bugger off". He followed this up by calling me a "cheeky cow", then threatened to take his belt to us.' Again she chuckled. 'Mind you, their faces were nothing compared to Tom Phillips's face when Gordon Bowers asked, "Are you threatening my wife?" Yer see, he hadn't seen Gordon and Joe come up behind him.'

'I'd love to have been there,' Danny said. 'I just hope that Gordon and Joe put the fear of God into him. Perhaps he'll calm down now, and the family see an improvement in their lives. Jenny is a lovely girl. She shouldn't have to put up with a father like that.'

'If yer want me honest opinion, I'd say I don't think anything that happened tonight will make a scrap of difference to Tom Phillips. The man is completely bonkers. I wouldn't be the least bit surprised if, right this minute, he's back to making life hell for Annie and the kids. The only way to cure a man like him is with a dose of arsenic.'

Jimmy raised his brow. 'That's a bit drastic, isn't it? I agree he needs a good hiding, but I draw the line at murder.'

'That was a slight exaggeration on my part, sunshine,' Ada said. 'And notice I said a slight exaggeration, 'cos if I had married Tom Phillips, I'd have either killed him or left him two days after the wedding. He's a dreadful man, an insult to all males. I feel heartily sorry for Annie, and the kids. Although I do think Annie is partly to blame for not cutting him down to size many years ago.'

'It's not too late, Mam,' Danny said. 'Something has to be done, 'cos they can't spend the rest of their lives with a madman. Jenny and Ben can't, anyway. When they're earning enough money they'll want to spread their wings and enjoy life.' He shook his head. 'Having said that, I don't think they'll ever leave their mother. They're devoted to her.'

Ada tilted her head. 'How did yer get on with Jenny at the dance? Was her dancing good enough for yer?'

'She's very stubborn, Mam. Insisted on paying her own tram fare, and I had to argue with her before she'd let me pay for her dance ticket. She's definitely got a mind of her own.'

'If she seems a bit difficult to get on with, yer've got to make allowances for her. Having a father like Tom Phillips is bound to have had an effect on her. Not only on her, but the whole family. They've been hounded out of every home they've had, because of his rotten behaviour. And Jenny is bound to feel ashamed, knowing we know what's going on. She probably feels embarrassed, and that's why she was on the offensive with yer. I doubt she's ever had a boyfriend in her life.'

'She might not have had a boyfriend, Mam, but I bet it's not because she's never had the chance. We'd only been in the dance hall for two minutes before she was asked up. I know the bloke . . . his name's Tony . . . he'd have had her up for every dance if I'd let him. It wouldn't surprise me if he hadn't asked her for a date.'

'Oh, that's nice!' Ada said. 'I'm glad she enjoyed herself. Yer'll have to ask her to go with yer again, sunshine. She needs to get out more.'

'Don't tell him that, love,' Jimmy said. 'Yer'll have his regular partners getting upset.'

Danny grinned. 'They pulled me leg over her, but they all thought she was very pretty. Tony certainly did, he was really taken with her.'

'Is she a good dancer, then?' Ada asked. 'Or not to your standard?'

'She's a good little dancer, I was surprised.' Danny's dimples showed. 'Mind you, I haven't had the tango or rumba with her yet.'

Ada gathered the empty cups and pushed her chair back. 'Be a good lad and ask her to go with yer again, sunshine. Get her out of that house and away from that rotter for a change.'

'I can't ask her to come with me, Mam! That's like asking her for a date, and I've only known the girl a few days. She'd probably tell me to get lost.'

Ada looked down at him and shook her head. 'No, she wouldn't do that. But if yer like, I'll ask her for yer.'

Danny looked horrified. 'Mam! Don't you do no such thing! She'll think I can't get a date meself, if me mam has to ask for me.'

258

Jimmy was in complete agreement with his son. 'Yer can't do that, love. Yer'd put the girl off. She'd think Danny didn't have a mouth of his own. Besides, Danny has his own friends. He might not want to feel obliged to ask Jenny.'

'I don't know what all the fuss is about,' Ada said. 'I don't see any harm in it. I'm not asking Danny to marry the girl, just to be a bit thoughtful. I bet with the father the way he is, she hasn't got many friends, and it wouldn't hurt to take her to the dance now and again. He doesn't need to stay with her once they get there. From what he's said, she's capable of getting her own partners.' She began to make her way to the kitchen with the dirty cups. 'I've always thought a little kindness goes a long way.'

Danny looked across at his dad and grimaced. 'Now she's making me feel like a heel.' He got to his feet and walked through to the kitchen. 'Look, Mam, I don't want yer to say anything to Jenny, 'cos she'll think I'm a right baby. But if I see her to talk to, I'll ask, casually, if she'd like to come to the dance with me. Does that make yer feel any better?'

Ada patted his cheek. 'I know yer don't need me to tell yer what to do, sunshine, so I'll leave yer to get on with it. And as it's well past our bedtime, I think we should make tracks for bed, otherwise we'll never be up in time.' She put her arms around him and kissed his cheek. 'Good night and God bless. See yer in the morning.'

Jimmy was in bed when Ada slipped her legs between the sheets. 'Ooh, let's snuggle up, sunshine, and keep ourselves nice and warm.'

Jimmy held her tight. 'We won't be long getting warm, love. And I won't be long getting off to sleep. I'm dead tired.' He nuzzled her neck. 'Let our Danny live his own life, love, don't try to live it for him.'

'Oh, I've got the message, sunshine, and I'll mind me own business.' She pulled his arm across her waist. 'Unless he changes his mind, of course.'

The next morning, Hetty brushed past Ada, eager to sit down at the table to hear the news. 'Well, how did yer get on? I kept watch through the window, and I saw yer coming out with the Bowerses and the Bensons. I was dying to know what happened, and I would have come over to yer, but Arthur put his foot down and told me not to be so nosy.'

'D'yer want me to tell yer now, or shall I make us a cuppa first?'

'Ooh, er.' Hetty pretended to be all of a quiver. 'Decisons, decisons.'

'Knock it off, sunshine, or yer'll have me a nervous wreck,' Ada said. 'Come to the kitchen and I can be telling yer while we're waiting for the kettle to boil. And before yer ask, I haven't got a biscuit of any description in the house. When we go to the shops, you can buy a packet of ginger snaps and treat me for a change.'

Hetty's face went through a range of expressions as she sat listening to her mate's account of the goings-on the night before. 'Oh, I'd love to have been there. Being told something isn't the same as seeing it with yer own eyes.'

'I know what yer mean, sunshine, and I really did feel lousy about leaving yer out. After all, yer are me best mate. But like I said, Annie's only got the four chairs, and it was more important that Jean and Edith were there than you. They're the ones who would be on hand if Annie or the kids needed help. And in the end, the little plan worked out a treat. For it gave Gordon and Joe the chance of seeing for themselves what Tom Phillips is really like. They were absolutely disgusted, and they'll be ready for the blighter if he starts any shenanigans.'

Hetty leaned forward. 'Ay, I saw your Danny going out with Jenny. How did he get on with her? Will he be taking her out again?'

'My lips are sealed on that subject, Hetty. Last night I was told in no uncertain terms that I was to mind me own business. By Jimmy, as well as Danny. So like meself, sunshine, yer'll just have to look, listen and wait.'

Chapter Twenty-Four

There were a lot of wagging tongues and raised eyebrows amongst the workmates of Tom Phillips. Instead of the surly expression they were used to, he was walking around with a half-smile on his face. He was even humming as he helped two dockers to load the crane which would swing the cartons on to the ship. And he hadn't skived off once to have a sly smoke behind the crates. 'They say there's always a change before death,' one of the gang said, 'but we wouldn't be that lucky.'

It was about ten o'clock when John Griffiths, the gang foreman, called a meeting with the men under his command. 'This ship has to be loaded and ready to sail by Sunday. So I need half a dozen men to work overtime on Saturday afternoon. Put your hands up if you want to earn some extra money.'

A couple of men shook their heads. Liverpool were playing at home on Saturday, and they wouldn't miss a match for the sake of a few bob. Their wives might have thought differently, given the choice. They wouldn't know, though, because their husbands weren't daft enough to tell them they were missing out on overtime. But Tom Phillips was one of the six who volunteered. And for the rest of the shift his smile stayed in place, and his humming became so loud, and so tuneless, he was told to put a sock in it. Which he did with good humour. Nothing was going to spoil this day for him.

It was going dusk when Tom Phillips walked towards the pub, his eyes peeled for sight of the prostitute who'd approached him a few days previously. He had thought of the possibility she wouldn't be there, for there was always business for women like her when the men were finishing work for the day. He wouldn't have far to look for another woman touting for business, but he was hoping to find the same woman, for she was younger than most. And his heartbeat began to race when he spied her leaning against the wall at the side of the pub. He would have liked to down a few pints first, to heighten his desire, but if he went into the pub she might be snaffled up by someone else and he'd miss his chance. So he nodded to her as he approached, and she moved away from the wall and came towards him. 'Out for a bit of fun, are yer, lad?'

Tom licked his lips. 'How much, how long and where?'

'Sixpence paid in advance, as long as it takes to make yer happy, and I'll tell yer where when yer give me the tanner.'

'How do I know I'll get me money's worth, if I pay yer in advance? Yer could take me money and then bugger off.'

The woman, who would have been pretty without the thick make-up plastered on her face, huffed. 'I wouldn't last long in business if I did that. Yer'll get yer money's worth, I'll promise yer that.'

Tom took the silver sixpence he'd been hoarding from his pocket and passed it over. 'Treat me well and I'll be back for more.'

'I'm not always available,' the woman told him. 'I have me regular punters.'

In case, at the end of the day, Tom didn't think her services were worth sixpence, he didn't take that conversation any further. He'd wait to see if he was satisfied, first, then he could well become one of her regular punters. The very thought excited him. 'Come on, let's go.'

'We're not walking together,' the woman said. 'I'll go first, you follow.' She nodded to a side street opposite. 'Go into that street, turn into the entry on yer left, then turn to yer right into the long entry behind the houses. Ten doors up, yer'll see a yard door with a circle in white. Open the door and step into the yard. I'll be there waiting for yer.'

Tom looked surprised. 'Yer mean we're going in your house?'

'Not on yer bleedin' life! Only me best punters, what pay me well, get inside me house. I've got a couple what pay me for the whole night, and they spend a full night going to heaven and back. I've got two young kids, but they know better than to come into the yard when I'm doing business.'

'Yer mean yer've got kids who know what yer do?' Tom was having second thoughts. It seemed a queer set-up to him. 'I don't like the idea of being watched by two kids.'

'I think more of my kids than to let them see what I do. They just think they've got a lot of uncles, that's all. And they won't see you, there's no chance of that. They go in me neighbour's next door, she looks after them if I'm busy. I need to earn money to keep them, and me neighbour is glad of the few coppers she gets for minding them, and for keeping her mouth shut.' The woman looked him up and down. 'Yer can have yer money back if it doesn't suit yer. I don't mind, there'll be another punter along soon. Please yerself.'

Tom had geared himself up for this, and he wasn't going to be put off.

'Go on, and I'll follow yer. I'll walk slow, to give yer time.' As she moved away, he asked, 'What's yer name?'

'As far as you're concerned, me name's Bella. And don't be too long following me, 'cos in my trade, time is money.'

When Tom found the entry door with the white circle on it, his hands were shaking and his heart pounding so loud he thought the whole street would hear. If he hadn't paid the sixpence, he would have seriously thought of walking away. But it was the money, plus the thought of his wife and her new friends, that moved his hand to the latch on the door. He was a red-blooded man and he needed a woman.

He opened the entry door, stepped inside and found himself facing Bella. To the left of her was the outside lavvy, and she opened the door to it. 'Inside with yer, and undo yer trousers. Make it snappy, for as I told yer, time is money.'

It was fifteen minutes later that Bella opened the yard door and stepped into the entry with Tom. 'Well, from the sounds yer made, and the way yer carried on, I'd say yer got yer money's worth twice over.'

Tom Phillips's head was reeling. There were times in that small outside lavvy when he'd thought his heart would burst. He'd never known anything like it. Had never even thought of half the tricks this woman had up her sleeve. 'Yer know yer job all right. And I'll be back for more.' He thought of the overtime he'd be doing on Saturday. He wouldn't get the money until next week, but what a way to spend it. 'How are yer fixed for Saturday, about half six?'

Bella shook her head. 'Saturday's me best day. I don't do any quickies.'

'What's the usual for a Saturday, then?'

'I'm booked up by one of me regulars for the night, so he'll be sleeping over. And I'll be doing a couple of punters who come every Saturday. The kids go next door, and I service the men in me house. They get half an hour for a shilling, and they leave very happy men.' There was sarcasm in Bella's voice when she said, 'It's amazing how many men have wives who don't understand them. Still, it takes all sorts, and at least it gives me a living.'

'Haven't yer got a husband?'

'Me name's Bella, and that's all yer'll ever find out about me. Ask no questions and yer'll be told no lies.'

'Suits me, girl. I'm Tom, and that's all yer need to know. I'll not ask yer any questions, except the one. Can yer fit me in on Saturday? You know, in yer house for a shilling.'

'I'll fit yer in if yer can be here for half six. Any later, there's nothing doing, 'cos I start getting busy at seven o'clock.'

Tom was eager. 'I'll be here. Shall I come in the back way, like now?'

Bella nodded. 'Better not be late, or yer won't get the full time. If ye're late, then it's you what loses the money, not me. And I want the shilling in me hand before yer get in the door. Is that understood?'

Tom wasn't used to being spoken to like that by a woman. If Annie spoke out of turn he'd belt her one. But he'd take it from this woman, for she'd given him a taste of the ecstasy and delights she could provide. His body was still tingling and his heart still pounding. And on Saturday, he'd have double the time. 'Yeah, I wouldn't expect any different. But I bet there's fellers who would let yer give them the works, then walk out without paying yer.'

Bella shook her head. 'They wouldn't get far, I can promise yer. A few buggers tried it on when I first started, but not now. I can read a feller inside out by just looking at them.'

'I'll see yer Saturday then, Bella,' Tom said, and began to walk back down the entry. 'I'll be here dead on half six.'

'Yer dinner will be dried up by now,' Annie said when Tom walked in. 'We had ours ages ago, and the kids have gone out.'

'Just see to me dinner and keep yer gob shut.' Tom flopped into the fireside chair. His body was still alive, a bit tender in parts. And when he tried to relive the feelings he'd felt when Bella's experienced hands had worked their magic, a quiver ran down his spine.

Annie put the plate down on the table. 'Get it while it's hot.' She watched out of the corner of her eye as he pushed himself out of the fireside chair and sat down at the table. He was very quiet tonight, no shouting or swearing. It's to good to be true, she told herself, it certainly won't last. But Tom ate his dinner in silence, the only sound in the room being the ticking of the clock.

He finished his dinner, wiped a hand across his mouth, and moved back to the fireside chair. 'Get off yer fat arse and bring me a cup of tea.'

Annie stood in the kitchen waiting for the kettle to boil. There was something not right here. Tom was far too quiet for her liking. She'd expected a torrent of abuse off him, and a few thumps, at least. He was bound to pay her back for letting the neighbours know their business, and humiliate him. As she poured the boiling water into the teapot, a little voice in her head warned her to watch out, and not to get too close to him.

With the warning still in her head, Annie didn't hand her husband the cup and saucer, but put it down on the end of the table where he could reach it easily. Then she sat on one of the wooden chairs on the opposite side. Not a word was spoken for several minutes, then Tom snarled, 'What the bleeding hell are yer staring at, yer gormless cow?'

'I'm staring at you, yer bad-tempered so-and-so.' Annie had been telling herself all day that she had to start standing up to him. She'd left it late, perhaps too late, but she couldn't expect her friends to do what she wouldn't do herself. And that was to put Tom Phillips in his place. 'I was just wondering if yer were sickening for something, with yer being so quiet.'

'I'm quiet because I want to be quiet, not because I'm sick.' Tom glared at his wife. What a dried-up old prune she was. She didn't know how to make a man happy, not like Bella. Now there was a woman for yer. She was the one he'd be going to to fulfil his needs. A red-blooded man needed a woman with experience. One who could thrill him and make him happy. He sneered, 'Yeah, I am sick, sick of the bleeding sight of you.'

'The same goes for me, Tom Phillips,' Annie was stung into saying. 'What the hell I ever saw in you I'll never know. But I've lived to regret ever setting eyes on yer.'

From habit, Tom had a strong urge to get up and give her a good hiding. But just at that moment he felt a tremor down his spine, and in his head he brought up the feeling of Bella's hands running over his body, gently rubbing in the right places. He closed his eyes, to enjoy the sensation, and forgot the woman he'd married some twenty years ago.

Annie looked on, perplexed by the change in her husband's face. His eyes were closed, and there was a smile playing around his mouth. He's been drinking, she thought. It's either that, or he's in for a cold. My best bet is to stay quiet and keep away from him. He's not his normal self, unless he's pretending, to lull me into a sense of false security. Whatever it was, she was going to keep out of his way. The children wouldn't be out long, they'd only gone round to a mate of Ben's, who had a few comics he was going to lend. Jenny had gone with her brother for the walk, so she'd be out of the house when her father came in.

Annie sat quietly at the table, not making a sound, just listening to the time tick away. Now and then Tom would half open an eye, stare at her for a second, then close it again. Ten minutes passed, then twenty, and the strange tension in the air was making Annie feel nervous and uncomfortable. In the end she couldn't stand it any longer, and asked, 'Are yer not going to the pub tonight? Ye're usually out well before this.'

Tom opened his eyes. 'It's got nothing to do with you whether I go to the pub or not, yer nosy old cow. I might go, then again I might not.' He was thinking that the money he spent in the pub would buy him another fifteen-minute session with Bella when he finished work the following night. Then the day after was Saturday. He'd be working overtime to get the ship loaded ready for sailing the next morning, but he'd get away in time to be in her yard at half six. The boss couldn't expect the crew to work any later than that. If he did, then he was going to be disappointed. A shilling was a lot of money, and Tom intended to get every penny's worth.

'No, I won't bother going to the pub tonight.' Tom decided to play games with his wife. He loved nothing better than to see her squirm. 'I think I'll go to bed now, and I want yer to come with me. The kids are out, so we can make as much noise as we like. Yer can be good to me, make me happy.' He saw the colour drain from her face, and it made him feel good. 'Go on, up the stairs, and I'll follow yer in a minute.'

Annie could feel her heart racing. But she wasn't going to let him see she was afraid. 'No, I am not sleeping in the same bed as you. Never again. I sleep with Jenny now.'

His laugh was pure evil. 'I've got a really good idea. I don't know why I've never thought of it before. You go to bed now, into Jenny's bed, and get a good night's sleep. And when me daughter comes in, she can come in my bed. She's growing up, is Jenny, nicely rounded and ready for picking. How about that then? I wonder if I'd be the first for her, or whether she's had a few before?' He snorted and shook his head. 'No, she's probably as cold as her bleeding mother. Mind you, I could teach her a few tricks the young lads wouldn't know. Wet behind the ears, most of them.'

Annie was off her chair like the shot out of a gun. She rounded the table and stood in front of him. 'You wicked bugger. May God forgive me for swearing, but yer'd make a saint swear. You are wicked through and through. There is not one bit of you that is good. Yer'll make a good mate for the devil, for hell is where yer'll end up. Only someone wicked to the core would talk about his own daughter like that.' Annie leaned forward and put a hand on each of the chair arms. 'I wonder what yer workmates would say if they'd heard what yer've just said? Or the neighbours what yer hate so much? I know what would happen, yer filthy-minded, wicked, dirty devil. Yer'd be hounded out of yer job and out of this street. Yer wouldn't be able to show yer face anywhere. Yer'd be a pariah, made to hide away from decent people. And so help me, I've a good mind to go down to the docks tomorrow and tell yer boss. And then I'd come back and tell everyone in this street. They all know ye're a good-for-nothing, but never in a million years would they think yer were bad enough to talk about taking yer own daughter into bed with yer.' She paused for breath. 'I

266

feel like scratching yer eyes out, but me flesh would crawl if I even touched yer.'

Tom had never seen such hatred in his wife's eyes before. He was used to seeing fear. But now he was the one in fear. For he knew Annie would do anything to protect her children, and right now she was capable of carrying out her threats. And if she did, he could lose his job and his home. His brain became active, seeking a way out. In the end he resorted to bluff. 'What's the matter with yer, yer silly old cow? Can't yer take a bleeding joke?'

Annie didn't think it possible to hate someone as she now hated her husband. What a wicked, filthy mind he had. He was pretending it was a joke, but she didn't believe him. He was bad enough to act out his evil thoughts. Look what he'd done to her over the years. Stripped her of her pride and dignity. Well, she wouldn't let it happen to the two people in the world she loved most. He'd not get the chance. The only way he'd ever hurt either of the children again would be over her dead body. 'Don't try and bluff yer way out of it, Tom Phillips, 'cos it won't work. I've lived with yer for twenty years, and found out the hard way exactly how twisted yer mind is. Twenty years living with a madman would be enough to drive most people insane. It's the love I have for my two kids that's kept me going over the years. Because of them I let you treat me like an animal. But those days are dead and gone now. They're not forgotten, for I'll never forget what you've put me through. But yer'll not rule the roost in this house any more. I'm not going to jump when yer tell me to. And I'll make ruddy sure the kids don't jump to yer bidding, either.'

Tom couldn't meet her eyes. 'I don't know what ye're getting so het up over, I was only joking. As if I'd touch me own daughter. It's you what's twisted in yer mind, not me.' He waved his arm towards the door. 'I said I was going to have an early night, so will yer move away and let me get to bed?'

'I'll gladly move out of yer way. The further away, the better. But I'll not forget what yer said tonight, Tom Phillips, so yer'd do well to keep yer nose clean in future. Leave me and the kids alone. I'll feed yer and do yer washing and ironing, but that's about it. Yer can come and go as yer please, as long as yer don't get drunk and make a show of us. If yer get too drunk to walk, then doss down in an entry. Don't bother coming home, 'cos yer'll not get in.'

Annie moved to put a distance between them when he got out of the chair. 'Perhaps yer'd be more comfortable dossing down in the gutter. More at home, like, for that's where yer came from.' And as he passed, she said softly, 'And that's where yer'll end up.'

267

Tom Phillips had been in bed half an hour when Jenny and Ben came in, and Annie was sitting at the table waiting for them. 'I thought yer'd be back before this. Yer did say yer were only going to pick up some comics.'

Ben's eyes went to the kitchen before he took his coat off. 'Where's me dad?' he asked in a whisper. 'Is he in, or gone to the pub?'

'There's no need to whisper, sweetheart,' Annie told him. 'The days of being afraid to speak are gone, never to return. So hang yer coats up, and tell me why yer've been out longer than yer expected.'

But Jenny couldn't wait. 'We'll tell yer our tale after yer've told us yours. Has me dad gone to the pub?'

Annie had spent the waiting time in getting a tale together that would be part truth and part lies. One that the children would believe. There was no way she would tell two young, innocent children that their father had mentioned taking his daughter into his bed. No one would ever hear that from her, for she'd be too ashamed to allow the words to leave her lips. So the story Ben and Jenny were told was a very watered down one. 'I've had a really good talk to yer father, and I think this time the words have sunk in. I really lost me temper and went for him, so it wasn't just a talk, more of a blazing row. I threatened to tell his workmates, and everyone in this street, what a devil he really is.' Annie looked from one surprised face to the other. 'I can't repeat it word for word, sweethearts, but I do know that the way I carried on, it left yer father speechless. I told him he can come and go as he pleases, but if he comes home drunk he won't be allowed in. He can sleep in an entry or the gutter. He's to leave me and you two alone. I'll feed him, do his washing and ironing, but more than that I won't do.' She gave a deep sigh. 'Yer father didn't have much to say for himself at all. After I'd finished, he took himself off to bed and I haven't heard a sound since.'

'That won't last, Mam,' Jenny said. 'You'll see, tomorrow he'll be back to his horrible self. But yer weren't half brave, and I'm proud of yer.'

'Yer were taking a chance, Mam,' Ben said. 'I wish we hadn't gone out now. I'd have loved to have seen me dad's face. But I think our Jenny's right, he'll be back to normal tomorrow. What is it they say about a leopard never changing its spots? Well, that's what I think about me dad. He'll never change.'

'Let's wait and see, sweetheart,' Annie told him. 'I've put the fear of God into yer father, and I'm prepared to guarantee yer'll have no more trouble from him. I know him a bit better than you do, and I know he's a coward. Once I mentioned telling his workmates, and all the neighbours, what he's like, that was enough for him. However, while I doubt very much I'm wrong, I'll be willing to eat me words if it turns out I am.'

'I can't get over him being in bed this time of night, when the pubs are still open,' Jenny said. 'It's never been known before.'

'Well, just forget about yer father for now, I've had enough of him. Tell me why it took the pair of yer so long to pick a couple of comics up.'

'Don't blame me,' Ben said. 'I'd have been there and back in half an hour. It was Danny Fenwick who kept us talking.'

'He was waiting at the tram stop when we were passing,' Jenny explained. 'He was on his way to the dance. We stopped to talk to him, that's all. We couldn't very well just walk past him, that would have been rude.'

'Yeah, I know we had to say hello to him,' Ben said, 'but we didn't have to stand talking for an hour.'

'Ooh, yer don't half exaggerate, our kid,' Jenny told him. 'We didn't stay that long.'

'He let two trams go.' Ben winked at his mother. 'He did, yer know. Twice he let one go, saying he'd take the next. I think he's got his eye on our Jenny, 'cos he asked her if she'd like to go to the dance with him.'

Annie sat forward. 'That was nice of him. Why didn't yer go, Jenny? Yer'd have enjoyed yerself.'

Jenny huffed. 'Oh, yeah, I'd have gone to a dance in me working clothes. Besides, he was only asking because he thought he should. I bet his face would have dropped if I'd said I'd go with him.'

'Oh, that's not a nice thing to say, sweetheart. Danny's a lovely lad, and he wouldn't have asked yer to go to the dance if he hadn't meant it. Why would he do that?'

Ben added to his sister's discomfort by telling his mother, 'He's asked her to go on Saturday, Mam. He wouldn't have done that if he hadn't got his eye on her, would he?'

'Oh, shut up, will yer, Ben.' Jenny was annoyed with herself for blushing. 'I'm not going to the dance on Saturday, so don't keep harping on it.'

'Why not, sweetheart?' Annie asked. 'Yer really should get out more, and Danny's a nice boy. From what Ada's told me, he's got three regular partners at the dance, so yer wouldn't have to stay with him.'

'Oh, it's not that, Mam. I know he's got partners, I've seen them. That doesn't worry me, 'cos I'd get asked up meself. The reason I don't want to go with Danny is because he wants to pay for me, and I don't think that's fair. I mean, why should he pay for me? All he knows about me is that I've got a drunken father who makes a holy show of us. He's helped bring me dad in a couple of times, and I don't want him to get the impression we're always expecting other people to help us. I've got pride, Mam, and I don't want to lose it.'

Ben was sorry he'd pulled his sister's leg now, because she seemed really upset. 'Wait a couple of years, Jenny, until I'm grown up enough to go dancing. We'll go out jazzing every night, and I'll pay for yer.'

His sister smiled at him. 'That's a lovely thought, our kid, and I appreciate yer thinking of me. But what am I to do with meself for the next few years, while I'm waiting for yer to grow up? I can't stay at home and twiddle me thumbs every night. Mind you, I could take up knitting, and knit meself a man who fulfils all the requirements I'd like in a boy friend.'

Annie clicked her tongue on the roof of her mouth. 'Surely that's doing things the hard way, sweetheart. Why not go to a dance where there'll be lots to choose from? Yer could do a deal with Danny that would suit you and also put my mind at rest.'

'Ah, ay, Mam. It'll have to be some deal that'll suit me and Danny, and also put your mind at rest. What are yer thinking of?'

Annie chuckled. 'We'll do me first, eh? Yer see, I always worry when you and Ben are out on these dark nights. Ben I don't have to worry about so much, him being a lad and big for his age. And he's always in at a respectable time. It's you I worry about more. But if yer went to the dance with Danny, I wouldn't have to 'cos yer wouldn't be coming home on yer own in the dark. And to keep yer independence, which seems to be important to yer, well, yer could buy yer own tram and dance ticket. That way yer'll not be under any obligation.'

Jenny's shoulders started to shake with a low titter behind her hand. Then the sound grew into full scale laughter as she rocked back and forth on the chair. 'Oh, Mam, ye're priceless! Yer've got it all worked out, haven't yer?' She wiped away the tears of laughter. 'But has it never entered yer head that Danny might take one of the girls home when the dance is over? Or that he'd be embarrassed if I sat next to him on the tram and insisted I paid me own fare? And when we get to the dance hall, I'll let him hold the door open while I rush in and buy me own ticket? I'm sure he'd love that.'

Annie frowned. 'But I'm sure Danny would understand if yer explained to him that yer'd feel better paying yer own way. He's very easy-going, and he's not the kind to take the huff over a little thing like that.'

Across the table, Ben shook his head. 'No, Mam, our Jenny's right. When I'm a bit older and take a girl out, I wouldn't want her to pay for herself. I mean, it's the feller's place to look after his girlfriend, and pay to take her out.'

'I know that, lad, 'cos I had a couple of dates before I met yer dad, and the lads always paid. But it's different with Danny. He wouldn't be courting Jenny, only travelling there and back to the dance with her. I don't see what's wrong with that.'

'Poor Danny,' Jenny said, 'I'm beginning to feel sorry for him. Here's us, sitting here planning his life for him. And while I can see the funny side, I'm blowed if I can see Danny thinking it funny and laughing his head off. So, if yer don't mind, Mam, we'll leave Danny to lead his own life, eh? He seems happy enough as he is, so why should we, who are almost strangers to him, come along and spoil things?'

'If that's the way yer want it, sweetheart, then we'll say no more about it.' Annie was disappointed but not defeated. She was determined her daughter wasn't going to marry a rotter, like she had. And Danny Fenwick was certainly no rotter. And as the saying goes, 'Hope springs eternal.'

Chapter Twenty-Five

'Yer never did get yer living room decorated in time for Christmas, did yer?' Ada looked past Hetty, to where Annie was walking on the outside. 'Even if yer got the paper yer wouldn't have it done in time now.'

'I haven't got quite enough money for it, sweetheart,' Annie told her. 'I've enough to buy the paper, I think, but as yer know, yer can't put paper up without doing the ceiling and the woodwork.'

'It's a pity that,' Ada sympathised, ' 'cos if we all got stuck in to help yer, we could still have it done in time.' She chuckled. 'We'd be at it until midnight on Christmas Eve, like, but it would be nice for Father Christmas to see when he comes down the chimney.'

'If Annie hasn't got the money, girl, then there's no use talking about it,' Hetty said. 'We could give her a hand after the holiday's over and she's got the money to buy what she needs.'

'Yeah, I know that, sunshine, but I was only saying it would have been nice for her. Put a bit of colour in the room and cheer it up a bit.' Ada nipped in front of her friend and placed herself between Hetty and Annie. 'That's better, I can see what I'm saying now.'

Hetty tutted. 'Don't mind me, girl, you just look after yerself. It's about time I put me foot down with yer, and thought of meself for a change.'

Ada put an arm across her mate's shoulder and squeezed. 'That's right, sunshine, you start sticking up for yerself. I would if I were you, and it would liven things up a bit.'

'What Hetty said about putting her foot down,' Annie said, 'well, I did that last night, good and proper. I had a real go at my feller and got everything off me chest.'

Ada pulled the trio to a halt. 'And yer got away with it? Go 'way, yer couldn't have told him off that much, or yer wouldn't be here to tell the tale.'

'I did though, and I am.' Annie still couldn't believe she'd found the courage to stand up to Tom Phillips. She probably wouldn't have had the nerve to say half she did if he hadn't said what he did about Jenny. That was the straw that broke the donkey's back. Something she couldn't stand there and listen to without retaliating. But no one else would be told what he'd said in case it got back to Jenny. 'He had everything flung in his face that he's done to me and the kids over the years. He tried to be cocky at first, but I'd got meself so riled up I pushed him down in the chair and made him listen to everything I've wanted to say for so long.'

'Ooh, I want to hear this,' Ada said with relish. 'I want to hear every word, yer mustn't leave anything out.'

Hetty gave her a dig. 'Ye're not going to hear it now, girl, 'cos here comes Ivy Thompson the troublemaker. Every word yer say, she doubles, then adds anything she can think of to spice it up.'

'Damn and blast her,' Ada said. 'I had geared meself up for a bit of excitement. But never mind, yer can come back to mine when we've finished shopping, sunshine, and give me and Hetty the news over a nice cup of tea, and the biscuits what Hetty is going to bring in.'

Hetty just had time to say, 'Ye're a cheeky article, Ada Fenwick,' before the neighbourhood gossip and bully came up to them. Most people in the area would scuttle away, or cross the street, when they saw Ivy Thompson, for she had a terrible mouth on her, and if yon tried to argue with her she'd think nothing of belting you one. So, all in all, she was very unpopular, and afraid of no one. No one except Ada Fenwick, who, when it came to fisticuffs, could give as good as she got. Not that Ada was a bully, like Ivy, for she wasn't. Ada was very popular with everyone, whereas Ivy liked nothing better than to pick on someone she knew was afraid of her.

Ivy stopped in front of the trio, effectively barring their path. 'Good morning, Ada.'

'Good morning to you, Ivy,' Ada answered. 'Not that it is a good morning, mind yer, 'cos it's ruddy freezing. Still, we have to be polite, don't we?'

Ivy was a big woman, easily twenty stone, and with muscles any man would be proud of. And now she was eyeing Annie up and down. 'This yer new neighbour, is she? The one that took over Eliza's house?'

Ada nodded. 'Yeah, this is Annie Phillips. Annie, this is Ivy Thompson, otherwise known as the neighbourhood bully. Yer'd do well to cross the road when yer see her coming towards yer, sunshine, 'cos she packs a very hard punch.'

As Ada was wearing a smile when she spoke, Ivy looked uncertain. She didn't know whether to treat it as a joke, or an insult. After a few seconds' debate in her head, she decided there was no use picking a fight, not with Ada Fenwick. She'd tried a couple of times but in the end had had to admit defeat. 'Take no notice of Ada, queen,' she told Annie. 'If ye're a friend of hers, then ye're a friend of mine.'

And to the surprise of everyone, Annie did something no one else had ever done. She held out her hand to the local bully. 'Pleased to meet yer, Ivy.'

Ivy looked down at the outstretched hand, and a second later she was pumping it up and down. No one had ever shaken her hand before, and she was over the moon. She squared her shoulders and her mountainous bosom stood proudly to attention. Over the next hour, the whole neighbourhood would hear about this. Ivy Thompson was going up in the world, and woe betide anyone who wouldn't stop to listen, and nod their head in agreement. 'Nice to make yer acquaintance, Annie. As I said, any friend of Ada's is a friend of mine.'

'Well, it does me heart good to know we're all friends,' Ada said, smiling to take the sting out of her next words. 'But I'm afraid I'm going to have to break the party up, 'cos I've got a load of shopping to do. I've no spuds and not a crust of bread in the house. It's been nice talking to yer, Ivy, and we'll see yer around.' She gripped an arm either side of her and marched her friends forward. 'Come on, ladies, time and tide wait for no man.'

When they'd walked what Hetty thought was a safe distance, she said to Annie, 'I hope yer know how privileged yer are, girl, 'cos If Ada hadn't been with us, Ivy Thompson would have made mincemeat out of you and me.'

'She's a big girl, all right,' Annie said. 'I wouldn't like to get on the wrong side of her.'

'There's no reason to get on the wrong side of her,' Ada said. 'If yer see her before she sees you, then run to the nearest entry. But if she sees yer, then give her a big smile, and be as polished as Hetty's sideboard on a Monday morning.'

Hetty screwed up her eyes, thought for a few seconds, then asked, 'Why Monday, girl, and not any other day of the week?'

'Because Monday is yer day for hard work, sunshine, that's why. I know yer dust every single day, but Monday is the day for using yer elbow grease.'

'Yer haven't half got sharp eyes, girl, 'cos I think me furniture looks highly polished every single day.'

'Now don't be taking the huff, sunshine, just because yer took what I said the wrong way. The only reason I mentioned yer sideboard was because it's the first thing anyone sees when they go in yer living room. And one Monday I called to yours for something, and me eyes were so dazzled by the shine I couldn't see properly for over an hour. All I could see was flashes before my eyes.'

'This is one of yer made up stories, isn't it?' Hetty asked. 'I know it is, so yer've no need to deny it. I'm used to yer by now, I know all yer little tricks. And what makes me so sure is that yer've never been in me house on a Monday morning.'

'Or any other morning, sunshine, don't forget that. I have never once been over the threshold of your door in the morning.'

Annie was finding this very interesting, but was hard put to it to know if the two friends were really having a serious conversation, or whether it would end up as a leg-pull. 'Does this story have an ending, or is it one of the tales Hetty mentioned? I'm only asking so I'll know whether to take sides if it comes to blows.'

Ada shook her head. 'No, it's all right, sunshine, 'cos that's what I use while Hetty is busy sweating using elbow grease.'

Hetty's head quivered and her lips became a straight line. 'I do not sweat, Ada Fenwick. Even on a really hot day, yer'll not see any sign of perspiration on my brow. And would yer mind answering Annie's question? What is it you use when I am supposedly sweating?'

'Oh dear, oh dear, oh dear! Yer do take on so, Hetty! If yer'd listened carefully, yer would have heard me telling Annie that while you polish yer furniture, all I do is blow the dust away. I know it only goes from one end of the sideboard to the other, but on the second blow I can sometimes get it as far away as the kitchen.'

'Go 'way!' Annie was chuckling inside. 'D'yer know, I've been taught more in the last ten minutes than I was in the whole nine years I was at school. Do you two often have these deep conversations?'

Hetty looked at Ada and raised her brows. 'How often would yer say, girl? Once a week or once a month?'

The women were standing outside Irwin's the grocer's by this time, and Ada rubbed her chin. 'No, ye're miles out, sunshine. I'd say twice every day.'

'Yer must have learned a lot from each other,' Annie said, straight-faced.

'Oh, we have, girl, ye're so right. We are twice as daft now as we were when we first moved into the street and became neighbours.'

Ada nodded her head vigorously. 'I blame the landlord. If he hadn't given us houses next door to each other, we would have been much saner people now.'

'Yeah,' Hetty agreed. 'Not as happy, like, but much more sane.'

'Well, no matter how it came about, the pair of yer would be lost without each other. And for meself, I have good reason to be grateful to the landlord for putting yer next door to each other. And for letting me have the tenancy of number twenty-two. My life has been changed completely since yer were kind enough to make friends with me. It's not perfect by any means, but much better. And after I tackled Tom Phillips last night, I know there's going to be a real improvement.'

'Yes, I was going to go back to what yer said about last night,' Ada said. 'I'm really interested to know whether yer were as firm with him as yer sounded. So how about you getting yer shopping done, while me and Hetty do ours? We'll all meet up at my place in an hour's time. How does that suit yer?'

'Wonderful, sweetheart. I'll be knocking on yer door in an hour's time. Ta-ra for now.'

When Ada opened the door to Annie later, she let her neighbour pass, then said, 'Not one word until we've got a cup of tea in front of us. I can always think better with a cup in me hand. And Hetty has mugged us to a cream slice each, so that's two things to look forward to.'

While Ada was making the tea, Hetty asked, 'What are yer having for yer dinner, Annie? Me and Ada bought some pig's liver, and we're doing it with onions and mashed potatoes. It's quick, easy and tasty.' She gave an exaggerated wink. 'At least that's what me mate told me when she talked me into buying the same as her.'

'Ay, buggerlugs, I heard that.' Ada came in carrying a tray set with cups, saucers and a plate with three cream slices on. 'I hope when ye're enjoying yer very tasty dinner tonight, yer tell yer family it's all thanks to me.'

'Oh, I will, girl! I'll even get them to knock and thank you.'

The tray was set down on the table, the cups of tea were handed out, and the plate of cakes was put down in the centre. The cream slices were filled with lots of mouth-watering fresh cream, and Ada insisted they leave the talking until the cakes were eaten, for it was torture to sit and look at them. So it was ten minutes later before Annie got to tell her tale. And she told it well, with actions and words. Her changing facial expressions added to the drama. She finished by saying, 'He ate his toast this morning, drank two cups of tea, and left for work without one word leaving his mouth. No punches, no bad language, not even a sneer. Now, whether it will last or not is something I can't be sure of. But I've got a feeling that Tom Phillips will be a different man from now on. Please God.'

'Good for you, sunshine. I'm proud of yer.' Ada was really pleased to see Annie looking relaxed and confident. 'What a difference it'll be for you and the children not to be looking sideways all the time.'

Hetty spoke her thoughts aloud. 'It seems too good to be true. Can a person as bad as yer husband change so quickly? I wouldn't have believed it possible.'

'Ye're as wise as me, sweetheart,' Annie said. 'I can only wait and hope for the best. But if he does start his bullying again, and coming home drunk, then I will do what I threatened to do. I'll go and see his boss, then his workmates will know him for what he is. That is one thing that would put the fear of God into Tom Phillips. I could tell I'd frightened him when I said that, 'cos I could really see the fear in his eyes. He's brave when he hits me or the kids, but he'd be terrified if his workmates gave him a hard time.'

'What do Jenny and Ben think about it?' Ada asked. 'If their father has changed, it'll make a big difference to their lives.'

'When they came in last night and I told them Tom had gone to bed early, and how I'd had a big row with him, they shrugged their shoulders and said it was a flash in the pan. They were surprised he hadn't gone to the pub, but I couldn't convince them that there were going to be big changes in the future. Jenny pulled a face and said give it a day or two and her dad would be back to his old ways.'

'Well, for what it's worth, sunshine, my gut feeling is that yer hit the right spot when yer told him yer would expose his wickedness to his workmates. And although I don't think he's ever likely to be a nice person, I've got a feeling yer life is going to improve from now on. In fact, if I had the money to spare, I'd buy a bottle of sherry and drink a toast to a good future for you and the kids.'

'It would be wonderful if yer were right, sweetheart, but I haven't got the high hopes you have. I don't expect a miracle. I'll settle for a quiet and peaceful life for meself, and for Jenny and Ben. I'd like to see them enjoying their teenage years.'

Hetty had been listening with interest. She had grown fond of Annie, and wanted to give her some hope. 'My mate Ada here is not very often wrong, girl. In fact, I sometimes think she has what they call second sight. I often think she's making things up, for a laugh, like, but more often than not the joke's on me. I'll bet a pound to a pinch of snuff that she's right about your feller. Give it a week or so, and see if she's not right.'

'I'll keep me fingers crossed, sweetheart, and I'll keep yer up to date with the goings-on. And now I've told yer that news, I've got something else to tell yer.' Annie uncrossed her legs so she could get them under the table and lean forward. Her eyes were bright with excitement and the words she'd had trouble keeping under control poured from her mouth. 'After I left yer this morning, I nipped along to the wallpaper shop, just to have a look at the paper and find out the prices. And while I was looking at the paper on display, I saw a notice saying a part-time worker was wanted. From nine to one o'clock, six days a week.'

Ada grinned. 'And yer got the job.'

Annie gasped. 'How did yer know that?'

'I could tell by the look on yer face. Like when yer were telling us about Tom Phillips, yer eyes were glistening. I am right, aren't I?'

'Yeah, I start on Monday!' Annie's face showed her surprise. 'I'm beginning to think Hetty is right, and ye're a mind-reader, sweetheart. Anyway, I went in the shop pretending to look at the wallpaper, and as yer know, I'm not a one for pushing meself. I'm a defeatist, really, and I was telling meself I didn't stand a snowball's chance in hell of getting the job 'cos I was too old and not the type to be able to talk to customers. But even though I thought I didn't stand an earthly, a little voice in me head told me I was a coward. And that is what gave me the courage to ask the man behind the counter. It's his shop, and the assistant he had left last week to go to a job what paid better. We got talking, and the man asked if I was interested. I told him I'd never worked in a shop before, but he said that wasn't important. He asked me age, where I lived and what ties I had at home. Well, with it only being a morning job, I told him there was nothing to tie me down at home and I'd be grateful if he'd give me a chance. So I start on Monday, and I'll be on a two-week trial. If I don't like the job, or he thinks I'm not cut out for it, then I can leave with no hard feelings.'

Ada was sitting with a satisfied grin on her face, while Hetty's jaw had dropped and she was shaking her head. 'If you two are pulling me leg, then I don't think it's very funny.'

'I'm not pulling yer leg, sweetheart,' Annie told her. 'I'm not clever enough to have made all that up. And I'm so happy, I really can't believe me luck. It only pays sixpence a morning, but that mounts up to three shillings a week, and that's a lot of money to me. Wait until I tell the children, they'll be really surprised.'

'And what about Tom Phillips?' Ada's eyes were wide as she asked, 'Will he be pleased, or will he cut yer housekeeping money down, for spite?'

'Oh, I made up me mind first thing that I wouldn't tell him. I know for certain he'd cut down on what little money he gives me. There's no way he'll know I'm working, 'cos I don't start until nine, and I'll be home again at one o'clock. He won't even notice the difference. He calls into a pub on his way home every day, so he won't notice any change.' Annie was determined her husband wouldn't gain by her working. 'I just wish it had come along a few weeks ago, then I could have saved up enough money to give the children some decent presents for Christmas. As it is, I'll only get one week's wages before the holiday. But even that will be a blessing.'

Ada leaned across the table and patted her hand. 'Annie, ye're a different woman from the one that moved into number twenty-two just a short while ago. Yer've gradually gained in strength of character, and ye're showing more backbone.' She turned to her mate. 'Hetty, am I right in saying that Annie has been changing gradually over the time we've known her, but the change since yesterday has been drastic?'

Her mate quickly agreed. 'She has surprised me, girl, I can tell yer that. And I'm hoping that husband of hers doesn't spoil it with his shenanigans.' Hetty was usually very mild-tempered, but just the thought of the things Annie had suffered was enough to raise her blood to boiling point. 'I'd even take the poker to him meself if he starts his messing again.'

Ada chuckled. 'Now, that is saying something, sunshine. That's probably the first time I've ever heard yer threaten to have a go at someone. And I hope Annie realises yer must regard her very highly if ye're prepared to go into battle on her behalf.'

'Oh, don't for one second think I don't appreciate what you two have done for me. If you hadn't come along and offered the hand of friendship, then I know only too well that I would still be terrified of opening me door to anyone, hiding behind the curtains to see who was knocking. And I'd still be cowering whenever Tom Phillips looked at me, or ordered me to do something that would humiliate and degrade me.' Annie shook her head slowly, and there was a hint of tears in her eyes. 'No, you two have been my salvation, and I'll never forget that. Neither will my two children.'

Ada tried to lighten the atmosphere by changing the subject. 'Talking of children, I believe our Danny asked Jenny if she wanted to go to the dance with him on Saturday?'

'Your son takes after his mother for being thoughtful and kind. But unfortunately, my lovely daughter hasn't been brought up to appreciate those qualities in people, because she's never known them. Because of her father, she doesn't trust people as she should. But don't blame her, Ada, 'cos it's not her fault.'

'Not for one moment would I do that, Annie, for Jenny's a lovely girl. And Danny understands because he's very caring. We'll just leave the kids to go their own way, eh?' Ada scraped her chair back. 'As I said before, if I had a bottle of sherry we could drink a toast to yer good fortune. But as we're not members of the idle rich, we'll have to make do with tea. I'll put the kettle on for a fresh pot.'

* * *

Tom Phillips saw Bella standing against the side wall of the pub, and his senses reacted in anticipation. As she walked towards him, he was thinking she'd be a nice-looking woman if she didn't plaster the thick make-up on. Mind you, that was part of her trade. She wanted to stand out to attract the punters. He nodded his head in acknowledgement.

'I didn't expect to see you tonight,' Bella drawled, a cigarette dangling from the side of her mouth. 'Got the money, have yer?'

'Yeah, I've got sixpence.'

She turned away. 'Same as yer did yesterday. Walk behind me, turn into the entry and then into me back yard.'

As Tom turned into the back entry, he could feel his passion growing. His appetite for sex was insatiable. He only had to look at an attractive woman, and in his mind he stripped her of her clothing and let his imagination run away with him. He'd had many dark looks thrown at him by men who were parading a pretty woman on their arm, and caught him staring.

The yard door opened before his hand had reached the latch, and Bella's low voice told him to get in sharpish. 'They're a nosy lot of biddies round here, and the less they know of my business the better.' She wasted no time in shoving him into the lavatory, then squeezed in herself and closed the door. Then she held out her hand. 'Sixpence, before I lay a finger on yer.' Time was money, and he was only a punter to her. So she was abrupt and straight to the point. 'Same as yesterday, undo yer trousers.'

Tom was so eager, he would have crawled if she'd told him to. But she didn't. Instead she did the job she was good at, and had him groaning with pleasure. When his cries became louder, she put a hand over his mouth so her next-door neighbour wouldn't hear. When his time was up, he was snaking like a leaf. His heart was thumping so hard he thought it would burst out of his chest. Bella left the lavatory while he made himself respectable, and when he came out, she asked, 'Was this visit instead of tomorrow?'

He was quick to answer, for all he could think of, while at work or lying in bed staring up at the ceiling, was Bella attending to his needs in her house. 'Oh, no, I'll be here tomorrow all right. Six thirty, like we said.' Then he couldn't resist confirming, 'It will be inside yer house, won't it?'

She nodded, then made sure he remembered, 'Yes, and it'll be a shilling.' She opened the yard door and peered into the entry. 'It's all clear, so scarper. And make sure ye're not late tomorrow. Saturday's a busy night for me.'

280

'Don't worry about that, I'll be on time.' As he walked down the entry and into the main road, Tom Phillips was a very happy, satisfied man. And he had great hopes that tomorrow would be better still. It would be warm in her house, there'd be more room, and he'd be able to watch Bella at work. It was a much better way of spending his money than going to the pub. He reached the tram stop and lit a cigarette. There'd be a tram along any minute, but as he drew on his cigarette, he let his fantasies run wild. He couldn't afford to call in the pub tomorrow before going to Bella's, but he'd have to try it some time. Next week, perhaps, when he drew his overtime money. Two pints of beer to increase his desire, and an hour with a woman who could fulfil his every dream.

Chapter Twenty-Six

There was silence round the breakfast table in the Phillips house on the Saturday morning. It was an uneasy silence, charged with suspense. And the ticking of the clock made the scene seem like something from a drama movie. Tom ate his breakfast and drank his two cups of tea without raising his head to look at anyone, while Jenny and Ben watched with bated breath out of the corner of their eyes. They were afraid to speak, or move, in case their words or actions broke the spell and caused their father to revert back to his bad-tempered self. They feared he was biding his time, just waiting for a sound or look that would spark off his temper. But there were no sneers, nor lashing out of fists, as Annie put the plate of toast down in front of him and poured out his tea. He didn't even look at her. The atmosphere was so strange, the silence so eerie, she was glad when he'd finished his breakfast and scraped back his chair.

Tom could feel the tension in the room, and it made him feel good. Let them wonder why he was acting out of character, he didn't care. He could still lash out at them any time he liked, so he'd keep them on pins. It just so happened that he hadn't felt the need for confrontation last night, and he didn't this morning. His life had taken a turn for the better now he'd met Bella; he didn't need his wife in his bed any more. But he still got satisfaction from knowing she and the kids were afraid of him, and that's the way things would stay.

Although he could feel three pair of eyes boring into him, Tom made his way to the hall without looking back. He took his donkey jacket down from the hook and slipped his arms into the sleeves. It was as he was opening the door that he called back, 'I'm working all day today, so I won't be home until half eight or nine o'clock.'

Annie moved swiftly, and she caught her husband as he was stepping down on to the pavement. 'Yer'd better bring some chips in with yer then, 'cos I can't keep a dinner until that time of night. And me and the kids are going out.'

Tom Phillips walked away as though he hadn't heard, leaving Annie to shut the door tutting and shaking her head. Jenny and Ben were waiting for her, and were soon talking fifteen to the dozen to get what they wanted to say out of their system before they went to work.

'I don't know what yer said to me dad the other night, Mam,' Ben said, 'but it certainly seems to have changed him. Two nights running he's gone to bed early, and no beer. I didn't think anyone could change so quickly.'

'He hasn't changed,' Jenny said, 'he just wants us to think so. He's playing cat and mouse with us, it's sticking out a mile.' She shivered inwardly as she remembered her father's hands mauling her. Oh, how she hated him. 'He's rotten through and through. Always has been, and always will be.'

'We haven't got much time to discuss it now, sweetheart,' Annie said. 'You and Ben will have to be on yer way in a few minutes. So let's just leave things and see what happens. But first, can I just say that I'm going to live me life as I want to from now on, and to hell with yer father. I'm starting work on Monday, as yer know, and I intend to get as much pleasure out of life as I can. Just to make up for the last twenty years. At least I'll be meeting people when I'm in the shop, and I'm going to be pleasant and friendly, so I'll be kept on after me trial period.'

'Yer told me dad we were all going out,' Jenny reminded her. 'Were yer only saying that, or are yer going over to Mrs Fenwick's for a game of cards?'

Annie shook her head. 'I meant what I said.' She turned to her son. 'I'll take yer to the pictures if yer feel like it? But if yer've made arrangements to go to yer mate's, I won't mind. I'll go to the pictures on me own.'

Ben's face lit up. 'Can we go to the Astoria? James Cagney's on there.'

'If that's what you want, sweetheart, then the Astoria it is. Ada did say I could go over for a game of cards, but I told her I'd take me son out for a change.'

'Will it be all right if I go to a dance with me mates from work, then?' Jenny asked. 'I could meet up with them outside the Grafton.'

Annie tried to sound as though she wasn't really interested, just curious. 'So ye're not going to the dance with Danny, then?'

'No, Mam, I'd rather go with me mates from work. I don't want to tag on to Danny all the time, it wouldn't be fair. He's got stacks of girlfriends in Blair Hall, he doesn't want me hanging on all the time, spoiling things for him.'

'I understand, sweetheart, and I want you and Ben to do yer own things in future. Yer don't have to worry about leaving me alone with yer father. He doesn't frighten me any more. In fact, I feel sorry for him. He doesn't know what it is to have a happy, loving family life. But that's his loss, not ours. So you and Ben cut yerselves free from him, and get out and enjoy the good things in life.'

Jenny looked thoughtful as she chewed on a piece of toast. 'Mam, yer'll still be friends with Mrs Fenwick, won't yer?'

'Of course I will, sweetheart, the very best of friends. The change in our fortunes is down to Ada, and Hetty. Especially Ada, who is uncanny. Everything has turned out as she said it would. If she hadn't talked me into sticking up for meself with yer father, I'd still be running around after him like a scalded cat. Oh, yeah, Ada has been one really good mate. And next door either side, Jean and Edith, I can't leave them out, they've been smashing. I'm not as close to them as I am to those over the road, but good friends none the less. It's their husbands who can take the credit for stopping yer father in his tracks, and I'll always be beholden to them for that. I've made a promise with meself that after Christmas, when this room has been decorated, I'll invite all me friends and neighbours in for a drink. As a way of thanking them, like, for being there when we needed them.'

'That would be nice, Mam,' Jenny said, 'very thoughtful of yer.'

Ben was grinning from ear to ear. What a change there'd been in his life in the last few days. 'When ye're swanking with yer posh room, Mam, can I bring my mates round? I'm always at their houses, and they must wonder why I never invite them here.'

Annie raised her brows. 'Before I commit meself, just how many mates are yer talking about? Two or twenty-two?'

'Only two, Mam. Spud Murphy and Joey Williams.'

'Oh, that's all right, then. I'll invite them round for tea one Sunday, but not for a few weeks, so don't mention it to them yet.' Annie glanced at the clock. 'You two should have been out of this house five minutes ago. So get yer skates on, or yer'll be late clocking on. I'll wash the dishes and give this room a quick flick with the duster, then I'm going to Ada's to give her the latest report. She was the one who gave me a kick up the backside, and she deserves to be kept up to date with the goings-on of the mighty Tom Phillips.' She walked to the door with her children and waved them off. Then she went back into the living room feeling lighter in her heart than she had for years. And as she worked, she hummed a lilting melody she remembered hearing on her mother's knee.

Ada was near her front window when she saw Annie closing her front door. She smiled when she saw how her neighbour crossed the cobbles with her head held high and a spring in her step. It would appear events were taking a turn for the better in Eliza's old house. The old lady would have been sad if she'd known of the heartache suffered in the house she'd lived in nearly all her life. They hadn't seen her since the day she left, because the weather had been bad, but she had written to them, and in her letter she'd sounded happy and settled in with her son and his family. And she'd promised to come and see them when the weather was kinder. With a bit of luck, Annie would have decorated by then, and the old lady would have no cause for sadness.

Before opening the front door to Annie, Ada knocked on the wall to let her mate next door know it was time for a cup of tea and a natter. 'Yer look on top of the world this morning, sunshine.' Ada held the door wide. 'Yer crossed that road like a spring chicken.' She followed her neighbour into the living room, leaving the front door ajar. 'I've knocked for Hetty, she'll be here in a few minutes.'

'Never mind a few minutes, I'm here now.' Hetty breezed in wearing a smile as big as a week. 'I came as soon as I heard the knock, so yer wouldn't have time to pull me to pieces behind me back.'

'When have I ever pulled yer to pieces, sunshine?' Ada asked, putting a hurt expression on her face. 'I'm cut to the quick that me very best mate can think that of me. Me, what has a mind as pure as the driven snow.'

Hetty pulled a chair out and plonked herself down. 'What about the time I walked in the butcher's when yer weren't expecting me, and I heard yer telling him about "that cat what lives next door to me". Now I'm sure Annie will agree that they are not the words of a so-called good friend what has a heart as pure as the driven snow.'

Annie waved a hand. 'Ooh, leave me out of it, sweetheart. I'm just getting me own life sorted out, I don't want to get involved in any more upset.'

Her elbow on the table and her head in her hand, Ada was shaking with laughter. 'Oh dear, oh dear! Before yer start getting upset, Annie, I'll let Hetty tell yer the tale about the cat next door. Go on, Hetty, the stage is yours.'

'There's not much to tell, really,' Hetty said. 'It did happen as I've just said, except I made a proper fool of meself. I walked in the shop just in time to hear Ada saying, "and that flaming cat what lives next door". Well, I didn't stop to think, I just took off, calling her all the sly articles I could lay me tongue to. That is until she put a hand over me mouth to shut me up, while she reminded me that the old lady on the other side of her had a cat which was a flaming nuisance. It used to sneak into everyone's back kitchen and steal whatever food was there.' Hetty was tittering as she relived the scene. 'Thinking about it now, it was funny, except Ada got a cob on over it, and she gave me a dog's life for days afterwards.'

285

'I might have given you a dog's life, sunshine, but the cat came off a damn sight worse. It got a kick up the backside, and it never ventured into me back kitchen again.' Ada raised her brows at Annie. 'I'd made a rice pudding that day, and left it on the draining board while I ran to the corner shop. I was only out five minutes, and got back to find the ruddy cat licking the top of the pudding. It flew when it saw me, otherwise I'd have strangled the ruddy thing with me bare hands.'

'It's funny that, but now I come to think of it,' Annie said, 'I've never seen a cat since I moved into the street.'

'Oh, there's plenty of cats around,' Ada told her. 'But there isn't one next door now, thank God. Mrs Fields got so many complaints about it going into people's houses and pinching food, she gave it to a woman in the next street who was plagued with mice. So the story had a happy ending, except for the mice.' She sat back and folded her arms. 'We've spent ten minutes talking about something that happened years ago. And I don't want yer to think I don't like cats, 'cos I wouldn't really hurt any animal. And as I said, there was a happy ending to that story. I'm now wondering if your story has a happy ending, sunshine? Or has the queer feller gone back to being his charming self?'

'He's as docile as a lamb, sweetheart,' Annie told her. 'So quiet, I'm beginning to think he's lost his tongue. In fact, me and the kids were uncomfortable and uneasy, for it was so unlike him. We expected him to kick off any time, but not one word crossed his lips all the way through breakfast. We were on pins, 'cos yer could have cut the silence with a knife. He ate his toast, drank two cups of tea, which I'd poured out for him, and left the table. Without a backward glance, he walked to the hall, took his coat down, and opened the front door. And then he spoke for the first time, to say he was working all day and wouldn't be home until half eight or nine o'clock. I went to the door after him, and told him he'd better get some chips on the way home because there wouldn't be a dinner for him at that time of night. And besides, me and the children were going out.'

Hetty rolled her eyes. 'Ooh, he wouldn't like that! I bet he had something to say?'

Annie shook her head. 'Not a dickie bird. He just kept on walking as though he hadn't heard. So it's his own fault if he starves, I don't give a damn any more.'

Ada was quiet, taking it all in. Her brain was ticking over as she tried to fathom out Tom Phillips's strange behaviour. The change in him was hard to understand, but she could think of one reason for the way he was acting. She would keep her thoughts to herself for the time being, though. Time

286

would tell if she was right or wrong. 'If he's going to be late home, sunshine, yer know ye're welcome to come over here for a game of cards. It would pass the time for yer, save sitting in the house on yer own. Unless the kids are staying in with yer?'

'Thanks for asking, sweetheart, but I wasn't lying when I told Tom Phillips me and the kids were going out. I'm taking Ben to the pictures, and Jenny is going out with some of the girls she works with. Not that the kids knew that until this morning. I lay in bed last night and made up me mind that there were going to be changes in the way we live. No longer am I going to let that rotter of a husband run my life, or my children's. And I was still of the same mind when I got out of bed. It hasn't sunk in with Jenny or Ben, for Tom Phillips was the only way of life they knew. We are all going out tonight, and I'm determined that from now on me and the kids are going to be free to do as we please. I'll keep me house clean, wash and cook as usual, but the rest of the time is me own.'

'Have yer forgotten ye're starting work on Monday, sunshine?' Ada asked. 'The mornings are not going to be free.'

'I haven't forgotten, Ada. I'm really looking forward to it. I haven't told Tom, and I don't intend to. It's only three shillings a week, but it'll give me that little bit of independence. A few bob in me pocket means I can buy the paper and paint to have me room decorated. And when that's done, I can buy meself some clothes. I've only got two dresses, as yer've probably noticed. I wear one while the other is being washed. Same with me underwear.'

Ada was nodding in approval. 'Good for you, sunshine, I'm really happy for yer. I'm sure Hetty will agree that yer look years younger now. That's what confidence does for yer. And I might as well warn yer now that if I ever think ye're slipping back into being a punch bag for Tom Phillips, then yer'll get the length of me tongue.'

'Ooh, yer wouldn't like that, girl.' Hetty's eyes spoke volumes. 'I've heard me mate giving someone the length of her tongue, and I can only tell yer that I was glad it wasn't me at the receiving end.'

Annie chuckled. 'Hetty, sweetheart, if I ever go back to hiding behind curtains, then Ada has my permission to give me more than the length of her tongue. But it will never happen, for I'm determined that Jenny and Ben are going to enjoy the rest of their teenage years, like I did. It's my fault they've had such a hard life so far, 'cos I'm the bloody fool who married Tom Phillips and gave them a father from hell. But I'll make it up to them, I swear it.'

Ada jerked her head at Hetty. 'Ay, sunshine, the way she's going on, she's going to be a force to be reckoned with. Ivy Thompson had better watch out.'

'Ivy Thompson,' Annie said, flexing her muscles. 'She's small fry, sweetheart. I could eat her for breakfast.'

'Ooh, er,' Hetty said, 'I'm beginning to feel sorry for Andy.'

'Who's Andy when he's out?' Annie asked. 'I don't know any Andy.'

'Yer will do on Monday, sunshine, 'cos he'll be yer boss.'

'Mr Saunders? Is his name Andy?'

'It is, sunshine, but I don't think yer should call him by his first name until he says yer can. He's a nice bloke, yer'll get on well with him.'

Annie looked puzzled. 'When I told yer I'd seen him about the job, yer didn't mention that yer knew him.'

'Everyone knows Andy,' Ada said with a wide grin. 'There isn't a house in this neighbourhood that hasn't been decorated with paper bought from his shop. He's a nice bloke. Pleasant, kind, and very reasonable.'

'It seems as though I've hopped in lucky, then.' Annie was cheered by what she'd heard. She hadn't worked since she was married, and had been worried on the quiet about whether she could do the job. What Ada had said made her feel much better. 'Things are looking up for me. I thought he seemed a genuine bloke, even though I was only talking to him for about ten minutes. What yer've told me now has really bucked me up.'

Hetty chuckled. 'Yer'll be able to sell yerself some wallpaper. And yer could ask for a discount, seeing as yer work there.'

'Ay, don't be putting ideas into Annie's head, sunshine, 'cos it would be really cheeky to ask for a discount when she's only just started working there.'

'I was only joking, girl.'

'I know yer were, sunshine, 'cos ye're the last person in the world to be cheeky enough to ask for something for nothing. And anyway, if I know Andy, Annie will get a discount without having to ask.'

'I wouldn't take a discount, even if he offered,' Annie said. 'Everyone has to make a living, and the man's probably got a family to keep.'

Ada and Hetty exchanged glances, then Ada said, 'He's had a lot of sadness in his life, sunshine, and me and Hetty think we should tell yer about it, so yer understand. We're not telling tales out of school, but just to put yer wise in case yer asked him about his family.'

Annie looked from one to the other. 'Hasn't he got a family?'

'I'll tell yer from the beginning, sunshine, then yer won't be getting it in bits and pieces. He and his wife used to run the shop between them. They had a fourteen-year-old son who had just left school and got a job as an apprentice mechanic. I'm not sure how long ago it was, time goes so

288

quickly. Probably ten or eleven years ago now. His wife was suddenly taken ill, and within two weeks she was dead. It was a brain haemorrhage. Anyway, everyone was shocked, for she was only forty-two. One day she's laughing and joking in the shop, then two weeks later she's dead. Andy, God help him, was out of his mind with grief. The shop was closed for weeks, and it took him a long time to come to terms with it.'

'It took him years,' Hetty said. 'But the son is married now, and he and his wife have been wonderful. They had a baby son last year, and they've called it Andrew. It's given Andy a new lease of life. He loves his grandson, and likes nothing better than to talk about him. He's happier than he's been for years, and so proud of being part of a family. He'll talk the leg off yer about his grandson, but whether he'll tell yer about his wife, well, I don't know.'

'I'm glad yer've told me all that, 'cos otherwise I might just have put me foot in it.' Annie spoke softly. 'The poor man must have been heartbroken. Yer don't expect to lose yer wife so young.' She gave a deep sigh. 'They say only the good die young. It doesn't seem right when there are some rotters who live to a ripe old age.'

'We have to take life as it comes, sunshine, we have no control over it. But Andy's a lovely man, and I'm sure yer'll get on really well with him. Yer'll go a long way to find a better man for a boss.'

'I'm looking forward to Monday, but a bit scared as well. I've never worked in a shop, and I hope I don't let the man down.'

'You won't, sunshine, yer'll be great. I've got every faith in yer. And now it's time for us to get off our backsides and do some shopping. I think I'll give mine sausage and egg tonight, it's quick and easy.'

Hetty and Annie smiled at each other and nodded in agreement. 'It seems the Fenwick family, the Watsons and the Phillipses will all be having the same.'

'Not all the Phillipses, sweetheart, only three of them. The other one can get some chips from the chippy if he's hungry.'

While Annie and Ben were being led to their seats in the stalls by an usherette, Tom Phillips was walking up the back entry to Bella's yard. He was ten minutes early, so he'd probably have to wait a while. But better early than late. He glanced behind him before he opened the door, just in case there were any nosy parkers around. Not that they would worry him, for they wouldn't know him from Adam. But he knew Bella didn't like her clients to be seen and he didn't want to get on the wrong side of her. She was the best thing that had ever happened to him, and he was keen not to fall out of favour with her.

Once he'd closed the entry door behind him, Tom opened the lavatory door and stood just inside. This was in case the neighbours either side happened to be looking out of their bedroom windows. He lit a cigarette to pass the time, and also to calm himself down. His whole body was alive with anticipation. But he'd barely had time to draw on the cigarette before Bella appeared before him. He thought she'd come to tell him off for being so early, and he threw his cigarette on the ground and sheepishly began to apologise.

Bella brushed his words aside. Speaking in a whisper, she said, 'A bloke knocked on me door a few minutes ago, said he'd been recommended by two of me regulars. I'm not sure about him, but I'll take him on 'cos I need the money. But I've had reason in the past to know yer can't trust men not to be violent, so I'm going to ask yer to stand in me back kitchen just in case this bloke causes me any trouble. He won't see yer, 'cos I'll keep the door closed, but I'd feel better if I knew I had someone to call on. Will yer do that for me?'

Tom was more than eager. He felt so important his chest swelled with pride. 'Yeah, of course I will.'

'Yer'll hear voices and groans, but take no notice. Only come in if I call yer. Don't make a sound, or yer'll put the punter off. Do that for me and I'll see yer right.'

When Bella went into the living room, closing the door behind her, Tom leaned back against the sink. He could hear a man's voice but the wireless had been turned on and he couldn't make out what was being said. Then over the next half-hour all he could do was stand and listen to grunts and groans, and wish they'd hurry up. Then he heard Bella's voice, but she wasn't calling for him, so he knew she'd had no problem with the man and was showing him out of the front door.

When Bella opened the kitchen door, Tom moved away from the sink. 'He was all right then, was he? No trouble?'

'He was fine, as good as gold and very grateful. He'll be coming next Saturday at the same time, wants to be a regular. But I'm always on me guard when I'm with a client for the first time, 'cos they can be as nice as pie when they come in, and then turn nasty if yer won't do some of the things they want yer to. I've had many a black eye, and worse.'

'I'll be asking yer to let me come next Saturday.' Tom was jealous that the other bloke might get in first. 'And yer should know now that yer can trust me.' Then he had a crafty thought. 'I'll do what I did tonight, if yer like. I don't mind standing guard in case anyone turns nasty on yer. How about it?'

Bella stared at him for so long he began to feel uncomfortable. Then she said, 'Perhaps you and me could come to some arrangement. I could make a lot more money on a Saturday night if I could let the punters come here, 'cos as yer know I charge a shilling.' There was a look of hardness about her when she added, 'Yer won't get paid for it in cash, mind, but yer'd get paid in kind. What d'yer say?'

'I'll make a deal with yer. I'll come every Saturday night, whatever time yer say, and I'll stay as long as yer want me to. I'll make sure no one hurts yer, or tries to pull a fast one on yer. In return I'd expect yer to see to my needs without any charge. I think that's fair to both of us. And I'll still come through the week for me tanner's worth.'

The hardness was back in her eyes. 'That sounds fair enough to me, as long as yer can handle yerself. Yer'd be no good to me if yer ran a mile at the first sign of trouble.'

'I can handle meself, don't you worry about that. I'd take good care of yer, and make sure no one took advantage of yer. So, is it a deal?'

Bella narrowed her eyes. 'How do I know I can rely on yer being here every Saturday? What about yer wife and family?'

'That's something else yer don't have to worry about. If I say I'll be here, then I'll be here. There's no one to stop me.'

His wife's downtrodden, Bella told herself as she led him into the living room. But if I had to feel sorry for the wife of every punter, I'd soon be out of business. 'I've got the first of me regulars coming in half an hour, so get those buttons undone.'

Chapter Twenty-Seven

Jenny was standing on the platform of the tram as it shuddered to a halt just yards from the Grafton rooms. She saw her two workmates standing outside, and she waved before jumping down and running towards them. 'I hope yer haven't been waiting long?'

'It's a wonder yer ears haven't been burning,' Pat said. 'We've been pulling yer to pieces for the last ten minutes.'

'We thought yer were going to let us down again.' Barbara's nose was red with the cold. 'I said if yer didn't turn up, we'd never ask yer again.'

'Well, I'm here now, so stop moaning.' Jenny had come without her gloves and her fingers were like ice. 'I've got a lot further to come than you two, don't forget.'

'Blimey!' Barbara said as the threesome made a dash for the doors. 'She'll be asking us to pay her the extra penny tram fare.'

In the cloakroom, with the circulation back in her fingers and feet, Jenny's spirits were high as she laughed with her friends. It was a lovely feeling, knowing that she didn't need to worry about what was happening to her mother. The sense of freedom, of being with friends of her own age, was exhilarating, and she had every intention of enjoying the evening.

Pat turned from the mirror on the white-painted wall to ask, 'Is this lipstick too red? It looks to me as though I've cut meself and me lips are bleeding.'

'I don't think it's too red.' Barbara was combing her mousy-coloured hair, which hung down to her shoulders. 'But if yer think it makes yer look like a tart, then kiss the back of yer hand and it'll take some off.'

'Look like a tart! Well, you cheeky beggar, Barbara Watkins. If I look like a tart, you look like a tart's mother with all that powder and rouge plastered on yer face. I bet if yer smiled, yer face would crack.'

Jenny stood by, smiling. Her two workmates were always pulling each other to pieces, but it was all in fun, for they were the very best of friends. 'If you two don't get a move on, we'll just about make it for the last waltz.'

'Huh! Just listen to her!' Barbara said, her nostrils flared for effect.

'She doesn't need any make-up. Eyes big enough to swim in, and hair thick enough to get lost in.'

'Yer both look gorgeous,' Jenny told them as she linked their arms. 'I bet yer both get asked up as soon as we go through the door. And I'll be the wallflower that sits every dance out.'

The girls were laughing as they walked through the double door into the dance hall. They walked towards the seats that were set along the full length of the wall. 'We'll leave our bags under the chairs,' Pat said. 'We'd look silly dancing with them, and no one is going to pinch them, anyway.'

'They wouldn't get much if they did pinch mine,' Jenny told them as she bent to push her handbag under a chair. 'There's only a comb in it, and a few coppers.'

She was running a hand down her skirt to smooth it into shape, when she felt a tap on her shoulder, and a voice asked, 'Would yer like to dance?'

Jenny spun round to find herself facing the blond-haired boy she'd met when she went to Blair Hall with Danny. 'Oh, hello! I didn't expect to see you here.' She could see the surprise on the faces of her friends, and said, 'These two are mates from work, Pat and Barbara.' She put a finger to her chin, then said, 'Oh, it's Tony, isn't it?'

He nodded, and his white teeth flashed when he imitated Johnny Weissmuller. 'Me Tony, you Jenny.'

'Yer daft ha'p'orth.' Jenny grinned. 'I thought yer went to Blair Hall every night?'

'I do most nights, but lucky for me I decided to come here tonight for a change.' He grinned. 'Are yer going to dance with me, or what?'

Jenny looked at her friends. 'D'yer mind if I leave yer?'

'Listen, kid, yer came here to dance, so dance!' Pat gave broad wink. 'Put in a good word for us. Ask if he's got any mates.'

Barbara agreed. 'Yeah, go on, kid, and enjoy yerself. But when yer come back I'll be telling yer what a dark horse yer are. Yer tell us yer hardly ever go out, but yer just walked in this door and got spoken for.'

Jenny was smiling as Tony took her hand and led her on to the dance floor. 'They're as crazy as coots, but good mates.'

It was a slow foxtrot, and as they danced Tony asked, 'Does Danny know yer were coming here tonight?'

'No, he wouldn't know that. Why?'

'I thought yer were good friends. He seemed very protective of yer.'

'Danny lives opposite me. I suppose yer could say we were friends, but that's all.'

Tony laughed as though pleased, and he pulled her close. Until then, Jenny had been enjoying the dance, but feeling him so close sent a cold shiver up her spine. Her father's face flashed before her eyes and suddenly the pleasure was taken from the dance. She pulled herself back, intending to make an excuse and say she'd twisted an ankle or something. But when she looked into Tony's face, he was smiling as though he was happy, and she didn't have the heart to spoil his enjoyment. The poor lad probably saw nothing wrong in holding her tight, and would be horrified if he knew what was running through her mind. He had an open face, not leering like her father's, and she was being childish. All the couples on the floor were holding each other close, and the boys weren't all bad. They could hardly dance with a yard separating them, she was just being stupid. She mustn't let her mind be poisoned because of a father who was rotten to the core. For if she did, she'd be looking at every boy through jaundiced eyes, and she would have allowed her father to ruin her life. And that was something she wasn't going to let happen.

The music came to an end, and Tony put his arm on her waist to walk her back to where her friends were. 'Seeing as Danny isn't here to claim yer, can I have the next dance, and the one after that?'

'Only if yer do me a favour.'

'Anything at all.'

'Then in between dancing with me, would yer ask me mates up? They've danced with each other for the slow-fox, and I don't want them to think I'm being big-headed by dancing with you for every dance. So will yer do that favour for us?'

'Yeah, of course I will. But don't you go dancing with every other Tom, Dick and Harry.'

They were nearing Pat and Barbara when Jenny said, 'If I get asked up, I'll ask them their name. If it's Tom, Dick or Harry, I'll tell them I'm spoken for.'

As soon as Tony left Jenny with her friends, there came a barrage of questions. 'Ay, girl, where did yer find him?' With her eyes narrowed, and a cigarette in the side of her mouth, Pat did what she believed was a good impression of Humphrey Bogart. 'He's a bit of all right.'

'Yeah,' Barbara agreed. 'I could go a bundle on him.' Not to be outdone by her best mate, she chose Mae West to impersonate. Her top lip curled, and her head tilted, she drawled, 'It's not the men in my life I worry about, it's the life in my men.'

Jenny chuckled. 'Go on, yer daft things. I've only met him the once, and that was when I went to Blair Hall. I had a couple of dances with him, that's all. So don't you be putting two and two together and getting it to six.'

'Well, if you aren't fussy on him, girl, yer can pass him over to me and Barbara. He'd be very welcome, wouldn't he, Babs?'

'He'd be more than welcome, Patsy, we'd smother him with ruddy kindness.'

'Babs and Patsy?' Jenny grinned. 'Why the nicknames?'

'They sound more friendly.' Barbara blew a smoke ring into the air. 'If I'd known we were going to meet a handsome blond man, then I'd have brought me cigarette holder.'

Pat raised her brows. 'I didn't know yer had a cigarette holder! I go everywhere with yer, and I've never seen yer with one.'

'That's 'cos I haven't got one, soft girl. But Jenny's blond, handsome friend doesn't know it, so if he comes over again, and I happen to remark that I've gone and left me cigarette holder at home, don't you dare call me a liar or I'll strangle yer.'

Pat threw back her head. 'Oh, I can see it all in me mind. The lad comes over to ask Jenny for a dance, and you suddenly grab hold of his arm and tell him ye're feeling really lost 'cos yer forgot to bring yer cigarette holder.'

'Ye're getting carried away, girl! It's not his arm I want to grab, yer daft nit, it's his ruddy attention. How many girls do yer see with cigarette holders? Not many, eh? So he'll think I'm a cut above the rest of yer.'

'Can I remind yer, Barbara,' Pat said, 'that in the cloakroom yer were talking about Jenny having eyes yer could swim in, and hair yer could get lost in. Now ye're saying she doesn't hold a candle to a ruddy ciggy holder!'

The night had started off well, and so it continued. Jenny thought she'd never laughed so much in her life. With no worry on her mind, she let herself go, and revelled in her new-found freedom. Tony kept his promise and divided his time between Jenny and her friends. The only time a smile left his face was when he saw another bloke ask Jenny to dance while he was on the floor with Barbara. 'He's got his eye on yer, Jenny,' Pat said. 'I think he's fallen for yer.'

'Don't be daft, I hardly know him. He's a nice lad, but that's about it.' However, her friend's words gave her food for thought. 'Pat, if he asks me if he can take me home, I'm going to tell a little fib and say I'm going home with you. It's not that I don't trust him, anything like that, I just don't want to get too friendly with him and give him ideas. So will yer back me up if I say I've promised to go home with you and Barbara?'

Pat nodded. 'Of course I will. And I'll tell Babs, so she doesn't put her foot in it. I think ye're right, girl, it pays to be careful. He's probably a really good bloke, but I agree yer should get to know him a bit better. After all, it's late and dark out, so better to be sure than sorry.'

Jenny felt relieved, but at the back of her mind was the thought that she might be jumping the gun. 'Ay, Pat, it would be the price of me if he has no intention of asking if he can take me home. It would serve me right for being big-headed.'

However, when the last waltz was announced, Tony wasted no time. Before she knew it, Jenny was in his arms, on the dance floor, and he was asking, 'Can I take yer home?'

'Oh, I'm sorry, Tony, but I'll be getting the tram with Pat and Barbara. We made arrangements to stick together, and I'd feel mean if I backed out.' Jenny felt awful telling lies when Tony had been so good, and he looked really disappointed. 'Perhaps next time, eh?'

'I'm sure yer mates wouldn't mind if I took yer home. D'yer want me to ask them?'

'Leave it for tonight, Tony, please. I work with them, and I don't want to be the one to break our arrangements.'

'Will yer be going to Blair Hall through the week?' Tony was doing his best not to let his frustration show. He'd taken a liking to Jenny when he first set eyes on her, but Danny had stopped him from getting close enough to ask for a date. And now it was Jenny's workmates who were the obstacle. 'If yer are, then tell me what night, and promise yer won't bring yer friends. It's not that I don't like them, but it would be nice to have yer to meself for a night. I could have every dance with yer then.'

Jenny rolled her eyes. 'I know yer'll think I'm making excuses, but bear with me. Yer see, I have a very strict father. In fact, he's a lousy father, and he gives me mother a dog's life. If he's in one of his bad moods, I won't go out and leave me mam alone with him.' She could see the doubt on Tony's face, but told herself she couldn't do anything about that, for what she was telling him wasn't all lies. 'I know yer go to Blair Hall nearly every night, so I'm bound to meet yer there. I won't say what night, 'cos as I've said, I can't always be sure of getting out. But I promise I will definitely be there one night next week.'

'Without yer mates?'

Jenny sighed inwardly, and wished she had the courage to say what she really thought. That he was a nice enough lad, but she didn't want to get involved with anyone right now, and would prefer to come and go as she pleased. After being held back all her life, she was enjoying her first real taste of freedom tonight, and she really didn't want to be tied down. 'I doubt they'll be with me, for they're not keen on Blair Hall.'

The music came to an end, and Jenny was pleased to see her two friends standing on the edge of the dance floor. Pat had her coat draped over an arm, and Barbara was swinging her handbag. 'We got yer things out of the cloakroom, Jenny,' Pat said. 'Save yer being caught in the rush.'

There was little Tony could do but wish them good night with a smile on his face. 'See yer at Blair Hall, Jenny. Don't let me down.'

She smiled and waved a hand. 'See yer, Tony.'

Pat waited until he was well out of earshot. 'He's got it bad, kid. Yer'll have a job getting rid of him if yer don't want him.'

'It's not that I don't want him, Pat. How do I know whether I want him or not when I hardly know him! It's just that tonight is only the second time I've seen him, and I don't want to be rushed into making a date which I might live to regret.'

'It's not for me to tell yer what to do, girl,' Barbara said as they walked towards the tram stop. 'But if I was in your shoes, I'd grab him with both hands. I think he's smashing. Nice to look at, dresses well, and can certainly move on the dance floor. What more can a girl ask for? If you don't want him, kid, then pass him over to me and Pat.'

Pat chortled. 'Yeah, you pass him over to us, kiddo, and we'll tear him limb from limb.'

They had just reached the tram stop when a tram that would take Jenny home came trundling along. She hopped on board, and waved when Pat called, 'We'll finish this discussion in work on Monday, kid.'

Annie was smiling when she opened the door to Jenny. 'Hello, sweetheart. Have yer had a nice time?'

Force of habit kept Jenny's voice low. 'I've had a smashing time, Mam. Did you and Ben enjoy the picture?'

Annie nodded as she closed the door quickly to keep the cold out. 'It was a good picture, and yer brother was well pleased with himself. Now get in by the fire and warm yerself through.'

Jenny was surprised to find her brother sitting in the fireside chair. 'Where's me dad? Isn't he back from the pub yet?'

'Yer father's in bed, sweetheart.' Annie took Jenny's coat and hung it up. 'He came in about half nine, with a bag of chips. I couldn't smell beer on him, so I don't think he'd been to the pub. I made him a cup of tea, and when he'd finished the chips and drunk his tea, he took himself off to bed. Never spoke one word to me or Ben.'

'There's something wrong, Mam,' Jenny said, warming her hands in front of the fire. 'It's not natural.'

Ben chuckled. 'I don't care whether it's natural or not, I just hope he stays like that. I was in this chair when he came home, and I expected a clip round the ear. But he didn't say a dicky bird, so I stayed put. Me dad

297

sat at the table to have his chips, then waltzed off to bed. If he stays that way it'll suit me fine.'

'Is there any tea left in the pot, Mam?' Jenny asked. 'I could do with a cup to warm me up.'

'There's none in the pot, sweetheart. I was waiting for yer to come in before making a fresh one. I'll put the kettle on, and while we're waiting for it to boil, yer can tell us what sort of a night yer've had.'

'Then I'll tell yer about the picture,' Ben said. 'It wasn't half exciting. I was sitting on the edge of me seat at times.'

On her way out to the kitchen, Annie winked at her daughter. 'If he was to tell yer the truth, he'd say he had his eyes closed for most of the time.'

Ben was indignant. 'Ah, ay, Mam, no I didn't! I had to sit a bit sideways 'cos the woman in front of me was the size of a mountain. And she had a ruddy big hat on.'

'Oh, I know the feeling, our kid,' Jenny said. 'That's happened to me as well, and yer get a kink in yer neck moving it from side to side.'

'I think anyone as big as that woman should have to pay for two seats.' Ben's head nodded in agreement with his words. 'The woman behind me was moaning because she couldn't see the screen, either.'

When Annie carried the cups of tea through, she asked, 'Did yer meet anyone nice at the dance, sweetheart? Did yer get asked up?'

Jenny thought carefully, for she didn't want to let her mother think she hadn't enjoyed herself. But at the same time she didn't want to give her ideas if Tony was mentioned. 'I had a great time, Mam, and so did me mates. We all got asked up to dance, and we laughed a lot 'cos they're very funny. I really did enjoy meself.'

'I hope yer've made arrangements to go out with yer friends again, sweetheart. Yer need to get out and about more often. The Lord knows yer deserve it. In the future, you and Ben go where and when yer please.'

'I know one thing,' Ben told them. 'Next time I go to the flicks, I'll make sure the usherette doesn't stick me behind a fat woman with a big hat on.'

'I know I shouldn't encourage yer to make fun of people, son. Particularly people older than yerself. But I've got to be honest and say the woman was getting on my nerves as well. She had a bag of sweets, and every time she wanted one she would take it out of the bag and then rustle the paper to close it up again. I'll swear she did it on purpose, just to let everyone know she had those ruddy sweets.'

'I heard the man sitting next to her telling her off,' Ben said. 'I felt like giving him a pat on the back for being so brave, 'cos he was only half the size of her.'

Mother and children were so used to doing everything quietly, they didn't make a sound as they climbed the stairs. But there was a difference from other nights, for they all had a smile on their face.

Ada was carrying a shovelful of coal up the yard when she heard her neighbour's back door open. 'Is that you, sunshine,' she called, 'or are yer letting yer fancy man out, hoping he won't be seen?'

'Chance would be a fine thing, girl,' Hetty called back. 'Not that I'd have any inclination for a fancy man, I've gone past that. I'll stick with my feller. Yer know what they say about the devil yer know being better than the devil yer don't know.'

'Yeah, I know that saying, sunshine.' Ada's smile was wide as she tried to imagine her mate having a fancy man. Hetty would run a mile if a bloke looked at her. 'I'm just putting some coal on the fire, making meself a cuppa, then resting me legs for a while. D'yer fancy coming in to keep me company?'

'Ye're early with yer cuppa, aren't yer? Yer don't usually make one until just before we go to the shops.'

'Well, it's like this, sunshine, I feel like throwing caution to the winds today. Yer know what I mean, 'cos yer must have had days like that yerself. When yer feel like saying sod the washing, and letting yer hair down.'

Hetty's chuckle came over the yard wall. 'Yeah, I've often felt like going mad and breaking eggs with a big stick.'

'Then I'm safe to invite yer in for a cuppa, sunshine, 'cos I haven't got an egg in the house until we go to the shops.'

'Have yer got any biscuits?'

'I think I can manage one each. Will that tempt yer?'

'I'll be over in ten minutes, girl, so have the room nice and warm.'

'What are yer doing in the yard, anyway?' Ada asked. 'I came out for a shovel of coal, which I'm still holding like a lemon. What did you come out for? It's no use putting any washing out, it's freezing.'

Hetty screwed up her face before saying very quietly, 'I was going to the lavvy, girl.'

'What did yer say, sunshine?' Ada held her tummy while she shook with laughter. She'd bet any money her mate was blushing. 'I didn't quite catch what yer said.'

'I'll tell yer later,' Hetty called as she scurried down the yard. She was freezing now, but would be a damn sight worse when she'd sat in the lavatory which gave no protection from the wind and cold. Oh, to live in a house with an inside toilet.

A short while later, the two friends faced each other across the table. Both had their hands curled round a cup of hot tea. 'When we go to the shops, girl, shall we call in and see how Annie's getting on? It wouldn't be out of our way, we've got to pass it to get to the greengrocer's and Irwin's.'

'Oh, we can't do that, sunshine, she'd be embarrassed. She won't have the hang of things yet, and she'd die if we walked in and she was trying to serve. Besides, I wouldn't like Andy to think we were going to be a nuisance.'

'I thought it would be matey, like, to show a bit of interest. And Andy wouldn't get a cob on, he's too nice for that.'

But Ada shook her head. 'We can call in next week, when she's got a bit of confidence. Besides, she's coming here when she's finished work, to tell us how she got on.'

'Yeah, ye're right, girl, as usual. She would probably get all hot and bothered if we walked in.' Hetty took a sip of tea. 'The goings-on in her house are funny, don't yer think so, girl? I've never known anyone like her husband, he's queer. For years he's knocked Annie and the kids around, done some terrible things to her, and then suddenly he's as quiet as a mouse and doesn't open his mouth to them! There's something fishy there, if yer ask me.'

'I've got me own ideas on what the queer feller is up to,' Ada said. 'People like him, who think they're the pig's ear, and lord it over everyone, they don't change. Not unless there's a good reason behind it.'

'What d'yer mean, girl? What good reason could Tom Phillips have for changing from a loud-mouthed drunkard to a quiet man who doesn't go to the pub every night or knock his wife and kids around? I mean, I'm glad he has changed, for Annie's sake, and the two children's, but I still think there's something fishy going on.'

'I agree with yer, sunshine, there is definitely something fishy going on. Men as old as Tom Phillips don't suddenly change. As I said, I have me own ideas on what he's up to, but I'm not saying anything in case I'm wrong.'

'What d'yer think it is, girl? Go on, yer can tell me. Yer know I won't repeat it to anyone. I'll be the soul of discretion.'

'What about when ye're in bed with Arthur, and having a little natter before yer put the light out? And yer think to yerself, well Arthur doesn't speak to no one, so there'd be no harm done.'

Hetty got on her high horse. 'My Arthur doesn't go round telling tittle-tattle! He hardly speaks to anyone. He doesn't even go for a pint unless it's with your Jimmy. So who would he have to gossip to?'

'Don't be getting yer knickers in a twist, sunshine, 'cos I know for certain that Arthur has got more to do than gossip. And you have my heartfelt apology for bringing his name into the conversation.'

Hetty made a clicking sound with her tongue. 'Yer've no intention of telling me what yer think, have yer, girl? If I had something to blackmail yer with, then I would. The trouble is, ye're too ruddy good to be true.'

'Listen, sunshine, ye're me best mate, and if I had anything to tell, then yer'd be the first one I'd tell it to. But I honestly don't know why Tom Phillips has changed. What I do have is an idea of what he might be up to, but I don't know anything for certain. And Annie, God bless her, hasn't a clue about what's going on.'

'Well, why can't yer tell me what yer think? If ye're not right, then there's no harm done, 'cos no one but me would know what yer had in yer head.'

'We've got Christmas on top of us, sunshine, and that should be enough to keep our minds occupied. A few weeks after the holiday, I've got a feeling we'll all know what Tom Phillips is up to. Whether it'll make life better for Annie and the kids, well, we'll just have to wait and see. It'll all come out in the wash, sunshine, believe me.'

Chapter Twenty-Eight

'And yer think ye're going to do all right in the shop, do yer, Mam?' Jenny's face was alive with interest. That the mother she adored was going to have a life of her own made her feel very happy. 'And the man was nice with yer?'

'He's a real gentleman, sweetheart. His name is Mr Saunders, but he told me right away to call him Andy.'

Ben's eyes were shining. 'Did yer serve any customers, Mam? I'd love to work in a shop, but with being a boy, I suppose I'm better off serving me time as an apprentice. The money's good when I get to twenty-one, and I'll always be sure of a job.'

'Ye're much better off having a trade, son, yer did the right thing. I know yer don't earn much now, but yer've always got to think ahead, to the future.'

'Me dad still doesn't know about yer working, does he, Mam?' Jenny asked. 'Are yer going to tell him?'

Annie shook her head. 'Not unless I've got to. If he knows I'm earning a few bob, he'll give me less housekeeping every week. He'd be the one to gain by me working, not me. So unless he finds out for himself, I ain't going to tell him. My few bob every week will make life a lot easier. I'll be able to pick and choose what we have for our meals, and spend a few coppers on meself. I could do with something decent to wear. The few clothes I've got make me look like a real frump.'

'It's not before time, Mam,' Jenny told her. 'Ye're still a young woman, yer've got a nice face and figure, and it's about time yer started to do yerself up.'

Annie chuckled. 'The few bob I earn isn't going to stretch like a piece of elastic, sweetheart, but if I put some coppers away each week, I'll soon have enough saved to buy something half decent for meself. And I'll be able to help you and Ben out if yer find yerselves skint in the middle of the week.'

Jenny's mouth set in a stubborn line. 'Mam, me and Ben get enough pocket money for the time being, so forget us and see to yerself. And I

302

hope me dad never finds out, 'cos as yer said, he'd drop yer housekeeping.' Her brow creased. 'Speaking of me dad, what's happened to him the last week or so? No shouting or bawling, no clouts or blows, and no rolling home blind drunk. I thought he was sickening for something at first, but there doesn't seem to be anything wrong with him.'

'Your guess is as good as mine, sweetheart. But I have to say I don't care what's happened to make him change, I'm just hoping he stays that way and doesn't go back to being a drunken bully. I'd be the happiest woman in the world if he never spoke to me again, and I didn't have to be looking over me shoulder all the time.'

'It is queer, though, Mam,' Ben said, his mouth half full of mashed potato. 'If he's working overtime every night, then he must be rolling in money. And having money in his pocket, why isn't he out boozing every night like he used to be? It makes yer think.'

'Your father has always been a dark horse, son. I didn't realise before I married him that he was a loner. I never noticed he had no friends then, and to my knowledge he's never, ever, had a real mate. He treated me all right when we were courting, so I never gave any thought to such things. I certainly had no inkling he would turn out the way he has. And it was only after we'd been married for a while that it struck me he didn't have one friend, and didn't allow me to have one.'

'I'm not surprised he's no friends,' Jenny said, 'he's a miserable man, with no sense of humour. He goes out on his own and comes back on his own.' She nodded to the clock on the mantelpiece. 'Look at the time now, it's half seven and there's no sign of him. He must know yer've got a dinner ready for him, and it won't be worth eating by the time he shows his face. It serves him right if it's all dried up.'

'It's all right you saying that, our Jenny,' Ben said, 'but it's me mam he'll take it out on.'

Annie shook her head. 'No, son, he won't be taking his spite out on me. Not ever again.'

'But what if he walked in now, Mam, and started throwing his weight around? You know, like, if he went back to how he was before.' Ben set his knife and fork down on his now empty plate. 'What should we do? Sit quiet and say nothing, or what?'

'If he does decide to honour us with his presence, and he starts any shenanigans 'cos his dinner isn't fit to eat, then we'll all move away from the table. And without saying a word, we'll put our coats on and walk out of the house. If he's spoiling for a fight, then let him fight himself. And if his dinner is ruined, then let him starve. I've given up worrying about what mood yer father's in, for I'm not afraid of him any more.' Annie glanced across to the window. 'I haven't drawn the curtains over yet, and with the light being on, anyone can see in. Not that there's much to see, but I always feel uncomfortable thinking people passing can see in.'

'Stay where yer are, Mam, I'll draw them.' Jenny scraped her chair back. 'If folk are nosy enough to peep in, they wouldn't be able to see much through the net curtains because the aspidistra is in the way.' She was pulling the draw curtain over when the door opposite opened and Danny Fenwick stepped down on to the pavement. Her breath caught in her throat for a second as her heartbeat raced, but she quickly drew the curtain while telling herself not to be stupid, she hardly knew the lad. Besides, although he'd been friendly towards her on the few occasions they'd met, it was only because he was that type of person. He was the same with everyone. And knowing what her father was like, he probably wasn't really interested in her as a person. Not as a girlfriend, anyway. And who could blame him for that? 'Danny's just come out, Mam. He must be off to a dance as usual.'

'Are you not going out tonight, sweetheart?'

Jenny shook her head. 'No, I'm having a night in.'

'Why don't yer go to the dance? Yer don't have to go with Danny, yer could follow him on. He wouldn't think anything if yer walked in a quarter of an hour after him. I'm sure lots of girls go on their own. And boys.'

But Jenny wasn't persuaded. 'No, I've made up me mind to stay in tonight. I'll be going out with me mates from work one night this week. I always have a good laugh with them, they're really good company.'

Annie sighed. She'd done her best, she couldn't do any more. But her daughter would never meet a nicer lad than Danny Fenwick.

Danny was gliding down the dance hall with Dorothy, really enjoying the strains of a slow foxtrot, and the harmony of his partner's steps. They were dancing as one, and it was bliss. But his concentration was broken when Tony danced alongside him and called, 'Ay, Danny, I had Jenny all to meself on Saturday night, it was great.'

Danny's step faltered and he trod on Dorothy's toe, causing her to groan. 'Oh, thanks very much, Danny, yer've only broken me blinking toe.'

'I'm sorry, Dot, but it wasn't my fault, it was that stupid nit for putting me off me stride.' Danny glared at Tony, who was dancing on the spot with a pretty brunette. 'What did yer do that for? Yer should have more sense than to act daft in the middle of a dance. Yer've got a queer sense of humour, that's all I can say.'

Tony was enjoying the situation, and intended to milk it for all it was worth. 'What are yer getting all het up for, Danny? I only told yer I had the pleasure of dancing with Jenny on Saturday night at the Grafton. I didn't expect yer to be daft enough to stand on one of poor Dorothy's toes.'

'Me toe's all right now,' Dorothy said, pulling on Danny's arm. 'If yer don't mind, and if it's not too much trouble, can we get on with the dance, please? It'll be over before we get halfway round the flipping floor.'

Danny raised his brows at Tony. 'I'll see yer when the dance is over.' Then he smiled down at Dorothy. 'Sorry about that, Dot, but Tony likes winding me up. He's always pulling someone's leg. The trouble is, he's not grown up proper.'

Falling into step with her partner, Dorothy chuckled. 'Oh, yer'll not find many in this room to agree with that, Danny. He's a very popular lad, is Tony. Almost as popular as you are.'

The dimples in Danny's cheeks deepened. 'Yer redeemed yerself just in time there, Dot. For a minute I thought yer were going to say I wasn't in the meg specks.'

Dorothy's timing was perfect as the couple navigated the corner. 'I'm saying no more, Danny Fenwick, 'cos ye're big-headed enough as it is.'

When the dance was over, Danny walked Dot back to where her friends were standing, then looked around for Tony. He finally spotted the blond head and made his way towards it. 'What d'yer think ye're playing at, Tony? Right in the middle of a dance and yer start acting daft. Dorothy's going to have a sore toe all night because of you and yer jokes.'

'I wasn't joking, mate, I just thought yer'd be interested. I went to the Grafton on Saturday for a change, and blow me if Jenny didn't turn up with some friends from work. It was a good night, we enjoyed ourselves.'

'Yer don't half exaggerate,' Danny said, while a little voice in his head asked why he was concerned anyway. After all, it was a free country. 'Yer've only met Jenny once, yer don't know anything about her. Even if yer are telling the truth, which I'm beginning to doubt, I can't see how yer could spend the whole night with her and her mates.'

Tony shrugged his shoulders as though he couldn't care less what Danny thought. But inwardly he was smiling. 'I don't care whether yer believe me or not, it's no skin off my nose. I wouldn't be bothered telling lies about something so trivial. After all, anyone that goes into a dance hall intends to dance. And that's what Jenny and me did on Saturday. Oh, and I danced with her mates, as well, 'cos she asked me to.' He forced out a sigh. 'I don't know why I bothered saying anything to yer about it. I wouldn't have done if I'd known I was going to get the third degree.

What's it got to do with you if Jenny happens to be in the same dance hall as me, and I ask her to dance? I mean, she's not yer girlfriend, is she?'

'No, she's not me girlfriend,' Danny admitted. 'She lives in the same street as me, and my mam is a very good friend of her mam. That's why I like to keep an eye on her, and make sure she's all right. Just to be neighbourly, like.'

'That's all right then,' Tony said, ' 'cos she's promised to meet me here one night this week. And seeing as ye're not romantically linked, I'm going to ask her for a date. She's a nice girl, is Jenny. The type yer could take home to meet yer mam.'

Danny's dimples appeared when he laughed. 'Now I know ye're kidding. Yer've met the girl twice, and now ye're talking about taking her home to meet yer mam! That's a good one, that is.' He turned away when the music started up. 'I'll believe it when I see it with me own eyes, Tony.'

'Ay, Danny Fenwick, if you think I'd let yer come with us when I take Jenny to meet me mam, then yer've got another think coming.'

Danny stopped and turned round. 'Don't count yer chickens before they're hatched, Tony, 'cos yer might be in for a surprise. Jenny might have set her sights elsewhere, for she's a good-looking girl and could have her pick. Yer might find yerself in a long queue.'

After making sure there was no one in the entry, Tom Phillips opened Bella's door and stepped into the yard. He was a regular nightly visitor now, preferring to spend his sixpence on pleasures of the flesh rather than hand it over the pub counter. He didn't have to make an appointment with the prostitute, he was a regular and expected. She would tap on the window or come out to him when she was ready, and while he waited he lit up a cigarette. He'd been instructed to stand in the lavatory, out of sight of prying eyes, and whatever Bella told him to do, he did without question. He was delighted with the way his life was now. His appetite for sex was being fed as it had never been before, and it filled his mind each day. The irony of the situation never entered his head. Where he had once been the slave driver, he was now the slave. And a very willing one.

He'd only taken a few puffs on his cigarette when he heard the kitchen door opening, then Bella's high-heeled shoes tapping on the cobbled yard. He quickly threw his cigarette down the lavatory, expecting to be told she was ready for him. However, as he made to step into the yard, Bella put a hand on his chest and pushed him back. In a low voice, she said, 'I've got a punter inside, a bloke I've never dealt with before. I don't usually take a chance on bringing a stranger back to me house, but he's nicely dressed and seems a decent enough bloke. And I can use the money. But as yer

306

can't always tell when a bloke is going to turn nasty, I want yer to keep an eye out for me. Will yer do that?'

Tom's chest swelled with importance. 'Yer want me to stand guard in the kitchen again?' He didn't mind, he'd done it a few times now and got a kick out of hearing the sounds reaching him from the living room. Sounds that whetted his appetite, making his heart pound and raising his desire. 'Of course I'll do it, anything to help yer.'

Bella jerked her head. 'I'd better get back or he'll be wondering what's keeping me. Give me a minute, then come up to the kitchen. But don't make a sound, d'yer hear?'

'I never have so far, so yer've nothing to worry about. I'll not let yer down.'

As Bella turned away, she whispered, 'I'll make it worth yer while. Yer'll get special treatment tonight.' With that she was gone, only the tapping of her heels still audible. But what she'd said was going round in Tom's head. After he'd let himself into the kitchen as quietly as he could, he leaned back against the sink and rubbed his hands together. Special treatment, eh? He hoped it meant something he'd been longing for, but had so far been denied.

Bella was good at what she did, and no punter ever left feeling let down. At the tender age of fifteen, she'd been lured into prostitution by a mate, who'd been on the game for a while. It was the money that drew Bella, for her family were very poor and many's the time there was no food in the house. The only clothes on her back were rags, and the prospect of money was too great an attraction to turn down.

Tom knew all this because Bella had told him. And the reason for her telling him, was to put a stop to his pleading for full sexual intercourse. He'd tried to touch her breasts one night while she was attending to his needs, and she pushed his hand away. In no uncertain terms she had told him she had only had sexual intercourse with two men in her whole life. Hence the two children. No man had ever got near her since, and no man ever would. She treated her clients like children, slapping them when they tried to touch her. She had respect for the money they handed over, but none for them. But as Tom listened to the sounds reaching his ears from the living room, his desire became strong, and he hoped that this time she would allow him to be the dominant one. If she would only give him the chance, he knew he could satisfy her.

The mumble of voices had Tom moving away from the sink. The session was over, and the punter would be leaving when he'd paid his money. A sneering smile crossed Tom's face as he muttered, 'That poor bugger's had his fun, now it's my turn.'

The kitchen door opened. 'Yer can come in now.' Bella passed him to wash her hands. 'He was a decent bloke. Nicely spoken and well dressed. And so satisfied, he's coming again tomorrow night.'

This didn't please Tom. 'I'm coming again tomorrow, so what time's he booked?'

Bella reached for the towel to dry her hands. 'Same time as tonight. I did ask him to come earlier or later, but he's on his way home from work and the other times wouldn't be convenient. And I wasn't going to turn down another sixpence, so I'm hoping yer'll do the same as tonight.'

'I'm on me way home from work, too, yer know. Why couldn't he come half an hour later?'

Bella could read Tom inside out. There was very little she didn't know about men, and she was adept at worming them round. 'Ah, I didn't think yer'd mind, not when yer get better treated than any of me other clients. It's a case of I rub your back, you rub my back.'

Tom grew two inches in stature. 'Do I get extra special treatment now?'

'Yer get extra time, lad, that's all. I know what ye're hankering after, but yer may as well get it through yer thick head that it will never happen. If ye're not satisfied with what yer get from me, then I suggest yer try one of the other women.' Bella put her face closer, and her voice was husky and coaxing, for this was one punter she didn't want to lose. He was too useful to her. 'I don't want yer to go to another woman, I'd rather yer stayed with me. But I can't make yer stay if ye're not satisfied.'

And Tom fell for it. 'I don't want no other woman, they're dirty and as ugly as sin. No, I'll do as yer say. And if yer get more offers, then I don't mind standing in the kitchen to see yer come to no harm. After all, yer treat me very well.'

When they were in the living room, Bella pushed him down on to the couch. It was always covered in a clean cloth, for she kept her house, and herself, clean. She watched him fumble with the buttons on his fly, and wondered about him. How could he come here every night and stay the extra half-hour? Didn't his family worry about what time he got home? 'Doesn't yer wife have anything to say about yer getting home at different times every night? She must have a dinner made for yer.'

'Me and the wife don't see eye to eye. There's no love lost between us, never has been. She's a cold fish in bed, thinks sex is dirty. She doesn't care what time I get in, and for meself I wouldn't care if I never saw her again. She does make me a dinner every night, but half the time it goes in the bin.'

'Have yer any children?'

'Yeah, a boy and a girl, both working. I've no time for them, either, they're all for their mother. We don't get on at all.'

Bella knew exactly what she was doing when her hands began to work on his body. 'So, I'm not keeping yer away from yer family by asking yer to stay here sometimes?'

His whole body tingling, Tom would have sold her his soul. 'I'll be here whenever yer want me. Every night, if yer like.'

Under the influence of Bella's expert hands, Tom Phillips's mind was incapable of any thought beyond his desire for sexual fulfilment. Bella's head, however, was very clear. She was used to the sounds made by men in various stages of satisfaction; they meant nothing to her except bread on the table and clothing on the backs of her children. But Tom Phillips was someone who gave her food for thought. He was a sucker if there ever was one. And she was sure that if she treated him right, fuelled his ego, he would come in very useful to her.

Danny was thoughtful as he ate his dinner. Because he was usually so talkative and full of humour, his preoccupation brought a frown to Ada's forehead. 'Ye're very quiet tonight, sunshine. Are yer all right? No trouble at work, I hope?'

'No, I'm okay, Mam, no trouble at work. I was just thinking about what a bloke at the dance said last night. Yer've heard me talking of Tony? Well, he said he'd seen Jenny and a couple of her mates at the Grafton on Saturay night. Nothing wrong with that, like, and he wouldn't say it if it wasn't true. But I've been thinking about it today, and it doesn't seem right. He'd only met her the once in Blair Hall, and yet he said he was with her all night in the Grafton, and she's promised to come to Blair Hall one night this week. And if she does he's going to ask her for a date.'

Ada pretended to scratch her nose to hide the smile which threatened. Oh dear, she thought, this sounds like jealousy raising its ugly head. 'Well, if he's a nice lad, there's nothing wrong with that, sunshine, is there?'

'But she hardly knows him, Mam! I mean, I get on all right with him, but then I'm a bloke. How he treats girls, I really can't say.'

'Yer can hardly tell Jenny who to go out with, and who not to go out with. She'd be within her rights to tell yer to take a running jump. On the other hand, she may tell this Tony to take a running jump. It's up to her, isn't it?'

'If you say this Tony is all right, son,' Jimmy said, 'then why worry? I'm sure Jenny will be able to look after herself. She seems a sensible enough girl to me.'

Danny was shaking his head. 'I still think she hasn't known him long enough to go out on a date with him. I mean, she hasn't got a decent father to keep an eye on her, so she should be warned about going out with strange boys.'

Ada's brows shot up. 'There's nothing strange about the lad, is there? I mean, he's not common, or tough, is he?'

Danny was fast losing his patience, which was most unlike him. 'I didn't mean he was strange, I meant he's a stranger.'

It was young Paul who came to his brother's aid. 'Ay, Danny, why don't yer tell Jenny not to go out with this lad until she knows him better?'

Danny feigned surprise. 'D'yer know, that's a good idea, Paul. On me way out, I might just give her a knock and tell her.'

Ada winked across at her husband. There'd never been any doubt in her mind that Danny would be knocking on the Phillips's door that night. Nor had there ever been any doubt in her mind that her son had more than a neighbourly interest in the girl from number twenty-two. So she patted herself on the back for being right on two counts.

When the knock came on the door, Annie got to her feet. 'You stay where yer are, sweetheart, I'll go. It won't be yer dad, or he'd use his key.'

'It might be our Ben,' Jenny said. 'Perhaps his mate was out when he got there.'

'Only one way to find out, and that's to open the door.' Annie was patting her hair into place when she opened the door to Danny. 'Hello, lad, come on in.'

'No, I won't disturb yer, Mrs Phillips, I just wondered if I could have a word with Jenny?'

Annie held the door wide. 'Of course yer can. But surely yer could do it better if yer came in for a few minutes?'

Jenny came up behind her mother. 'Did I hear my name mentioned?'

'It's Danny, sweetheart, he wants a word with yer. He won't come in, I've asked him.'

'He's probably dashing off to Blair Hall,' Jenny said, her head popping over her mother's shoulder. 'You go in out of the cold, Mam, it's no good two of us freezing.'

Danny smiled when Jenny moved to the edge of the top step. 'I believe yer went to the Grafton with yer mates on Saturday, Tony told me.'

Even though it was pitch dark except for the faint glimmer of light from the street lamp, Jenny could see Danny's white teeth gleaming, and his dimples deepen. He really was a very handsome boy, there was no getting away from it. He knocked all the other lads into a cocked hat. But he wasn't the one for her. He knew too much about her, and the life she led. 'Yeah, me and a couple of me friends from work went to the Grafton. And yeah, Tony was there. Is that all yer've come to talk to me about?'

Danny was mentally questioning his motive, now he was face to face with Jenny. Well, not really questioning his motive, but the way he'd gone about it. He hadn't changed his mind or his opinion, but standing on a front step wasn't exactly the place to say what he wanted to. 'I'd have taken yer to the Grafton if yer'd let me know. Save yer coming home on yer own in the dark. Unless yer mates live near by, and yer came home together?'

Jenny leaned against the door jamb and folded her arms. It was far too cold to stand talking, but just looking at Danny was enough to keep her there. 'No, me mates live in the opposite direction. But I'm capable of getting home safely on me own. I'm not exactly helpless, yer know.'

'I never thought for one minute that yer were helpless, Jenny. But yer have to be careful 'cos yer never know. And yer have to be careful who yer make a date with, as well. Don't go out with anyone unless yer know them well enough to trust them.'

'I'm not soft, Danny. I'm a big girl now.'

'Well, how about coming to the dance with me one night? I know yer can't come tonight 'cos it's too late for yer to get ready. But how about tomorrow?' He had his fingers crossed for luck. 'And yer can pay yer own fare if it makes yer feel better.'

'Are yer asking me because yer think I can't look after meself?'

'No! Of course not! I'm asking yer as a friend, a mate.'

'So once we get to Blair Hall we can both go our separate ways? You dance with yer usual partners and I dance with whoever asks me?' Jenny was thinking it was one way of keeping her promise to Tony. She could dance with him, then have a good excuse for turning him down if he asked to bring her home. 'Okay, I'll go with yer tomorrow night. But only on the understanding that yer don't have to be lumbered with me. You dance with who yer like, and I do the same. Agreed?'

Danny was so intent on looking into her pretty face, he didn't hear his heart singing. 'Yeah, agreed. And you tell yer mam she's not to worry about yer, 'cos I'll make sure yer get home safe and sound.'

'Will yer go now, Danny, because the dance will be over before yer get there. Those three girlfriends of yours will think ye're not coming.'

'They're not girlfriends, Jenny, they're only dancing partners.'

'I'll take your word for it, Danny, and now I'll say ta-ra. Enjoy yerself.' Jenny was smiling as she closed the front door. You couldn't fall out with Danny Fenwick, he wouldn't let you.

Annie was too happy to try to pretend she hadn't heard nearly every word of the conversation. 'I'm glad ye're going to the dance with Danny tomorrow. He's a nice lad.'

Jenny took a seat by the table. 'Mam, don't be getting any ideas about me and Danny. He knows what me dad's like, and if he's got any sense he won't touch this family with a bargepole. He is a nice lad, but he's not only nice to me, he's nice to everyone. So don't let yer imagination run away with yer.'

'But yer do like him, sweetheart, don't yer?'

'Mam, it would be very hard not to. But that's as far as it goes, so let's change the subject, eh?'

Chapter Twenty-Nine

Ada pulled the door shut after herself and was just about to link arms with Hetty when she spied two familiar figures walking up the street on the opposite pavement. 'Oh, look, there's Jean's mam and dad! It's ages since we saw them, let's cross over.'

Joe and Enid Button came to a standstill when they saw the pair crossing the cobbles. Joe was a fine-looking man of sixty, with hair still more mousy than grey. And like his daughter, Jean, he had dimpled cheeks and a face that was happy when it was smiling. His wife, Enid, was small and slim, with dark hair and eyes that were ever changing from brown to hazel.

'Top of the morning to yer both.' Ada put on a Irish accent when she stood in front of them. 'I won't bother asking how yer are, 'cos yer both look the picture of health.'

'We're both fine,' Enid told her. 'But neither of us like this cold weather, and we'll be glad when the winter's over.'

'No work today, Joe?' Hetty asked.

'I've been working a lot of overtime for the last few weeks, so the boss let me have a day off. We haven't been able to let Jean and Gordon know, there wasn't time, so I hope we haven't had a wasted journey. D'yer know if Jean's in?'

'If she's not, she'll only be at the shops.' Ada handed her basket over to Hetty. 'Hold this, sunshine, while I run and see if Jean's in. If she's not, Enid and Joe can come in mine and wait for her. I'll make a pot of tea, and we can have a natter. It would be better than hanging around in the cold.'

'We don't want to put yer to any trouble, lass,' Joe said. 'We're well wrapped up, so we won't freeze to death if we have to wait a while.'

'Nonsense! I wouldn't dream of letting yer stand around in this weather! But before we come to blows over it, I'll run and see if Jean's in or out.'

In answer to Ada's knock, Jean opened the door with her hands covered in flour. 'I'm up to me eyes baking. I thought I'd give the family a treat and make a steak and kidney pie.' She stood aside and jerked her head. 'Come in, but don't look at the place.'

'I won't come in, sunshine.' Ada grinned. 'And I hope yer've made a big pie, 'cos yer mam and dad are here.'

Jean rubbed her nose and left a streak of flour across her face. 'Ooh, where are they?'

'I left them talking to Hetty, but they've seen yer now and are on their way up. I hope yer've got a fire going, 'cos they must be cold, even though they say they're not.'

Jean stepped down on to the pavement, both flour-covered arms bent at the elbow. 'I can't give yer a kiss, Mam, or yer'll get flour all over yer. Come on in, where it's nice and warm.'

'At least bend yer head and let me give yer a kiss on the cheek.' Enid and Joe were very proud of Jean, who was their only child. She had given them two grandchildren whom they doted on, and who had brought much happiness into their lives.

Before Joe put his foot on the step, he turned to Ada. 'Thanks for the offer, lass, it was really kind of yer. Me and Enid were both beginning to feel the cold.' His dimples appeared. 'Yer can't take it when yer get to be an old fogey like me.'

'Away with yer, Joe Button, ye're as spritely as a twenty-year-old. I bet yer outlive the lot of us.' Ada gave him a broad wink. 'It's good to see you and Enid looking so well. And I hope we'll see yer again soon.'

'Yeah.' Hetty took Ada's arm. 'We're bound to see yer sometime over Christmas. Take care now.'

'Lovely couple,' Ada said as they walked down the street. 'Jean's lucky to still have her parents. I wish mine were still alive.'

'Never mind, girl, we've got each other. Think what life would have been like if we hadn't moved in as next-door neighbours.'

'Doesn't bear thinking about, sunshine. I can't imagine life without you.' Ada squeezed her mate's arm as they turned the corner into the main road. 'I'm going to pop me head in the shop to see Annie. I won't go in, I don't want to get her into trouble. I'll just call from the doorway to remind her we'll be expecting her for afternoon tea.'

'Yer don't need to remind her, girl, she'll come anyway.'

'I just want to make sure she does. I want to know what happened when our Danny went over to speak to Jenny last night. Me and Jimmy were in bed when he got home from the dance, and we didn't have time to talk over breakfast this morning. Yer know what a nosy cow I can be, sunshine, I can't wait until he comes in from work to find out how he got on.'

'I'm glad you said that and not me.'

Ada chuckled. 'If you'd said it, sunshine, I'd have clocked yer one.'

'But seriously, girl, Annie might not like yer popping yer head in. She hasn't been there long, and she'd be embarrassed if Andy is serving.'

'Oh, Andy won't mind, he's known us long enough.'

However, when Ada put her head inside the shop door, it was to find Annie standing alone behind the counter. 'Where's Andy, sunshine?'

'He had to go to the warehouse for some stock we're running short on. He won't be back just yet, so yer can come in.' Annie was looking as pleased as Punch. 'Ay, I've served two customers while he's been away. One wanted a paint brush, the other a bottle of turps.'

'Good for you, sunshine!' Ada was happy for her neighbour. It was about time she got some pleasure out of life. 'Andy will be very pleased with yer.'

'I was nervous at first, me hands shaking like a leaf. But Andy had put the price on every item in the shop, so it was easy. I'm really chuffed with meself.'

'Me and Hetty were passing, and we've called in to remind yer that ye're expected for tea at the usual time.'

'Oh, I haven't forgotten, sweetheart, I'm looking forward to it. Afternoon tea in your house is the highlight of me day.'

'Just a quick word in case Andy comes back.' Ada leaned across the counter. 'What happened last night when Danny paid a call on Jenny?'

Hetty gasped. 'Don't tell her, Annie! She's just admitted to being a nosy cow . . . and they were her very own words. So make her wait until this afternoon. A couple of hours is not going to make that much difference to her.'

Ada lifted both hands in surrender. 'Okay, okay, I give in, I'm a nosy cow. But a certain person standing just inches away from me is not getting off scot-free. If I'm a nosy cow, then she's a miserable cow.'

'What are yer talking about?' Hetty's shoulders were squared and a hurt expression crossed her face. 'Why am I a miserable cow?'

'Because yer won't let me be a nosy cow, that's why.'

Annie's loud laughter filled the air. 'If any more cows come into this shop, Andy will be able to sell milk.'

'Well, seeing as yer can see the funny side of life these days, Annie Phillips, I think you, me and Hetty, could become like the Three Musketeers. Only we'd be three cows. The nosy one, the miserable one, and the laughing one.'

Annie held her chin in her hand and pretended to give that some thought. 'Ooh, I don't know whether to look on that as an insult, or treat it as an honour. It's a "to be or not to be" question, that is.' She saw her boss's small van draw up outside and the smile left her face as she stood to

315

attention. 'On yer way, ladies, here's me boss. I'll see yer this afternoon, but I've decided I'd like to be a member of your gang, even if it is a herd of cows.'

Ada and Hetty were out of the shop as Andy crossed the pavement carrying a heavy cardboard box. 'Morning, ladies!'

The friends answered in unison, 'Morning, Andy.' Then they went on their way to the butcher's for stewing steak to make a hotpot for the evening meal.

The kettle was on the boil when Annie called that afternoon, so within minutes the three neighbours were sat round the table with a cup of tea in front of them. There were no cream cakes, hadn't been for a while now. With Christmas only days away, every penny was being counted for extra food and goodies. The shops were filled with everything needed for the festivities, and excitement was building up.

'Don't keep me in suspense, sunshine,' Ada said after being patient for five minutes. 'Give us the low down on what transpired between Danny and your Jenny. And don't worry about me repeating what yer tell me, 'cos me lips will be sealed.'

'I'll make it short and sweet then, shall 1?' Annie had blossomed in the last few weeks, she'd really come out of herself. Life had some meaning for her now, and she was taking more care with her appearance. Her hair was no longer combed back in a severe style, but left loose in soft curls, and had really taken years off her. 'I didn't hear the whole conversation, 'cos I could hardly stand there and listen, could I? But when Danny left and Jenny came in the room she told me he'd asked her to go to the dance with him tonight and she'd agreed.'

'Ooh, er,' Hetty said, her eyes rolling. 'D'yer think there's romance in the air?'

'I think there would be if Danny had his way,' Ada said, looking pleased with the news. 'He'd deny it if he heard me saying this, but I've got a feeling my son was smitten from the time he first set eyes on Jenny.'

Annie looked from one to the other, then lowered her gaze for a few seconds while she considered her words. 'I can only tell yer what I personally think, but Jenny might not agree with all I'm going to say. I know she definitely has a soft spot for Danny, but I doubt if she'll let him know that. Yer see, she is so ashamed of her father, she won't let herself get close to any lad. She's never had a boyfriend, even though I know for certain that she's had plenty of chances. It breaks my heart when I let meself think about it, because life would have been so different for her and Ben if I hadn't been stupid enough to marry Tom Phillips.'

'Oh, come on, sunshine, yer can't blame yerself for that! How were you to know he was going to turn out to be a rotter?'

'I've had cause to go over that hundreds of times through the years, sweetheart, and no matter how I try to find excuses for meself, it always boils down to the fact that my two children are suffering because of my stupidity. Whichever way yer look at it, if it weren't for Tom Phillips, life would have been much better for me and the kids. Give them their due, they have never once blamed me for putting them through a life of hell. They have always taken my side, and tried to shield me when things got bad. And for that, I love them more than any other mother could love their kids.'

'Our Danny knows what Tom Phillips is like,' Ada said softly. 'He certainly wouldn't think any the less of Jenny because of the way her father is. My son is not like that. He's just the opposite, in fact.'

Hetty seldom took the initiative in asking questions, for usually her mate did all the asking. But this time Hetty was running out of patience. 'Yer don't have much to say about yer husband these days, girl. In fact yer never mention him.'

'Not much to mention, Hetty, 'cos I see very little of him. I don't think we've exchanged twenty words in the last fortnight. He comes in late every night, eats his dinner if it's still fit to eat, then goes up to bed without saying a word. Not that it worries me, for I wouldn't care if I never, ever, had to speak to him again. Or even set eyes on him. The kids are bewildered, they don't know what to think. They've never said anything, but underneath I believe they think it's a flash in the pan, and one night he'll come in from work and be back to what he was before.'

'I can't see that, sunshine,' Ada said. 'For my money, I'd say Tom Phillips will never revert back to the rotter he was. Something tells me yer'll never again be troubled by him. Those days are gone for ever.'

'What makes yer say that, sweetheart? I only wish it was true.'

Ada was remembering how embarrassed and ashamed Annie had been when telling them of her husband's unhealthy appetite for perverted sex. A man with such needs didn't turn into an angel overnight. 'Time will tell, sunshine, time will tell.' She scraped her chair back. 'I'll make a fresh pot of tea, eh, and we can talk about what we're going to be doing over the two days of Christmas.'

Jenny was ready at seven fifteen that night. She had taken special care with her appearance, and her wonderful thick auburn hair had been brushed until it shone. She kept telling herself there was no need to look too good, it was only a dance she was going to after all. But what the head thinks is often very different from what the heart feels, and her heart was beating very quickly. She also had butterflies in her tummy.

Annie was trying not to fuss, or seem over-interested, but inside she was praying that tonight was going to be the start of a new life for her lovely daughter. Since the dramatic change in Tom Phillips, young Ben seemed to have grasped his freedom with both hands, and he spent every evening round at his mate's now. But Jenny hadn't taken advantage of their circumstances, probably because she didn't believe it would last.

The banging of a door had Annie moving to the window. 'Here's Danny crossing the street, sweetheart. Shall I let him in?'

Jenny picked up her handbag from the sideboard. 'No, I'll open the door, Mam, and I won't ask Danny in, we'll go straight out.' She hesitated at the living room door. 'Don't wait up for me, Mam, you have an early night. I'll try not to wake yer when I'm getting into bed.'

'We'll see, sweetheart,' Annie told her. 'If I'm tired I will have an early night. But I won't go to bed until Ben's in, yer know that. Anyway, you go off and enjoy yerself, and don't worry about me, I'll be fine.'

Danny saw Annie peeping through the window as they were passing, and he waved before cupping Jenny's elbow. 'Is yer mam all right about yer coming out with me?'

'Of course she's all right about it, why shouldn't she be? After all, we're only going to a local dance, not miles away.'

'Then she won't mind if yer come to the same local dance with me again.' Danny was bending his head sideways to look into her face. 'You know, the one that's not miles away.'

Jenny could hear the laughter in his voice. 'What are yer talking about, Danny Fenwick? Yer've got me all muddled up.'

'Well, it's like this, yer see. Last night they were selling tickets for the dance on Christmas Eve. It has to be ticket only, otherwise they'd be packed in like sardines. And I wouldn't like to be packed in like those poor sardines are, would you?'

Jenny rolled her eyes towards him. 'I'm sure ye're doing this just to confuse me. First it was tickets to a dance, and now we're on to sardines being packed tight into a tin.'

'Now I didn't mention no tin, Jenny Phillips. Dance tickets, yes, Christmas Eve, yes, but definitely no tins.'

'There's a tram coming.' Jenny tugged her arm free. 'Let's run for it.'

'No, we can get the next one.' Danny pulled her to a halt. 'I want to get things straight about the dance on Christmas Eve. Yer see, the tickets were selling like hot cakes, and I was afraid there'd be none left by tonight. So I bought two, in the hope yer'd come with me.'

Jenny watched the tram passing them. 'What is so important about the tickets that we have to miss a tram while yer sort it out?'

'Yer can't talk sitting on a tram, 'cos the people sitting in the seat behind will be listening in. There's some nosy beggars around.'

'Why would it matter if they did listen in?' Jenny was trying hard to keep her face straight. Danny was very like his mam, always acting the goat. 'Yer said yer'd bought yer ticket last night, so it's safe. Why worry about anyone knowing?'

'My mam does that, yer know.'

'Yer mam does what?'

'Listens in to the conversation of people sitting in the seat in front of her.'

Jenny put a finger to his lips to shut him up. 'Danny, will yer just tell me why we didn't get on that tram? Was it because yer didn't like the look of the driver? Or perhaps the conductor was an old school friend and yer didn't feel like going over old times with him?'

Danny grinned. 'That's more like it. Now I know yer can be as daft as me, I'll lay the whole thing out for yer. First, I've got yer a ticket for the dance on Christmas Eve, and I want to know that yer'll come with me? Willingly would be nice. But I'm prepared to carry yer over me shoulder if all else fails.'

'And yer couldn't wait until we get to the dance hall before asking me this?'

'I could have waited, yes, but I didn't want to. Yer see, the stakes are too high. I know that as soon as Tony sets eyes on yer, he'll be over to ask yer up for a dance. And I'll bet a pound to a pinch of snuff that he'll also ask yer to go to the dance on Christmas Eve with him.'

'Yer shouldn't bet on something that's not a certainty, Danny Fenwick. What makes yer think Tony will ask me?'

Danny's chuckles came out at the same time as his dimples deepened. 'Because he was in the queue behind me last night. And he bought two tickets.'

'He could have bought them to take another girl. He wouldn't buy a ticket for me without asking me first. That would be daft.'

'Are you saying I'm daft, Jenny?'

'Now yer've got me all confused, Danny Fenwick. What did yer tell me about Tony for?'

'So yer'd be prepared, like, and not caught out by surprise. Now yer know, yer can turn him down gently.'

319

'And what makes yer think I'd turn him down?'

'Well, it stands to sense, doesn't it? I mean, yer'd look daft going with both of us. And if yer tell him tonight, it'll give him time to ask one of the other girls.'

'Danny Fenwick, are yer always so sure of yerself, or does being big-headed come naturally to yer?'

'I'll be anything yer want me to be, Jenny. Yer see, I've set me heart on taking yer to Blair Hall on Christmas Eve.'

'But yer've already got three dancing partners there, isn't that enough for yer?'

'I didn't buy four tickets, Jenny, I only bought two. The other girls are partners, yes, and they're smashing dancers. They're like mates to me, as well. But it's you I want to take to the dance with me on Christmas Eve. I've set me heart on it, and I know yer wouldn't be cruel enough to turn me down when I've told yer me heart's set on it.'

'I can't dance as well as the other girls, Danny, I'm a novice compared to them.'

'I don't care if yer've got a wooden leg, Jenny Phillips, I still want to take yer to the dance.'

Jenny was thinking she'd be over the moon to go to the dance with Danny, for he had certainly captured her heart. But she wasn't going to let him know that. 'I suppose I'll have to go with yer, 'cos I don't want to be responsible for breaking yer heart. Yer mam would have me life if I did that. Besides, yer'll come in handy for carrying me wooden leg.'

When a tram came along, the couple were laughing as they climbed on board, bringing a smile to the driver's face. What it was to be young, eh, he thought.

At the same time as Jenny and Danny were stepping on to the tram platform, Tom Phillips was stepping into Bella's back yard. He wasn't so concerned about being seen now, and didn't worry about nosy pokes. Nor did he have to wait until Bella came for him, for he'd been given permission to go straight to the kitchen and she'd give him the wire when she was ready for him. The fact that she was a prostitute didn't bother him one little bit. He considered himself to be the luckiest bloke alive to be so well catered for by Bella. He walked with a swagger these days, very cocky because she'd told him he was treated better than any of her other clients. And whatever Bella told him, he fell for. She could wrap him round her little finger. He'd even met her children twice, and the kids had been told he was their Uncle Tom. And he treated them far better than he'd ever treated his own children, Bella saw to that. He knew without being told that if he raised his hand or his voice to them, he'd be on his way out. And that would be the worst thing that could happen to him. So he went out of his way to keep her sweet. Little did he know she was making her own plans.

Tom was lost in his thoughts when the kitchen door opened and Bella called, 'Yer can come in now, Tom.'

He lost no time in taking his place on the couch, and soon his eyes were closed and he was groaning with pleasure as Bella's hands worked their magic. She was watching his face, and although she was smiling, it was not a smile of pleasure, but of expectation. Her hands became still, and Tom's eyes flew open. 'Me time's not up yet. What have yer stopped for?'

'Don't worry, yer won't lose out. I'll make sure yer get more than yer money's worth. You are one man I'll look after, 'cos yer look after me. No, I'd let me mind wander. I was asking meself what I'm going to do on Christmas Eve, 'cos I've got about eight clients booked in. The first is at four o'clock, then every half-hour after that. Business is always brisk around this time of the year. There's a couple of punters asked if I'd cater for them on Christmas morning, while their wives are at church.'

Tom was restless but interested. 'Ay, yer could make a few bob there.'

'Yeah, I know, but I don't know how I'd manage. Christmas Eve can be a bit frightening, 'cos some men have a few drinks before they come and I'm always afraid of one of them getting rough. I'm all right when I know you're here, I feel safe then. But with you not here, I think I'm going to have to turn a few down. I know the money is good, but it can't be helped.'

Tom lifted himself on his elbows. There was real interest in his eyes now. 'Don't be turning money away. I can be here for yer.'

Bella was crafty, and a damn good actress. No one would ever have known that her surprise wasn't genuine. 'Christmas Eve and Christmas Day! Yer can't be here then. What would yer family think? They'd wonder what the hell yer were up to.'

'I don't give a bugger what the family think. I've told yer I don't get on with the wife or kids. And I know they'd be over the moon if I wasn't there. If I left home tomorrow, and they never saw me again, they'd put the flags out.' Tom's mind was racing, as he imagined the extra he'd get from the woman who had become so important to him. 'Just say the word, and I'll be here as often as yer want me to be.' He lowered his eyes. 'I'd expect special treatment though.'

'Yer'd be entitled to it, and I promise yer wouldn't go short in that department.' Bella had succeeded in her plan so far, but the next part needed a little extra coaxing. 'It's a pity we've only got two bedrooms, or yer could move in permanent. We'd be good for each other. With you working during the day, and looking out for me at night, I could take more punters on. Just think of the money we'd make. We'd be on easy street.' She pushed him back gently, her mind on track. 'I really shouldn't be saying this when yer've got a wife, it isn't fair. I know yer two children are working, but yer wife couldn't manage a house on their money.' Her hands were working now, and Tom's eyes closed. 'Unless yer give her a couple of bob a week to help her out. Then I wouldn't feel so bad about taking yer away from her.'

Tom was at the stage where he would have promised her anything. She brought his senses alive in a way he had never thought possible, and he'd die rather than give her up. Bella had set a trap, and he'd walked straight into it. 'I'll do that. I'll tell her tonight that I've met another woman, and I'll move in here tomorrow, after work.'

'Don't forget to tell her yer'll be giving her money every week. I don't want to be the cause of a woman being left penniless. Tell her she'll get a half-crown postal order every week.' And when Bella's hands stopped for a few seconds, it was a warning that she meant what she said. If he didn't do as he was told, he would suffer for it. 'I'll get the order from the post office, and to make sure she gets it, I'll send it off to her meself. But don't tell her who I am or where I live. I don't want no angry woman coming down here and making a show of me.'

'I've told yer, she'll be glad to be shut of me.'

And Bella didn't doubt him for one minute. He'd be a lousy husband and father if he was allowed to have his way. He'd probably given his wife and kids a dog's life. Then again, she was hardly in a position to criticise anyone. She wasn't a decent or respectable woman herself. Certainly not an upstanding member of the community.

While Bella's hands worked, so did her mind. Her and Tom were two of a kind. Neither of them were angels.

Chapter Thirty

Annie sighed when she heard the key turn in the lock of the front door. She left her chair and made her way to the kitchen, dreading having to face her husband. The very sight of him was enough to make her feel sick, never mind having to spend time in the same room as him. She turned the gas off and opened the oven door. The dinner she'd been keeping warm for him would be shrivelled up by now, but that was his own fault for coming home so late.

Tom Phillips threw his coat on the couch and pulled a chair out from the table. He wrinkled his nose when Annie put the plate down in front of him, but picked up his knife and fork and began eating without saying a word. It was only when he saw her walking towards the stairs that he broke the silence. 'I want a word with yer.'

Annie turned to face him. 'I'm tired, and I really don't think we've got anything to say to each other.'

'I've got something to say to yer, so shut up, sit down and listen.'

'If yer intend shouting and bawling, then don't bother, 'cos yer'll be talking to an empty room. I'm off to bed.'

'There'll be no bawling or shouting, 'cos I've got things to do before I go to bed. Yer see, I'm packing me bag and getting out.'

Thinking it was a joke, Annie huffed. 'That'll be the day when I see the back of you, Tom Phillips. I should be so lucky.'

'I'm telling yer, I'm packing me bag and leaving yer. I've found another woman, one who understands me needs, and I'm moving in with her.'

'I'll believe it when I see it,' Annie said. 'If it's true, it'll be one of the happiest days of me life, Tom Phillips. But is it true, or just a cruel joke?'

Tom pushed his plate away. 'It's no bleeding joke, yer silly cow. We've never been happy together, yer never catered to me needs. I'm leaving yer for a woman who gives me everything you wouldn't. She's got red blood in her veins, not bleeding ice.' He waited for Annie to rant and rave, or at least show some signs of shock, but she just sat and stared at him. 'I'll be sending yer some money every week, to help out. Not as much as yer get now, 'cos I'll need money for where I'm going. But there'll be a half-crown postal order sent to yer every Saturday. Yer'll get it through the letter box every Monday without fail.' He waited, but there was still no sound from his wife. 'What's the matter with yer, have yer got no bleeding tongue? Don't think yer can get me to change me mind by making me sorry for yer. Tears won't cut no ice with me. I'm off tomorrow whether yer like it or not.'

Annie was having trouble with her conscience. One part was telling her she should tell him that she was working and earning three shillings a week. By not telling him she would be acting a lie. But another voice in her head was saying she'd be crazy to tell him. After the way he'd treated her and the children over the years, he didn't deserve any sympathy or consideration. The half-crown he said he'd send every week would enable her to buy things for the house, make it nice, like Ada's. And it would mean no scrimping on food or clothes. She didn't doubt he would send the money, for he'd be afraid of her turning up at his work and causing trouble. Not that she would, she had more pride than to go down to the docks and make an exhibition of herself. But Tom wouldn't know that, for he didn't know what the word pride meant.

'There'll be no tears, not from me, anyway. And if there are any tears from your two children, they'll be tears of thankfulness. For yer've been a lousy husband and father, and this house will be a much happier place without yer.' She left her chair, and making fists of her hands, she leaned on the table and looked down at him. 'I'm going to bed now, and I'll stay in bed in the morning until yer've left. Yer can see to yer own breakfast for once. And I won't wake the children until I hear yer closing the front door. I bear yer no ill will, Tom Phillips, but I hope I never have to set eyes on yer again.'

With her back straight and her head held high, she left the room and climbed the stairs. But she had no intention of undressing or getting into bed, for her brain was over-excited. She would have to tell the children tonight. If she kept the news to herself until tomorrow she wouldn't be able to get a wink of sleep. Never in her wildest dreams had she imagined such a dramatic thing happening, and she couldn't wait to see the faces of her two children as she broke the news to them.

Annie sat on the bed, her arms folded, and listened to her husband's heavy footsteps on the stairs. Then she heard him walking the floor in the next bedroom, and the sound of drawers being opened and closed. In her mind's eye she could see him getting his clothes together to take with him in the morning. Not that he had many clothes worth talking about. He preferred to spend his money over the pub counter than buy himself any decent underwear. She'd often thought over the years that if he had an accident and ended up in hospital, she'd die of shame because of the state of his clothes.

It must have been twenty minutes before Annie heard the sound of twanging bed springs coming from the next bedroom, and knew Tom Phillips must be settling down for the night. But to make sure, she waited a few more minutes before quietly opening the bedroom door and creeping down the stairs. It was nearly half past ten now, and Ben would be in soon. She made up her mind she would ask him not to go to bed until Jenny came in, but wouldn't tell him why. She wanted them to be together when they heard the news that would hopefully change their lives for ever.

Jenny and Ben listened wide-eyed as Annie told them their father was leaving home. They remained silent as she repeated almost word for word the exchange between herself and her husband. She didn't make heavy weather of the situation; there was no sense of drama, shock or sadness in her voice. In fact she felt as though a weight was being lifted from her shoulders. She could see disbelief on the faces of her two children and was quick to assure them that what she'd told them was the truth. 'So there yer have it, sweethearts, that's all that was said. And there was no shouting or arguing.'

'I don't believe it, Mam,' Jenny said. 'He's playing tricks with yer.'

'I wish it was true,' Ben said, 'but I think Jenny's right, he's playing a trick on yer. It's the sort of thing he would do. He's so twisted in his mind, he'd think it was a huge joke.'

'That's what I thought at first, son, and I told him so. But no, he was dead serious, and I am firmly convinced this is the last night he'll spend in this house. Please God.'

'D'yer really believe he's got another woman, Mam?' Jenny wasn't totally convinced, even though she knew her mother was sensible enough to know when she was being told a lie. 'I can't see another woman wanting him. I mean, he's not exactly God's gift to women to look at, is he? And he's certainly no angel to live with. Who'd put up with his shenanigans? His drinking, and foul language. Not to mention his violent temper.'

'I'm not going to worry about that, sweetheart, I don't care who or what the woman is. She's doing me the biggest favour anyone could. I feel as though a ton weight has been lifted from me shoulders and I feel light at heart. To live a normal life, without having to look over me shoulder all the time, or worry about being shamed in front of neighbours. Since I got married I've lived under a cloud that I never thought would go away. Now, perhaps, I'll be able to live a normal life, like Ada and Hetty, or Edith and Jean. I know they've got good husbands, which I'll never have, but I won't ever have to feel inferior to them. From tomorrow onwards I'll be able to laugh and joke without worrying about what Tom Phillips has in store for me.'

'Oh, wouldn't it be wonderful, Mam, if it's true?' Jenny was slowly beginning to believe her mother, for two reasons. The first was that her mother seemed quite sure of her facts, and the second was because Jenny wanted with all her heart to believe it. 'We'd be like a normal family, able to invite our friends here. And think of how different Christmas will be without me dad getting blind drunk and spoiling everything for us. If he goes, it will be the first and only good thing he's ever done for us.'

Ben was smiling as his brain worked overtime to digest the news. Think of the freedom he'd have! 'I'll be able to ask me mates round here for a game of cards, save me going to their houses all the time.' He pulled on each of his fingers and chuckled at the sound of his knuckles cracking. 'It's like a dream. I don't think I'll be able to sleep tonight, but if I do, I hope I don't wake to find it was only a dream after all.'

'Talking of sleep, I think it's time we went to bed.' Annie scraped her chair back. 'Don't get up in the morning until I give yer the wire. Even if ye're wide awake, stay there until I'm sure yer dad has left the house. It will mean yer being tight for time, and it'll be a mad dash for yer. But I don't want to face Tom Phillips before he leaves, and I'm sure you don't. So it'll be a case of getting yer skates on. Yer should get to work on time if ye're lucky enough to catch a tram handy.'

Jenny stood up and pushed her chair back under the table. 'Ay, Mam, wait until yer tell Mrs Fenwick and Mrs Watson. I bet they'll get a shock.'

'I haven't been able to get Ada Fenwick out of me mind since yer dad told me he was leaving,' Annie said. 'I'm sure the woman is a clairvoyant, 'cos only this afternoon she told me I'd never again get any trouble from Tom Phillips. I didn't pay any attention to it at the time, but she was right. And it's not the first time she's told me something which turned out to be true, either! She must have a gift for seeing into the future.'

'Ay, she could make money telling people's fortunes,' Ben said, following his mother to the stairs. 'There's a gypsy at the fairground what tells fortunes, and she asks yer to cross her palm with silver.'

With her foot on the bottom stair, Annie put a finger to her lips. 'Be as quiet as mice, now, we don't want to wake a certain person up. We'll have plenty to talk about tomorrow, please God. A little prayer from each of us wouldn't go amiss, either.'

When Annie heard the front door closing the next morning, she hurried to the window to make sure her husband had actually left the house. And as he passed the gas lamp, she saw he had a rolled-up bundle of clothes under his arm. 'Thank God for that,' she murmured as she crossed the cold lino in her bare feet. 'Come on, kids, it's time to move. Yer father has just left, so the coast is clear.'

Annie was first down the stairs, followed closely by Jenny and Ben. 'I'll make the toast while you two get washed and dressed.' It was when she was picking up a plate which bore the remains of toasted bread that she saw the half-crown at the side of it. 'Ay, look at this!' She held the silver coin in the palm of her hand for the children to see. 'I'm beginning to wonder whether yer father has lost his marbles, or seen the light!'

'Don't worry about him any more, Mam,' Jenny said. 'From the looks of things he's done what he said, and gone for good.'

'Good riddance to bad rubbish,' Ben said with feeling. He'd suffered at the hands of his dad, been the whipping boy when things didn't suit. He'd been wishing his life away, wanting to grow up quickly so he could square up to the father who had no love for him, his mother or his sister. He'd always promised himself that when he was older, he'd protect the two people he loved most in the whole world. But he wouldn't have to worry any more now, there'd be no more clouts lashed out, no more rows or filthy language. In their place would be love, warmth and laughter. 'It'll be a good Christmas, Mam.'

'Yes, it will, son.' Annie turned the bread over under the grill. 'And this half-crown will help things along just fine. Plus I get me first week's wages, so that's five shillings and sixpence I'll have.'

'And our money, Mam,' Jenny reminded her. 'There should be enough for the extra food, and to buy each other a little present.' On impulse she wrapped her arm round her mother. 'Things are looking up for the Phillipses, Mam.'

'And not before time, sweetheart. But if yer don't leave go of me, it'll be burnt toast you and Ben will be having for yer breakfast.'

'Are yer going to see Mrs Fenwick before yer go to work, Mam,' Jenny asked, 'to tell her the news?'

'Oh, no, sweetheart, I won't have time. I've got this place to tidy and dust, the dishes to wash, and meself to see to. But my first priority is the bed in the front room. I'm going to strip every stitch off it and put the lot in the dolly tub to steep in warm soapy water while I'm at work. Then when I'm putting all clean bedclothes on the bed, I'll have the window open to get the smell of yer father out of the room. For tonight I'll be back in me own bed, and I want it to smell nice, clean and fresh. Then I'll be able to enjoy the best night's sleep I've had in twenty years. And, oh boy, am I looking forward to it.'

Annie worked like a Trojan for the next hour. But it was work done willingly, with a heart that was lighter than it had been for many a long year. And she sang while she worked, something else she had never done before. Tom Phillips had only been out of the house two hours, and already it had a different feel about it. There was no trace of him, or smell, when Annie had finished the bedroom and took the bedding downstairs to put in steep. She was hard pressed for time, so when she finally left for work, she could only glance at the house opposite. She would have loved to tell Ada and Hetty what had happened, but she didn't want to be late for work. And she'd be having tea with them at three o'clock.

As Annie hastened down the street, she felt like a young girl again. There was a new life ahead of her, and she felt she was walking on air. And adding to her happiness was the knowledge that her two children would be sharing her lightness of heart and feeling of good will. She vowed to live her new life to the full, but her real priority was to make up to Jenny and Ben for the dreadful childhood they'd suffered at the hands of Tom Phillips.

Andy Saunders was serving a customer when Annie entered the shop, and after passing the time of day she quickly made her way to the stockroom to don a coarse apron. When she came out there were several customers waiting to be served. It seemed everyone was intent on brightening up their living rooms for the festive season. And because she was feeling so happy, Annie was more outgoing than usual, and laughed and joked with the customers she served. Both she and her boss were kept busy for the first half-hour, and then, when the shop was free of customers, Andy looked down the counter to where Annie stood, her face showing traces of a smile.

'Ye're looking very happy with yerself, Annie. Has Father Christmas come early to your house and left yer a nice present?'

Annie had never mentioned her husband to her boss, and wasn't going to do so now. 'I'm looking forward to Christmas, Andy. It's my favourite time of the year. In fact it seems to have an effect on most people, for everyone seems more happy than they do the rest of the year.'

'I'm looking forward to it meself,' Andy told her. 'I'm going to me son's for the two days, and I'm really looking forward to it. I always think Christmas is a time for children, and I'll be in me element with me two grandchildren. I'd be a lonely old man without them. Me son and his wife are very good to me, and I'm lucky. But it's the grandchildren who have brought light into my life.'

'Ay, less of the lonely old man, Andy,' Annie said. 'Listening to yer, anyone would think yer were in yer dotage. I bet there's not many years between you and me, and I'm blowed if I'm going to think of meself as old.'

'I'm a lot older than you, Annie. I was fifty last birthday.'

'Ye're still a young man, so stop feeling sorry for yerself.'

A customer came in then, and for the rest of the morning the shop was quite busy. In fact at one o'clock, the time they closed for the dinner hour, there were still customers there. 'You finish now, Annie,' Andy said. 'I can manage. As soon as I've served these few, I'll put the bar on the door.'

'Are yer sure? I don't mind staying, yer know.'

'I'm positive. You get off and I'll see yer tomorrow.'

Annie flew to the butcher's and was just in time to stop Ronnie from locking the door. She put her hands together as though in prayer, and begged him to let her in. 'I only want a pound of sausage, lad, it won't take yer a minute.'

'I've been working all morning, missus, rushed off me ruddy feet! Can't yer come back when I've had me dinner?'

'I've been working meself, sweetheart, ye're not the only one. And if yer don't serve me, I'll go somewhere else for me turkey tomorrow, and I'll take me mates Ada and Hetty with me.'

Ronnie rolled his eyes to the ceiling. 'Ruddy blackmail now! Come in, but be quick about it. Otherwise, as sure as eggs, a few other customers will come along and I could say goodbye to me dinner.' He dragged Annie in by the arm, then pulled the blind down on the door. 'One pound of sausages yer asked for, and that's what yer'll get. So don't even think of adding anything else.'

'God love yer, son,' Annie said when the butcher handed the sausage over. 'Yer'll get paid for yer kindness when yer get to heaven.'

'Yer can pay me back tomorrow by bringing yer mates with yer for their chickens or turkeys.' Ronnie grinned. 'I'm only pulling yer leg, girl, 'cos Ada and Hetty have got their order in. They're picking their birds up in the morning.'

'Put a small turkey away for me, if yer will, and I'll ask Ada to pick it up and pay for it when she comes for hers. I'll be working in the morning, so I'll be pushed for time.'

As he opened the door to let her out, Ronnie said, 'Have a nice Christmas if I don't see yer before, girl, but keep off the gin. Mother's ruin, that is.'

Annie waved as she hurried away. 'That'll be the day when I have a glass of gin,' she muttered under her breath. The most she'd ever drunk was a glass of sherry. She had more to do with what little money she had

329

than spend it on booze. Besides, one drunkard in the family was enough. Tom Phillips had put her off drink for life.

It was half past two when Annie decided she couldn't keep the news to herself any longer. Ada was very easy-going, she wouldn't mind her being early. And all she had to do to bring Hetty running was to knock on the wall.

'I know I'm early, sweetheart, but don't shout at me 'cos I've got news for yer.'

'No need to apologise, sunshine, 'cos ye're not the only early one. Hetty came in half an hour ago, and without so much as a by-your leave she plonked herself down as though she owned the place.' Ada held the door wide, a welcoming smile on her face. 'It would have been all the same if I'd been in me nuddy, splashing away in the tin bath in front of the fire.'

Hetty was chuckling when Annie walked in. 'What a sight for sore eyes that would have been, eh, girl? My best friend in all her glory. It's enough to make yer go giddy.'

Ada stuck her tongue out at her mate. 'There's worse sights I can think of than seeing me in me nuddy. And don't ask me what, or yer might hear something yer don't like.'

After pulling a chair out, Annie sat down. 'Now don't you two start an argument, for I want to take centre stage. Yer see, I come bearing news of epic proportions, and I want your undivided attention.'

Ada and Hetty leaned their elbows on the table. 'I know,' Ada said. 'Andy Saunders has asked yer to marry him.'

Annie chuckled. 'That would be news of epic proportions, sweetheart, but what I have to say puts that in the shade.' She sat back in the chair and faced the two mates. 'My husband, Tom Phillips, has left me for another woman.' She saw two pair of eyes widen. 'Yes, it's true. He left home this morning, and he looked rather like Charlie Chaplin as he walked down the street with a rolled-up bundle of clothes under his arm.'

Hetty's body shook with laughter, thinking it was a huge joke. But Ada kept her eyes fixed on their neighbour from number twenty-two. 'Well, that's the second piece of news we've had today. But I have to say that yours knocks the other into a cocked hat.'

'Ah, yeah, but Eliza's wasn't a joke,' Hetty said. 'Not like Annie's.'

'Annie's isn't a joke, sunshine,' Ada said. 'She means it.'

'Go 'way.' Hetty tutted. 'I'm not as green as I'm cabbage-looking.'

'It is true, sweetheart,' Annie assured her. 'Tom left home this morning, and he's gone to live with another woman. A woman who, he said, "understands me needs".'

'Whoever she is, she's done yer a real favour.' Ada's face was serious. 'I am so happy for yer, sunshine, and for the kids. Yer can have a real life now, say what yer want, do what yer want, when yer want. But tell us the whole story, how he told yer, and what your feelings were.' She leaned across the table and patted Annie's hand. 'Not that I need to ask yer how yer feel, 'cos I can tell by yer face. It's sticking out a mile that ye're happy to see the back of him.'

Annie told them the sequence of events, and apart from a few gasps from Hetty, it was done quietly and quickly. 'Me and the children are over the moon. We haven't got used to it yet, but just the thought of him never coming into the house again is enough to make us happy. We can do what we've never been able to do, and that's to walk with our heads held high.' With a sigh of relief and contentment, Annie sat back. 'And now yer can tell me what other news yer heard today.'

With her brows raised, Ada said, 'If yer hadn't told us your news, than I wouldn't be telling yer about the letter I had this morning from Eliza. You know, the lady who lived in the house before you. Well, she's written to say she'd like to see her old house again, just for a visit, if the new tenants wouldn't mind. She often thinks about it, and would love to see it, just for a few minutes, for old times' sake.'

'We weren't going to tell yer, girl, 'cos we knew yer'd be embarrassed if yer husband was there when she called.' Hetty took a deep breath and let it out slowly. 'She's a real lady is Eliza, and we love the bones of her. Ada was going to find an excuse to put her off, but she won't have to now, will she? With yer husband not living at home now, yer wouldn't have to worry about Eliza visiting yer.'

Annie looked troubled. 'I couldn't let her come with the place the way it is. I haven't done a tap to it since I moved in because I've never had the money. I'd be ashamed, for yer've always told me she kept her house like a little palace. I'd love to meet her, 'cos she sounds like a wonderful woman, but not with the house as it is now.'

'Hear me out for a few minutes, sunshine,' Ada said. 'In her letter, Eliza said it would be lovely if she could call on New Year's Eve. Not to stay for any length of time, but just to see once again the house she lived in for sixty years. It's only natural she'll pine for a place she's spent the best part of her life in. She'd be content if she knew there were good people living there now. And there's over a week to go before then, plenty of time for us all to get stuck in and help yer decorate yer house. We'd all help, and we'd have it done in no time. Jimmy, Danny and Arthur would willingly help, and I know Gordon Bowers and Joe Benson would put their heart and soul into making it look lovely for the sake of Eliza. They all love the bones of her.'

The troubled look was easing off Annie's face. 'D'yer think it could be done? I'd love to meet Eliza.'

'Where there's a will there's a way, sunshine,' Ada said. 'It won't cost much for paper and paint, and we could all help with a few coppers if yer were stuck.'

Annie was beginning to get excited. What a wonderful day this was turning out to be. 'Andy told me, when I started in the shop, that anything I bought there I would get a discount on. So I could probably manage at a pinch.' She clasped her hands together. 'Wait until I tell the kids, they'll be absolutely delighted. How lucky we were the day we moved into the house across the street. It's not very long ago, but just think how it has changed our lives. Your Eliza must have put a magic spell on the house, God bless her.'

Chapter Thirty-One

Danny was cupping Jenny's elbow as they walked down the street. He was so elated he couldn't stop talking, and the words poured from his mouth. 'There's so many things happened in a matter of two days, I can't take it all in.' He had programmed his brain not to mention the leaving of Tom Phillips in case it upset Jenny. Actually it was his mother who had put the idea into his head, by telling him it was Christmas Eve, a time for enjoyment, and he shouldn't spoil it by saying anything out of place. 'It'll take me a few days to get me head round the changes.'

'Danny, will yer slow down a bit?' Jenny asked. 'I don't know what ye're doing the fastest, talking or walking. But I do know yer've got me out of breath.'

'That's 'cos I'm so excited, Jenny. I don't usually talk so much. But with it being Christmas Eve, and taking you to the dance with me, well, I feel like a little boy who's just seen Father Christmas go past on his sleigh.'

Jenny clicked her tongue as she shook her head. 'We're only going to Blair Hall, Danny, not to a ball. And in case yer haven't noticed, I'm not Cinderella.'

But nothing could dampen Danny's high spirits. 'I'm glad ye're not Cinderella, 'cos she had two ugly sisters. And another thing, you are much prettier than Cinders.'

Jenny was just as excited as Danny, and just as happy to be in his company. There were hundreds of butterflies in her tummy, and her mouth was dry. She told herself it was because she wasn't used to going out on her own with a boy, and was too shy to let him see how she really felt. 'It's dark here, Danny, yer can't see very well. When we get to the dance, in the bright lights, yer might find I look more like one of the ugly sisters. If so, I won't be upset if yer want to dance with one of yer regular partners.'

'Not on yer life! I'm taking you to the dance, and I'm staying with you all night. Dorothy and the others will understand. And if Tony thinks for one minute he can hog yer for every dance, then he's got another think coming.'

'Danny, ye're doing it again!'

Looking puzzled, Danny asked, 'Doing what again?'

'Talking too much.'

'If me mam was here, she'd be nodding her head to agree with yer.' Danny was so overjoyed to have her walking next to him, touching his elbow, he couldn't contain himself. 'She once told me that when I was born and the nurse put me in her arms for the first time, I was talking then.'

Jenny couldn't keep the giggle back. 'And did yer mam tell yer what yer were talking about?'

'Apparently I didn't hold a full conversation, but ycr have to remember I'd only just been born. All I said was, "Can I have a drink, Mam, 'cos that was thirsty work." '

'Here's a tram coming,' Jenny said. 'Let's make a dash for it.' She would have run on ahead, but Danny's hand pulled her up short.

'Hang about a minute, Jenny, till we get something straight. There'll be another tram along in a couple of minutes.'

'What is it yer want to get straightened out? Before we left the house yer said yer wanted to get to the dance early, and now ye're making us late.'

'I just want to remind yer that this is the season of good will to all men. No arguing over little things like a tuppenny tram ticket. So don't be making a scene on the tram when I stop yer from getting yer purse out. You're my date for tonight, and no date of mine is going to sit next to me on the tram and pay her own fare.'

'But yer've paid for the dance ticket, Danny. I can't let yer pay for everything.'

'I bet yer've never been out on a date with a boy who let yer pay yer own tram fare. If he did, he must have been a drip.'

Jenny looked up into his face, and wondered whether to tell a lie, or tell the truth and shame the devil. 'Danny, I've never been out on a date with a lad before.'

Danny's surprise had him stepping back a pace. 'Are yer trying to pull me leg, Jenny Phillips? If yer are, then it'll be your fault if we miss the first few dances.'

Jenny's pride began to make itself heard. 'It's not that I've never had the chance, Danny, 'cos I've been asked out on dates loads of times. But I've always turned them down before. Not because there was anything wrong with the lads, but because I knew I would never be able to bring one of them home with me because of me dad. I know it's wrong of me, and I shouldn't class everyone the same, but my dad is so horrible he's put me off boys for good.'

There was a catch in Jenny's voice, telling Danny that if he wasn't careful about the words he chose, tears would soon be running down her cheeks. And his heart went out to her. But sympathy wasn't the answer, it would only make her more miserable. 'Jenny Phillips, are yer telling me yer think I'm horrible? If yer are, I'm going to set me mam on to yer. She'd give yer a right ticking off if she thought yer'd insulted her lovely son.'

Jenny sniffed, a shaky smile on her face. Tears had been very close, and for one dreadful moment she had thought she was going to blubber like a baby. 'I'm sorry, I don't know what came over me. I had no right to say what I did, and I regret it. Tonight of all nights I should be feeling on top of the world, not miserable. I should put me dad out of me mind now, and get on with me life. I know all men are not like him, Danny. I shouldn't have said that to yer.' Again she sniffed, at the same time thinking she'd have to powder her face when she got to Blair Hall, and do it before Danny saw her in the light. Her nose must be as red as Rudolph's, the reindeer. 'Here's another tram, Danny, and I promise I won't take me purse out.'

He put his arm round her waist and helped her up on to the platform. Then he whispered in her ear. 'Yer might have to, Jenny, 'cos if I'm not mistaken, I've left all me money on the table at the side of me bed.' His dimples deep, he chuckled. 'Only kidding, don't look so worried. We are going to have the time of our lives tonight, Jenny Phillips, I promise yer.'

Danny's forecast started to come true for Jenny the moment she went into the cloakroom to hang her coat up and repair the damage to her face. For standing in front of one of the mirrors on the wall was Jane Bowers, her next-door neighbour. The girls had never been in each other's company, they'd only ever exchanged smiles, waves, and the time of day. But as they titivated themselves up in the cloakroom they chatted as though they were old friends. Jane was very like her mother in looks, having Jean's colouring, dimpled cheeks and friendly disposition. She knew Jenny hadn't had a happy life because of her father, and when she was told last night that Tom Phillips had left home, she had been pleased for the family in number twenty-two. But Jane was a very sensible girl, and to her Christmas Eve wasn't the time to rake up something best forgotten.

'I didn't know yer came here,' Jenny said. 'D'yer come often?'

'Now and again,' Jane told her as she patted her nose with a powder puff. 'But me and me mate like to go to New Brighton Tower, or Barlows Lane.'

'Is yer mate with yer tonight?'

335

'Yeah, she was going out of the door when you came in. She said I was taking too long to get ready, and she'd see me inside.' Jane grinned at Jenny's reflection in the mirror. 'Are you with a mate?'

Feeling embarrassed, Jenny said, 'My mates from work had brought tickets for the Grafton, so Danny Fenwick offered to bring me here, save me staying in on Christmas Eve.'

Jane's mouth was as round and wide as her eyes. 'Well, you lucky beggar! He's a smashing dancer is Danny, and really handsome. Yer'll be getting cow eyes off some of the girls tonight, for there's a lot who fancy him.'

'There's nothing in it,' Jenny was quick to say. 'I think he just felt sorry for me.'

'Listen to me, kid.' Jane's blue eyes were twinkling. 'If you get the chance to nab Danny Fenwick, then go for it before somebody else gets their claws into him. A feller like Danny doesn't come along very often.'

Jenny didn't think she should be discussing Danny in his absence, so she closed her handbag and turned towards the door. 'I'd better go. I'll probably see you inside.'

'Hang on,' Jane said. 'I'll come in with yer.'

Leaning against the wall facing the cloakroom were Danny and Tony. And as soon as the girls walked out, the lads came towards them. Danny's face showed surprise when he saw Jane, but he didn't express it until he'd laid claim to Jenny by putting his arm round her waist. 'Hi, Jane, this is a surprise. I didn't expect to see you here.'

'I'm with my friend. We knew everywhere would be packed tonight, so we bought tickets for here to make sure we had somewhere to go.'

Tony had been weighing up the two girls. He'd come to the dance in a fighting spirit, intending to win Jenny's hand by fair means or foul. But if he was to be honest with himself, he'd have to admit he didn't stand much chance against Danny Fenwick. And the new girl on the scene was really pretty. 'Where are yer manners, Danny Fenwick? Are yer not going to introduce me to yer friend?'

Danny was full of apologies. 'Oh, I am sorry, Tony, please forgive me for my lack of manners. This young lady is a neighbour. She lives in the same street but on the opposite side.'

'How come that two very pretty girls live in the same street as you, but on the opposite side?'

'Ah, well, yer see,' Danny said, grinning, 'they were crafty. They reckoned they would see more of me if they lived opposite than they would side by side. But let me introduce yer, so we can get in the hall for some serious dancing. Tony, meet Jane. Jane meet Tony. And I can vouch for him, Jane, he's not dangerous.'

Tony raised his brows at Jane. 'Would yer like to have this dance with me, or have yer got to find yer friend?'

Thinking the blond boy was quite handsome, Jane said, 'I'll have this dance with yer. My mate has probably got a partner by now.'

Sure enough, Jane's friend, Eva, was enjoying a waltz with a slim, dark-haired, good-looking young man. And when the dance was over, she walked hand in hand with him to join the other two couples, and introduced him as David. From then on it was fun and laughter all the way. Three young couples out to enjoy themselves and have fun. And if Jenny was a little more subdued than the others, nobody noticed except Danny. They swapped partners now and again, but after the interval, when tea and biscuits had been served, they stayed with the same partner. This was brought about by Danny, who was feeling very protective towards Jenny, and was reluctant to part with her. But nobody cared, for they were enjoying themselves so much. Tony was definitely smitten with Jane, and they'd already made a date for the following week. And the signals coming from Eva suggested she'd found a soulmate in David.

Jenny was enjoying the freedom, and the fact that she didn't have to worry about her mother now, with her father gone. But it would be a while before she was able to let herself go, and be as outgoing as Jane and Eva. The inferiority complex she'd carried all her life would take more than a few days to disappear. She had no idea how pretty she looked, with her thick mop of rich auburn hair, deep brown eyes glistening with happiness, and a permanent smile on her face. Nor did she notice the looks of admiration which came her way from some of the men standing near. And Danny was completely captivated. He couldn't take his eyes off her. She wasn't as smooth a dancer as Dorothy or Betsy, but he wouldn't have cared if she had two left feet. She was the only partner he wanted. But he couldn't tell if she shared his feelings, and he was afraid of pushing things too quickly in case he scared her off.

When the last waltz was announced, there was a mad dash to get on to the dance floor before it became too crowded. It was a romantic number, sung by a member of the band, and the men were holding their partners close, dancing cheek to cheek. But Jenny drew back, putting a little space between herself and Danny. He was sensitive to her feelings, having been involved with her father during two of Tom Phillips's drunken rages. And the words he'd uttered about his own daughter had so enraged Danny he would never forget them. So he understood it would take time for Jenny's wounds to heal, but he didn't mind, she was well worth waiting for. That's if she would have him, of course. 'Have yer enjoyed yerself, Jenny?' he whispered in her ear. 'Are yer glad yer came?'

Jenny wasn't to know that when she looked up at him his heart flipped. 'Oh, yes, Danny, I've really enjoyed meself. Thank yer for bringing me.'

'It was my pleasure. And I'll make sure yer get home safely. And don't forget we'll be seeing a lot of each other in the next few days.'

Jenny looked puzzled. 'What makes yer think that?'

'Didn't yer mam tell yer? Me and me dad, and Mr Watson, are decorating yer living room. I thought yer mam would have told yer.'

'Me mam did say something about decorating the room, but I was busy getting ready and not really listening. I did hear her say something about the lady who used to live in the house, though.'

'Yeah, that's Mrs Porter. She's coming to see all her old friends sometime over the holiday. I'm looking forward to seeing her, she's a little love.'

The dance came to an end then, and, to Jenny's surprise, people were hugging and kissing and wishing each other a merry Christmas. She didn't mind when Danny gave her a bear hug, but when she saw his lips coming towards her, she turned her head quickly and his kiss landed on her cheek. 'That was mean, that was,' Danny told her, pulling the corners of his mouth down to look like a brokenhearted clown. 'Christmas Eve and not even a kiss.'

Jane was standing near with Tony, who, having been well and truly kissed, was looking like the cat that got the cream. And Jane took pity on Danny. 'Don't be so miserable, Jenny, give the lad a kiss. It won't hurt yer.'

Not wanting to appear a spoilsport, Jenny lifted her face. 'Oh, go on, then, but only a peck.'

The meeting of the two pairs of lips was more than a peck. It was a kiss that took Jenny's breath away, and left Danny believing his heart was doing somersaults. He understood what his dad meant now, when he'd said he knew Ada was for him as soon as he kissed her.

'That was a nice peck, that, Jenny,' Danny said. 'I'd say it was the best I've ever had.'

Jenny was about to say it was the only one she'd ever had, but thought better of it. Jane was standing near and she didn't want her to think she was childish. 'I'm glad yer enjoyed it, Danny. I aim to please.'

He put an arm across her shoulder and gave her a squeeze. 'Go and get yer coat, babe, I don't want yer mam after me for keeping yer out late.' But that wasn't strictly true. There was method in Danny's madness. In his mind's eye, he could see himself standing outside the Phillipses' front

338

door, and he had his arms round Jenny, kissing her. And it was a proper kiss, not a peck. And, oh boy, was he enjoying it.

'I'm ready, Danny. What are yer waiting for?'

Danny shook his head to scatter his thoughts. He'd been miles away. And now, the girl he'd been dreaming of was standing in front of him. 'I'm sorry, Jenny, me mind was elsewhere.'

She tutted and shook her head. 'That's not very complimentary, Danny Fenwick, telling a girl yer mind was anywhere but on her. Are yer trying to give me an inferiority complex?'

Danny's hand cupped her elbow as he led her from the hall into the street. 'If yer must know, Jenny Phillips, I was standing outside your house, saying good night to yer, and yer were giving me a kiss that was taking me breath away.'

'Yer were dreaming, were yer, Danny?'

'I was enjoying meself, yeah! Not for long, though.'

'Why, what happened?'

'Yer mam came out and hit me over the head with a frying pan.'

Jenny was giggling when she pulled him to a halt. 'Danny, I want to thank yer for a lovely night. I've really enjoyed meself.'

'Will yer come out with me again, then?'

'Ye're a sucker for punishment, Danny, but if yer want me to come out with yer again, then I will.'

'How about New Year's Eve? That's the best night of the year to go out and enjoy yerself.'

'Why do yer have to pick the one night of the year that I won't come out with yer? I'd never leave me mam alone on New Year's Eve. Especially not this one.'

A tram came along and Danny helped Jenny on to the platform. 'I understand, and I think ye're right. All the neighbours get together that night, and they have a knees-up and sing-song in the street. We could join them.'

'I'll see what me mam and Ben are doing before making any arrangements. It's a week off. I'll see yer loads of times before then.'

'Jenny, yer'll be sick of the sight of me next week. I'll be in yours every night helping to decorate. But just to keep me spirits up, will yer at least promise me another of yer pecks on New Year's Eve?'

Keeping her voice down, so the people in the seat behind them couldn't hear, Jenny said, 'As long as yer make a good job of papering our living room. Is that a deal?'

'More than a deal, babe, a promise. Your living room will be the best in the whole street. In fact, yer'll be able to sell tickets just to let people see it.'

Jenny held out her hand. 'Let's shake on that, Danny.'

'Ah, ay, babe! Why can't we seal it with a kiss?'

'Let's wait and see what sort of a job yer make of the room first.'

'Yer drive a hard bargain, Jenny Phillips. I can see I've got some ground to cover before I get a real kiss off yer. But we Fenwicks never give up, I warn yer. We fight to the finish.'

Danny didn't see as much of Jenny the following week as he'd hoped. For while the men worked like Trojans, scraping, papering and painting, she and her mam went to sit with his mam and Auntie Hetty. Apart from taking drinks over to the men, the women left them alone so they could work to get the room finished by New Year's Eve. But Danny's disappointment was forgotten when the room was finished. The looks of surprise and pleasure on the faces of Annie and her two children made the wait and hard work worthwhile.

Annie had a hand to her mouth as she surveyed the room. In all her married life she'd never been allowed to live in a house long enough, or given enough money, to have a room looking like this. The wallpaper was light beige, with a small green leaf pattern, and the glossy paintwork and ceiling were white, making the room look light and airy. It was all too much for her, and she couldn't keep the tears back. 'God was certainly looking after us when we got this house. We've never before had neighbours who befriended us like you have.' There was a catch in her voice. 'I haven't got the words to thank you enough.'

Ada went to stand beside her and put an arm across her shoulder. 'Come on now, sunshine. Just look at the faces on my feller, and Arthur and Danny. They've worked their guts out for the last four nights, and what happens? You cry yer ruddy eyes out!' She could feel Annie's body shaking, and gave her a squeeze. 'It's been our privilege and pleasure to get to know yer, sunshine, and you and the kids are part of our gang now. But if yer don't stop crying, yer'll have us all at it. The room looks lovely, the men have done a grand job, so let's all be happy that everything has turned out well. And finished in time for Eliza's visit.'

Ben was struck dumb. He was too young to know what to say, and could only look around the room with wonder. But Jenny was so happy that something nice had happened for her mother, she wiped the tears away with the back of her hand, then plucked up the courage to cross the room and stand in front of Danny. 'We had a deal, Danny, and you kept your part.' She stood on tiptoe and kissed his cheek. 'Now I've kept my part.'

'Blimey!' Danny feigned a look of disgust, but deep down he was thrilled that Jenny had kissed him in front of everyone. And after all, a peck was a kiss really, wasn't it? 'Yer don't call that a kiss, do yer?'

Jimmy and Arthur were grinning. 'Ay, son,' Jimmy said, 'don't push yer luck. A kiss from a pretty girl is not to be sneezed at. What do you say, Arthur?'

'Oh, I agree, Jimmy. If it was me what had been kissed, I'd be going to sleep tonight with a smile on me face.'

Jenny didn't hesitate. She crossed to where the two men stood and planted noisy kisses on their cheeks. 'Thank you, from me, me mam and our Ben.'

Ada gave a little nod, well satisfied at the way everything had worked out. 'I think it's time to call it a day. And Hetty's not going to be too pleased at me leaving her with my two children for longer than the minute I promised. Yer know how she hates to miss anything. So let's away to our homes, families and beds. We'll all sleep soundly, knowing there's been a job well done.'

On New Year's Eve, Eliza's son, John, brought his mother by taxi to the house she would always look on as home. She was well looked after where she was now, with her own room for privacy, and well cared for and loved by himself and his wife. But the small two-up-two-down terrace house had been her home for sixty years, and there were times when she pined for the house and the memories it held for her. And when she was helped from the taxi her eyes lit up at the sight of the number 22.

Ada and Hetty were in Annie's waiting for Eliza, and they were pushing each other out of the way to get to the door first. Edith and Jean knew she was coming, but had wisely said they would wait for half an hour to give the old lady time to settle down. And Annie and Jenny waited in the kitchen, so Eliza could be welcomed by two of her best-loved neighbours.

'Come in, sunshine, and get a warm.' Ada and Hetty had taken an arm each, and their faces were lit up with pleasure. 'Hasn't Vera come with yer, John?'

John was gazing around the room as he took his hat off. And out of habit he was about to put it on the sideboard when he realised this was no longer his mother's home, or her sideboard. 'Our grandchildren have some friends coming to see the New Year in, so Vera thought she'd better stay to help out. But she sends yer her best wishes, and she'll be up to see yer soon.'

'The house looks well cared for.' Eliza was nodding her head in approval. 'I'm glad the new people are looking after it.'

'Talking about the new people,' Ada said, once the old lady was seated,

'I think it's about time yer met them. They're standing in the kitchen waiting to be called in.'

'Oh, they shouldn't have done that. This is their home.'

Hetty called, 'Come in, Annie, and meet the woman we've been talking about all week.'

Annie came in, followed by Jenny and Ben. She took one look at Eliza and fell in love with her. The old lady was frail, but her eyes were alert and friendly. No wonder she'd been well loved by everyone in the street. You only had to look at her to know she was a real lady. 'I've heard so much about yer, I feel I know yer. And yer've given me the hard task of trying to live up to yer.'

Her hands folded in her lap, and looking completely at home, Eliza smiled. 'I'm sure yer'll do well here, my dear, and be as happy in this house as I was for most of my life.' She looked past Annie to where Jenny and Ben were hovering. 'And yer have a very pretty daughter and a handsome son. I bet they're looking forward to the jollity there'll be in the street tonight when the bells ring in the New Year.'

It had been decided that Tom Phillips's name wouldn't be mentioned in case it upset Eliza. She belonged to an age where if you got married, you stayed married for life. So Ada helped to skirt round the issue by changing the subject. 'Edith and Jean will be on pins, sunshine, they were just giving yer time to settle down before coming in. I'll knock on the walls and let them know ye're ready to receive them.' She grinned as she hammered on Jean's wall with her fist. 'That's what the Queen does, Eliza, she receives people. She doesn't have mates in, like us common as muck folk.'

The time passed quickly after that. The men came home from work and had their dinner, then men and women alike put on their best bib and tucker. And still Eliza made no move to leave. 'Mam,' John said, 'we'd better be going. Vera will wonder what's keeping us.'

'I don't want to upset yer, son, or have yer think I don't appreciate all that yer've done for me. You and Vera, and the grandchildren, are marvellous, and I love yer dearly. But, for the last time in me life, I would love to be the one to let the New Year in, in this house. That's if you and Vera wouldn't be upset, and Annie would let me.'

'We'd love to have yer, sweetheart,' Annie told her. 'But it's up to yer son.'

'I'll go home now and tell Vera.' John set his hat on his head. 'I'll order a taxi for half past twelve and come and pick you up. So try and stay awake, Mam, and have a good time with all yer old mates. I'll see yer later.'

DATE DUE

SEP 07 2011
JUN 06 2012
FEB 07 2013
FEB 25 2013
APR 03 2013
JUL 16 2013
AUG 12 2013
SEP 25 2013

JAN 18 2006
JUN 06 2006   JAN 08 2008
JUN 13 2006   FEB 24 2009
SEP 11 2006   JUL 21 2009
JUN 24 2010   DEC   2009
GAYLORD   JAN 02 2009   PRINTED IN U.S.A.

So it was that when the bells rang out on the stroke of twelve, and the ships and barges on the River Mersey hooted their horns to welcome in the New Year, Eliza felt like a young woman again as she knocked on the door of number twenty-two. Surrounded by all her old friends, the Fenwicks, Watsons, Bowerses and Bensons, and welcomed as a first footer by a smiling Annie, she was as happy as could be, and her heart was at peace.

Danny felt quite emotional as he watched Eliza from the back of the crowd. 'I've loved that old lady all me life.' Then, through the crowds of neighbours who were hugging, kissing and singing, he pulled Jenny towards the street lamp. 'I want to see what I'm doing. So, can I have my New Year's kiss, please? And pecks are not on the menu. I want a proper kiss.'

And when Jenny lifted her face, and Danny's lips met hers, Cupid worked his magic. They saw stars twinkling, heard fireworks going off, and their heartbeats felt like the beating of a drum. When Danny finally lifted his head, he said, 'I feel dizzy. Me head is going round.'

Jenny said softly, 'I feel faint.'

'Don't you dare faint on me, Jenny Phillips. Not until yer've given me another kiss, and an answer to me question.'

'What question is that, Danny?'

'Will yer be my girl?'

'That's a daft question, Danny Fenwick. Of course I'll be your girl. I might not have known it at the time, but I think I'd made up me mind on that the first time I set eyes on yer.'

His dimples deep, Danny put a finger under her chin and lifted her face. 'That's all right then. And now it's official, will yer stop talking so much and give us a kiss to seal our bargain?'

DATE DUE

SEP 07 2011	
JUN 06 2012	
FEB 07 2013	
FEB 25 2013	
APR 03 2013	
JUL 16 2013	
AUG 12 2013	
SEP 25 2013	
JAN 18 2006	
JUN 06 2006	JAN 08 2008
JUN 13 2006	FEB 24 2009
SEP 11 2006	JUL 21 2009
	2009
JUN 24 2010	DEC
	JAN 02 2009

GAYLORD   PRINTED IN U.S.A.